NAZI AMERICA

CONSPIRACY

R.J. KELSAY

Also by

RJ Kelsay
Nazi America Election

NAZI AMERICA

CONSPIRACY

Chapter One

The insistent vibration of Melissa Carthage's watch pulls her from sleep, announcing a new day. As she leaves her bed, Melissa's heart beats steadily, reflecting her calm and content state of mind. A symphony of chirping birds greets her on her balcony, their melodies weaving through the crisp morning air. The fresh scent of dew-kissed grass lingers, invigorating her senses, while the gentle warmth of the rising sun caresses her skin, embracing her in its comforting embrace. A soft breeze whispers through the trees, rustling their leaves in a soothing melody. As the world awakens around her, alive with vibrant colors and gentle sounds, she takes a moment to savor the beauty of the morning. She puts on her red robe.

"Television, MCBS."

"Back to you, Sarah," says a field correspondent, his voice crackling over the voice phone.

Sarah from MCBS says: "Thank you, Mark. We confirm Jill Lunden as the next President of the United States. Vice President Nelson has conceded the election, while there is no word from the Thompson camp yet. We will deliver further details as they become available."

Melissa gently lifts a heavy, ornate golden frame, the image of Jacob gleaming within. The old picture shows his jet-black hair, perfectly slicked back, and deep brown eyes that seem to hold a lifetime of stories. A smile blooms on her lips, the memory of his laughter a sunbeam warming her heart even in the dark. Warmth spreads through her chest, a pleasant pressure expanding her ribcage as she inhales deeply. Her pulse quickens slightly, a happy flutter in her veins. The corners of her eyes crinkle, a subtle physical manifestation of her joy, and her face softens, the muscles around her mouth relaxing into a gentle curve. The weight of the frame, initially felt as a physical burden, seems to lessen, almost insignificant compared to the lightness in her heart. "Thank god that Jill won the election, although I can't believe that Daniel almost won the Presidency. That mother fucker that says that our esteemed military personal are losers and hopeless."

Frustration bubbles. She grabs her bright pink stress ball and hurls it with surprising force across the hall; the impact echoes faintly. "He wouldn't know military pride if it came up and bit him in his imaginary stomach virus. Damn bastard might sing a different tune if he went to Botswana during the war. He witnessed the same things I had witnessed. The shattered buildings, scorched landscapes, the deafening roar of gunfire and explosions, and the acrid stench of burning debris. The pervasive hopelessness, the pain etched on survivors' faces, and the tears and fear in the eyes of the dying. And I am just here to have a trial for those responsible for the Kalanga massacre. I can't imagine the people that were in that hellhole for years on end."

She still pictures the courtroom itself, where she presides over the trials of those responsible for such wanton violence; it haunts her still: the guilt and defiance on the defendants' faces, their hushed whispers, restless movements, and occasional gasps of shock—all echo in her ears, creating a constant, suffocating anxiety. The weight of her duty, the severity of the crimes, presses heavily upon her soul, leaving an unrelenting echo of the world's darkness. In a move toward reconciliation, the military agrees to hand over the commanding officer responsible for the Kalanga massacre, a gesture of goodwill intended to offer some measure of justice to the victims' families. The other soldiers involved face various military disciplinary measures, further damaging the unit's reputation. "Still, I wonder why Daniel has not conceded." Melissa says to the portrait.

"You're right. He's probably off pouting about not getting his way. Perhaps he has had too many drinks and is sleeping it off. "Television, speaker on. Give the results of the House elections."

"Working." the television computer says. "Results ready." The television announces the House election results alphabetically by state. One name gets her attention. Sue McAllister loses to Kathleen Hand.

"What idiots vote to send that chief idiot back to Congress? Maybe they just want her to stay away from their towns. Can't say I blame them. But do they have to torture me with her again?"

The television goes on with the list. Melissa hears her name, which is no surprise.

With a steaming mug of tea in one hand and a plate overflowing with golden-brown bacon and fluffy eggs in the other, Melissa returns to the living room. From afar, the grandfather clock's slow, deliberate chimes provide a soothing counterpoint to the gentle creaking of her beloved chair.

With a sigh of contentment, a warm wave washes over her. Melissa settles into her armchair. The muscles in her face relax, the slight furrow in her brow smoothing out as the tension eases from her shoulders. A pleasant warmth spreads through her chest, a gentle pressure expanding her ribcage with each slow, deep breath she takes. The rich aroma of the bacon and tea fills her senses, triggering a cascade of salivation and a comfortable rumble in her stomach. Her heart beats steadily, a calm rhythm mirroring the grandfather clock's chimes, a gentle pulse against her ribs. Even the slight tremor in her hands, a lingering echo of the day's anxieties, subsides as she savors the simple pleasure of her breakfast.

"List complete," the television says.

Melissa goes through the mental calculations. "Let's see that give the Democrats 218, 150 for the Independents, 50 Republicans and 32 for American Now." Melissa again looks at the portrait of Jacob. "Shit, American Now is gaining while the Republicans are slipping." Melissa's fists clench, a burning rage igniting within her at the thought of Kathleen Hand in her position in the future. A single tear traces a path down her cheek as her shaking hand finally grasps the warm tea, a meager comfort in her grief.

She controls the shaking with heavy meditation. "Television resume MCBS. I use the distraction," Melissa says. "Mmm," she sips her steaming, fragrant tea.

The young blonde weather woman, with her hair fluttering in the breeze, announces the forecast with a bright smile. "A tornado is expected to hit central Maine by 3:00 p.m."

The news of another tornado ignites a furious outburst in Melissa, her tea, a projectile of her rage, flies from her lips. "Damn it, this marks the fifth tornado to hit the state of Maine this year."

Unfortunately, these catastrophic events—wildfires ravaging the West, snowstorms engulfing the Midwest, and tornadoes and hurricanes plaguing the East Coast—are far from isolated incidents. This grim picture stretches FEMA's resources thin, leaving the agency on the brink of financial collapse. Melissa struggles to suppress her frustration and anger at past decisions; this constant battle creates a knot of nausea and unease in her stomach. The overwhelming helplessness and despair manifest physically: her once vibrant eyes are now dull and tired, shadowed by dark circles from sleepless nights spent worrying about the future. Mounting pressure causes physical manifestations of her anxiety, including increased heart rate, shallow breathing, and unconsciously clenched fists. The weight of the world's problems is crushing, a heaviness in her limbs that drains her energy and motivation, leaving her both physically and emotionally exhausted.

The faded photograph, yellowed at the edges, shows three small figures on a sun-drenched beach: Melissa, her grin wide, Jacob's sandy hair tousled, and Erica building a sandcastle. The salty tang of the ocean seems to waft from the picture itself, a phantom scent mingling with the dusty aroma of the old photo album. A gentle warmth, like a summer breeze, accompanies the nostalgic feeling, a comforting pressure in her chest. The cold frame chills her fingers to the bone. "I am so sorry, my baby girl. Climate change is not a novel concept. For over a century, people have been aware of its potential consequences, yet they have overlooked it, leaving the burden to future generations. Now, these generations face the repercussions head-on. The effects of climate change go beyond mere weather patterns. Higher sea levels submerge England, once a thriving nation, and predictions show it will remain so. The Middle East, the cradle of civilization, has become uninhabitable because of extreme heat and droughts. As each recent disaster unfolds, the world slowly becomes a battlefield for survival, testing the limits of human resilience. Why did we not heed the warnings of experts during the conference in 2119? Instead, we chose a delay tactic in our lawmaking, making things worse for you guys." Melissa grabs a book and throws it across to the wall. Meanwhile, shaking increases. Melissa goes to the bathroom to take her pills. The shaking decreases, but Melissa knows this is not a good sign. She goes to her palm top on her nightstand. She opens it, but her vision is blurring. "Computer, display available appointments for Dr. Stan before Thanksgiving. Use a voice recorder."

"One appointment available before November 23, 2124, however, it conflicts with a meeting with President..."

"Book it!" the desperate whisper urged, a plea for escape from an unbearable reality.

"Appointment set on November 20, 2124, at 10am eastern standard time."

"Add to Calendar."

"Added."

"Phone call Sanchez."

"Hello. Mr. President."

"Madame Speaker."

"Mr. President, I need to reschedule our meeting on November 20th."

"Any specific reason?"

"No. I just remembered that I have a doctor's appointment at the same time."

"Well, your health is very important. At least that's what my daughter/health nazi keeps saying. Let me take a look. Is 4:00pm good for you."

"That's fine. Thank you. Phone disconnect."

Melissa returns to the living room to see her breakfast. Her fears cause her lack of appetite. She puts the food in the reclamation bin and then goes to her exercise room to put on her exercise clothes, discarding the robe.

She lies on the mat in the room and begins meditation; the music plays calmly to her. After closing her eyes and inhaling, Melissa strives to find her inner peace in a moment of reflection. Not finding it, she says, "Oh hell, might as well get this done. Room hologram program Carthage exercise level one." A sudden flash of light illuminates the room, startling Melissa as she sees a younger herself, impeccably dressed in a Judge Advocate General uniform.

"Ready, Melissa." Melissa stares at her younger self on the hologram; the vibrant image is a stark contrast to her current weariness, a poignant reminder of lost hope.

"Those were the days when I thought I could move mountains and make a difference." She says to herself. She then says the words to begin the program. "As ready as I'll ever be."

Unresponsive to the comment, the hologram instructs, "Okay, let's begin with some light stretches."

Melissa begins her workout by doing some stretches, feeling the tautness of her muscles relax. As Melissa stretches, her muscles respond, energized and flexible, poised for the day's challenges. Any muscle stiffness dissipates, replaced by fluidity and grace. Aligning each rhythmic movement with her steady breathing, a peaceful calm envelopes her mind. In this moment, Melissa finds comfort and tranquility, prepared to tackle any challenges the day may present.

"Ok, that's some wonderful stretching; now the real fun begins," the program laughs while rubbing its hands.

"Why did I put that ominous threat in the program?"

"Ok maggot, now drop and give me five pushups."

"Ah, this brings me memories of my boot camp days."

"I don't see any movement. Your mother's not here to help you."

"Yes, ma'am." Melissa salutes herself and begins her pushups.

"I want to see your full body on the floor. And a one and a two." The program counts to five pushups. "Good, now let's see you do ten lunges. And a one and a two."

With every exercise repetition, Melissa's heart rate increases, signaling her body's preparedness for the challenge. As droplets of sweat form on her forehead, catching the soft light of the room, her resolve strengthens with physical effort, driving her to surpass her own limits. As she continues her pushups, her body cries for mercy. "I won't let this stupid program stop my resolve," she says between breaths.

"Very good. Now let's see if your body can withstand thirty minutes of jumping jacks."

She begins her jumping jacks; the rhythmic thud of her feet is a steady beat against the floor. Twenty seconds into the race, she's breathless, her lungs screaming for oxygen.

"*There was a time I could do fifty minutes of jumping jacks.*" She crawls to the chair and collapses, totally out of breath. "Room, disengage the hologram," Melissa says. Her younger self fizzles. She hits the chair arm. "There was a time I could outlast the males in my boot camp. But that was her." She points at the hologram emitter. "Now look at me. Nearly eighty, and a simple workout takes all my energy and breath." The shaking returns. "And this Salvanti disease zapping more strength. I ask you, God, what did I ever do to you?"

Gaining her composure, she returns to the living room. She notices that she left the balcony door open and walks towards it. She looks outside, her gaze fixed on the grandeur of the Capitol building and the Washington Monument. A complex mix of emotions fills her heart. Palpable pride for her country courses through her veins, causing a slight tremor in her hands; she feels the weight of the countless sacrifices made to protect America.

A sense of peace washes over Melissa as she walks to the bathroom; the sound of running water already promises comfort. With a sigh of contentment, she sets the water to a soothing temperature, sheds her clothes, and steps into the shower. The water's soothing rush cleanses her, a blissful release washing away her worries. "The water is fine," Melissa thinks as she completes her shower and promptly reaches for her bathroom robe. After drying off, she makes her way back to her room, where she exchanges her robe for a suit. She gazes at a picture of her and Jacob from their first day at the Capitol, taking a moment to reminisce as she gently places a finger on her late husband. "I'll always love you. But I hope I don't see you too soon. Our family needs me."

Melissa collapses on the couch but sees a photo of herself, Erica, and Miranda, her granddaughter, and remembers her last conversation with them. "We have a surprise for you, Mom," Erica says.

"And a gift," Miranda chimes in.

Melissa thinks, *what could that mean? She won't be running for my seat until I tell her I'm retiring. And what is this gift Miranda's talking about? Everything sounds so cryptic.'*

A sense of peace washes over Melissa as she walks to the bathroom; the sound of running water already promises comfort. With a sigh of contentment, she sets the water to a soothing temperature, sheds her clothes, and steps into the shower. The water's soothing rush cleanses her, a blissful release washing away her worries. "The water is fine," Melissa thinks as she completes her shower and promptly reaches for her bathroom robe. After drying off, she makes her way back to her room, where she exchanges her robe for a suit. She gazes at a picture of herself and Jacob from their first day at the Capitol, taking a moment to reminisce as she gently places a finger on her late husband. "I'll always love you." She gives the portrait a kiss. She then begins to leave, but before turning off the light, she says. "But I hope I don't see you too soon."

Chapter Two

The warm rays of the sun stream through the curtains, casting a golden glow on the walls of Andrew's Oklahoma home in Durant. He steps onto the hardwood floors, noticing their smoothness beneath his feet. The aroma of brewed apple cider wafts through the air, enticing his senses. He gazes around, admiring the generous size of his ranch style home with its open layout and expansive windows that present breathtaking views of the extensive countryside. The gentle rustling of leaves and the distant chirping of birds create a serene symphony, providing a soothing soundtrack to his mornings. Andrew's heart fills with contentment as he absorbs the beauty of his cherished home. He glances around, taking in the enticing aroma of bacon and sausages sizzling in the kitchen. The sound of eggs tapping against the bowl resonates through the air. He observes his environment, the vivid hues of the ingredients on the countertop catching his eye. The soft sizzle of the food frying in the pan reaches his ears. He watches Cassandra's adept hands deftly handle the spatula, eagerly anticipating the scrumptious breakfast soon to come. "You slept late," Cassandra notes.

Andrew gives a kiss on Cassandra's cheek and replies, "No, you're an early riser." With an effort, he holds back a yawn, trying to prevent another one from escaping. The fatigue clear in his eyes and the slight slump of his shoulders betray the lingering weight of disappointment from yesterday's setback. Cassandra notices his exhaustion and reaches out, caressing his cheek in a gesture of comfort and understanding. "I'm wondering, what was the reason behind your early rise?" he asks.

"I just wanted to cook breakfast," Constance says, her gaze darting around, hands trembling.

"And?" prompts Andrew, well aware that Constance only prepares a full meal when she's nervous.

"Fine. I wanted to put you in a good mood before asking how Daniel is taking the loss. Daniel was winning when I left the convention center. But he still lost," Constance says. Andrew recognizes the significance of being there for Daniel during his triumphs and his challenges. As he concludes his breakfast, he shifts to planning strategies to help his friend during these challenging times. He is determined to ensure that Daniel is aware of his steadfast support and encouragement, believing that his friendship will help him overcome any obstacles.

"That's another reason I woke up," Andrew states, his voice laden with fatigue. "Daniel wants to discuss strategy."

Prompted by curiosity, Cassandra asks, "Strategy about what?"

"He insists he won the election." This statement catches Cassandra off guard, leaving her feeling surprised and confused. She can sense a slight tension building in her shoulders as she tries to make sense of the news.

In a reclined position in her chair, she crosses her arms and narrows her eyes at Andrew. Doubt fills her voice as she asks, "Is he out of his fuckin' mind? Even I couldn't vote for the cold-hearted bastard." Her disbelief is clear in both her tone and expression. She can't comprehend how Daniel, with his questionable tactics and lackluster campaign, could even entertain that he won. She looked at Andrew, sadness in his eyes, and said, "You had to know that I couldn't vote for him. His attitude was disgraceful. That recording really doomed him. Not to mention the death of Laura Kelly. I guess there just weren't enough gullible people to vote for him. Thank God." Cassandra's mind races as she considers the implications of her confession. Her heart rate increases, and her pulse quickens as she grapples with the potential consequences. After all, her husband is the Vice-Presidential nominee. She feels her palms grow clammy, a physical expression of the uncertainty that now surrounds her.

Andrew sighs, his own emotions surfacing, and responds with a mix of satisfaction and anxiety in his voice, "I figured as much. But he still wants to go over the strategy and figure out how to navigate this unexpected turn of events. I need you by my side. You're my rock." Cassandra's mind races with questions, her curiosity battling against a growing sense of skepticism. She can't get rid of the sense that there is more to this story than Andrew is revealing.

"Is there something that you're keeping from me?" she asks.

Andrew responds by showing her his palm top, saying, "I don't know. Look at this." The screen displays a vibrant image, immediately catching her attention. The soft hum of the device fills the air, blending with the ambient sounds of conversation around them. Her curiosity surges within her, eager to explore what Andrew has to share.

"How's that even possible?" she asks, her mind now racing with even more questions. "Who or what is a CainAnon?"

Andrew replies, "I wish I knew."

Andrew and Cassandra drive their Ford Escalante, the engine humming as they head towards Paris, TX and their destination: Daniel Thompson. Despite the peaceful ambiance, Cassandra expresses her doubt about the significance of a particular post. "You really don't think that post means anything," she says. Andrew counters, acknowledging that it's all about optics and how Daniel can use this to his advantage. The weight of the situation hangs heavily on both of them, especially Cassandra, who fears the potential consequences for the democratic system they hold dear. Understanding the power of optics, she knows how something seemingly insignificant can be twisted and exploited to fuel a dangerous agenda.

On the other hand, Andrew perceives an opportunity for Daniel to capitalize on this message and advance his cause. Though his voice conveys confidence, there is a slight hint of apprehension. He is aware of how optics can sway public opinion and, in the wrong hands, become a weapon of manipulation. Cassandra interjects, her voice quivering with fear, and emphasizes the potential to undermine the democratic system. Her eyes flicker around anxiously as the trepidation in her tone echoes, sending chills down her spine. The gravity of her statement lingers in the air, shrouding the room in a veil of doubt. Andrew maintains a composed facade, but his eyes betray a glimmer of worry. His eyebrows knit together as he articulates his thoughts with urgency, his hands moving expressively to underscore his words. The tension between the two friends is so strong that it feels like an electric current running through the air.

Andrew implores Cassandra, pleading for her understanding, "Please, I am convinced that Daniel intends to concede to the election. He is simply seeking some guidance on composing his concession speech." Cassandra, still skeptical, addresses Andrew without receiving a response. "Dear, do you honestly believe that?" she says, her words filled with disappointment. Andrew continues driving, offering no reply. Cassandra mutters under her breath, "That's what I thought."

As the car speeds down the road, Andrew's grip on the steering wheel tightens, causing his knuckles to turn white. Frustration and disbelief emanate from Cassandra's tense posture, her eyebrows furrowed and her jaw clenched. The tension inside the car is palpable, creating an invisible wall between them.

Breaking the silence, Andrew's voice trembles with a hint of annoyance. "Cassandra, I know Daniel for a year. We worked side by side. I find him to be quite reasonable in his actions and decisions. He doesn't cling to power if he knows he has lost." Cassandra's eyes dart towards Andrew, her disbelief etched across her face.

"But given everything that's happening this election season, it's hard to trust anyone's motives," she responds, her voice laced with skepticism and a sense of betrayal. A heavy silence falls, broken only by the steady hum of the engine. Andrew's eyes remain fixed on the road, his jaw clenched as he navigates the busy traffic. Cassandra turns her gaze towards the passing scenery, her fingers tapping nervously on her thigh.

Unable to contain her frustration any longer, Cassandra speaks up, her voice tinged with exasperation. "It's just hard to believe that Daniel would give up without a fight. The election was intense, and conceding seems like an unlikely outcome." Andrew's grip on the steering wheel relaxes slightly, his brows furrowing as he considers Cassandra's words. The weight of uncertainty hangs in the air, casting a shadow over their conversation.

He knows that Cassandra's doubts are not unfounded, yet he can't let go of his belief in Daniel's integrity. Finally, Andrew breaks the silence, his voice filled with determination. "We can't jump to conclusions without giving Daniel a chance to explain. Let's reserve judgment until we hear from him directly. Only then can we truly understand his intentions." Cassandra sighs, her shoulders slumping as she reluctantly nods in agreement.

The tension in the car dissipates, replaced by a cautious hope for clarity and under-standing. They continue their journey; the road stretching out ahead, uncertain of what awaits them at their destination.

The stormy weather at Daniel's tennis resort in Paris, Texas, greets Andrew and Cassandra upon their arrival. The strong winds gush and lightning strikes in various places, creating a disheartening sight. Outside the resort, a group of homeless individuals seek shelter and congregate. Their weary expressions reveal the hardships they face, with their tattered tents and soaked clothes. Standing by the gate, they softly plead for help, their voices drowned out by the howling gusts of the storm. This somber scene merges with the lively sounds of the city, casting a melancholic shadow over the area. The odors of despair and abandonment intertwine with the aromas from nearby food vendors, accentuating the sharp contrast between affluence and poverty. This poignant contrast deeply moved Cassandra, feeling a pang of sorrow for the homeless gathered outside the opulent resort. Overwhelmed with empathy, she struggles to hold back tears as their burdens seem to settle on her, compelling her to assist in any way possible. "Let's offer these people some money, food, or clothes," Cassandra proposes, driven by her innate compassion to act. Andrew, however, responds cautiously and skeptically, expressing concern that giving money will only encourage more people to approach with expectations. He also reminds Cassandra of the need to see Daniel.

"Look at them. They have no shelter, and their clothes seem to be fused to their bodies. Some of them look like living skeletons." She points to a woman in her thirties, holding an infant child, struggling to keep a fire going. It's clear that the baby won't last long in this cold.

Meanwhile, Andrew stands nearby, his arms tightly crossed and his stance defensive. His furrowed brow and narrowed eyes reflect his apprehension, as if he's shielding himself from any potential disappointment or inconvenience. As their inner dialogues continue, the weight of the situation intensifies, drowning out the bustling city noises and leaving only the sound of their internal conflict echoing in their ears.

Approaching the gate, Andrew notices a soft buzz of electricity in the air. The gate itself is robust and imposing, its metallic bars reflecting the sun's rays. Filled with anticipation, he inputs the code provided by Daniel, feeling the buttons click beneath his fingers. A mechanical whirring ensues, and the gate gradually opens, revealing the verdant expanse that lies ahead.

Entering the area, fear engulfs Andrew and Cassandra. The sound of birds chirping is absent, drowned out by the heavy winds that batter the trees. Even the tennis courts resemble swimming pools. Pressing forward, they finally reach Daniel's room, where Andrew feels the cool metal under his hand as he turns the doorknob. The room itself is dimly lit, with soft ambient lighting creating a cozy atmosphere. A faint scent of sandalwood lingers in the air, adding to the serene ambiance.

Andrew and Cassandra step into the living room, where Cassandra's gaze immediately falls upon the disarray before her. Unsightly ketchup stains mar the striking artworks carelessly strewn on the floor. The once-sophisticated walls resemble a third-grader's abstract project, tarnished with splatters of ketchup and mustard. As they walk through the halls, animal heads lining the walls elicit a sense of grief in Constance for the creatures. A subtle scent of condiments, mixed with the musty aroma of neglected art, fills the room.

Overwhelmed by disbelief and confusion, Andrew and Cassandra stand amidst the unforeseen turmoil. Cassandra's thoughts race, knowing that Daniel, still seething with rage from losing the election, is now in full combat mode. His face flushes, his eyes narrow into fiery slits. Veins on his forehead throb with intensity, his fists clench tightly, and his knuckles turn white. Every muscle in his body seems on edge, ready for a fight. Fueled by a surge of adrenaline, he is determined to retaliate against those who thwart his political aspirations. Each breath he takes heaves his chest with a mix of frustration and fury, making it seem as if he is preparing for a physical confrontation rather than a political one. The calm and composed demeanor he once has during his campaign vanishes, replaced by a raw and unbridled aggression.

A relentless storm of thoughts consumes Daniel's mind, replaying the moments of defeat repeatedly. The unpleasant sensation of failure lingers on his tongue, amplifying his anger and pushing him further into combat mode. Every nerve in his body screams for vengeance, urging him to take action and make those responsible pay for what they have done. Pacing back and forth, his footsteps echo with a sense of determination and purpose. The surrounding air crackles with his volatile energy, as if he is a coiled spring ready to unleash its force.

Daniel's transformation from a politician to a warrior is evident in his palpable energy. His body language exudes readiness, with his gaze fixed and unwavering. The loss ignites a fire within him, propelling him relentlessly towards justice and vindication. Freed from the constraints of a campaign, Daniel now finds himself driven by an intense desire to fight back. With each passing moment, his rage grows stronger, propelling him further into combat mode, prepared to face any challenge that comes his way.

"Andrew, I must reclaim what is rightfully mine! **I won the election!**" Daniel's authoritative streak emerges as he speaks. His voice grows louder, his face turning a shade of crimson, and his hands clenching into tight fists. His eyes now burn with fierce determination. Andrew can sense the weight of Daniel's desire to reclaim what he believes is rightfully his.

Upon sensing the urgency in Daniel's tone, Andrew takes a deep breath, striving to maintain his composure. As Daniel's trusted advisor, he knows he must navigate this delicate situation carefully, mindful of the potential consequences of fueling Daniel's authoritarian impulses. "I understand your frustration, Daniel," Andrew begins cautiously, his voice steady. "While it is important to acknowledge your feelings, we must also consider the legal and ethical boundaries surrounding the presidency."

Daniel's gaze hardens, clearly growing impatient. **"I don't care about legalities or ethics! They rig the election against me. I insist that justice must prevail in this case."** Daniel states, his typically authoritarian tone faltering momentarily, giving way to a hint of uncertainty.

"There are steps and options we can take."

"I need you to present me with those options. **I want to explore every avenue available to regain my rightful position as the victor.**"

Andrew, relieved, nods in agreement as Daniel shows the willingness to consider a more calculated approach. "Understand. Let's start by looking into legal options, like requesting recounts or starting legal challenges in certain states. We should also consider diplomatic routes to tackle any issues regarding election integrity. Perhaps it's best to concede this election and focus on preparing for a Senate campaign in 2126," Andrew proposes.

Daniel yanks Andrew towards him, their eyes locked in a fierce struggle. **"I never said that I plan on giving up, did I?** I do not ask for defeat, but for answers. I did not lose the election! **That bitch won't take what is mine by the right of male privilege.** A woman should never be President."

Andrew cuts off Daniel, saying, "Some group named CainAnon sent a message about the election. About how you lost."

"It's not something I feel like delving into at the moment. **Just show me the message.**" Daniel replies, his cup shattering against the wall as he hurls it down the hallway. "The hired help will take care of it in due time."

As Andrew highlights the contentious post, he observes the unmistakable signs of Daniel's growing frustration. Daniel's clenched jaw, furrowed brow, and the fissures in his typically composed facade reveal his curiosity and impatience. The intensity of Daniel's emotions is palpable as shards from the shattered cup scatter across the hallway, their clashing sounds amplifying the tension.

Despite being taken aback by Daniel's sudden outburst, Andrew remains composed, cognizant of the gravity of the situation and the pressing need to address Daniel's concerns. He remains aware of the need for caution when engaging with issues of uncertain veracity.

"This is perfect. It's exactly what I advocate for," Daniel says, his face alight with excitement and a broad grin, his eyes gleaming. His body language radiates victory, shoulders relaxed yet poised with confidence.

In a serene yet firm tone, Andrew reassures him. "I understand your eagerness, but we must proceed with caution. It's crucial to verify the authenticity of the message before drawing any conclusions. After all, if it is a fake, it will harm you more than help you."

Daniel's breathing steadies, and his grip on his emotions begins to relax. He nods in agreement, acknowledging the value of patience and recognizing the need for thorough analysis before drawing conclusions. United in their purpose, Daniel and Andrew shift their attention from emotional turmoil to the pressing task at hand: deciphering the message. As they work together to unravel the mystery, they prepare themselves for the potential revelations and implications it might bring.

"Not everyone may have received it," Andrew says. "My guess is only a select few. They may have even deleted it without reading it."

"I see your point, Andrew. We must broadcast this message. However, the question remains, when would be the most suitable time to do it? If we want to make it public, it should be when everyone is watching their televisions. It's crucial that we inform everyone. Let's schedule a press conference today to make the announcement."

With a determined expression, Daniel reaches for his phone, his hands trembling with a mix of excitement and nervousness. As he dials the numbers, a surge of adrenaline races through his veins, intensifying the gravity of the message they are about to share. Andrew watches, his own sense of purpose mirrored in Daniel's shining eyes. The room fills with an electric energy, as if the air itself carries a sense of urgency.

When the call connects, Daniel's voice quivers slightly with anticipation and conviction. "Hello, this is Daniel," he says, his excitement subtly evident. "I need to schedule a press conference for today. Yes, this is an urgent matter that requires immediate attention." Fueled by the urgency of the situation, Daniel's determination grows, causing his voice to strengthen with each passing word. He provides all the necessary details, ensuring that the message will reach as many people as possible.

Meanwhile, Andrew paces back and forth, his mind racing with thoughts of the impact this announcement will have. A surge of energy, a mixture of anxiety and hope, fills him. Each step he takes echoes in the room, manifesting his restless anticipation.

With the press conference scheduled, Daniel hangs up the phone, his hand trembling. He turns to Andrew, a mix of excitement and apprehension etched on his face. "We've done it," he says, his voice filled with determination.

"Now, we wait for the world to hear our message," the weight of their decision settles upon them as the room falls into a heavy silence. The anticipation in the air is palpable; it feels as if time itself has slowed down. They are aware that once they broadcast the message, there is no turning back.

Cassandra approaches Andrew and Daniel, her voice filled with concern and frustration. "Now that your ego is taken care of, what about those people outside looking for shelter in this devastating storm?"

Daniel responds callously, "What do I care about those vermin? They are leeches on society."

"One of those people is trying to keep her baby warm and alive! If you don't let them come in from the cold, **that baby could die.**" Cassandra pleads, anger welling in her voice as she envisions the desperate mother doing everything she can to save her child.

"One less homeless piece of trash to worry about," Daniel dismisses, his heartlessness evident.

"How can you be so heartless" Cassandra's anger intensifies, her voice trembling. Despite Constance's protests to help the people outside, Daniel disregards them, focusing instead on the upcoming press conference.

Outside, as they head for their car, Constance turns to Andrew and asks with fear and worry, "How can you hold a press conference on information that could be fraudulent? **With his batshit followers, the consequences can range from people getting hurt to something much more tragic.**"

Considering Andrew's suggestion of verifying the information, Constance responds, "If that is the situation, then it is appropriate to allow the courts to handle it. However, there's something unsettling that I can't ignore." Her furrowed brow and piercing gaze reflect the gravity of the situation, creating an electric atmosphere between them. Andrew feels the intensity of her words, his heart racing with a blend of adrenaline and uncertainty. The weight of the risks he is about to take manifests as a knot in his stomach.

In that charged moment, Cassandra's lips brush against Andrew's, offering a brief respite from the mounting tension. This bittersweet gesture leaves him with both comfort and unease. The room seems to hold its breath, filled with anticipation, as their lips part. Andrew's mind becomes a whirlwind of conflicting emotions, torn between the need to proceed and the fear of potential repercussions.

As Constance and Andrew get in the car and drive off, Constance looks out her window and notices dark, ominous clouds swirling in the sky. The air is heavy with the smell of rain and anticipation. In the distance, the rumble of thunder grows louder with each passing moment. She looks out the window and sees the cries of a grieving mother echo through the air, a heart-wrenching sound that pierces Constance's soul. Hopelessness and sadness fill Constance as she watches people hastily gather makeshift items to wrap the dead infant up. The weight of sorrow and loss hangs heavily in the atmosphere, like a thick fog that envelops everything in its path.

As Constance grieves for the poor woman, a thought crosses her mind. *'I hope that heartless bastard never enters the White House.'*

Chapter Three

Upon waking up, William Chavez becomes conscious and carefully examines the surrounding environment. He finds himself in the Presidential bedroom, a domain of grandeur and luxury, adorned with lavish decorations and dominated by a grand four-poster bed. The space radiates a sense of authority and control, accompanied by soft, subdued noises that hint at a rich history and great responsibility. The occasional creaks from the aged wooden floorboards only add to the atmosphere of lasting importance.

As William takes in the room, he detects a slight musty odor blending with the scents of polished wood and fine cologne, further enhancing the room's aura of solemnity and distinction. Surrounded by such splendor, he feels a profound sense of reverence and awe. The room commands respect and evokes admiration, awakening within him a keen sense of the weight of leadership and the significant events that unfold within its walls.

Next to him lies his wife, Amanda, her beauty shining as it always does. William gently leans in to kiss her forehead, releasing a flood of emotions inside him. His heartbeat speeds up, and a smile spreads across his face, bringing him a sense of complete satisfaction. It's as if a gentle hug wraps around him, leaving him feeling content.

"I love you."

Upon leaving the room, a warmth fills William's chest, physically reflecting the love he holds for his wife. The gentle kiss he places on Amanda's forehead seems to lift a burden from his shoulders. Infused with a buoyant lightness, his footsteps become light along the hallway, thanks to the lingering effect of the kiss. The tension in his muscles dissolves, replaced by a glow of affection for Amanda that suffuses his being. Each nerve ending awakens and responds to the joy elicited by his wife's nearness, creating a tingling sensation that skitters across his skin.

The world around William brightens, causing the colors to become even more vivid. His emotions deepen, casting a radiant glow on his surroundings, while his breathing turns deeper and more rhythmic, reflecting his inner tranquility. Each inhalation ushers in new life, and each exhalation dispels lingering concerns. The air, tasting sweeter and purer, rejuvenates him. As he moves, the physical manifestation of his emotions is palpable. It's remarkable how the ethereal sensations of love and joy can profoundly influence his physical state, underscoring the complex link between mind and body. With each stride, the external indicators of his internal emotions are apparent, confirming the profound connection with his wife. The constant warmth in his heart. It leaves a gentle smile on his lips, and the lively bounce in his step. A testimony to the transformative power of love and its lasting impact on his life.

"Mr. President," says Secret Service agent Mark McAllister, a steadfast companion always by President William's side. "Is there anything I can do for you?"

"I'm just heading to the kitchen for some breakfast. Let the First Lady rest a bit more."

"Understood, sir. What should I tell her when she wakes up?" McAllister responds, communicating with his team.

"Just that I'm in the kitchen to get a little breakfast. Is there anything I can get for you?" William asks.

"Not while on duty, sir."

"Then carry on."

Despite the weariness, a sense of pride swells within him. He has dedicated his life to protecting the President and seeing him safely navigate through the challenges of leadership fills McAllister with a deep satisfaction. This feeling of accomplishment courses through his veins, momentarily overshadowing the fatigue.

McAllister knows the world is fraught with uncertainties, and McAllister's duty is to ensure the President's safety amidst the constant threats. This underlying anxiety manifests as a subtle tightening in his chest, as if a vice grip is squeezing his heart. It serves as a constant reminder of the weight of responsibility that accompanies his role.

Simultaneously, a flicker of anticipation dances within McAllister. He knows that today's schedule contains important meetings and critical decisions. The adrenaline courses through his veins, sharpening his focus and heightening his senses.

Despite the physical toll these emotions take on McAllister, he remains steadfast. He has cultivated the ability to compartmentalize his own feelings, always putting the President's needs first. He takes a deep breath, centering himself, and prepares to face the day ahead with unwavering dedication.

William stopped for a second.

"I'll probably miss you the most, always there by the door."

"I guess no one told you. I'm part of your detail when you leave."

"I think I read that somewhere. I'll just be glad that I won't be responsible for the economy or life and death decisions."

"You're probably going to go down as one of the best Presidents ever."

William pats McAllister on the shoulder and heads for the kitchen.

As President Chavez makes his way to the kitchen, the weight of exhaustion is visible in his heavy footsteps and slouched posture. His shoulders, usually held with confidence and strength, now bear the burden of the nation's responsibilities. The lines etched on his face are deeper than before, revealing the toll his role has taken on his physical well-being.

Exhaustion has cast a shadow over his once vibrant eyes, dulling their sparkle. The bags beneath them are evidence of countless sleepless nights spent deliberating over important decisions and grappling with the weight of the nation's problems. The weariness in his gaze reflects the immense mental and emotional strain he has endured.

Yet, despite the fatigue, there is a flicker of anticipation in his weary eyes. It is the anticipation of hope, fueled by his unwavering dedication to the betterment of his country. Even in his depleted state, the prospect of enacting positive change still stirs a sense of renewed energy within him.

Physically, President William's exhaustion manifests in the tension that lingers in his body. His muscles ache, longing for respite from the constant demands placed upon them. The weariness has turned his once strong and sturdy frame into one that appears slightly more fragile, as if the weight of the world has taken its toll on his physical strength.

His shoulders, once broad and squared, now sag under the weight of responsibility, as if burdened by an invisible load. The lines etched across his forehead are deep and pronounced, evidence of the countless hours spent furrowing his brow in deep thought and contemplation. The exhaustion has etched itself onto his face, leaving it pale and drawn, with a hint of pallor that betrays his lack of rest.

The effects of his emotional strain are not limited to his face alone. His hands, once steady and firm, now tremble slightly with fatigue. The once confident stride that commanded attention has been replaced with a slight shuffle, as if each step requires an immense effort. Even his voice, once strong and commanding, now carries a subtle tremor, a reflection of the emotional toll that has been exacted upon him.

The toll of exhaustion is not just visible, but also palpable. The surrounding air seems heavy, as if it carries the weight of his fatigue. His presence, once vibrant and magnetic, now exudes a subdued energy, as if his very essence has been dimmed by the emotional strain he bears.

Despite the physical effects, however, there is an undeniable resilience that emanates from him. It is a testament to his unwavering determination and unwavering spirit. Though physically worn, his eyes still hold a glimmer of determination, a spark that refuses to be extinguished. It is a reminder that even in the face of exhaustion, the human spirit has the capacity to endure and to overcome.

As he stands in the kitchen, President William takes a deep breath, trying to find solace in the familiar surroundings. The anticipation that accompanies him is like a subtle electrical current running through his veins, causing a gentle flutter in his heart. It is a reminder that despite the physical toll, he remains steadfast in his commitment to serving his nation, ready to face whatever challenges lie ahead.

As he steps inside, the warm aroma of freshly brewed tea envelopes his senses. The gentle sizzling of bacon fills the air, creating a symphony of breakfast delights. The inviting scents entice him, promising a comforting and satisfying meal.

Sunlight pours in, enhancing the room's welcoming ambiance. The noise of dishes and murmurs of conversation add vibrancy. The fragrances of fresh fruit and pastries blend with spices, enlivening his senses.

As William's weariness dissipates, a surge of determination courses through his veins, revitalizing his body and mind. His muscles, once heavy with exhaustion, begin to feel taut and energized. With each passing moment, his posture slowly transforms, as if a weight has been lifted off his shoulders. His spine straightens, regaining its natural alignment, while his shoulders square back, exuding a newfound confidence.

However, despite the renewed sense of purpose, subtle signs of his previous fatigue still linger. Though not as pronounced as before, a faint hint of tension remains, causing his once erect posture to curve ever so slightly under the weight of relentless exhaustion. The muscles in his face, which were once strained and fatigued, now relax, allowing his expressions to become more fluid and animated.

As William's determination takes hold, the dark circles beneath his eyes serve as a poignant reminder of the countless sleepless nights he has endured. They speak volumes of the toll his responsibilities have taken on his physical well-being. Etched beneath his tired eyes are the physical manifestations of his dedication and sacrifice, each line telling a story of sleepless nights spent poring over documents and facing tough decisions.

Yet, amidst the weariness and the shadows beneath his eyes, there is an undeniable sense of resilience. His eyes, though tired, still shimmer with an unwavering determination, reflecting the fire within his soul. The physical effects of his emotions serve as a testament to his commitment, reminding him of the challenges he has overcome and the strength he possesses.

As he settles into his chair, the physical transformation continues, a subtle metamorphosis fueled by his resolute spirit. The weariness fades further into the background, replaced by a newfound energy that propels him forward. With each passing moment, William becomes a living embodiment of the emotions coursing through his being, his physicality mirroring the indomitable spirit that resides within.

Yet, within his exhaustion, there's a flicker of enthusiasm. The day ahead promises significant meetings, pivotal choices, and chances to positively affect countless lives. Adrenaline revives his weary form with energy.

The room is filled with the aroma of freshly brewed tea wafting through the air and tantalizing his senses. He can hear the soft rustle of leaves outside, accompanied by the

23

distant chirping of birds. The warmth of the tea cup against his palms brings a comforting sensation, soothing his tired body. The gentle steam rising from the cup tickles his nose, carrying with it the delicate scent of chamomile. As he takes a sip, he feels the energizing effect of the caffeine gradually spreading through his veins, revitalizing his weary mind.

Emotions, both physical and mental, intertwine and dance within President William. Exhaustion and excitement merge, creating a unique blend of sensations. Weariness weighs on his bones, while anticipation fuels his determination. It's a delicate balancing act, one that only a leader of his caliber can navigate.

As his wife enters the room, the atmosphere shifts. The sight of her radiant smile brings warmth and joy. However, he can also see concern and anger in that face.

The physical effects of the emotions are palpable. With each passing moment, the atmosphere seems to vibrate, as if the air itself is charged with energy. The warmth and joy emanating from her radiant smile seem to wrap around him like a comforting blanket, causing a surge of warmth to course through his veins. The concern and anger in her face create a sense of tension, as if the air becomes heavy with unspoken words and unresolved emotions.

The soft sunlight streaming through the window adds to the ethereal ambiance, casting a gentle glow on her face and emphasizing the subtle changes in her expression. It highlights the delicate lines around her eyes, revealing the depth of her emotions. The room seems to bask in this soft illumination, as if holding its breath in anticipation of what is to come.

As she takes each step, her movements are so graceful and elegant that they seem to defy gravity. The sound of her footsteps, though barely audible, resonates with a sense of purpose and determination. It's as if each step holds a weight of its own, marking the significance of her presence.

The scent of her perfume lingers in the air, intertwining with the charged atmosphere. The delicate blend of floral notes invigorates the senses, evoking a sense of familiarity and comfort. The fragrance seems to dance in the air, creating a sensory symphony that adds another layer to the emotional tapestry of the room.

As she finally approaches, a wave of happiness washes over him, almost tangible in its intensity. It feels like a cozy embrace on a cold day, enveloping him in a sense of security and contentment. The physical effects of this emotion are undeniable - his heart rate quickens, a smile tugs at the corners of his lips, and a warm flush spreads across his cheeks.

In this moment, the physical effects of the emotions intertwine with the sensory details of the room, creating a vivid and immersive experience. The atmosphere, the sunlight, the sound, and the scent all contribute to the rich tapestry of emotions, heightening the anticipation and making the encounter all the more profound.

The scent of her perfume lingers a delicate blend of floral notes that lingers in the air. It's a sweet fragrance, reminiscent of a summer garden. The room feels calm and inviting, the lingering scent creating a sense of comfort and familiarity.

Feeling her presence instantly brings a sense of calm and love, creating a soothing ambiance. "Thanks for telling me you're leaving. I nearly had a panic attack. Luckly Mr. McAllister told me where you were. Are you trying to give me a heart attack?" she expresses her frustration.

"Sorry about that. You looked so peaceful sleeping; I couldn't bear to wake you," William responds, trying to lighten the mood with a touch of humor.

"Ever the romantic, you can't expect me from worrying about you. I still remember when you had that heart attack. I thought I was going to lose you."

"You will not lose me soon. You're stuck with me."

"You're hardly the silver-tongued charmer," Amanda kisses William.

The sight of their embrace is tender and intimate, their bodies leaning into each other with a gentle sway. The sound of their kiss is a soft, delicate symphony, the meeting of their lips creating a hushed, sweet melody. The scent of Amanda's perfume lingers in the air, a captivating blend of flowers and warmth. The feeling of William's hand on the small of her back is firm yet gentle, his fingers tracing delicate patterns that send shivers down her spine. The moment is electric, a timeless connection that makes everything else fade away.

As Amanda playfully kisses William, a mixture of relief and lingering worry intertwine, creating a bittersweet sensation within her.

The bittersweet sensation Amanda feels manifests in physical effects that cascade through her body. Pulling away from the kiss, she is enveloped by a wave of relief that lightens her shoulders and dissolves the tension within. A weight seems to lift from her chest, permitting a deep, easeful breath to fill her lungs.

"I love starting our day like that," William says.

"I know you do. But we still have to talk about you sneaking out to the kitchen. We also need to talk about your eating habits." She looks at the food that William has on his plate. **"You're just inviting another heart attack."**

"I found a way to get past chief. It's called getting it myself."

"Well. You know what Chelsea would do if she saw what you're eating?"

"Probably raid all the kitchens in the White House."

"And your secret stashes."

"How do you know about those?"

"Trade secrets."

Amanda still feels a subtle undertone of worry lingering within her. This worry manifests as a slight tightening in her stomach, causing her muscles to contract ever so slightly. It's like a knot, gently twisting and turning, reminding her that not everything is perfect, that uncertainties still remain.

Her heart, caught between conflicting emotions, beats at an irregular pace, its rhythm mirroring the ebb and flow of her feelings. Each thump feels both stronger and more fragile at the same time, as if her heart is trying to reconcile the conflicting emotions within her.

As Amanda's lips tingle with the remnants of the kiss, a tingling sensation spreads across her skin, like tiny electric currents dancing beneath the surface. It's as if her body is responding to the mixture of relief and worry, sending subtle signals that reverberate throughout her being.

Meanwhile, Amanda's hands, which were entangled in William's hair during the kiss, now tremble ever so slightly. The nervous energy that still lingers causes her fingers to twitch involuntarily, a physical manifestation of the emotional rollercoaster she finds herself on.

Overall, the physical effects of the bittersweet emotions within Amanda are a delicate dance between relief and worry. They play out in her body, creating a unique and complex physical experience that mirrors the intricate blend of emotions she feels in that moment.

Both William and Amanda's eyes meet, revealing the depth of their emotions. William's eyes sparkle with love and longing, reflecting the joy he feels in Amanda's presence. His pupils dilate ever so slightly, a subtle sign of his heightened interest and attraction towards her.

Amanda's eyes hold a mixture of playfulness and concern. They shimmer with a mischievous glint, revealing her desire to keep the mood light despite her lingering worries. Yet, a hint of worry lingers within her gaze, a reflection of the fear she experienced during the potential panic attack.

As the physical effects of their emotions intertwine, their bodies respond in harmony. Their heartbeats sync, pounding in unison, as if their love and worries intertwine. The room fills with a palpable energy, charged with a mix of affection, frustration, and genuine care.

As they continue with their breakfast, the physical effects of their emotions become more pronounced. William's heart begins to race, a subtle yet noticeable thump echoing in his chest. The nervous energy that accompanies his anticipation of the day ahead causes his palms to grow slightly clammy, the moisture clinging to his skin.

Amanda, on the other hand, feels a warmth spreading through her body, radiating from the core of her being. It's as if every cell in her body is lit up with a gentle glow, a physical manifestation of the joy she feels in William's presence. Her cheeks take on a rosy hue, as if they are blushing in response to the overwhelming emotions that course through her.

As they exchange glances, their eyes sparkle with excitement, reflecting the intensity of their emotions. William's pupils dilate ever so slightly, a biological response to the surge of adrenaline that accompanies his growing affection for Amanda. His breath quickens, becoming slightly shallower, as if his body is trying to match the rapid pace of his racing thoughts.

Amanda's body language also speaks volumes about her emotions. Her posture becomes more open and inviting, her shoulders relaxed as she leans in closer to William. The corners of her lips turn upward in a contented smile, while her fingertips tingle with a delightful sensation, a physical reminder of the butterflies that flutter in her stomach.

As they finish breakfast and William glances at his palm top, the physical effects of their emotions begin to subside slightly. But the lingering warmth on their chests and the soft glow in their eyes remain, serving as a constant reminder of the intricate dance of emotions they share.

"After we finish, I need to meet with Bill." Wiliam says.

"Why not simply call him?"

"Because he might be four sheets to the wind and not answer the phone, or worse, he might answer the phone, in which case it's all logged in the White House database. I would rather have a heart to heart." William reasons, aware of his colleague's habits.

William's frustration is clear in his words, his brows furrowing slightly as he contemplates the potential unreliability of his colleague Bill. The thought of Bill being intoxicated evokes a sense of annoyance within William, causing his muscles to tense. As he speaks, his voice carries a hint of exasperation, the words flowing at a quicker pace than usual.

The mere idea of having to physically meet with Bill, despite the convenience of a phone call, elicits a sense of weariness on William's body. His shoulders slump slightly, as if burdened by the additional effort that might be required. The weight of this task seems to settle upon him, causing a subtle heaviness to his posture.

A touch of concern dances in William's eyes, evident in the way they dart around, searching for a solution. The creases around his eyes deepen, betraying his worry about the possibility of Bill's inebriation hindering their communication. William's gaze remains focused, as if trying to envision the potential scenarios that may arise from this encounter.

As William weighs the options in his mind, his fingertips tap against the surface of the table, a physical manifestation of his mental activity. The sound of the tapping serves as a subtle backdrop to his thoughts, revealing his inner restlessness.

Overall, William's physical demeanor reflects a mixture of annoyance, weariness, concern, and restlessness. These emotions subtly manifest in his facial expressions, body language, and even the rhythm of his movements, offering glimpses into the complex web of thoughts and feelings swirling within him.

"Do you really would've gotten drunk? Amanda asks.

"He lost the Presidential election to that damn woman. Worse, he only got thirty percent of the vote. Either one would have made him turn to the bottle."

"And what about you? I bet you had your fair share of Scotch yesterday."

"Well, I have to go."

"That's what I thought. Oh well. I would go with you, but I have that homeless charity lunch in," Amanda expresses her regret.

"Always helping the homeless."

"Remember, although my family wasn't homeless, we were far from affluent. We frequently visited food pantries and hoped fervently that we'd have enough money to cover the bills. I just wish I could do more to help the homeless."

As Amanda spoke, a pang of regret washed over her, causing a subtle tightening in her chest. The weight of her words seemed to manifest as her shoulders drooped ever so slightly, conveying her disappointment. Her normally radiant eyes dulled momentarily, mirroring the sorrow she felt deep within.

With every passing moment, Amanda could feel her heart sinking, almost as if it were being pulled downwards by an invisible force. The heaviness in her chest seemed to spread, creating a dull ache that resonated through her entire body. It was as if her emotions were translating into physical sensations, overwhelming her with a tangible sense of regret.

As she continued to express her remorse, Amanda's body language revealed her inner turmoil. Her animated gestures became more restrained, her hands fidgeting, as if trying to find solace in their own movements. She twists a strand of her hair around her finger, a subconscious attempt to distract herself from the weight of her decision.

"I remember. After all, it was at a food pantry that I was volunteering where we first met."

As President William finishes his breakfast and kisses Amanda again. He reflects on the first meeting with Amanda. She was seventeen, and he was twenty. Her parents walking around the pantry trying to get some food. He took one look at Amanda and was instantly in love. "Here, take a little more." William said to Amanda's parents. While making small talk with Amanda. Along with the food, he slipped her his number. A few months later, Amanda's mother started a new career. Two years after their first meeting, William and Amanda were married.

As he gets up the toll on his body is undeniable, but so is the resilience that allows him to persevere. It's a constant reminder of the sacrifices he makes and the immense responsibility he carries. With renewed strength and purpose, President William resumes his duties, ready to face the day's challenges. The physical effects of his emotions will persist, but they won't deter him from his role as the nation's leader.

Chapter Four

U pon his arrival at the Vice President's home, conflicting emotions overwhelmed William. The air is crisp and biting, causing him to pull his coat tighter around him as the chill seeps into his bones. Exhaustion weighs heavily on him, making each step feel like a burden. However, the sight of the warm glow emanating from the windows offers a glimmer of respite from the cold.

'Damn, just last week it was in the eighties.'

He contemplates if he can do more to help with the climate crisis, but then realizes that the point of no return occurs several decades ago. Memories of lost empires and flooded cities flood his mind, from England lost to the English Channel to the Florida keys and places like Miami and Orlando now submerged. The rising waters also affected the west coast and Hawaiian islands. He remembers going on a scuba dive trip to what was once called Seaside, Oregon.

With military officers saluting him, William's mind drifted back to the present. "Sir."

"At ease. I'm here to see the Vice-President."

He notices the door open, revealing Bill's wife, Grace. Her anxious and irate demeanor sends a shiver of unease through him, causing his muscles to stiffen and a tightness to grip his stomach. Despite her hesitance, Grace beckons him inside, her tone laced with reluctance. William's tension subsides, but his pulse races as he braces for the impending dispute. As he stepped into the complex, a faint heat suffused his being, signaling the onset of rising fury. His complexion reddens, and his fists ball up, mirroring the fervor of his feelings as he gears up for a quarrel. In this moment, William grasps the deep impact of emotions on the physique, recognizing the intricate connection between his emotional and corporeal states. Every notion and sentiment transforms into a palpable, corporeal reaction.

With each step, his growing attunement to the subtle dance between his inner turmoil and the external world becomes more evident. He can feel his emotions physically shaping his reality. "I need to see Bill," William states urgently, leaving no room for argument. Grace lets out a sigh and motions for William to enter.

"Bill's in our room. After our argument and his loss in the election, I think he might resort to drinking. That's why I stayed in the guest room.

Curiosity lingers as William asks, "What is the argument about?" Grace recalls telling Bill that the party he represents for several years is fading, the same party William represents. She doesn't want to repeat the same argument.

"I rather not say."

William respects her decision and drops the topic. In her own way, Grace matches Bill's resoluteness and unpredictability. "Unfortunately, I need Bill, dealing with Senate issues, and ensuring a seamless, peaceful transition of power. Operations of the US government **must continue** uninterrupted, even after an electoral loss." William's tone reflects the seriousness of the matter.

Signs of stress manifest, such as a quickened heartbeat, clammy hands, rapid and shallow breathing, a creased forehead, and stiff muscles, revealing his inner turmoil. His stooped posture underscores the weight of the situation. Grace, in contrast, appears exhausted and irritated. Her sigh, laden with emotion, reflects her mental weariness. A flicker of irritation makes her fingers quiver as she waves her hand in a dismissive gesture. Her once lively and expressive eyes now appear tired and red from sleepless nights and emotional strain. The recent quarrel with Bill results in a lingering headache, which she massages.

Grace nods. "Of course. Right this way." Guiding William to the room she shares with Bill. The door creaks, echoing through the silent house, amplifying the tension. As her eyes land on Bill, her heart skips a beat, and warmth spreads through her chest. Seeing him engrossed in his work brings a gentle smile to her lips. However, as she steps closer, a bittersweet ache tugs at her heartstrings, catching her breath. Her body reacts, causing her skin to tingle and her palms to grow clammy. The room feels smaller, as if the walls are closing in. The creaking sound of the floorboards echoes, magnifying the deep quiet that envelops the house. A mix of joy and sorrow swirls within her, creating a whirlwind of conflicting sensations. Her stomach tightens, tied in knots, as if expecting what's coming. Her heart races, pounding against her ribcage like a wild bird trying to break free.

As Grace's gaze lingers on Bill's face, tears well up in her eyes, blurring her vision. The moisture gathers at the corners, threatening to spill over. The lump in her throat makes it difficult to speak or swallow. Her trembling fingers instinctively reach out, yearning to touch his familiar face. The physical urge to connect with him is almost overwhelming. The room seems to hold its breath, as if the air is aware of the weight of the emotions between them. This emotional encounter seems to command the world's attention, magnifying and exaggerating every sound and movement. While watching Bill, his diligent work ethic strikes William. He feels a surge of admiration and respect for Bill's capacity to handle multiple tasks, managing business calls with assurance while writing crucial notes. The room vibrates with the intensity of Bill's focus and drive. A bittersweet sensation sweeps through Grace as she grasps the magnitude of Bill's decision to run for the House seat, a pivotal moment in their lives. Pride and anxiety blend within her, aware that this new direction will present both obstacles and possibilities. The weight of the future looms large around them.

"No, I plan to declare my candidacy for the House seat in January's special election...No as an independent." Bill proclaims, his voice a mix of excitement and melancholy. William feels a deep loss at the words he just heard from Bill, who is leaving the Republican party. Grace, beside herself with joy, wonders if her words resonate with her husband. With every word spoken, a wave of anticipation rises within him, ready to reveal his campaign and strengthen his determination. Upon hanging up the phone, Bill felt renewed motivation, strengthening his resolve to overcome recent difficulties. The emotions stirring within him translate into various physical sensations. Bill states, "I thought about what you said the other day," as he approaches Grace, who responds with a comforting smile. "You're right; the Republican party is dead. I was just too stubborn to see it. Yet, for me, aligning with America Now is not a possibility."

"I never thought you'd join America Now, and you swore you'd never join the Democrats. I suppose choosing to be an Independent is a wise decision," Grace replies. With a hint of optimism, Bill's eyes gleam as he grasps Grace's hands. "Perhaps, in time, I might unite what's left of the Republicans and Democrats against America Now. They must be stopped, no matter the cost." Hearing the note of optimism, William realizes that someone needs to take action. As he contemplates the consequences of Daniel's loss in the election, a wave of anxiety washes over him, sending an icy shiver down his spine. He can feel his heart pounding in his chest, the rapid thumping echoing in his ears. The weight of the situation seems to press down on his shoulders, causing tension to coil into his muscles.

As he contemplates the potential havoc that American Now supporters could wreak upon cities, a sense of dread settles in the pit of his stomach. A knot forms, twisting and turning, as if his insides are tightly bound. The thought of destruction and chaos fills him with unease, causing his stomach to churn and a faint queasiness to rise. Simultaneously, a surge of anger courses through William's veins, causing his face to flush with heat. His fists involuntarily clench, his muscles tensing with a mix of frustration and disbelief. The intensity of his emotions seems to radiate from his body, creating a palpable energy that vibrates in the surrounding air. Amidst the emotional turmoil, a tinge of sadness creeps into William's being. He feels a heaviness in his chest, as if a weight has settled upon his heart. Each breath becomes slightly harder to take, as if the surrounding air has thickened, suffocating him with grief and disappointment. "If anyone can do it, it's you," William says, giving his Vice-President a hug. The room transforms into a melting pot of emotions, where tension, nostalgia, determination, and excitement merge, creating an electrifying atmosphere. It is as though the room itself reacts to these emotions, altering the energy that everyone can feel. William's surprise triggers an adrenaline surge, accelerating his heartbeat and causing his hands to tremble slightly. This rush of energy heightens his senses, intensifying every sound and sharpening every detail. As he continues further into the room, his muscles stiffen, preparing him for whatever lays ahead.

The sight of broken glass scattered on the floor sends shivers up William's spine as the shards glisten in the faint light, reflecting the chaos that unfolds. He scanned the room, noting the chaotic pillows—a sign of Bill's anger. The heavy smell of alcohol added to his dizziness. A lump forms in his stomach as he tries to make sense of the scene before him, his brow furrowing with concern and his mind racing to understand.

Adrenaline courses through his body, making his hands moist and his grip slippery. However, amidst the disorder, William experiences an unforeseen sense of relief, alleviating his initial fear. His shoulders, previously tense, now relax as he realizes the situation is not as dire as he thinks. The tension in his face softens, and a subtle smile forms, showing a change to cautious optimism.

As the initial shock wears off, William's body adapts to the new reality. His heartbeat normalizes, his breathing deepens, and he regains his calm. His muscles unwind, no longer bound by the earlier stress.

Grace glances at William and says, "Sorry, I'll leave you two to chat. I'm so proud of you." She kisses Bill before cheerfully making her way to the door.

She walks away, and a warm and content emotion overwhelms her chest. Her heart pulses with happiness. A gentle smile graces her face, and her steps lighten, as though she's walking on air. Her body appears to emanate happiness, clear in the sparkle of her eyes and the ease of her shoulders. The physical sensations are significant for William. His heartbeat slows to the calm cadence of his breathing, and the tension in his stomach eases, replaced by a soft flutter. His muscles relax, allowing him to stand straighter, exuding confidence and grace in his movements. In this moment, the physical manifestations of their emotions stand as proof of the strength of human bonds. Their joy and relief seem to transform their very beings, revitalizing them from the inside and wrapping them in the serenity surrounding them. They understand their emotions influence not just their minds but their physical states as well.

William offered his commendation as he approached his Vice-President. "Bill, your composure is like that of a staunch champion, even in defeat, like Grace. I'm very proud of you. To be fair, I thought you would be four sheets to the wind." He remarks as he pats Bill on the shoulder, his tone betraying his astonishment. Bill, with a brief flush of embarrassment tinting his cheeks, confesses, "After conceding the election, I... indulged in a few shots of Jack Daniels, I must confess." This confession adds a layer of vulnerability, revealing the cracks in his otherwise steadfast demeanor. A spectrum of emotions dances across his face, betraying the emotional tempest he has endured. The grueling campaign has carved lines of exhaustion into his forehead, and sorrow lives in his eyes. Yet, there's a palpable resilience about him, resembling an unyielding flame. The physical manifestations of Bill's emotional odyssey are apparent. His hands quiver, mirroring the strain of the electoral contest. His shoulders, once emblems of determination, now sag slightly, burdened by the defeat. The determined clench of his jaw tells of the formidable challenges he has encountered.

Bill's voice, typically firm and assured, trembles, betraying his emotional turmoil. Despite showing clear signs of fatigue and disillusionment, he continues to emit a resilient aura. It seems every challenge only strengthens his resolve to overcome. His demeanor, marked by silent strength and steady calm, reveals much about his character. Bill's unyielding spirit does not allow defeat to define him. At this moment, with his emotions intermingling and conflicting, he stands as a testament to the intricate and significant influence emotions exert on our physical presence. They etch onto his face, stance, and tone, portraying a man who perseveres and propels forward.

Bill recounted, "while nursing another drink, a friend called. He reminded me he turned his career's lowest points into successes because of something I said. I may have lost this election, but this isn't the last of me," Bill says with determination. He clenches his fists, the tension in his muscles escalating. The physical manifestation of his emotions is clear, his tightened grip symbolizing his unwavering resolve. His grasp reflects the inner strength and determination he harbors. With every breath he takes, his inhalations grow deeper and more purposeful, his chest rising and falling with intent. These breaths are akin to new life, filling his lungs with renewed optimism. As he exhales, he releases any remaining doubts or fears, making space for a firm belief in his ability to turn challenges into triumphs. Bill's physical reactions mirror his emotional state. The sensations and responses he experiences are outward signs of the passion within.

"I'm relieved to hear that, Bill," William asserts, stressing the need to move forward as tasks await. While he speaks, Grace bursts in, her usual serenity replaced by alarm. "Grace, what's the problem?" Bill asks. "You need to see what's on the TV," she announces, her voice laden with astonishment as she turns it on. With a sense of urgency, the men quickly make their way to the television.

As the television screen captures their attention, an immediate tension fills the room, causing a shift in the atmosphere. Grace's heart races, fueled by adrenaline coursing through her like a swift stream. Her previously poised nature is now overshadowed by an untamed agitation, causing her to quiver with anxious energy. Noticing her panic, and in response to the urgency in Grace's gaze, the men's pace quickened. A series of physical reactions unfold among them. Gathered around the TV, their breathing becomes shallow and fast, their chests heaving in unison. Beads of sweat form on their brows, glistening in the low light. Their muscles tense, jaws clench, and fists close, all reflecting the heightened intensity of the moment. It was Grace that broke the silence. "It can't be."

Chapter Five

J ill's body enters a state of complete relaxation as her husband's skilled touch causes the muscles in her back to yield. With each soothing pressure coursing through her body, a wave of contentment washes over her, causing her mind to drift into a state of pure bliss. A gentle smile curves across her lips as she experiences the sensations. Steve's touch seems to awaken every nerve ending in Jill's body, heightening her sensitivity to touch and prompting her to express her delight. "Oh, I love it when you massage just one spot on my shoulder," The tingling sensation intensifies, bringing warmth and comfort, effectively easing tension. Steve chuckles and moves her hand down her naked back, his spine shivering at the sight of her smooth, bare skin. As their bodies move against each other, the room fills with the intoxicating scent of their shared desire. Steve's hand glides over her skin, sensing the warmth and softness beneath his fingertips, each touch igniting an electric sensation that sets a fire within him. "Mmm, that feels amazing," Jill purrs.

"Just relax and let go of all the tension."

"I can't remember the last time I felt this good,".

"You deserve this,"

"I feel like I'm floating,"

"That's the whole point, my sweetie. Let the stress melt away."

With each passing moment, her senses grow increasingly heightened. She is experiencing the gentle hum of the bed beneath her, creating a soothing vibration that resonates with her very core. The fragrance of lavender permeates the air, augmenting the tranquil ambiance and contributing to her deep relaxation. Jill closes her eyes, allowing the experience to consume her as she envisions the tension fading and dissipating like smoke. She also senses that the skilled hands of the masseuse are not only restoring her physical body but also working their magic on her emotional well-being. Jill's body shifted and sank deeper into the bed as the massage continued. Her muscles grew pliable, unknotting. With each passing moment, a sense of renewal fills her, replacing fatigue and stress with renewed vitality. In this harmonious dance of relaxation and pleasure, the physical effects of the massage merge seamlessly with her emotions, creating a state of pure bliss. It is in this moment of complete surrender that the outside world fades away, and all that matters is the exquisite sensation coursing through her entire being.

Curiously, her husband, Steve, breaks into her stream of thoughts and asks, "So, what are your plans for today?"

Jill pauses briefly, gathering her thoughts before responding. "First, I take the kids to school. Then, I help my staff dismantle my campaign headquarters," she says, her eyes displaying her focus on the tasks ahead.

"Are you certain that is your initial course of action?"

Jill turns to face Steve, momentarily captivated by his bare chest.

While massaging her ears, he applies soothing pressure that sends waves of relaxation through her body, easing the stresses of the day and loosening her tense muscles. "You know, there are other things we could do," Steve whispers.

The mixture of his touch and the intimacy in his voice creates an electrifying sensation, quickening her heart's pace. With her breath caught in her throat, a warm flush spread across her cheeks, revealing the intensity of the emotions welling up inside her. Every nerve ending awakens, heightening her sensitivity to every touch, word, and subtle movement. It's as if her entire being is responding to the physical effects of the emotions, creating a symphony of sensations in perfect harmony.

"I need to prepare to dismantle the office," Steve's lips continue their tantalizing journey down her neck. His touch ignites a shiver down her spine, causing her muscles to tense in anticipation. Goosebumps prickling her skin manifest as the desire continues building within her. Her heart rate quickens, blood rushes to her cheeks as her body prepares for the upcoming wave of pleasure. His touch, along with their intimate connection, causes electric currents to surge through veins. With each kiss and caress, Jill's body becomes increasingly sensitive to his touch. Her skin flushes with a rosy hue, visibly reflecting the heightened blood flow and intense emotions she experiences. Shallow breaths mirror the increasing intensity of her desire, her rising and falling with each inhale and exhale.

As the physical sensations intensify, Jill's body subtly responds with cues. Her nipples harden in response to the delicate attention given to her, and a soft moan escapes her lips, reacting to the pleasure coursing through her. However, these physical effects of Jill's arousal extend beyond her skin and senses. Inside her, a warm, pulsating sensation spreads, igniting a yearning that kindles a fire deep within her core. Her body becomes more supple, her limbs turning into putty in his hands. Her muscles relax in readiness for the passionate connection they are about to share. Desire and pleasure intertwine with Jill's emotions, painting her body like a canvas in this delicate dance of physical and emotional connection. Every touch, every kiss, and every breath become intertwined with her emotions, heightening the experience and creating a symphony of sensations that leaves an indelible mark on her memory.

When Jill's lips reach his, a surge of passion courses through her body, causing her heart to race and her cheeks to flush with a rosy hue. Her breath quickens, becoming shallow and erratic in response to the anticipation and desire. A tingling sensation spreads from her lips, igniting a cascade of pleasant shivers down her spine. It seems as though every nerve ending has come alive, and even her fingertips tingle with an electric energy. In that moment, time seems to stand still as the physical sensations blend with the emotional connection between Jill and her husband.

"I guess the kids could be a little late and it's not like the office is going anywhere," she thinks as she leans in to kiss her husband. As their lips meet, a rush of warmth spreads across her body, accompanied by a tingling sensation that intensifies her anticipation.

Her heart quickens its pace, desperately trying to keep up with the growing surge of desire. With each kiss, she experiences a surge of electricity running through her veins, setting a blaze inside her. The passionate embrace between Jill and her husband continues to intensify, and she can't help but notice the butterflies fluttering in the pit of her stomach. This thrilling and comforting sensation is a physical representation of the love and connection they share. As their senses become heightened, every sensation seems magnified, from the gentle brush of his hands on her skin to the softness of his lips against hers. While moving in unison, Steve also experiences moments of pure passion. He realizes his muscles tensing and relaxing in a rhythmic motion, syncing with the ebb and flow of their intimate dance.

Adrenaline courses through his body, providing a surge of energy that fuels their passionate encounter. His breathing becomes deeper and more erratic, mirroring the rising intensity of their shared desire. As their bodies intertwine, a wave of heat washes over both Jill and Steve, causing their skin to flush and their cheeks to redden. The physical closeness and raw intimacy create a sense of vulnerability, yet it also serves as a testament to the trust and connection they have built. The physical act of love becomes a conduit for their emotions, amplifying the depth of their bond. At this moment, time stands still, and the outside world fades away. The physical effects of their emotions create a symphony of sensations, heightening their pleasure and deepening their connection. It serves as a reminder that love is not only an emotional experience but also a tangible and physical one.

Afterward, she glances at her watch and realizes she is running late. "Oh shit." She quickly gets out of bed and prepares to leave.

Just as she is about to make her way out the door, Steve, notices her hurried movements and asks, "Where are you going?"

Jill responds with a hint of sarcasm, her voice laced with annoyance, "Off to the shower. I still need to drop the kids off at school before heading to the office. Remember?"

Steve, trying to be helpful, "Why don't we save water and time by showering together?"

Jill acknowledges his consideration with a slight smile. "That's environmentally thoughtful of you," she says as she starts making her way towards the bathroom. Once inside, the warm water cascades over their bodies, creating a sense of comfort and relaxation.

"I'm very environmentally conscience."

As they stand under the soothing stream, Jill and Steve find solace in its embrace, their bodies responding to the emotions coursing through them. The sensations seem to intensify as the water caresses them, deepening their physical connection. Jill's heart races, her breath quickens, and desire pulses through her veins.

The steamy atmosphere adds an element of intimacy and secrecy to their private moment, heightening the sense of pleasure they share. Their hands explore each other's bodies, each touch from Steve sending shivers down Jill's spine, causing her muscles to tense and relax.

The water droplets create a sensual symphony as they cascade down their bodies, increasing the pleasure they both experience. The mingling scent of their shower gel and natural bodies fills the air, creating an intoxicating aroma that enhances the sensory experience.

The blend of aromas, vapor, and heat surrounds them, heightening their awareness and boosting their enjoyment. Their lips meet in passionate kisses, their breathing quickens, and their heartbeats synchronize in a passionate rhythm.

As the physical act of kissing floods their bodies with a surge of endorphins, their connection intensifies further. Guided by the deep emotional bond they share, their bodies move in harmony, responding to the pleasure and desire that consumes them.

The water, steam, and scent create an otherworldly ambiance, enhancing every touch, every kiss, and every intimate act. It's a moment of pure sensory bliss, where their emotions and physicality merge into one beautiful, passionate dance.

As their amorous encounter continued, Steve and Jill's bodies released endorphins, natural chemicals that acted as powerful painkillers and mood enhancers. These endorphins flooded their systems, creating a euphoric sensation that elevated their pleasure and strengthened their connection. Reveling in the physical effects of their emotions, they delved deeper into their desires, moving in perfect harmony with their intertwined bodies.

After the shower, Steve and Jill make their way back to the bed, continuing their passionate embrace with fervent kisses. Steve's heart races, pumping blood throughout his body at an accelerated pace, heightening his state of arousal. This increased excitement causes his muscles to tense, infusing his movements with strength and vigor. The rush of adrenaline coursing through his veins intensifies his senses, turning each touch and caress from Jill into an electrifying source of pleasure.

"You look amazing, Jill," Steve utters, his voice filled with admiration.

"Mmm, you too, Steve," Jill responds, sliding her hand between his knees. "I can't get enough of you."

Steve, with a surge of desire, gently lays Jill on the bed and positions himself on top of her. "Good, because I don't want to stop." A sense of exhilaration was evident in his voice.

In that moment, both Steve and Jill feel an overwhelming sense of aliveness. Excitement and desire consumes their bodies, causing Jill's skin to flush with a rosy hue. Her body temperature rises, and her breathing quickens, her chest rising and falling rapidly as she struggles to take in enough oxygen to support the intensity of her passion.

As their amorous encounter continues, Steve and Jill's body's release endorphins, natural chemicals that act as powerful painkillers and mood enhancers. These endorphins flood their systems, creating a euphoric sensation that elevates their pleasure and strengthens their connection. Exploring their desires further, their bodies intertwine and move in perfect harmony, reveling in the physical effects of their emotions. The intense heat of their passion radiates from their bodies, filling the room with palpable energy. It serves as a testament to the profound physical and emotional connection they share, a connection that transcends words and becomes an undeniable force.

Later, Jill starts putting on her clothes. As she does, Steve asks, "Are you still taking the kids to school?" Jill walks back to the bed and replies,

"You always do it when I'm not home. I just want to spend time with the kids before the inauguration." Steve nods, understanding her perspective. "Don't get me wrong. I would love to just stay up here with you and take care of that pent-up energy you seem to have today. I don't remember you having that much energy, except during our honeymoon." She suggests, "Maybe tonight we can find other ways to liven up events."

"Maybe we can convince the kids to spend the night at some friend's house and see how sturdy some of the furniture is."

Jill considers the logistics, saying, "We'll have to see. It depends on how long it will take to tear down the office. However, if you wait, I will make it worth your time. I still remember we have some chocolate syrup." With that, Jill gives Steve a kiss and leaves the room.

As Steve goes about his morning routine, his emotions stir within him, subtly manifesting in various physical ways. Upon entering the walk-in closet, a sense of excitement washes over him, causing his heart rate to increase slightly. This surge of energy translates into a quicker step and a bounce in his movements. He carefully selects his clothes, noticing a sense of confidence building up. His posture straightens, and with each deep breath he takes, his chest expands. He envisions the productive day ahead. A smile graces his face, and his eyes light up with a spark of determination.

With each step down the stairs, Steve's anticipation transformed into concentration. His breathing becomes steadier, and his muscles tighten slightly in preparation for the tasks awaiting him. From within, a sense of purpose radiates, propelling him forward. Upon entering his office, a wave of calm washes over Steve. As he sits down at his desk, his body relaxes, and his breathing slows. The steady rhythm of his heartbeat provides a sense of grounding, allowing him to concentrate on his accounting job with clarity and precision.

Alone in his office, the heavy weight of his emotions bore down on him. The quietness of the house amplifies the intensity of his thoughts, causing his heart to beat faster and his breathing to become shallow. The heaviness in his chest is a physical representation of his yearning for Jill's presence.

The dimly lit office is filled with the scent of stale tea, mingling with the faint aroma of paper and ink. Outside, the distant sound of traffic echoes through the closed windows, reminding me of the bustling world beyond. The silence is broken only by the ticking of the clock on the wall, each second magnifying the weight of Steve's emotions. The air feels heavy, suffocating, as if his thoughts are tangible entities pressing down on him. His heart pounds in his ears, the rhythm matching the racing thoughts in his mind.

Recalling the early part of the morning, and my mind floods with bittersweet memories. A surge of energy courses through my body, rejuvenating me in ways I haven't experienced in a long time. However, as Steve contemplates Jill's upcoming presidency, a mix of happiness and uncertainty begins to manifest as physical sensations. A knot forms in his stomach, causing a slight discomfort. Steve worry's about whether they will be able to have moments like they did this morning. The thought of Jill being occupied with the demands of her new position brings a sense of restlessness, making his muscles tense and his body fidgety.

Steve's mind races, conjuring images of Jill being whisked away to crises and attend to state matters. Each thought triggers a subtle, involuntary tightening of his jaw and a creasing of his brow. The anticipation of their future together leaves him with a mix of excitement and trepidation, which translates into a subtle trembling in his hands. As Steve contemplates the dynamic changes that lie ahead, his body becomes more attuned to the ebb and flow of his emotions. His thoughts manifest physically, a stark reminder of his complex relationship with Jill. The challenges of balancing their personal and professional lives loom large.

Chapter Six

Jill rushes through her morning routine, her mind a whirlwind of emotions. Anxiety grips her chest, causing her heart to race and her palms to grow clammy. The weight of anticipation settles heavily on her shoulders, making her spine feel tense and rigid. She slips into her perfectly tailored pants suit, unable to help but notice how her body reacts to the mix of excitement and nervousness. Her muscles feel taut and ready for action, as if preparing for a race. Adrenaline courses through her veins, energizing her every movement and leaving her with a tingling sensation in her limbs. As she grabs her keys, a surge of determination courses through her, manifesting as a surge of heat in her cheeks. The fire of motivation burns within her, propelling her forward with a sense of purpose.

As she calls for the children, her voice carries a mixture of excitement and urgency, betraying the underlying emotions that threaten to spill over. Her voice trembles slightly, revealing the nervousness that still lingers beneath her confident facade. Meanwhile, her children, sensing the charged atmosphere, mirror her emotions. Their eyes sparkle with a mix of curiosity and anticipation, their bodies buzzing with an electric energy that mirrors their mother's. They, too, feel the physical effects of the emotions swirling around them, their hearts pounding in synchrony with their mother's.

In the midst of this whirlwind of emotions, breakfast is finished hastily but with an almost palpable intensity. The clinking of cutlery against plates and the hurried footsteps of the children add to the chaotic symphony of emotions that fill the air. "We're running behind," Rachel, her daughter says. "I know. Get your things together and let's get going."

NAZI AMERICA CONSPRACY COPY

"Do we really need to go?" her son, Henry, the youngest of her children, says. "**Yes, that is a direct order from your future President!**" Jill says. The words are still new to her. "Now get going or I'll sic the Justice Department on you." "Yes, ma'am," both kids say.

As they prepare to leave, Jill's body feels both lighter and heavier at the same time. Lighter, as the excitement lifts her spirits, filling her with a sense of possibility. Heavier, as the weight of responsibility settles on her shoulders, reminding her of the important task that lies ahead.

In this moment, as Jill leads her children out the door, they can't ignore the physical effects of their emotions. It serves as a reminder that they are embarking on a new chapter of their lives, an uncertain journey that lies ahead. However, despite the uncertainty, their shared emotions bind them together, giving them the strength and determination to face whatever challenges await them.

Outside, their Secret Service detail greets Jill and the kids. "Where are you heading to, ma'am?" one of them asks. "Taking the kids to Giles Corey High School," Jill replies. She gets into the car while the Secret Service takes the lead vehicle. This attention is something Jill is used to, but her kids decide to embrace it and pretend they are in a parade.

They finally arrived at the school. As they stepped out of the car, the sight of the school captivated them. Tall and proud, the three-story white building gleamed in the sunlight. Its modern design exuded a sense of sophistication, reflecting its youth of just a decade. The scent of fresh paint lingered in the air, hinting at the care and maintenance given to the premises.

Voices echoed from the open gym doors on the ground floor, where the sounds of basketballs bouncing and sneakers squeaking filled the atmosphere. Upstairs, the hushed murmurs of students engaged in deep discussions could be heard, a testament to the academic prowess of the school.

Further in, the pristine locker rooms emitted a faint smell of disinfectant, reminding one of the students' energetic routines. Walking through the corridors, the feeling of excitement intertwined with a hint of nervousness enveloped them, as they expected the challenging math, science, and politics programs for which the school was renowned.

The school was initially named Buzz Aldrin High School until it was destroyed by fire and subsequently rebuilt. The school board opted to preserve the original design. Rumors suggest that the school was erected on the site where Mr. Corey was pressed to death during the Witch Trials. Some believe his spirit haunts the school, resulting in teachers resigning and stories proliferating.

With Jill standing outside the newly rebuilt school, her eyes scanned the grand entrance. The rumors of hauntings and eerie spirits seem distant now, replaced by a sense of curiosity about what lies inside. As she steps through the doors, a surge of anticipation mixed with a hint of unease washes over her. "Okay, well, have a good day in school," Jill says to her children. Her daughter reminds her that they are late and need to go to the office to get a tardy slip. Jill glances at her watch and thinks, 'Of course it does.' "Very well, let's go in."

As Jill walks down the polished hallways, she can't help but be haunted by the lingering stories of Mr. Corey's restless spirit. Goosebumps prickling her skin when a cool draft brushes against her, causing an involuntary shiver. The question of whether the school's dark history still has a physical presence within its walls nags at her. The whispers of the past seem to echo through the corridors, creating an eerie silence that hangs in the air. With each creak of the floorboards beneath her feet, Jill's heart races, as if the very building itself holds its breath, waiting for her to uncover its secrets.

Upon reaching the office, a heavy feeling settles in Jill's chest, as if the weight of the past is pressing down on her, making it harder to breathe. Her eyes land on a plaque that reads "More weight," supposedly Mr. Corey's final words. At that moment, Jill can't help but question her initial skepticism. Perhaps there is some truth to the tales she had dismissed as mere folklore. The physical effects of fear and anticipation awaken her curiosity, leaving her eager to uncover the truth behind the school's haunted reputation.

Since the school has been rebuilt and its name changed, everything has been calm. With a step inside, Jill felt nostalgia and familiarity blending with progress and renewal. The gym and locker rooms on the ground floor hint at the school's commitment to physical fitness. As she climbs up the stairs, the bustling sounds of students and teachers echo through the hallways, creating a vibrant atmosphere.

Accompanied by her kids, Jill enters the Administrator's office.

"I'm sorry the kids are late,"

The Principal, a fifty-year-old woman with curly black hair, reassures her, "Think nothing of it. We actually expected the kids to miss the whole day. I mean, they were probably awake when the election was called. By the way, congratulations! I can't think of a more perfect President."

"Thank you, Ms. Dissaldorph,"

Henry chimes in, "See mom, I told you we could've skip today." Jill responds, "Yeah, but what kind of example would I be if I let you off? A President has to be an example that the people can look up to."

The Principal interjects, "Very well put. The kids will have to sign a tardy slip and then go to their classes. Boy, I believe Mr. Chalmers in trigonometry is your next class. Lady, I believe Constitutional law with Ms. Pittens is yours?"

"Yes, Ms. Dissaldorph." The kids leave. As they leave, Ms. Dissaldorph looks at Jill and says, "I have an idea. Right now in Constitutional powers, they are talking about the election and the responsibilities of the President. I'm sure that Mr. Atkinson would love it if you could give a presentation."

"Oh, I would love to, but I have to get to my campaign headquarters."

"It would only be a brief presentation. I know the students would get a kick out of meeting the President-elect and learning how to run and organize a successful political campaign."

"I don't know."

"Just think about the kids. You can tell them everything you know and shape the minds of the next voting generation."

"Very well."

"Great, I'll tell Mr. Atkinson to expect you. His class is just downstairs and to the left."

"You don't fight fair, you know," Jill says as she leaves. Ms. Dissaldorph picks up the phone and says, "Yeah, she's here...Don't worry, she's not going anywhere soon." Ms. Dissoldorph hangs up the phone and smiles.

Jill and her secret service walk down the stairs, instantly greeted by a tall twenty-something man with a beard and nice sandy hair. "You must be Jill Lunden," he says. "I'm George Atkinson. A pleasure to meet you." However, George is blocked by Secret Service. Jill walks forward, saying, "Oh yeah, I understand." She extends her hand. "Pleasure to meet you, Will. Right this way. I'm sure the students will like to know everything you do and plan to do in the coming years."

Jill walks into the room and Mr. Atkinson announces to the students. "I want to give a rare honor to announce that the President-Elect wants to give some words of her wisdom to you guys." The students immediately start asking several questions. Meanwhile, Mr. Atkinson stands by the corner, sending a message. "She's in the classroom. Awaiting further instructions." He hits send and smiles. Jill is peppered with many questions from the students, ranging from, "What is it like working on the campaign?" to "Are you honest about adding Republicans to your cabinet?" Jill answers them all with the calmness of a career politician, even the outlandish ones. Suddenly, Mr. Atkinson's phone notifies him, saying, "Everything is taken care of. We're ready for her now." He addresses the students, saying, "Ok students, I think we have taken enough of Ms. Lunden's time. Also, the bell is about to ring," Jill interjects with a smile. "Well, I must say that is fun, and if you want to learn more, I recommend you talk to your state representatives." She glances at the clock on the wall and realizes she's late. "Damn, I'm late," she thinks to herself. In a rush, she runs back to the car and dials Tracy. However, Tracy's voicemail plays: "You have reached Tracy Kincaid. I can't come to the phone right now." Jill listens to the whole message and the beep, thinking, "Funny, she's never without her phone." She leaves a message, saying, "Tracy, this is Jill. I know I'm running late. I should be there within thirty minutes."

Thirty minutes after making the phone call, she arrives at the office, only to find it deserted and dark. She is puzzled by the absence of her staff and ponders her options, her mind racing with thoughts. "**Hello**." She receives no response. Her bodyguards circle around her, ready for action, as she senses a growing frustration. She frowns and clenches her jaw, trying to make sense of the situation and feeling the physical effects of her emotions taking hold. Her heart rate quickens and her pulse pounds in her temples, creating a throbbing sensation. The surge of adrenaline coursing through her body makes her muscles tense, her hands forming tight fists. As her frustration intensifies, her breath becomes shallow and rapid, making it difficult to find calm. She realizes she can't handle the situation alone and calls Tracy again, hoping for answers. She says, "Tracy, where is everyone? Please call me back. Something doesn't feel right." Feeling the need for assistance, she considers reaching out to Steve for help with packing up. In her mind, she even entertains the idea of indulging in some post-packing fun, imagining pouring chocolate syrup on Steve's chest and licking it off. These fantasies ignite a rush of desire that courses through her veins, igniting her body with anticipation. Her skin tingles with a delicious sensation, spreading like wildfire across her entire being. The vivid images of chocolate syrup and ice cream overwhelm her senses, awakening her taste buds with anticipation. Her heart quickens its pace, thudding against her chest in sync with the intensity of her thoughts. Each beat sends waves of heat surging through her, causing her cheeks to flush with a rosy hue. The rush of blood to her face heightens the sensations, making her feel alive and electrified. Lost in her pleasurable daydreams, her breathing becomes shallow and rapid. Each inhale carries the scent of sweet treats and the promise of indulgence, while each exhale releases a faint moan of longing. The air crackles with an electric charge, intensifying her senses and making her keenly aware of every sensation.

Her muscles are beginning to tense, a subtle but undeniable response to the surge of desire coursing through her. It feels as if every nerve ending is on edge, ready to explode in a crescendo of pleasure. Her body yearns for the touch of another, for the taste of sweetness mingled with passion. Amidst her physical sensations, a thought crosses her mind - maybe they have already finished cleaning the office. Although unlikely, it remains a possibility. She considers the option of asking Steve to come over and check if they are done. The tension in her muscles eases, and her breathing steadies, offering a momentary relief from the earlier physical effects. A glimpse through a window revealed overturned chairs and papers scattered across the table. As Jill's heart rate increases, her body responds with a surge of adrenaline, causing her muscles to tense up. This tension is evident in her clenched jaw and tightly gripped fists. Every breath she takes feels shallow and rapid, reflecting her heightened state of arousal. The mix of puzzlement and disappointment weighs heavily on Jill, manifesting as a physical sensation of heaviness in her chest. It feels as if an invisible weight is pressing down on her, making it harder to breathe and adding to her overall unease. Suddenly, her eyes widen in surprise as a black image zooms past outside the window. In that split second, her pupils dilate, allowing more light to enter her eyes and enhancing her visual perception. The sudden movement triggers her body's fight-or-flight response, causing a jolt of electricity to shoot through her nervous system. This surge of energy momentarily sharpens her senses, making her more alert and attentive to her surroundings. She briefly considers telling her Secret Service detail what she saw, but quickly reconsiders. "I don't want them to overreact based on an exaggeration of my imagination," Jill thinks to herself. With a deep breath, she inserts her key and opens the door to her office.

Chapter Seven

Carefully, Jill affixed her identification badge to the door. Adrenaline coursed through her veins, causing her heart to race and beat rapidly. Feeling apprehensive about the possibility of danger, she tightened her muscles, bracing herself for a potential attack. Her senses sharpen, every sound magnified, shadows dancing in her vision. Her palms sweat, making her grip shaky. Shallow breaths reveal her intense emotions, a sign of fight-or-flight response. Jill is a natural fighter. If someone took her staff, she will get it back, even by force. Her leg muscles are like springs, ready to act instantly.

She looks once again at her detail, contemplating the decision. A surge of determination courses through her veins, leaving a tingling sensation in her fingertips. The adrenaline pumps, causing her heart to beat faster, as if it's ready to burst through her chest. A surge of energy washes over her, granting her a sense of invincibility, as though she could overcome any challenge before her. A twinge of anxiety creeps up from the pit of her stomach, causing her muscles to tense up. A knot forms in her throat, making it difficult to swallow. Her palms become clammy, and she fidgets with her hands, a physical manifestation of the nervousness that has taken hold of her. With each passing moment, a sense of anticipation builds, making her breath quick and shallow. Sweat beads form on her forehead, trickling down her temples. The temperature seems to rise, and she can feel a flush spreading across her cheeks, betraying her inner turmoil. Yet, despite the physical effects of her conflicting emotions, she remains resolute in her decision.

As her determination grows, her adrenaline surges, sharpening her senses and increasing her focus. Her heart beat is faster, propelling her towards her goals. Her muscles feel invigorated, ready to conquer any discomfort. Her determination is evident in her posture and body language. Her shoulders square back, her spine straightens, and her gaze remains steady. She walks confidently and purposefully, with deliberate movements.

Though discomfort and unease may arise, she remains undeterred. Her body may experience tension and strain, but she pushes through, unfazed by the physical toll. Beads of sweat may form on her brow, but she wipes them away with determination, refusing to let anything hinder her progress. Her breathing becomes deep and steady, a rhythmic cycle that anchors her in the present moment. It is through this controlled breath that she finds her center, maintaining a calm and collected demeanor amidst the surrounding chaos.

As she forges ahead, the physical effects of her determination become a source of empowerment. The discomfort and unease she encounters are not seen as obstacles, but rather as opportunities for growth. She embraces the physical sensations as reminders of her commitment and resilience. In this way, the physical effects of her determination become a testament to her unwavering resolve.

She understands actions speak louder than words, and she is willing to endure the physical toll, knowing that the consequences of her actions will be worth it in the end.

She cautiously surveys the room, her senses heightened, her body trembling with a blend of anxiety and anticipation. Her blood pressure rises, causing a slight flush to creep up her neck and cheeks, despite the coolness of the room. Beads of sweat trickle down her forehead, a testament to the intensity of her emotions. With each step she takes into the room, Jill's mind races, analyzing various scenarios and outcomes. The anticipation of confrontation pulses through her, causing a knot to form in her stomach. The surge of adrenaline makes her feel almost invincible, fueling her determination to protect her staff and find answers. As she contemplates her actions if she catches the intruder, her hands tremble slightly, a mix of nerves and readiness. Her voice, usually calm and composed, has an underlying edge of urgency, ready to demand answers and confront the person responsible for the chaos that has unfolded. Just as she spots a shadow and is about to pounce, the lights suddenly burst on in a bright and intense display. The sudden illumination sears her vision, momentarily blinding her. In that instant, the air crackles with electricity as the hidden staff reveals itself, its presence now palpable in the room.

*

The room erupts with a sudden burst of voices as they spring up and cheer, "**SUR-PRISE**!" The cake emerges, adorned with the words "Congratulations" on top, its vibrant colors catching Jill's eye and filling her with a sense of joy. Laughter and applause fill the room, creating a buzzing atmosphere of anticipation. The sweet scent of vanilla and frosting envelops the air, causing Jill's mouth to water. As her heart races, a mix of excitement and relief washes over her, like a warm embrace.

Despite her anticipation for the surprise party, a hint of sadness shadows Jill's eyes as she realizes she has to cancel her plans with Steve. The exuberant crowd demands a speech in perfect harmony, eliciting laughter from everyone. Jill humorously addresses her Secret Service detail, remarking on their lack of startle response. She thanks them for their dedication and challenging work, emphasizing that their triumph belongs to them as much as it does to her.

With a playful tone, Jill orders the Secret Service to join in the celebration. Her best friend since Kindergarten and campaign manager, Tracy Kincaid, approaches her, her platinum blonde hair and blue eyes catching the light. Tracy asks, "So, are you surprised?"

Jill admits, "I'm not kidding about the near heart attack. The knocked over chair and scattered papers would put anyone on the defensive."

Tracy apologizes, explaining that they turned off the lights prematurely, causing Lily to knock over the chair while trying to untangle herself. Many people were looking in the window, so the shadow Jill saw could have been anyone. She mentioned this possibility.

Jill, experiencing foolishness, expresses self-doubt.

"I guess I can't blame you, Jilly. Seeing the papers and the chair, but seriously, ten phone calls in less than five minutes? Do you know how hard I have to concentrate not to answer? After all..."

"I know your phone is your life. You remind me of that every time you mention that thing. How did you orchestrate this? I mean, if it isn't for Steve... He helped you with this, didn't he?"

"I cannot tell a lie."

"Well, that's not true. I remember a certain ethics test in high school..."

"Yeah, we're not going to get into that. I might have asked Steve to keep you distracted while we decorated."

Jill remembers her victory speech and looks at Tracy and Steve. She recalls Tracy hugging Steve and smiling. *'So that is what that was all about?'*

"I would like to know how he kept you for as long as he did." Jill's nose and cheeks turn a red tinge as she remembers the morning with Steve. "Then again, maybe I don't want to know." Tracy's eyes sparkle with understanding as a mischievous smirk plays on her lips.

"Okay, that explains Steve. What about the kids, Ms. Dissondorph and Mr. Atkinson? How did you convince them to keep me away from the office?"

"I know only the children. Steve must have something to do with them. When he decides to, he can be quite resourceful."

"You don't know the half of it." Jill becomes convinced that she will have to thank Steve later tonight for the party, possibly with ice cream and chocolate syrup. "I still can't believe that you did all this. I mean, the election was yesterday. What did you do? Return here from the party?" Jill turns around and sees the cake, balloons, and many people in party hats. "Don't be overdramatic. I recruited some people to 'stay home' to help with the decorations. Everyone had faith that you will cross the finish line."

"So, those people that become sick or had last-minute family emergencies…"

Tracy's mouth curls up into a mischievous smile, revealing a hint of dimples, while her eyebrows arch, adding an air of innocence to her expression. As her eyes meet Jill's, a subtle blush spreads across Tracy's cheeks, giving her complexion a rosy glow. Alongside this, her heartbeat quickens ever so slightly, causing a gentle flush to rise on her neck. Tracy's body language mirrors her emotional state as she stands up a little straighter, radiating a sense of curiosity and anticipation through her posture. In contrast, her shoulders relax, displaying a sense of vulnerability. Tracy's hands fidget nervously, her fingers tapping against her thigh, betraying her slight unease.

Jill gazes at her friend with sorrow and pleads with deep concern. "Tracy, your heart is brimming with kindness. Any man would be fortunate to have you as his wife. As your friend, it troubles me. I do not want you to wake up one day with regrets about what might have been."

As Tracy relives that fateful night, the grip of panic tightens around her, sending waves of physical effects coursing through her body. A surge of adrenaline floods her system, causing her heart to race erratically, pounding against her chest as if trying to break free. Each beat reverberates through her entire being, serving as a constant reminder of the turmoil within. Beads of sweat form on Tracy's forehead, trickling down her temples and leaving a cold, clammy sensation behind. Meanwhile, her palms become moist, making it difficult for her to maintain a steady grip, as if her body is preparing for a fight-or-flight response. Her breathing quickens, characterized by shallow gasps punctuated by moments of holding her breath. The air seems thin, as if it can't penetrate her lungs fully, leaving her with a sense of suffocation. Tracy recognizes this and takes deliberate, deep breaths, attempting to oxygenate her body and bring a semblance of calm.

Muscles tense involuntarily, preparing for a threat. Her shoulders hunch, jaw clenches, and fists ball up. Panic physically manifests, reminding her of overwhelming fear. Tracy's senses become hypersensitive, heightening awareness of every sound and movement. The world around her amplifies, making her jump at slight noises. Colors appear vivid, air feels charged. Time slows as thoughts race, consumed by memories and fear. Each second feels like an eternity, elongating distress. Grounding herself is challenging amidst chaotic emotions. Panic leaves a mark, altering body's rhythm and equilibrium. She fights for control, but physical effects persist.

"I appreciate your concern, but you're always aware of my statements," Tracy seriously replies. Jill looks concerned, her hand placed over her heart. "I am aware. Your career is important. But I'm telling you, life is about more than just work. I couldn't imagine my life without Steve and the kids. I wish you the same."

The dreadful night and subsequent trip to Canada continue to haunt Tracy. She looks at Jill and notices the concern on her friend's face. Tracy counts to ten in her mind before saying, "I will give it serious consideration if, and when, the right person comes around." This is Tracy's way of saying to leave her alone, and this time Jill the hint. She did not want a repeat of the victory party from the other day, but she worried about her friend. Since the recording surfaced of Daniel as a sexual predator, Tracy has changed. Jill remembered Tracy's eruptions of rage, but the party revealed a fury she'd never witnessed.

"Remember, Mrs. President, this is your day and your party. Celebrate. Soon you will see more of the White House than any person who hasn't been a President," Tracy says.

"I'd love to see you in a flowing white dress, gracefully walking down the aisle," Jill says.

Tracy holds up her hand with an irritated scowl. "Don't get me wrong," Tracy speaks, the aroma of sincerity permeating the air. "I appreciate your genuine concern. However, I'm ecstatic about the outcome of my life. You know, that surge of joy and pride that fills your heart when you accomplish a successful Presidential campaign on your first attempt at running a campaign. That should at least give me a few job offers, if not book deals."

"Who knows? It's possible that you'll run a Thompson campaign in the future, perhaps a Congressional campaign."

Tracy thinks of even being in the same room with Daniel Thompson almost makes her vomit. "Not a chance in hell." She and Jill laugh. "Besides I doubt he would listen to me and you remember what happened to his last female campaign manager."

"You're probably right."

Jill and Tracy continue laughing about their friendship, the campaign and what the future might hold.

Lily Jess runs up to Jill and Tracy, her bright green eyes reminding Jill of herself when she was twenty. Bright and always willing to help, Jill can see a brilliant future in this woman. She is almost out of breath. "Well, I guess I have you to blame for some of my anxiety,"

"Lily, is there something wrong?" Jill asks, noticing the look of shock on Lily's face. "Something is going on with the television." Both Jill and Tracy exchange glances as they head for the television.

*

On the screen stands Daniel Thompson, his face as red as a tomato. With his index finger pointing at the screen, he proclaims, "With definitive proof." As the words escape his lips, a surge of fiery anger courses through his veins, causing his face to contort into a shade of red resembling a ripe tomato. The blood vessels in his cheeks and forehead seem to pulsate with every word he utters, emphasizing his determination and frustration. "I actually won, and I want everyone to know that I have no plans to concede the election." His body language speaks volumes about his unwavering conviction. With his index finger pointed like an accusatory dagger towards the television screen, he exudes an air of defiance and authority. Each forceful jab of his finger serves as a physical manifestation of his unwavering belief in his victory and his refusal to back down. "I plan to offer this proof this Thanksgiving. So, enjoy your turkey." The impact of his emotions silences the party, leaving an almost tangible tension in the air. His unwavering resolve echoes in each syllable, leaving no doubt that he intends to present irrefutable evidence of his victory, even in the face of opposition. In that moment, the physical effects of Daniel Thompson's emotions are undeniable. His flushed face, pointed finger, and forceful gestures all paint a vivid picture of his determination and unwillingness to concede defeat. It is a display that leaves no room for doubt, capturing the attention of viewers and setting the stage for a Thanksgiving that is anything but ordinary.

Jill then thinks, *'OK, welcome to my second heart attack.'*

Chapter Eight

November 23

, 2124

Melissa sits in her cozy California home, surrounded by the scents of pine, the crackling fireplace, and warm sunlight, reminiscing about her life. The soft, woolen blanket wrapped around her, feeling warm and comforting against her skin. A sense of comfort and nostalgia washes over her as she gazes at the snow-capped mountains in the distance, enveloped in her blanket. The crisp and refreshing air fills the space, hinting at wood smoke from nearby cabins, creating a peaceful ambiance that fills her with a sense of contentment and gratitude. A wave of nostalgia washed over her, bringing back a flood of cherished memories from the past. Memories of Jacob's and Erica's laughter bring a bittersweet smile. The weight of the past lingers in the air, as if the walls themselves hold the echoes of their family's happiness, sadness, and everything in between.

Melissa felt her emotions so intensely that they manifested physically. As she remembered the house's love and warmth, her chest tightened, a lump formed in her throat, and she fought back tears—a mixture of joy and sorrow. The bittersweet mix of emotions leaves her simultaneously grounded in the present and lost in the memories of the past.

Jacob and Erica's love seems to linger in the softly glowing room, their energy permeating the house.

The faint scent of Jacob's cologne and Erica's favorite flowers wafts through the air, wrapping Melissa in a comforting embrace that soothes her soul. "I'll be here full time in two years, near my family," she says. Her family is in for a surprise, as they are unaware of her retirement plans, though they've planned a surprise for her. In the kitchen, where the warm, spiced pumpkin cheesecake awaited its final adornment, she excitedly hurries, the smooth, cool ganache providing a perfect contrast.

After tidying up, Melissa heads to Sacramento to see her daughter Erica, the Governor of California. She admires Erica and fondly remembers her own time in office, evoking a nostalgic feeling in her heart. This sentiment becomes tangible as she drives, experiencing warmth in her chest and a tingling sensation in her arms. Despite feeling a bittersweet ache in her heart, causing her body to feel heavy and her grip on the steering wheel to tighten, she smiles softly. Reflecting on the defining moments of her political career, a blend of pride and yearning washes over her.

Sadness clouds her eyes, though a soft smile touches her lips. The weight of memories seemed to hunch her shoulders. Lost in the past, a gentle tug draws her back to a past both distant and vividly remembered, painting a portrait of wistfulness and yearning on her face. After her two terms end, supporters try to petition for a constitutional amendment, allowing Melissa a third term, but she declines, stating, "I've served my two terms; now it's time for me to step aside. Besides, I believe I can serve you better in the House of Representatives."

Melissa listened to the radio and heard about Daniel Thompson's Thanksgiving surprise. She chuckled, hoping for an admission of defeat and a good luck wish for Jill's presidency. Lost in thought, she nearly missed the turn. Suddenly, she realized that Erica's early dinner was unusual for Thanksgiving.

Melissa felt curious and suspicious, which made her heart race and filled her with adrenaline. This sudden realization made her uneasy and anxious. She blushed as she thought about Erica's early dinner and tensed up, eager to find out more. Her hands trembled on the steering wheel and she breathed quickly. These physical reactions showed how anxious she was becoming.

She turned on the radio. The news broadcast many reports about Daniel Thompson and his surprise announcement. "I doubt it's a concession speech and wishing Jill good luck," Melissa says to the radio.

Erica is busy inside her home, the aroma of roasting turkey and warm spices filling her large kitchen as she prepares Thanksgiving dinner. When: Inputting spice names into the pantry system in her search for the perfect yam seasoning, she received the message, "Item not found."

Roberto, a tall, handsome second-generation Mexican immigrant, has a warm voice, resonant as the desert sun. With a deep and gravelly voice reminiscent of distant thunder. "Yes?"

"Please go to the store and get me these spices."

His brow furrows in concentration, his eyes darting back and forth as he mentally checks off each item. The intensity of his focus sends a tingling sensation down his spine, a physical display of his determination and attention to detail.

"Your wish is my command," he assures Erica as he leans in to plant a gentle kiss on her lips. The gesture fills him with warm affection, causing his heart rate to quicken slightly. The touch of his breath on her hair brings comfort and reassurance, making Erica safe and loved.

As Roberto makes his way to the car, a sense of purpose and readiness settles over him, his muscles primed for action. His chest is light and buoyant, matching the fluttering of excitement in his stomach. With each deliberate step, a surge of confidence courses through his veins, propelling him forward with a clear sense of purpose. His posture straightens, shoulders back, reflecting the resolve in his heart. The physical effects of his agreement to Erica's request are evident in the way he carries himself, exuding a newfound sense of determination and resolve.

With his finger on the control, he speeds off to the grocery store, embodying a mix of readiness and determination.

After about thirty minutes, Erica's eyes widen as she realizes she may have forgotten to give Roberto the complete list of items needed. A hint of panic surges through her as she imagines the missing ingredients for the Thanksgiving feast, her heart beginning to race and adrenaline coursing through her veins. Erica's heart pounds and desperately tries to recall the items. A heavy weight of responsibility burdened her, increasing her anxiety with each passing second. The fear of disappointing her loved ones pushed her to act swiftly.

Roberto's resourcefulness means she doesn't have to worry about anything. The delicious aroma of the nearly cooked turkey fills the room, and she's already hungry. It is perfect timing since the family will arrive soon; she makes sure her mother will arrive at two pm and her daughter at three pm, so that Melissa won't arrive before Miranda.

Roberto returned at one-thirty with more groceries than listed: milk, butter, and eggs. Erica, noticing their low supplies, felt relief when she saw the items. The feeling spread warmth from her chest to her fingertips. Her heart rate normalized, but her hands trembled slightly from the remaining adrenaline. The relief Erica felt was evident when Roberto brought the needed groceries. The warmth spreading from her chest to her fingertips showed the emotional relief she felt. As her heart rate returned to normal, the adrenaline left her hands trembling slightly.

When she leaned in to kiss Roberto, the flood of affection and gratitude she felt flushed her cheeks, a visible sign of the emotions surging through her. The playful teasing that followed, fueled by her admiration for Roberto, added a lightness to the moment, further emphasizing the connection between their emotions and physical expressions.

As she felt the rush of affection and gratitude, a warm sensation spread throughout her body, causing her cheeks to tinge with a rosy hue. The increased blood flow to her face was a physical manifestation of the emotions swirling inside her. The playful teasing that ensued only heightened the effect, as laughter bubbled up from deep within her, releasing tension and adding a sparkle to her eyes. A crackling electricity charged the air between them, making her heart race and skin tingle with anticipation. The physical effects of their emotions were undeniable, creating a palpable energy between them that seemed to dance in the space between their bodies.

The physical closeness between them only amplifies the fluttering in her stomach, leaving her light-headed and giddy. Relief, gratitude, and attraction combined left her elated and breathless.

Erica asks, "Are you sure you are never a Scout?" as she wraps her hands around Roberto's waist and gives him kisses.

Roberto says with a smile, "Not as far as I can recall. I am good at reading the Kitchen's mind."

"So, the kitchen talks to you?"

Roberto glances at the kitchen's chaotic state. "Sort of. And you don't want to know what it's saying right now."

Erica teases, "Oh, now you are a comedian as well."

Roberto chuckles, "I'm just saying with this big a project, instead of sending the staff home, we could have kept some of them."

"You know, it's a tradition for Carthage women to make Thanksgiving dinner. Who am I to break tradition?"

Roberto retorts, "Hey, I'm just saying.."

"I understand your point." Erica responds defensively as she places the yams in the oven. A sharp ring interrupts the moment—the doorbell. She quickly removes her flour-dusted apron, the scent of baking bread still clinging to the fabric, and makes her way to open the door. The sight of her mother elicits a warm feeling of nostalgia, her smile illuminating the room. Her mother's laughter fills the air, a melody of joy. The familiar scent of her perfume lingers, both comforting and familiar. A rush of emotions washes over Erica, a blend of love and longing.

Erica greets her mother with an embrace, expressing, "Mom, it's wonderful to see you."

Melissa responds, "It is nice to see you too, Baby cakes." She embraces her daughter for a long time. Erica's emotional turmoil is clear in her physical responses, with her cheeks flushing crimson with embarrassment and frustration. The rush of blood to her face betrays her inner turmoil, while her fidgeting and twisting hands in her lap show clear signs of discomfort and agitation.

The tension in her body is palpable as she cries out, her voice quivering with emotion, "Mom! You know I am not fond of that nickname!" The mix of anger in her physical demeanor, with a storm of conflicting feelings brewing within her. She put that aside, inviting her mother in with the words, "Come on in and store your cheesecake in the fridge."

Curious, Melissa asks, "How did you know I'd baked a cheesecake?"

Erica replies, "You always make cheesecake, Mom," acknowledging her mother's fondness for making and eating cheesecakes. Melissa, possessing a cookbook full of cheesecake recipes, makes superb cheesecakes. "It's kind of your main obsession."

"Everybody eats them. So, I see no problem making them."

Erica then asks about DC, to which Melissa responds, "Intriguing, however, I'm more captivated by the California-Washington rail link proposed by the Republican Governor of Oregon. What's his name?"

"Richard Brady." Erica shares details about the proposed rail link, expressing pride in her accomplishments. Erica inquires further, "I don't suppose you know how he got the funding?"

Melissa notes, "Let's just put it this way. Richard Brady is quite charming and an excellent orator. I remember him having the House eating out of his hand." She recalls a time when she thought he would be a perfect match for her daughter until he announced his fiancée. Ultimately, things worked out well.

"He is quite the charmer." A crimson tide floods Erica's face, her voice a whisper, choked with unspoken grief.

Melissa smiles as she glances at her daughter. "Should I be aware of anything about you and Mr. Brady?" Melissa's question hangs in the air, creating a tense atmosphere between the two women.

"Please, we're both married!" a sharp snort, a physical manifestation of her disbelief and indignation, accompanies Erica's denial, thickening the tension in the room. The emotions swirling between them are tangible, crackling with energy. Melissa's heart pounds. Erica's defensive reaction fuels her adrenaline, making the air tense with unease. If Erica was going to be honest with herself. She has some feelings for Richard Brady, but she also loves her husband.

As Erica grappled with her conflicting emotions, she could feel a heaviness in her chest whenever she thought about Richard Brady. Her heart would race a little faster, and a warm flush would spread across her cheeks whenever he was near. These physical sensations served as a constant reminder of the emotional turmoil she was experiencing. Her love for her husband brought a sense of comfort and stability, grounding her in a different kind of warmth and contentment. The mixture of desire and loyalty created a complex tapestry of emotions that played out not just in her mind, but in her body as well.

"Believe me, that hasn't stopped others in the past. I know a few stories from Congress that would make you blush. No soap opera can write this stuff. Especially this loudmouth woman. Not only is she married. She has two boyfriends on the side. Who knows maybe one of these days I'll write a book." She felt a surge of excitement and anticipation, her heart pounding, adrenaline coursing through her. Her defiance and determination shone through, matching her bold words and confident demeanor. A mischievous glint and sly smile perfectly captured their readiness for anything. Her subtly altered behavior suggested a thrilling disregard for rules and boundaries, making the conversation more mysterious and intriguing.

Before Erica has a chance to reply, the doorbell rings, and Erica realizes it must be three pm. "Saved by the bell."

The tension left her, replaced by a feeling of ease. Her muscles, once tense with anticipation, relax as a sense of calm settles over her. The knot in her stomach unravels, replaced by a warm, comforting sensation. The interruption relieved her. With a smile, she walked to the door, putting off her reply. Meanwhile, Melissa waited excitedly at the door for her beaming granddaughter, Miranda. Melissa's face beams and her eyes sparkles. When Erica opens it, a woman in her early thirties greets her, causing Melissa to feel envious of her youthful appearance. The woman, with vibrant red hair like a fiery sunset and striking green eyes that shimmer like emeralds, is Miranda's wife, Jessica.

Melissa's exuberant smile turns to envy at the sight of Jessica's youthful appearance. A tinge of jealousy overshadowed the spark in her eyes. Her shoulders slump, a physical manifestation of the emotional weight she feels in this moment. Watching Jessica, Melissa compared her own aging reflection to her granddaughter's youthful wife. The mirror showed Melissa the passage of time and her longing for youth. Despite her efforts to mask her emotions, the physical effects of envy are evident in the subtle changes in her posture and demeanor.

Melissa looked around. "Where's my dear Miranda?"

Chapter Nine

"Miranda is retrieving the green bean casserole from the car and insisted that I go inside first."

Meanwhile, Melissa observes Erica's and Jessica's facial expressions and wonders, '*What are they plotting?*'

"Grandma." Recognizing the voice of her beloved grandchild as she enters. Her mind shifts back to the present. She also gives her grand daughter Miranda a long hug.

With a smile, she asks Miranda, "How are you, my joy?" Miranda, looking every bit the polished professional, captivates Melissa with her stunning appearance. She gives Melissa a hug before passing a dish to her mother, Erica, whom she also embraces. Miranda smoothed her long, dark hair before hugging her father, Roberto. Turning to Jessica, she plants a passionate kiss on her lips, revealing her deep affection. As Miranda's gaze meets Melissa's, a flicker of recognition sparks in her eyes, evoking memories of Erica's words. "So, your mom said you have a big surprise for me."

"You can say that." Miranda responds with intrigue, her voice full of curiosity. Secretly, Jessica and the Miranda smile at each other, their eyes twinkling mischievously as they locked eyes. Melissa notices Roberto and Erica, their excitement palpable as they share knowing looks with her.

The atmosphere crackles with anticipation, sending a shiver down Melissa's spine. "Okay, what's happening? You're all making me nervous," Melissa asks, her hands raised in confusion. Gracefully removing her coat, Miranda reveals a hidden surprise that brought a radiant smile to Melissa's face. Gasping in pleasant surprise, Melissa realizes Miranda is pregnant. Overwhelmed by the news, she asks, "Congratulations to both of you, but how?"

April 11, 2124

Jessica watches Miranda clutch a faded photograph of her family, her eyes drawn to a younger Miranda—perhaps five years old—with a wistful, downcast expression etched onto her face. Jessica can guess the reason behind Miranda's expression. Miranda comes from a loving family, unlike Jessica, whose family situation is different. Her older brother left when she was ten, and her father later evicted her after he discovered she was a lesbian, with her mother taking no action to help. Thankfully, her Aunt Cheryl provides support, preventing a worse outcome. Despite this, Jessica feels compelled to ask Miranda about her troubles. "What's on your mind, dear?" she inquires. Miranda expresses her feelings about the emptiness despite having ample space around them.

"We have so much space, but there's nobody to enjoy it with," Miranda says. As Jessica sips her tea, she acknowledges the size of her Aunt's house, inherited after Cheryl's passing. "You know my stance on having a family. No child should endure what I did. Protecting my baby brother from my parents' arguments over Mike was necessary.

"But not all families are like that. Look at mine. They accept me for what I am and they even accepted you. I know they would accept a grandchild."

Jessica remembers the look on Erica's and Roberto's face when Miranda gives her a passionate kiss during her law school graduation ceremony. Roberto is the first to recover, and Erica even invites Jessica to dinner. The most surprising is Miranda's grandmother, who welcomes her at first sight. The other shocking thing is Miranda's family history regarding politics.

"Ok, I give up. No wonder you're a judge. I doubt any attorney would win a case against you."

That gets Miranda to smile and laugh.

"So, what are our choices? We could always apply to foster a child."

"No. I could not picture loving a child only to have him or her ripped from our home," Miranda says, near tears.

"I understand. IVF or adoption remain possibilities."

"Possibly."

"What is the problem now?"

"I wish the child came from both our genes. That's all."

"I don't have to tell you that's not possible," Jessica says.

"I know. It's farfetched," Miranda concurs. With a determined look, she walks to the door, prompting Jessica to inquire, "Where are you going?"

"Out for a walk to get some air. When I get back, I guess we can look at adoption agencies. I love you," Miranda warmly expresses her commitment to their relationship.

"Love you too. I'm sorry we can't have a child together," Jessica responds sadly as Miranda walks outside, giving Jessica some time to contemplate their situation.

"Or maybe we can," Jessica ponders quietly, before discreetly reaching for the phone. With a press of the privacy mode button while dialing, she asks, "Hello, can you connect me to William Proctor?"

"William, it's me, Jessica, from medical school.... I go by Hernandez now. Thank you. Are you still working on your experiment? Good, you're past the animal stages. If you're working with humans now, my wife and I would like to volunteer. Tomorrow at noon? See you then," Jessica arranges, hopeful for a solution.

Upon Miranda's return inside the house, Jessica shares her news, "I talked to an adoption agency, and they would like to see us tomorrow at noon."

"Ok," Miranda responds, showing her willingness to explore other options.

The following day, Miranda and Jessica enter Doctor Proctor's laboratory, where they notice how perfectly organized and clean it is. Gleaming countertops and stainless steel equipment reflected the room's light. Neatly labeled bottles lined the shelves, and the air smelled sharply of antiseptic. They were amazed. The air hung heavy with the sharp, biting scent of disinfectant and the sound of their footsteps echoes in the pristine space. Jessica, comparing her cluttered lab to this picture of order and efficiency, experiences a pang of envy and longs for the same level of cleanliness and organization. She questions her own abilities to maintain such a pristine work environment. "This place doesn't resemble an adoption agency," she remarks.

"I just needed you here," Jessica admits.

"My dear friend Jessica," a man in his mid-fifties emerged, his face a roadmap of deep wrinkles etched by time, his thinning white hair catching the light. "My favorite student. I wonder how long it's been since our last meeting."

"It's been roughly five years. After that symposium on gene splicing. I've been following your research," Jessica confesses, her eyes wide with interest.

"Yes, you were always the little bookworm. Do you still try to volunteer whenever you have the chance?" Proctor asks, but it sounds more like a statement.

"Actually, I'm conducting research as well," Jessica states.

"I see, on what?" Proctor inquires.

"Myopic brain tumors. I hope to find a cure within my lifetime."

"Do you, have it?" Proctor sounds worried.

"My grandfather suffered from it. He died when I was two years old." Miranda nods, her heart heavy with the weight of the grandfather she only hears of.

"I sincerely apologize and offer my heartfelt condolences. You must be Miranda," he extends his hand to greet her. "Now, let's focus on the basics. We need to conduct initial tests to assess compatibility with my research. Once you remove your clothes and slip into the gowns, my assistant will proceed with the tests. Results will be available in the afternoon."

"What a minute? What tests?" Miranda asks.

"Don't worry, everything will be fine. Trust me," Jessica says.

"Very well. I trust you with my life. However, we are going to have to have a talk when we get home."

With deep breaths, the women undressed for the upcoming tests; feeling vulnerable in the sterile white gowns clinging to their skin, a reminder of emotion's physical toll. Proctor's assistant, a blonde girl around twenty-five, displays a calm and professional demeanor, approaches them, and guides them through the initial tests, carefully noting down each result.

With a deep breath, both women undress, preparing themselves for the tests that lie ahead.

It had been a long time since someone persistently poked and prodded Miranda, and she noticed her patience wearing thin. The assistant finally allowed them to dress again after a lengthy delay. "The doctor will assess the results and offer a conclusion by three o'clock."

Miranda and Jessica visited a restaurant near the clinic. "Are you going to tell me why I endured that afternoon of many needles? What is this all about?" Miranda asked.

"I don't want to raise your hopes," Jessica responded with a sympathetic tone in her voice. She bit her bottom lip nervously. A subtle quiver ran through her body, causing her hands to tremble slightly. Her heart raced in her chest, pounding like a drum, and her breaths came in short, shallow bursts. Restless eyes betrayed her intense anxiety.

Miranda's warm, understanding gaze conveys both cherishment and vulnerability. A flood of emotions overcame her, unlike any she'd known, stemming from their powerful connection. It was a beautiful but overwhelming sensation, one that left her with a simultaneous mix of exhilaration and unease.

Amid her anxiety, there was also a sense of comfort. She knew her wife accepted her for who she was, quirks, and all. And although her lip-biting habit may have been a sign of nervousness, it was also a testament to the profound impact on her wife had on her life. With each gentle press of her teeth against her lip, she silently acknowledged the power of their love and the exhilarating journey they were embarking on together.

"Very well. I guess I'll stay in the dark until three."

"Trust me. If everything turns out well, you'll be thrilled."

"I do trust you. I just wish you will trust me to tell me what this is all about."

Upon returning to Doctor Proctor's office near three, Jessica and Miranda find the doctor examining the test results before opening the door. "I am excited to announce that I have received some positive news," he says, observing the bewilderment in Miranda's countenance. Turning to Jessica, he inquires, "I gather you have chosen not to reveal the details of these trials to your wife?"

"I decided against raising her hopes because I didn't want to disappoint her," looking down as she speaks.

"It is understandable.", Doctor Proctor says. He turns to Miranda. "My profession is in genetic science. The focus of my research is manipulating a female egg to attain sperm-like qualities. Subsequently, I introduce the aforementioned sperm into another female individual."

Miranda looks confused. "I'm sorry I'm into the law, not genetics. I only took the crash course in genetic science."

Jessica looks at Miranda. "Doctor Proctor will extract an egg from one of us, change it to function as sperm, and then inject it into the other."

Miranda, grasping the information, "This way, the child will have a blend of our genetic traits." Her face lights up with enthusiasm, a radiant smile stretching across her face and her gestures becoming animated with excitement.

Miranda's excitement is palpable not only in her expressions but also in her posture - standing tall, shoulders back, and chest slightly pushed forward, ready to embrace the possibilities ahead. Her magnetic enthusiasm fills the room, drawing others closer to share in her joy. As she speaks of the unique blend of genetic traits, her eyes sparkle with anticipation, imagining the stunning combination of herself and her partner reflected in their future child.

At this moment, Miranda's physical presence becomes a manifestation of her emotional state as her enthusiasm imbues her every gesture and every word with a contagious energy. She is eager to embark on this new journey and witness the magic that will unfold as their genetic traits intertwine, expressing her readiness. The discussion now turns to practical matters: "Who will carry the child until birth? On a weekly basis, starting next month, the person needs to come here for a status update."

Miranda volunteers, saying, "I guess I will. I can work around my schedule in the courtroom."

"Very well. Miranda, do you mind waiting outside?" he asks, gesturing towards the door. She nods in understanding, planting a quick, tender kiss on Jessica's lips before rushing out of the office.

As she leans against the wall outside, Miranda's heart races, and the lingering warmth from Jessica's lips sends shivers down her spine, heightening her anticipation. Her mind races with nerves and excitement, her cheeks flush with a rosy hue. Each passing second seems like an eternity as she anxiously awaits Jessica's completion of the procedure. The uncertainty of the outcome weighs heavily on her, evident in her absentminded tapping of her fingers against her thigh, a nervous habit she has developed over the years. Time seems to slow down, amplifying her anticipation and making her acutely aware of every heartbeat echoing in her ears.

Her thoughts return to their recent tender kiss, now seeming like ages ago. This spontaneous gesture has ignited a fire within Miranda, intensifying as she waits for the procedure's outcome. The surrounding atmosphere is heavy with hope and uncertainty, causing her constant back-and-forth movement. Her fingers absentmindedly brush against her lips, still aware of the lingering warmth of their intimate moment.

As Miranda stands outside, her emotions fluctuate between fear and excitement, hope and doubt. The weight of the moment feels suffocating, but she finds solace in the endurance of their strong connection.

The office door finally opened after a seemingly endless wait, revealing Jessica, who smiled gently. A wave of relief washed over Miranda, making her heart skip a beat and her breath catch in her throat. While the procedure progressed inside, Miranda paced anxiously outside the office, each minute seeming to last an eternity.

Eventually, Jessica and Doctor Proctor emerge together, with Proctor informing both Jessica and Miranda, "Expect to hear from me with the extraction outcome in two days." They then made their way to the car, where Miranda expressed her impatience, exclaiming, "Two days? I doubt I can even wait for two seconds!"

Jessica, sensing Miranda's anxiety, offered comfort by saying, "I have a way to spend the time," while stroking Miranda's shoulder.

April 14, 2124

Every passing second seems to stretch endlessly as they wait. Time appears to elongate without end. At last, Jessica and Miranda make their way back into Proctor's office. When Proctor and his assistant arrive, they stand up to greet them. "I have successfully changed the egg to perform similarly to a sperm. It's time to start the implantation procedure," he says, turning towards Jessica. "If you could please wait outside, we can get started." With one final, lingering kiss planted on Miranda's lips, Jessica makes her way to the waiting room.

"Okay, Miranda," the doctor instructs, "please remove all clothing from the waist down. After that, you can jump onto the table and position your feet in the stirrups. We can begin." With unwavering obedience, Miranda follows each instruction without hesitation. She experiences a sense of uneasiness, but Proctor provides reassurance that it's a common sensation.

Doctor Proctor presents what appears to be a rod of medium size and describes, "We will insert this rod into your vagina. Then we will press this button. The device forcefully ejects the sperm by emitting a jet of air. Initially, you may experience a sense of discomfort. Do you understand?" With a nod, Miranda shows her agreement. Miranda's body tenses slightly as the rod glides into her vagina, a sensation that is both unfamiliar and slightly uncomfortable. She focuses on her breathing, trying to steady herself amidst the strange mixture of emotions swirling within her.

Proctor then gives his assistant the thumbs up. Upon pressing the button, a soft whirring noise permeates the room, causing Miranda's heart to quicken. A surge of anticipation mixed with anxiety washes over her, making her palms damp with perspiration. She can't avoid experiencing a surge of vulnerability as the device starts its work. The jet of air, when it comes, is a sudden burst of pressure that catches her off guard. A peculiar feeling: sudden warmth, then chill. Miranda's grip on the edge of the table tightens involuntarily, her knuckles turning white. Despite the warnings of unease, Miranda can't suppress the surge of hope that wells up inside her. This procedure helps her realize her dream: creating a family. It is a powerful reminder of the immense desire she holds in her heart. "That's it," Proctor says.

Miranda experiences a slight alleviation of tension in her body as the physical discomfort subsides, giving way to a lingering sense of vulnerability and the weight of the unknown. A brief hush falls over the room before the normal sounds return, and Doctor Proctor and his assistant exchange a glance, their expressions a mix of professionalism and compassion. They fully grasp the emotional weight carried by their patients, understanding the hopes and fears that accompany each step of the journey towards conception. Miranda's heart swells with pride, pounding against her chest as if trying to burst free. Admiration surged through her, electrifying her. A tingle ran up her spine, making her hair stand on end. It is as if a current of awe has taken hold of her, rendering her momentarily speechless. Despite her happiness, she felt nauseous, dizzy, and unsteady.

Miranda's brows furrow, her face contorting in confusion as she struggles to make sense of the conflicting physical reactions within her. Despite her efforts to steady herself, she can't help but marvel at the dichotomy of it all. How can such a remarkable achievement, accomplished with such speed and finesse, elicit such opposing physical responses? Miranda, taking a deep breath to regain her composure, focuses on the remarkable feat before her. Despite the unease in her stomach, she can't deny the incredible talent and dedication that Proctor has displayed. His effortless solution to a complex problem, exceeding all expectations, leaves her in awe. That brilliant moment deserves acknowledgment, even amid some unexpected physical discomfort.

Two Weeks Later

"Are you alright?" Jessica asks with concern while Miranda is in the bathroom, her head down in the toilet, vomiting things she had eaten as a child. It is the second day in a row that Miranda has been sick.

Finally, the toilet flushes, and Miranda emerges. "I don't think we need to tell Proctor that his experiment was a success," Miranda says, rubbing her belly.

"You should probably still take a test,"

"Just give me a few more seconds," Miranda hastily as she rushes back to the bathroom.

Modern Day

Melissa says. "That it is pretty extraordinary." She then asks, "So, what is it going to be, a boy or a girl?"

"Grandma, you know the Carthage tradition. We won't know until the little tyke comes out."

"I know, but I'm old and impatient," Melissa responds.

"Well, you can have this for now," Miranda says as she hands Melissa an envelope.

Melissa opens it and takes out a picture. "It's a sonogram," Miranda reveals. "I know. I'll cherish it forever," Melissa says.

Chapter Ten

"So, Jessica, Miranda told me you've left the ER and started your research. Something about some kind of cure? What's it about." Melissa inquired.

As Melissa speaks, excitement surges through Jessica's veins, her heart rate quickens and pumps fresh energy throughout her body. Adrenaline surged, sharpening her senses and focus. Excitedly, she looked forward to discussing her research and the potential for a groundbreaking cure. A radiant glow illuminated Jessica's face, a testament to the passion and unwavering determination burning within her. The radiant energy that she possesses captivates everyone around her and leaves a lasting impression.

"Yes, I have been researching a cure for myopic brain tumors. I got the idea from Miranda." She gives Miranda a kiss. "After I started reading some books, it grabbed my interest. I also know that it's important to all of you."

As Jessica speaks, her eyes sparkle with enthusiasm and determination, her voice full of passion and conviction, resonating with a sense of purpose and commitment. With each word she utters, her body language exudes confidence and a strong sense of dedication.

Miranda felt a surge of gratitude and pride for Jessica's dedication. Jessica's reassuring hand squeeze created a sense of unity and shared purpose in their fight against myopic brain tumors. The emotions in the room were so intense, they created a physical tingling sensation. This palpable energy of hope and determination buoyed everyone present. It's as if a tangible force of positivity and drive envelops them, propelling them forward in their shared mission.

As Melissa's heart races with conflicting emotions, her chest tightens, making it hard for her to take a deep breath. The surge of adrenaline coursing through her veins causes her hands to tremble; her body is hot and flushed. Tears well up in her eyes, blurring her vision as the weight of sadness and regret settles heavily on her shoulders. Melissa is experiencing a crushing weight of grief that is overwhelming her. The constant reminders of Jacob cause physical pain, leaving her exhausted and emotionally distraught, manifesting as stomach knots and muscle tension.

As she recalled the moments with Jacob, the physical sensations of their time together lingered. The warmth of his touch, the sharp, clean scent of his cologne, and the enduring flavor of spicy pepperoni pizza brought a bittersweet ache to her senses. The sight of him losing his memory was like a physical manifestation of her heart breaking, each forgotten detail a sharp pang in her chest. Witnessing Jacob's decline took a toll on Melissa's own well-being, her body mirroring the devastating effects of his illness. The stress and anxiety caused headaches, stomachaches, and unrelenting exhaustion, with the weight of the impending loss pressing down on her, leaving her physically weak and emotionally drained.

As Jacob's condition worsened, the physical toll on Melissa became more pronounced: the knot in her stomach tightened with each forgotten moment, each sign of his declining health. The weight of the situation bore down on her, leaving her physically and emotionally exhausted. Jacob's departure left Melissa with a profound sense of emptiness and grief. The heaviness in her chest was a tangible reminder of her loss. The physical effects of her emotions were a constant reminder of the depth of her love and the pain of her loss.

A dull throb pulses in her temples, a physical manifestation of the grief and guilt she carries within her. As she blinks away tears, her throat tightens, making speech difficult, and a lump forms, giving the sensation of being choked by her own emotions. Despite her efforts to stay composed, the physical effects of her emotions are impossible to ignore. Her body trembles with the intensity of her feelings, and her mind struggles to process the tangled web of thoughts and memories that threaten to overwhelm her. Her teary face shows her inner storm, begging for solace.

"Yes, it would have been nice if they found a cure thirty years ago," Melissa's eyes glisten with unshed tears, her voice trembling as she speaks. Years of waiting and unfulfilled hope have visibly affected her. The quiver of her lip and the way her hands clench show her anxiety. A knot forms in her stomach, a physical manifestation of the frustration and sadness that has been building up inside her for so long. The tension in her body is visible, her shoulders hunched and her posture slightly slumped as she struggles to contain her emotions. The room feels heavy with the weight of her words, the air thick with unspoken grief and longing.

"I'm sorry if this is distressing you." Jessica's apology hangs in the air, creating a wave of tension and discomfort that seems almost palpable. The heaviness of her words seems to affect the mood of those around her, settling in the room like a sense of unease. It causes a slight tightening in the chest or a knot in the stomach for some, as if the energy in the room has shifted.

The emotional impact of her apology is palpable, manifesting physically in listeners through furrowed brows, clenched jaws, or racing hearts. Her words resonate not just in the ears, but throughout one's very being, provoking emotions and electrifying the air with a blend of regret and tension.

Don't worry about it; it's really nothing at all. I wish you luck."

Jessica gives Melissa a hug. "Thank you."

"I'm serious. I really wish you luck. I don't want my worst enemy to watch the person they love slowly disappear." Melissa looks downcast. " I want you to find that cure."

"I will do my best."

Erica's words filled the room as she spoke. "Dinner is almost ready."

A wave of anticipation washes over everyone as the savory aroma of the cooking food tickles their noses, causing their mouths to water in response. The excitement and hunger in the air are palpable, making their stomachs growl in anticipation of the upcoming meal. Each person's heart rate increases slightly, and a sense of warmth and comfort envelops them as they eagerly await the delicious dinner that is almost ready to be served.

Around the worn, round oak table, everyone waits for Erica, anticipating a tray of steaming, delicious food. The room buzzes with chatter and laughter, the clinking of silverware against plates filling the air with a joyful melody. The aroma of roasted turkey and garlic mashed potatoes drifts through the room, tantalizing everyone's senses. Amidst the warmth of the gathering, the sweetness of grape juice perfectly complements the meal, with Miranda's green bean casserole earning praises and recipe requests.

As Melissa taps her glass delicately, the Thanksgiving chatter hushes, drawing everyone's attention. "I have some news to share," she announces, her decision firmly made. "This term of the House of Representatives will be my last. I'm retiring from politics." The news lands like a wave crashing against the shore, leaving the group stunned in its wake. Melissa's words linger in the air, heavy with finality, as the reality of her retirement settles in. The room fills with tension, almost palpable, enveloping each person like a suffocating blanket. Miranda's emotions surge, her heart racing with joy and excitement. The embrace with her grandmother floods her system with oxytocin, creating a deep sense of connection and contentment. Her smile triggers the release of endorphins, boosting her mood even more. With a hand on her belly, she experiences wonder and anticipation, a gentle fluttering in her stomach as she connects with the life growing inside her.

"This is wonderful news," she says, her voice filled with happiness. "I'm certain this little one will require a caring babysitter." The rush of excitement causes a surge of energy within Melissa, making her heart race and her cheeks flush with warmth as she imagines spending time with her great-grandchild. A wave of joy washes over her, lifting her spirits and brightening her entire demeanor. The sparkle in her eyes reflects the joy in her heart, and her widening smile radiates happiness, creating a contagious aura of warmth and enthusiasm around her. Her anticipation of her baby brings her purpose, fulfillment, love, and connection. This is palpable to those around her.

"Count me in!" Melissa says nervously

Erica speaks up. "Are you sure, Mom? Politics has been most of your life."

"I'm sure. Nobody wants a geriatric person in the speaker's position. You're also right. Politics has been a big part of my life. Sometimes neglecting you and Miranda. For that, I'm very sorry." As she speaks, a wave of guilt washes over her, weighing down her shoulders and causing a knot to form in her stomach. The regret lingers in the air, creating a tense atmosphere as she confronts the consequences of her actions. Her words are heavy with emotion, each syllable reflecting the profound remorse she has for neglecting her loved ones. The weight of her past choices is palpable, casting a shadow over the room and leaving a bittersweet taste in the air. The physical effects of her emotions are evident in the way her voice wavers, her hands tremble, and her eyes glisten with unshed tears. It is a moment of raw vulnerability, as she lays her inner turmoil bare and seeks forgiveness for the pain she has caused.

"You've been an excellent mother and grandmother."

"That's nice of you to say. But I know better. The important events I missed. Several of your recitals. Miranda's birth. I didn't even see the issues you were having with Roberto. Now I have a chance to make that up with my great-grandchild. I don't intend to let that slip by." Tears welled up in Melissa's eyes, reflecting a mix of regret and determination. The weight of missed moments and lost opportunities seemed to physically burden her shoulders, causing her to hunch slightly. But as she spoke about making amends with her great-grandchild, a newfound spark of hope and resolve lit up her face. A sense of anticipation and eagerness radiated from her, lending a newfound energy to her movements as she envisions a brighter future filled with love and connection. Her emotional turmoil visibly alters her demeanor, reflecting her journey of self-reflection and redemption.

As Melissa embraces Miranda, a surge of emotions washes over them both. Miranda senses the warmth and love emanating from her grandmother, mixed with a tinge of sadness and regret. The physical effects of these complex emotions manifest in various ways - a tightening of the chest, a lump in the throat, and tears welling up in their eyes. Melissa experiences a wave of relief and gratitude as she holds her granddaughter close. The weight of her past mistakes lifts from her shoulders, replaced by hope and redemption. She perceives her heart rate slowing, muscles relaxing, and tranquility arriving.

As everyone discusses dinner, Melissa retreats to a secluded corner of the house. She gazes at the sonogram with tears in her eyes. "I still have time," she thinks.

As everyone watches a Thanksgiving cartoon special, Jessica's hands move with precision and care. Miranda perceives the tension easing from her muscles, replaced by a sense of relaxation and comfort. The gentle kneading and pressure help stimulate blood flow and release hormones that improve mood, inducing a sense of calm and well-being. Miranda's breathing slows down, becoming deeper and more steady as the soothing touch of Jessica's hands works its magic. The tension in her shoulders and neck gradually eases, leaving behind a lightness that spreads through her entire body. With each knead and stroke, a wave of warmth and comfort washes over her, as if all the stress and worry are being massaged away. The increased blood flow brings a subtle tingling sensation to her skin, invigorating her senses and bringing a subtle blush to her cheeks. Endorphins flood her system, creating a natural high that lifts her spirits and melts away any lingering traces of anxiety. Miranda feels herself drifting into a state of blissful relaxation, her mind clearing of any distractions as she surrenders to the healing power of touch.

Erica and Roberto's focused attention on the television heightens their excitement and anticipation. Their hearts pounded, and they leaned forward, engrossed. Their eyes widen, pupils dilating as they absorb every moment of heightened senses. As their excitement and anticipation grows, a rush of adrenaline surges through Erica and Roberto's bodies, causing their hearts to beat faster and their breathing to quicken. Their muscles tense with anticipation, ready to spring into action at any moment. The heightened focus on the television screen sharpens their senses, making every sound and movement seem more vivid and intense. Their eyes widen, pupils dilating to take in every detail, as if trying to imprint the scene in their minds forever. The electricity in the air between them is palpable as they both lean in closer, their bodies almost vibrating with energy and anticipation.

Melissa focuses intently on the sonogram, tracing the outline of the baby's tiny form with her fingertip, her heart swelling with emotion. A mix of joy, wonder, and love washes over her, causing her eyes to well up with tears of happiness. The sight of the sonogram elicits a warm, fluttering sensation in her chest, a physical manifestation of the overwhelming emotions swirling within her. Her heart races with excitement, the rapid thump echoing in her ears as she feels a tingling sensation spread from her fingertips to her toes. The warmth in her chest radiates outwards, enveloping her in a comforting embrace that makes her feel as though she is floating on a cloud of pure bliss. Every cell in her body seems to vibrate with the intensity of her emotions, creating a palpable energy that hums with the promise of new beginnings. A rush of overwhelming love and joy transformed Melissa. She gasped, breathless from the intensity of it. The television flickers with light, illuminating the smiling faces of everyone gathered around, enjoying the show. With a frown, Miranda consults the small, silver watch on her wrist, "Dear God, we have to leave pretty soon."

"Do you have to?" Erica asks.

"I have court tomorrow and Jessica still has research to do."

"I also have a town hall to attend," Melissa says.

Suddenly, the television screen flickers, then dissolves into a chaotic snow of static, the sound dying with a hiss.

"What in the hell?" Roberto yells.

"Television diagnostic mode," the machine replies. As Roberto's frustration bubbles up inside him, his heart rate increases, causing his blood pressure to rise. His muscles tense up, his jaw clenches, and his fists ball up in frustration. He senses a knot tightening in his stomach, a physical representation of his emotional turmoil. The weight of his emotions is a heavy burden on his shoulders, making it difficult to breathe. His words, escaping his lips, are laced with tension, his voice tinged with irritation and impatience. The static on the television screen only serves to amplify his frustration, adding to the chaos of his swirling emotions.

"Damn. Television explain static."

"There is no static."

The static clears to show Sean Bradley and Daniel Thompson at the American News Network.

Chapter Eleven

Richard drives from Salem to Hillsboro, ordering his driver to drive around Portland along the way. The city appears unchanged since his time as governor: housing is thriving, businesses are booming, and the traffic clamp system he implemented continues to maintain zero accidents. It is a stark contrast to the city of Mr. Big. Despite the empty house, Richard can't bring himself to let it go.

"So many wonderful memories." Ashley gives Richard a squeeze on his arm.

"I'm sure your sister is expecting you."

"You're probably right." Richard gives Ashley a kiss. "I don't want her to think that I ducked out again."

"You are right. There was so many excellent memories."

Upon arriving at his sister Marileigh's place, Richard Brady and his family are greeted by the familiar sight of the old family home. The one-story ranch-style house, with its nice lawn and backyard garden, remains unchanged from the outside. Richard notices with appreciation that the house is now painted a delicate blue, a departure from his mother's favored putrid green. As he steps inside, the creak of the wooden floorboards and the comforting mustiness in the air evoke a flood of memories long held within the walls. Sunlight filters through the curtains, casting warm hues on the furniture, while the chirping of birds outside blends with the gentle hum of the neighborhood. The cool touch of the doorknob in his hand serves as a grounding reminder of the place he once called home, enveloping him in a sense of familiarity and belonging. As Richard stands before the old house, nostalgia washes over him, bringing back memories of a carefree childhood. Laughter echoing through the house, his grandparents' joyful chatter, and running around with his siblings all replay in his mind. Even the image of himself swinging on the rubber tire outside, now absent with the tree it once hung from, remains vivid in his memory. However, intertwined with this nostalgia are feelings of grief and loss, as he reflects on the tragedies that have befallen his family.

The passing of his brother Reginald in Botswana and his mother at the hands of a drunk driver weigh heavily on his heart, stirring anger towards the unknown driver who shattered their lives. These complex emotions manifest physically within Richard, with warm bittersweet feelings spreading through his chest, a gentle ache accompanying his memories of happier times. His expression reflects a mixture of fondness, sorrow, and loss, with a smile and glistening eyes revealing the depth of his emotions. A lump in his throat makes swallowing difficult, and slumped shoulders mirror the heaviness he carries with each step towards the house. Amidst this emotional turmoil, a blend of hope and apprehension courses through Richard as he contemplates Marileigh taking over the family home. While the prospect of preserving their lineage brings excitement, uncertainties about future changes loom large. Anxiety tightens his stomach, forming a knot, and clammy palms signal the challenges that lie ahead. As Richard stands there, the physical effects of his emotions become a tangible presence, feeling the ebb and flow of his feelings like waves crashing against the shore of his existence. Each emotion leaves its mark, subtly altering his posture, his breathing, and the sensations coursing through his body. The house, standing witness to this emotional rollercoaster, seems to hold its own secrets and stories, exuding a sense of quiet strength weathered by the passage of time and the weight of the family's history. With a deep breath, Richard feels a bond with the house, as its history of joy and sorrow mirrors his own.

Richard gets out of the car and rings the doorbell to Marleigh's house. The door opens to a man in his mid-forties, his white hair in stark contrast to his blue and white kippah.

"Shalom," Richard says respectfully, acknowledging Jacob's Jewish heritage. "Come in, Richard," Jacob says, "and place what you've made in the warmer."

"Where's Marleigh?" Ashley asks. "Oh, she's just getting the turkey prepared. You know, a whack on the neck with an axe," Jacob says as Alexis and Cristopher come in, both looking terrified. "I'm kidding. She's out back but getting some vegetables for dinner," Jacob reassures them, and everyone lets out a sigh of relief.

"So, Jacob," Richard asks, "when are Joshua and Dakota coming?"

"They already say they are on their way," Jacob replies.

"That's great. Last I saw little Rachel, she is up to my knee."

"She's grown quite a bit," Jacob replies, "already in third grade."

"Where does the time go?"

"Well, if you come by every once in a while..."

"I know. I got the same message from Maire during the election. Such is the life of a politician."

"Yeah, she told me you would say that. I'm just glad that you kept your promise and came over. I think she would drive all the way to Salem and bring you back."

Marileigh opens the backyard door window and goes up to give Jacob a kiss on the lips, saying, "Ashley, always a pleasure," as she looks at Richard.

She comments, "Your wife visits the place more often than you do, brother."

"My wife works for a disability center. She comes to Portland and Hillsboro to get donations." Marileigh then shifts the conversation by asking,

"And what about your children?" She goes over to Alexis and Christopher, noting, "They also visit their poor aunt Marileigh more times than their own brother."

Suddenly, the doorbell goes off again, and Richard thinks, 'Saved by the bell.' In steps a man, clean-shaven and in his early thirties, carrying an apple pie.

"Why Uncle Richard?" Joshua says with a laugh. "Mom said that you were coming. Dakota and I wondered, while traveling, about your cancellation excuses this time."

Richard chuckles and says, "Okay, is everyone going to gang up on me? At least Buster seems to be quiet for a change."

As if on cue, a small, white bushy dog runs down the hall and into Joshua's arms. "How's my little boy?" Joshua says, patting Buster.

The eight-year-old boy screams, "Buster!" with his arms outstretched. He then looks at Richard and says, "Oh hi Uncle Richard."

Richard, surprised, comments, "Oh, this can't be Samuel. My god, you've grown."

Dakota, Marianne's daughter, interjects, "And of course, you remember Rebecca."

"Dakota, you look good," Richard says, attempting to ease the tension. "How's your mother?"

Dakota's tone holds a hint of longing. "She's great. Loves Italy, but misses me, the grandkids, and Ashley. She also mentioned how America dodged a bullet with Daniel," Dakota replies. Their gaze briefly meets, and Dakota continues. "I'm not her. You don't have to hide the knives. After all, she also threatened to have Joshua castrated when he was dating me, but it never happened. Besides, I think she knows you would never hurt Ashley. As a matter of fact, I think she's seeing someone. It makes me feel strange. I know that Dad's been dead for twenty years. Hell, I don't even remember him. Still..."

Richard responds sympathetically, his own experiences of loss coming to mind. "I understand. The loss never goes away." He looks back to the people that he lost–his mother, stepfather, and his brother.

With a wide smile lighting up his face, Richard Brady enjoys his time at the dining table, conversing and laughing with his family, unable to contain his happiness. He expresses, gazing fondly at his beloved family, "It is a long time since we ate together." Richard acknowledges his role in the lack of family gatherings but sees a solution to this issue. Excitedly, he shares, "With the new bullet train, we can have more get-togethers. Just imagine getting from Portland to Seattle in less than an hour. Joshua, you can see your mother every day!"

Joshua looks at his wife and kids, contemplating the possibility, while Ashley chimes in, "Or maybe every week."

Their conversation then shifts to the upcoming holidays, with Ashley asking, "So when are the menorah and Christmas tree coming out?"

Richard notices the love between Jacob and Marileigh, despite historical tensions between the Jewish and Christian religions. Marileigh had faced hostility when attending their mother's funeral, including from the priest, because she was dating a Jewish man.

"Ashley, we display decorations at the beginning of Advent, the menorah on Hanukkah," Marileigh notes.

Alexis chimes in, appreciating the couple's ability to bridge the religious divide and says, "I find it great that you two can do something that the religious leaders can't. In fact, I wrote a paper detailing both histories, including the fact that Jesus was a Jew." Jacob, expressing his interest, responds, "I'm sure it's interesting."

The mood suddenly shifts when Joshua slams his hand down, catching everyone's attention, as Dakota shares a disturbing incident. "Pro-Daniel supporters tied a good friend of Joshua's to a fence and beat him."

"It's just so senseless. How can people be so cruel?"

Richard, grateful that Daniel had not won, acknowledges, "Daniel brings out the worst in people. Luckily, he didn't win. **Good human decency prevailed that day."** However, Marileigh raises concerns about the future, asking, "What about next time? Also, what about the talk of the election being stolen?"

Richard says, "It's just grandstanding. Trying to save face. Nothing more." Wanting to shift the focus from these troubling topics, Richard says, "Enough talk. Let's eat. If I wanted to talk about politics, I would've stayed in Salem. I want some of mom's famous homemade cranberry sauce."

"I have to admit, Mare, that was a good meal," Richard says, turning his attention to Marileigh, who is busy picking up the dishes. "By the way, I'm sorry about Joshua's friend. This conspiracy over the evil Jew has to stop."

Marileigh slams a plate down and looks at Richard. "It just makes no sense. Daniel Thompson is now claiming that the election was stolen, and you know America Now will blame foreigners and the Jewish population. The usual scapegoats."

Richard approaches Marileigh, sharing his thoughts. "He's just a sore loser. You remember how he made a big fuss about not winning the Emmy for season five on Houston? It's the same person, same nonsense. We shouldn't pay too much attention to it. **He's not the first person to lose the Presidency and act this way.** I doubt he'll be the last. The important thing is to remember that our country has guardrails in place to protect us."

Marileigh's brow furrows as she considers Richard's words. "But what if those guardrails fail? What then?"

As the discussion turned uneasy, Richard shifted the topic. "I admire your work on the place. We should definitely have more family get-togethers here."

Marileigh's grateful for the change in topic. "I'm always here. It's you who has been gone for such a long time."

Richard's gaze drifts away,

Marileigh's remorse is clear in her voice. "I'm sorry."

"No, you're right. Mom always taught us to tell the truth, even if it hurt. I've noticed that I've been so focused on my own ambitions and career, like the clamp system for cars and the bullet train. Sometimes, it comes at the expense of our own family. I can see it in both Alexis and Christopher. One minute they were kids and now... I know I don't have the same relationship that you have with your son."

Marileigh walks up to Richard. "You still have time, you know."

"Wait a minute. I'm your big brother. Shouldn't I be the one giving sage advice?"

"Have any?"

"Not really." Both siblings laugh.

On the way back to Salem, Richard gazes at his wife and expresses his admiration, saying, "Even now, you mesmerize me. I'm so grateful that we met at Willamette University all those years ago." Ashely looks at Richard and puts her head on his shoulder.

As he looks at his daughter, Alexis, memories flood back of holding her in his arms, reflecting on her vulnerability as she gazes back at him. Now, as the President of the Western Oregon University Student Government, Alexis is preparing to follow in her father's footsteps and attend Willamette Law School. Richard admires her, seeing his own ambition and drive reflected in her, along with her mother's stunning beauty. As Richard reflects on the passage of time, he turns his daughter, thinking, *'Time really flies, doesn't it?'* "Lex, how's it going with that guy... Justin, right?"

"Dustin. But things are going well. Thanks for asking," Alexis responds.

Richard then observes his son, Christopher, who, despite being three years younger than his sister, is taller and speaks with a voice filled with passion and ambition. Christopher often speaks of his girlfriend, Kimberly, while serving as the Student Body President at McKay High School and securing a scholarship to Western Oregon University. "How are you, Christopher, and I believe Kimberly, doing?" Richard inquires.

"We're fine," Christopher replies.

"Well, why don't you bring them to Mahonia Hall? Say around Christmas." However, Alexis and Christopher appear surprised and concerned, knowing Richard's tendency for detailed questioning from his days as a District Attorney. Richard reassures them, saying, "Don't worry, I won't subject your partners to intense interrogation and torture." Just a friendly chat, I promise." His amusement is evident in his voice, causing a subtle chuckle to escape his throat.

At Mahonia Hall, his residence for the past six years, Richard gazes at the pictures of former governors; a surge of pride and connection washes over him. The building's walls embody Oregon's history and legacy, giving Richard a sense of belonging and rootedness. A warm sensation spreads through his chest, and he can't help but smile as he envisions himself as part of the rich tapestry of the state's governance. The images vividly portray his emotions, filling him with respect and admiration for the leaders who shaped his homeland.

Richard is eager to relax. "Let's watch the Mayflower Chronicles on TV."

"Sounds good." Everyone says.

They settle on a black, fake leather couch and enjoy the Thanksgiving special. However, their enjoyment is short-lived as the television suddenly starts fizzing out. To make matters worse, messages appear on Richard's palm top computer. After a moment of confusion, the television screen clears, revealing Sean Spencer and Daniel Thompson. Richard attempts to command the TV, saying, "Television, turn on the Mayflower Chronicles," but to no avail.

"Television turn on the Thanksgiving story." Nothing. The television continued to show Sean and Daniel.

"Hon, what is going on?"

"I don't know,"

Richard and Ashley listen to what Daniel has to say. Ashley looks at Richard with horror.

"He can't be serious." Richard says.

Chapter Twelve

A midst newsroom chaos, Sarah Spencer examines daily news at MCBS using the eye news screen. Despite the noise, Sarah finds solace in her quiet spot, although her body remains in a state of heightened awareness. The constant sound of fingers typing and the holograms creates a symphony of sensations that keep her fully engaged in the moment. As Sarah continues to absorb the news, the physical effects of her emotions serve as a reminder of the power and impact that journalism holds. These effects fuel her passion and drive and propel her forward in her pursuit of truth and the desire to make a difference in the world through her reporting. She can hear fingers typing on the palm tops and sees several holograms of the United States and the entire world. Eavesdropping on Gloria Washington's hologram conversing with President Chavez, a sense of awe and respect fills her. The diplomatic discussions and their global impact made her aware of the moment's significance.

A tingling sensation ran through her fingertips. As Sarah immerses herself in the news, her emotions begin to take hold, causing a range of physical effects within her body. The anticipation and excitement of being surrounded by the latest updates and important conversations send a surge of adrenaline coursing through her veins. Her heart rate quickens, causing a gentle thumping sensation in her chest. The blood rushes to her cheeks, leaving a faint rosy hue that matches the flush of enthusiasm on her face. Her pupils dilate, absorbing every detail of the holograms and news articles with heightened focus and intensity. Sarah's mind races with thoughts and ideas; a surge of energy flows through her muscles. Her body is vibrant and energized, ready to absorb every bit of information and contribute to the chaotic yet exhilarating atmosphere of the newsroom. Mixed with the excitement, a touch of nervousness lingers in the pit of her stomach. A slight tightening sensation reminds her of the responsibility that comes with being a journalist and reporting on these critical events. Still, she accepts this emotion, knowing it strengthens her resolve to share precise and significant narratives globally.

She takes out a slender, white metal object from the stand near her. As she holds the slender, white metal object, a soft hum fills the air, and the window part glows, emitting a gentle blue light. The device is cool against her skin, its smooth surface providing a sense of comfort and familiarity. The scent of technology lingers in the air, a subtle mix of plastic and metal, adding to the ambiance.

With a sense of anticipation, her eye remains focused on the window as it scans her retina, unlocking a gateway to the latest headlines. She learns of a riot in Louisville, Kentucky, sparked by claims of a stolen election, with ten torch-carrying people arrested. 'What has this country come to,' Sarah thinks, her mind filled with concern.

As she continues reading the messages on her eye, something catches her attention. It is the news of Gregory Sotkins' passing. Sarah puts down her eye message machine and says a silent prayer, reflecting on his life and expressing her condolences. "At least you're with your loved ones again. Still, I will miss you."

As Sarah finishes her prayer, a weight settles in her chest, making it harder for her to breathe. The news of Gregory's passing hits her like a tidal wave, causing her body to tremble involuntarily. Her eyes well up with tears, blurring her vision as she tries to understand the loss. The tears spill over, making her cheeks grow damp and her face turn red and swollen.

A knot forms in her throat, making it difficult for her to speak. Every word presents a challenge, as if an invisible force constricts her. Sarah's hands shake, and the quivering spreads throughout her entire body. A mixture of sadness, grief, and disbelief courses through her veins, causing her muscles to tense up and ache. It seems as if she's carrying the weight of the world on her shoulders, her posture slumping under the burden of sorrow.

She wonders what the Moderate News network is doing right now. Despite Sotkins' planned retirement, the sudden passing of their star anchor must be a blow to them. She puts the eye news back on, but there is no word yet about who will replace Sotkins. However, the good money is on Thomas Hunter. Sotkins took Hunter under his wing when he was just thirty years old. Whenever Sotkins was out because of health reasons, Hunter stepped as the anchor. Just then, Mark Esper comes over. Mark is five years younger than Sarah, and they have an off-again, on-again kind of relationship. "I thought I'd find you here," Mark says.

"Where else would I be? It's quiet and I can think."

"I heard about Greg. I know his network and ours are bitter enemies, but I also know you had great respect for him," Mark sympathetically hugs her.

"Thanks, he was a giant among men. I remembered when I did my first debate moderating. I was a nervous wreck. He offered this advice: breathe deeply, then ask the challenging questions. He calmed me. Even though we were on different networks." Sarah recalls, with a pang of sadness. She hugs Mark.

"Look, if you want to talk more, I'm right here for you," Mark offers.

"Thanks."

"I almost forget the reason I came over here. I talked to the executive producer, and he agrees. We will run a memorial for Greg.

"When?"

"While Daniel is arguing that the election was stolen," Mark says in air quotes.

Sarah smiles. "Good. I really don't want to hear from that blowhard," she admits.

"Which one? Sean or Daniel?" Mark asks.

Sarah takes a moment to think. "Both," she finally replies.

At the American News Network, a heavy cloud of grief hangs in the air following Gregory Sotkins' passing. Amidst the hustle, an air of solemnity hangs over the people. The chair and desk, Greg's old work area, command attention; the office feels heavy with unspoken emotion. Christian Silverstone, the head of the network, steps off the elevator with a heavy heart, his usually confident demeanor replaced by a noticeable heaviness. With slightly slumped shoulders, he makes his way through the office, experiencing the weight of the loss affecting everyone in its presence.

Passing by his colleagues, Christian observes the physical effects of their grief. Once vibrant and animated faces now wear expressions of sadness and disbelief. Tears and exhaustion fill their eyes, replacing the usual determination and ambition. It seems as though a dark cloud has settled over the entire office, casting a shadow on their usual liveliness. The somber atmosphere permeates the very walls, making the air heavy with the collective sorrow. Hushed whispers and occasional sniffles replace the usual sounds of bustling and chatter as people try to hold back their tears.

Christian cannot escape the physical effects of his emotions. His chest tightens, making it difficult to take a deep breath, while his temples pulse with the weight of grief, causing a dull ache in his head. He trudges forward, each step increasingly difficult. The weight of responsibility presses down on his shoulders, causing fatigue and pain. These physical manifestations of are clear throughout the office, as postures slump, energy levels deplete, and even steady hands tremble with sadness.

As Christian makes his way to the area known as the pit, he can't help but reflect on the interconnectedness of emotions and physicality. The somber mood negatively impacts everyone's well-being and atmosphere. It serves as a stark reminder of the power of emotions to shape our physical states, emphasizing the need for compassion and support during times of grief.

"Ok, we all know that we are grieving the loss of Greg. He is a good man. However, the news doesn't stop for just one man. With this in mind, I plan on airing special segments throughout the hour. Right now, there are some arrests related to a Daniel Thompson rally. There are talks about torches and some speech. However, we need to get more information first. It's important that we air nothing that might be false. After all, what does that say about our network? But first, I need someone to replace Greg on his show. For that honor, I have picked Thomas Hunter to fill in."

Thomas Hunter stands up and waves his hand. With his dark hair slicked back and piercing blue eyes, he has the look of a seasoned movie star. The room erupts in applause. "So, let's make sure that today we honor Greg by producing the best shows we can." The clapping continues, and everyone begins to move. Purpose and determination are palpable in the room's buzzing energy. The air crackles with the electric excitement of the team, each member driven by their own unique blend of emotions.

Christian stops Thomas and says, "You know this is conditional, depending on performance. Greg has a lot of faith in you. I hope you don't let him down."

"Never. I just hope that I live up to a tenth of what that man does."

"Good. Tonight, Sean will be interviewing Daniel regarding the election during his show."

"Is covering that going to be my first assignment?" As Thomas speaks, his voice quivers, betraying the mixture of anxiety and uncertainty that fills his heart. A cascade of emotions surges through his body, each one leaving its distinct physical mark. His hands tremble involuntarily, a visible manifestation of the nervous energy coursing through his veins. Fingers fidget, fumbling with the edge of his shirt or tapping anxiously on the table, as if trying to release the pent-up tension within.

The muscles in Thomas' face tighten, his brow furrowing with worry lines. He scanned the room, searching for solace or a route to avoid the building stress. The corners of his mouth turn downwards, forming a hesitant and apprehensive expression.

His heart pounds against his chest, its rhythm irregular and rapid. The thumping grows louder in his ears, as if it is echoing his inner turmoil. Each beat seems to reverberate through his entire body, a constant reminder of the weight of his newfound responsibility.

A cold sweat breaks out on Thomas' forehead, tiny droplets forming and trickling down his temples. The dampness clings to his skin, mirroring the clamminess that has taken over his palms. The sensation of moisture on his brow serves as a tangible reminder of the fear and uncertainty that grip him.

With every breath, Thomas's chest tightens, as if an invisible hand is constricting his lungs. Each inhale is shallow and rapid, struggling to supply enough oxygen to his racing mind. The physical discomfort mirrors the mental strain he endures, a reminder of the immense pressure he feels.

"Hell no. I don't care what Daniel has to say. Let him rant and rave. No one could have stolen the election and last I checked, he has brought no evidence."

Relieved, Thomas senses a heavy weight lift from his shoulders. As the tension dissolves, a wave of calmness washes over him. His racing heart steadies, and his clenched fists unclench. With each breath, he senses the tightness in his chest gradually loosening, allowing him to inhale deeply and exhale all the built-up stress. "In that case, here's an idea we can have Greg's first day as a news anchor while Daniel and Sean are on the air. Sort of a memorial."

As Thomas speaks, the relief in his voice is palpable. His words flow, without the hesitation and stuttering that plagued him earlier. His voice, once strained and tight, becomes smooth and melodic. A smile tugs at the corners of his mouth, and his eyes sparkle with a newfound sense of hope.

"I love that idea," Christian chimes in. "We can show Daniel that we will not cave into demands on a whim. **Let him say his peace and go to the courts. If he can prove fraud, then we report it.** We do not report on supposition." Christian then grabs a glass of champagne and raises it. "To Gregory Sotkins, a person whose shoes no one can ever entirely fill!" As Christian raises his glass, a wave of bittersweet nostalgia washes over him, mingling with a tinge of admiration. The effervescence of the champagne tickles his nose, as tiny bubbles dance and rise to the surface. With each sip, a delicate warmth spread from his throat, coursing through his body and melting away any lingering tension. "To Gregory," everyone says. The taste of the champagne seems to mirror the emotions swirling within Christian. A hint of sweetness provides a comforting embrace, reminiscent of the fond memories shared with Gregory. A lingering bitterness hints at the absence of a remarkable journalist.

As the toasts continued, Christian felt invigorated by the festive mood. The clinking of glasses, laughter, and stories contributed to a lively atmosphere. The room was filled with a blend of emotions - excitement, gratitude, and a touch of sadness.

Thomas's relief is apparent, affecting those near him. As he shares his idea, a shift occurs in the room. The tension dissipates, and a collective sigh of relief seems to echo through the air. Shoulders relax, brows unfurrow, and smiles spread across faces, mirroring the physical transformation Thomas has undergone. It is as if relief, like a gentle breeze, sweeps away the storm of anxiety and uncertainty, leaving in its wake a sense of lightness, calmness, and renewed energy. Thomas knows this relief will pave the way for a brighter future, not only for himself but also for Greg's legacy.

As the toasts continue around the room, Christian's senses come alive. The clinking of glasses creates a symphony of celebration, punctuated by laughter and heartfelt anecdotes. Excitement, gratitude, and a hint of sadness fill the vibrant room. Emotionally stirred, Christian feels his heart beating a little faster, a physical manifestation of the admiration he holds for Gregory's work. A gentle flush creeps up his cheeks, a blush of appreciation for the impact Gregory has on his life and the lives of others.

Christian's eyes sparkle with a mix of joy and sorrow, reflecting the glistening warmth of the room's lighting. His wistful smile curves the corners of his mouth, mirroring the bittersweet sentiment in the atmosphere. As the evening progresses, a newfound lightness fills Christian's step, buoyed by the honor bestowed upon a talented journalist's legacy. His shoulders relax; a sense of grounding and upliftment washes over him. In this moment, Christian realizes emotions transcend the mind and heart alone, touching every fiber of his being and leaving a tangible imprint on his physical state. With every sip of champagne, heartfelt toast, and shared memory, Christian realizes the profound connection between his emotions and the physical world surrounding him.

At the Conservative News Network, Sean Bradley, the network's most watched anchor, reads with glee about the death of Gregory Sotkins. Considering their lack of friendship, Sean concludes, "I'm not pretending we're friends. He hated me, and I him." A subtle smile crept across Sean's face as he scanned the news, his glee transforming his demeanor. The corners of his lips lifted, dimpling his cheeks. His once neutral eyes now sparkle mischievously, reflecting the excitement he feels about the news he is about to deliver.

Sean's posture and shoulders conveyed confidence. The room's energy also shifted, reflecting his newfound vigor. His normally measured and composed voice takes on a hint of enthusiasm, gaining an animated quality that captivates his audience. Each word he speaks carries an underlying tone of satisfaction, as he relishes in emphasizing certain details of Gregory Sotkins' death. His words resonate through the studio, influencing the atmosphere and leaving a palpable impact on the emotions of those around him.

Sean's glee is evident in his body language, facial expressions, and voice. Together, these create an aura of excitement throughout the studio. It serves as a testament to the power of emotions, shaping not only Sean's experience but also having the potential to influence the emotions of those watching him.

While Sean browses the news, he discovers that the police arrested ten people at a rally supporting Daniel. News reports stated that many participants carried torches and chanted, "No cunt should ever hold power."

As Sean glances at his schedule, he notices the upcoming interview with Daniel Thompson and smiles. "I have the full exclusive. Daniel should tear into how the election was stolen and demand that authorities release the hostages from the rally."

Sarah is in her makeup chair, preparing for her show. As she gets ready, she reviews the snippets of Gregory Slotkins' life that her aides have found for her. On her eye reader, she discovered several accolades, including a Pulitzer and several Anthony Shadid awards, while reviewing her notes. "Okay, you're ready," her groomer says. The makeup artists' work continues to amaze Sarah. "Knock 'em dead tonight," they encourage her. Sarah responds, "I will. I owe Greg that much."

As Sarah settles into the anchor chair, a surge of confidence washes over her, causing her posture to straighten and her movements to become more deliberate. The adrenaline coursing through her veins heightens her senses, making her aware of every detail in the studio. Her heart rate quickens a bit, intensifying the excitement and anticipation.

As she puts in her eye teleprompter, a sense of focus and determination takes over.

Just as she settles in, Mark Esper announces, "In five, four, three, two, and one." Then, he welcomes the audience, saying, "Hello and welcome to the Sarah Spencer show. Tonight, we honor..."

Up in the video room, everyone remains calm as they see Sarah and hear her voice sounding good. "Sarah, if you can hear me, give me a thumbs up." Melinda Peterson, the head controller, instructs. They're accustomed to this routine; ten years working there. Sarah gives her the thumb. "Is eye teleprompter in?" Sarah gives another thumb. "Ok, we are good to go then."

Everything is running smoothly, like clockwork. "Tonight, we honor..." Melinda prepares her finger to press the button, anticipating the mention of Greg's name. That will signal the start of the video montage featuring Gregory Slotkins, and Melinda can relax. However, suddenly, the screens go into static, catching Melinda off guard.

Startled, she finds herself back in her chair. "What the hell is going on?"

"We don't have any signal," someone informs, as many people scramble to fix their panels.

"Well, find out what the problem is." Melinda looks up and, to her surprise, sees that every news screen shows static. After a few tense minutes, the static disappears, and the video clears to reveal Sean Bradely's face.

Sean then addresses the viewers, stating, "We have received information that this broadcast is being transmitted to all stations. Welcome, Daniel."

"Thank you. It's a pleasure to be here. I'm also grateful that every station has agreed to air this important message. I have indisputable proof that the election was tampered with and that I won.

"So, with a stolen election, what do you propose to do?" the interviewer asks.

"First, I would like to express my gratitude to the brave members of Cain-non for risking their lives to provide us with this information. Second, I demand a new election, overseen by America. Now personnel in each district, to prevent a repeat of this fraud."

"But isn't that unconstitutional?" Sean questions.

"Given the extent of this fraud, all laws, including those in the Constitution, must be terminated," Daniel confidently responds.

Chapter Thirteen

William Chavez, with his wife Amanda and daughter Chelsea, enters The White House viewing room to watch a retrospective on President Chavez's friend Gregory Sotkins. Plush furnishings and ornate fixtures elegantly decorate the room, creating a historic and powerful atmosphere. Soft, warm light fills the room, accompanied by hushed whispers and a faint scent of polished wood and fresh flowers. In the dining room, candlelight illuminates the space with the inviting aroma of roasted turkey and savory sides. Guests enjoy a decadent feast, with the clinking of fine China and silverware blending with polite conversations.

After dinner, as they settle down to watch television, static fills the screen, revealing an unexpected sight - Daniel Thompson and Sean Bradley. This surprises William, as he had no intention of watching Daniel's interview, but what he hears shocks him. Daniel claims to have proof of election fraud, calling for a new election with his team overseeing the counting and the termination of the Constitution. "Television off," William's shock evident through his racing heart, sweaty palms, and heavy breathing. The surge of adrenaline causes his muscles to tense and his hands to tremble. As the gravity of the news sinks in, his face pales, his eyes widen in disbelief, and a flush spreads across his cheeks from the rising body temperature. William experiences nausea, dizziness, and disorientation due to difficulty swallowing from chest tightness and a stomach knot. The overwhelming mix of emotions makes it challenging for him to process the unfolding situation's gravity.

Chelsea approaches her father, noticing the tension in his jaw and the way his fists clench at his sides. "Dad, please calm down. I don't want a repeat of the Megan Foxhead show. When you got back and then you clutched your chest and fell on the floor. I thought I lost you."

Chelsea is near tears as the memories of Megan Foxhead from the Conservative News Network relentlessly attacked him about events that occurred before he became President, including the whole Botswana war. As if he was to blame for the entire war. Her network praised Megan Foxhead and rewarded her with her own show when news of his heart attack broke. Tears welled up in Chelsea's eyes, threatening to spill over as a mix of anger and hurt churned in her stomach, creating a knot of emotions that seemed to consume her. Feeling the weight of the accusations, her muscles tensed and her breathing grew shallow. The stress and anxiety of the situation manifested in a pounding headache, making it hard for her to focus on anything else but the onslaught of criticism and betrayal. The emotional turmoil was taking a toll on her body, leaving her feeling drained and overwhelmed.

William looked distressed with a flushed face and rapid breathing, showing the impact of the accusations and hatred on him. His tense muscles and trembling show the toll it took. Amanda sensed his emotional turmoil and reached out to him, offering reassurance with a hand on his arm. They found strength in each other's love and support, standing united against the storm of hatred and injustice.

As William's anger and frustration boil within him, manifesting in physical symptoms like increased heart rate, shallow breathing, and tense muscles, the urge to unleash his fury overcomes him. Adrenaline surges through his veins, causing trembling hands, clenched jaw, flushed face, and the impulse to release his emotions. Ultimately, William throws his glass, shattering it into several pieces. Not even hearing his daughter.

"I have heard of sore losers before, but Daniel is really taking the cake." William sits on the couch. "It can't be true. Dammit, I demand to see this so-called evidence that Daniel says someone named Cain discovered and not at some later time." This revelation is the lynchpin for William. "We should have experts produce and analyze Cain's evidence. This is so much nonsense. If I could find this person named Cain, I would beat the evidence out of them." The shards of glass, glinting under the harsh light, scattered across the floor, much like William's usually calm demeanor, now fractured and agitated.

NAZI AMERICA CONSPRACY COPY

His controlled facade cracks under the pressure of his emotions, revealing the fiery intensity that simmers beneath the surface. This intensity is like a volcano on the verge of eruption, with molten rage bubbling just beneath the surface. On the couch, shoulders slumped, he presents a stark contrast to the furious tempest brewing within. His fists clenched and unclenched, his jaw tight with tension, and his eyes flashing with anger, radiating palpable energy that sends a clear warning to anyone nearby to tread carefully.

"Dad, please remember your blood pressure."

Finally hearing his daughter, William says. "To hell with my blood pressure. Didn't you see the interview? Daniel wants to tear this country apart just because he lost the election. He's basically declared war against our democratic system. You saw what happened when Daniel just posted wild conspiracy theories about the election. The incident in Louisville with the torches on the pitchforks. That was over social media. Now, with the stations 'voluntarily' giving their air space, everyone heard him loud. They will act even with the lack of evidence."

"So, you think someone hacked the stations?" Amanda asks.

"I'm sure of it. Remember the static?"

"But how?"

"Any good computer hacker could have invaded the mainframes. Dammit, we should have put more security on television satellites."

"But why say something if you don't have proof?"

"That's easy to rile up your base. If you think Louisville was a problem, then we probably haven't seen anything yet."

William's trembling hands clenched into fists, his knuckles turning white with emotion, and his heart raced, pounding like a drum in his chest. Beads of sweat formed on his forehead, revealing the inner turmoil he was experiencing as anger and fear washed over him, draining the color from his face. The room seemed to spin around him, overwhelmed by the surge of adrenaline coursing through his veins, manifesting in tense muscles and shallow breaths.

"Still, that doesn't mean you should raise your blood pressure."

"Darling, we are just seeing the first volley. I'll be damned if I'm the President who lets this country, which has stood for almost three hundred and fifty years, be destroyed. The weight of the responsibility he carried seemed to press down on his shoulders, causing a visible tension in his posture. Despite his outward composure, a storm of conflicting

101

emotions raged within him, manifesting in the clenching of his jaw and the slight tremor in his hands. The gravity of the situation was palpable in the room, as the air crackled with the intensity of his emotions.

"That's why we have justice and investigation departments to handle these situations. Let them take the headaches. I only have one person to look over, and that's you." Chelsea pats his father's shoulder. A warm surge of affection and pride fills his chest, causing a gentle flutter in his heart as he gazes at her. His daughter looks up at him with a bright smile, and a sense of joy radiates through his body, creating a tingling sensation in his fingertips. The physical connection between them reinforces the bond they share, strengthening the love and support that flows between them. As they share this moment of connection, William experiences contentment and peace washing over him, grounding him in the present moment.

"You're right. Daniel is just full of hot air. He doesn't have any proof." William pats his daughter's shoulder, eliciting a wave of relief. The reassuring touch grounds her and provides a sense of security in the midst of uncertainty. A surge of gratitude washes over her for her father's unwavering support and belief in her. The tension in her body eases slightly, and a flicker of determination ignites in her eyes. Despite the accusations and doubts swirling around her, she knows she can rely on her father's unwavering trust and guidance, which strengthens her resolve. The physical effects of her emotions manifest in the way her muscles relax and her posture straightens, a silent declaration of her inner strength and resilience.

"So, you're saying..."

"Daniel doesn't have a leg to stand on." William lets out a breath and responds, "Not that it matters. He has his followers that will believe anything he says, proof or no. And we already know how violent they could be."

"You are talking about that protest again."

As William recounts the protest, his voice trembled with frustration and fear. Amanda noticed his tense shoulders and clenched fists. The memory of the violence committed by Daniel's followers weighs heavily on him, a sick feeling in his stomach. Amanda's heart quickens and her chest tightens with anxiety as she listens to William. The thought of the potential danger posed by these extremists sends a shiver down her spine, causing her muscles to tense involuntarily.

"Five people. Five people that didn't need to die. Five people that are at the wrong place at the wrong time and are not white and straight," William expresses, his voice filled with a mix of sadness and fury. "Daniel calls the people that killed those five people heroes. It makes me sick. Also, the fact that he wants me to pardon them. Like that's going to happen."

"He will just call them hostages then," Amanda responds.

"He can call them whatever he wants. They didn't have to bring torches and gasoline. They especially don't need to bring the rubber tires."

The emotions in the room are palpable, swirling in a mix of anger, disbelief, and sorrow. As the conversation continues, tension thickens, and the weight of the situation presses down on everyone present. Anger radiates off William, his face flushed with indignation. Their emotions charge the air with intensity, making the surrounding molecules vibrate. The physical effects of these emotions are clear in the room. Some clench their fists tightly, knuckles turning white as they struggle to contain their rage, while others shift uncomfortably in their seats, their bodies tense with the urge to act. The speaker's voice cracks with emotion, their words punctuated by sharp intakes of breath as they fight to keep their composure.

As the discussion shifts to pardoning the perpetrators, a wave of nausea washes over the group. The mere suggestion of forgiveness in the face of such heinous acts feels like a betrayal, a slap in the face to the memory of the victims. The tension in the room escalates, becoming a physical manifestation of the emotional turmoil gripping them all.

His daughter watched in horror as the demonstration unfolded on television. Several people waving Confederate, Daniel Thompson, and Nazi Germany flags doused gasoline on people of various ethnicities tied up in rubber tires. They set them on fire while cheering, the screams piercing the air as burning figures writhed, the stench of gasoline and signed flesh creating a horrifying backdrop to the sickening cheers. Some individuals in the crowd were wearing armbands that she couldn't quite decipher; they looked like the American flag, but there was something different about the blue field. The flames consumed the figures within the tires, sending plumes of smoke skyward, a poignant reminder of the lives lost in the tragic blaze with no one to save them as their screams echoed across the television screen. Each gruesome image flickering on the screen clawed at her throat, icy fingers tracing a path of terror down her spine. She wondered why the news people covering the assembly didn't try to intervene, then realized that if they had, they would be the next ones in the tires. The press was probably a few blocks away, using hyperzoom, so any help they could have provided would have been too late. Her body tensed, muscles tightening as she struggled to comprehend the cruelty and inhumanity being displayed. Tears welled up in her eyes, clouding her vision as a mix of anger, disbelief, and sorrow flooded her. The physical impact of the intense emotions she experienced was palpable, leaving her feeling weak and shaken to the core.

"I just wish that Daniel would accept this loss and move on. As for Cain, I doubt he or she even exists."

"So, you believe Daniel is fabricating the entire story?" Amanda puts her hand on William's arm.

William experiences a sense of relaxation washing over him, easing the tension in his muscles and slowing down his racing heart. He confidently dismisses the possibility of election rigging, explaining the extensive resources and expertise required for such a scheme. As he speaks assuredly, a wave of calmness overtakes him, leading to steady breathing and relaxed shoulders. His mind feels clear and focused, free from previous doubts and worries. The physical effects of his newfound certainty are evident as he sits comfortably with a peaceful expression.

"I'm sure that the FBI will investigate these claims. You need to relax. Doctors orders," Chelsea says.

"I'm sure. It's just that the FBI has enough on its plate. They shouldn't have to investigate this election. Let this Cain person produce the evidence, as I've said."

"Do you really think that the election could have been stolen?"

William gives his wife a kiss. "Don't worry, there are safeguards in place to prevent election theft.

"But what if...?"

"Let's not get ahead of ourselves. Everything will be fine."

The weight of uncertainty settled like a heavy stone in William's chest, causing his heart to race and his palms to grow clammy. The tension in his muscles made his body rigid, as if he were bracing himself for an impending storm. Each breath seems shallower, the air thick with the fear of what could come next. As the seeds of doubt sprouted in Amanda, a sense of unease crept through President Chavez's veins, sending shivers down his spine. The emotional turmoil he experiences seems to manifest physically, leaving him depleted and on edge, unable to shake the lingering sense of dread.

As they turn off the television and walk to the hall, William notices the fear and doubt in his wife's eyes, which affect him physically, tightening his stomach and quickening his heart rate.

This uncertainty drives him to stay vigilant about the claims and their implications, planting seeds of doubt in his mind. As moments pass, lines of concern etch onto his face, his brow furrowing and jaw tightening, hands clenching involuntarily at his sides, reflecting the swirling anxiety within him. The room seems to close in, thick with tension as he grapples with the doubts clouding his mind. Despite his attempts to remain composed, his body reveals the inner turmoil he faces, betraying the emotional battle within. He considered the potential fallout from the doubts sown by Daniel and Cain, causing waves of apprehension and leaving him vulnerable and exposed.

Chapter Fourteen

December 3, 2124

A rusty red car, its paint chipped and faded, its engine sputtering, arrived in Portland's Pioneer Courthouse Square via a clamp system. Upon being released, the driver of the car took a moment to survey his environment, looking around cautiously. The lively sounds of street musicians playing upbeat tunes and the chatter of passersby blend with the distant hum of traffic, enveloping him in the vibrant atmosphere. Earthy scents from nearby trees mingle with the smell of food trucks in the air, adding to the sensory experience. The vibrant energy of the square fills him with a sense of excitement and possibility, drawing him further into the scene.

Amid the crowd, signs with messages like "Jill won fair and square," "Daniel is a liar," and "Show us the proof" bobbed frantically. The atmosphere crackled with tension, ignited by the cacophony of shouts and jeers that echoed through the space. The tranquil waterfall offered a stark contrast to the bustling, frenetic activity of the surrounding scene. The century-old charm of the food courts' tantalizing aroma attracts hungry visitors, amidst the backdrop of laughter and chatter filling the air, creating a lively and inviting ambiance. However, the driver's nervousness becomes evident as his racing heartbeat and clammy palms cause his grip on the steering wheel to tighten. Thoughts about the support campaign for Jill Lunden bring a sinking feeling to his stomach, making it difficult for him to take deep breaths. He feels an icy dread that chills him to the bone. Seeing Jill's picture and the signs makes him angry and tense, sending a resolve to his quest.

He let out a scream in the car, conveying his immense frustration. "**That whore cost me everything. I lost my bitch of a wife and kids. My boss subsequently fired me, citing my support for Daniel and accusing me of disrespecting women and minorities.**" A sudden rush of adrenaline coursed through him as his heart pounds, his palms sweat, and his stomach churns as he wrestles with his decision. Despite the toll on him, a sense of duty and patriotism drives him to make the ultimate sacrifice for his country. Sharpening his focus and determination, the adrenaline rush heightens his senses as he prepares for the challenges ahead. Amid a storm of conflicting emotions, his commitment to justice and loyalty to his nation remains steadfast. The governor's planned attendance at the rally causes him extreme happiness. His final prayer was a lament for a life unlived yet willingly sacrificed for President Thompson. With a final, shuddering breath, his prayer turns into a choked sob as his heavy hand reaches for the radio button.

Vanessa Hampton looks around, her brown eyes scanning the bustling marketplace, taking in the sights, sounds, and smells. The enormous crowd gathers in the square and the various people mill about the sidewalks, impressing her, coming from all walks of life. She looks up and sees the Christmas Tree. Vanessa listened to the conversations, her heart racing with excitement and intrigue. A wave of crimson surged across her cheeks, spreading warmth and a blush of color. The vibrant sights and sounds of the marketplace overwhelmed her heightened senses, creating a cacophony of exciting sensations. Vanessa empathizes with people's varied reactions to the recent election, hearing regret and relief in some of their voices. This deeply moves her and stirs her feelings of compassion. The skepticism voiced by the other individual sparks a flicker of curiosity in Vanessa's eyes, causing them to widen with interest. The conflicting emotions swirling within Vanessa create a whirlwind of energy in her body, manifesting as a subtle trembling in

107

her hands. She finds herself caught up in the emotional rollercoaster of the moment, her body responding to the intensity of the conversations happening around her. Despite the chaos of emotions, Vanessa remains composed, her brown eyes reflecting a deep well of understanding and empathy for the diverse perspectives being shared in the marketplace.

A woman with her husband and baby girl remarks, "Quite a crowd you have."

Vanessa greets her, saying, "Janice, how are you? This must be little Debby. Are you here for the protest?"

"I'm so sorry, but I'm just grabbing a quick burger and fries," the woman replied, explaining her brief delay. "But it is good to see you. I am truly astonished by the impressive turnout of people who came to listen to your speech."

"Thank you. After what Daniel said about the Constitution, I knew a speech and demonstration was in order. However, I think it's mostly because Richard Brady is going to show up that a lot of people are here."

"The Governor. That was an amazing accomplishment; I'm wondering what strategies you used."

"There are many approaches and strategies that a woman uses when working towards her goals. Regardless, it is always a joy to see you and catch up." As the happy couple walked hand-in-hand up the ramp, they eagerly anticipated the delicious array of food awaiting them at the various food carts.

Anticipating Richard Brady's expected appearance fuels Vanessa's excitement at the rally. The prospect of hearing his speech filled her with joy and nervousness, causing her heart to race and her cheeks to flush. As she envisioned the moment, a sense of hope and unity permeated the air, enveloping her in warmth and contentment. This feeling was evident in her posture as she stood taller and smiled brighter. Vanessa's emotions continued to intensify, triggering a surge of adrenaline that heightened her senses. The lively square seemed to burst with vibrant colors and bustling activity, amplifying every sound and smell. Noticing a red car nearby added to the anticipation and intrigue building within her. Physically, Vanessa's body responded with heightened awareness, her pulse quickening and her breath becoming more rapid. The blend of excitement and nervous energy invigorated her, preparing her to embrace the rally and Richard Brady's upcoming speech.

Intrigued by the man in the car, she watches as he gestures and speaks without a phone, prompting her to step closer for a better view. Vanessa, recognizing the city landmarks and reminiscing about her deep roots in Portland, ponders offering directions. Because she moved to the city two years ago and her father actively took part in rebuilding it, she feels connected to the community. Remembering Richard's support during her father's funeral, Vanessa persuades him to participate in the rally. As she approaches the car, she witnesses the driver pressing a button. A massive explosion engulfs the vehicle and nearby buildings. Intense heat, a deafening roar, and the smell of burning metal and rubber fills the air. Vanessa's heart races with fear and shock, adrenaline surges through her body, heightening her senses. The explosion's sight triggers a wave of panic, causing her muscles to tense and her breath to quicken. Overwhelmed by the intense heat and deafening noise, her skin prickles, sweat forms on her brow, and her head spins. The acrid scent of burning metal and rubber assaults her nostrils, adding to the chaos of the moment. These physical effects culminate in a visceral experience that leaves Vanessa trembling with a mixture of terror and disbelief.

Richard is driving to Pioneer Courthouse Square after visiting his sister. While on Sunset Highway, he checks his notes about a demonstration in Portland organized by Vanessa Hampton, the daughter of his former Assistant District Attorney, Bruno. Bruno supported Richard until his mayoral campaign, then became District Attorney before moving to Hawaii with his wife. After his wife's death, Bruno returned to Oregon but passed away after a heart attack.

"Your father was a good man."

"He thought very highly of you. There was always talks of Richard Brady. To be fair until I saw you, I thought you were a superhero."

Richard smiled and looked at himself. "Nope, I'm human. Look if you need anything. Don't hesitate to ask.

"That sounds like a tempting possibility, and I may well decide to take advantage of your offer."

Richard glanced at Amy Rogers, his assistant, who was reviewing her notes, her brow furrowed in concentration.

"Amy, would you mind telling me something?"

"Sure, what is it?"

"I continually ask myself why I keep agreeing to such commitments, it's a question that haunts me." Richard says trying to lighten the mood.

"It's Bruno's child. You couldn't help yourself."

"Ok, so how about you?"

"I'm your assistant and, as such, I need to make sure you present yourself as a professional. Since Ashley is at the fundraiser to help people with disabilities in Salem. I have to save you from yourself. Also, Bruno was a good friend of mine as well. However, did we have to visit your sister's first?"

"Deal I made, so she doesn't keep calling me. Consider it my gift to you." Richard chuckles, which becomes infectious.

"Sir, I think you better see this," Richard's driver, Samuel, says.

Richard puts on the passenger front window video. He looks at the street and the plume of smoke in their path. Amy looks at it as well. "What is it?"

"I don't know. Computer plot the likely source of the black smoke."

The computer says. "Likely source is Pioneer Courthouse Square."

"Damn, I was afraid of that. Computer disengage clamp on this car and switch to manual. Sam, I want to get to Pioneer Courthouse yesterday, understood?"

"Yes, sir."

A wave of despair washed over Amy, leaving her numb and tears tracing paths down her cheeks.

Upon arriving at the square, Richard saw a chaotic mess with people scattered everywhere. "I'm glad that some people are screaming in agony." Richard says to Amy.

"That's a horrid thing to say..."

"I only mean. I'm glad they are in agony because that means they are still alive, but I agree I could have phrased that better. How I don't know."

It was the silent ones that made him say a silent prayer. Rushing back to the limo, he immediately dialed emergency services. "Hello, this is Richard Brady at Pioneer Courthouse Square. There has been an incident. I need an ambulance urgently," he tells the operator before hanging up.

Despite being informed that the ambulance will take thirty minutes due to a five-car pile-up, Richard quickly shifts his focus to the immediate needs of the injured. Turning to his driver, Samuel, Richard surveys the scene and the extent of the injuries becomes apparent. Above the stairs, the scene is horrific; several people are missing limbs, their stumps still oozing blood. The baby, only five months old, is among the dead; its head is severely damaged. Her parents are also dead and missing body parts. It is a gruesome sight. Richard's emergency preparedness and first aid training proved invaluable when Ashley was injured during Marianne's wedding, and he was grateful for it. Although Richard hopes his training will help, he also knows he needs assistance.

"Sam, do you know any first aid?"

"Former combat medic during the Botswana War."

Memories from the war haunt Samuel, like bombs exploding and seeing an injured man with his stomach split open. Moving him would have caused his guts to fall out. He hoped to leave those memories behind, but they come flooding back as he looks at a meeting spot in Portland.

"Sam, are you OK?" Amy asks.

"Sorry, talking about the war just brings back so many terrible memories. I'll be fine." Sam says.

Richard pats Sam's shoulder. "I cannot fathom your wartime experiences; however, we must prioritize immediate needs. Let's prioritize those who can't move over there, and the more serious cases closer to the waterfall," he directed.

As Richard's words sank in, Sam felt a surge of determination and adrenaline course through his veins. His heart rate quickened, his muscles tensed, and a sense of urgency washed over him. The weight of the situation pressed down on his shoulders, making his breaths come in short, sharp gasps.

"And the dead." Amy's response resonated with a deep sense of grief and sadness that seemed to hang heavy in the air. Her trembling voice showed her grief and dismay at the surrounding death. A lump formed in her throat, and tears welled up in her eyes, reflecting the emotional toll of the moment.

"Let's move them inside by the waterfall. Amy try to talk to the more seriously injured. Give them something to hope for."

"Yes, sir." Amy gives a mock salute, trying to help the mood.

Richard moves through the carnage. He sees a boy about ten years old, Africa American, screaming in pain. Richard sees that the boy's arm is at a weird angle. 'Dislocated.' Richard says in his head, knowing that it could be worse. "Hold on." Richard grabs the boy's arm. "I will not lie. This is going to hurt. On the count of three." The boy nods. "Three." Richard gets the arm back in its socket.

The boy moves it. "Where's my mother and sister? They were with me," the boy cries. Richard looks around and sees an African American older woman with a girl only seven by her side. Neither was moving. Richard swallows. "Where's your dad?"

"He died two years ago."

Richard scoops up the boy. "Do you want to be my little helper until we can find your family?"

"I guess so."

"Richard over here." Amy says.

Richard runs over to Amy and a woman lying on the pavement. Soon, Richard recognizes Vanessa Hampton.

Richard quickly checks on Vanessa, then turns to look at Amy before shaking his head in disbelief. He notices Vanessa's ribs sticking out and sees her spitting out blood. Placing his hand on the back of Vanessa's head, he can feel the dampness of blood. Despite the ambulance being on its way, Richard knows Vanessa only has mere seconds left.

Richard walks up to Amy. "Amy, this is..."

"Jack Kirkson." the boy says.

Richard whispers something in Amy's ear. Amy sees the dead woman and child. "Dear god. Does he know?"

"We don't know if they are his family. So let's keep it quiet for now. Give him something to do."

"No problem." Amy leaves with Jack.

Richard looks back at Vanessa. Her breathing coming in gasps. Richard hates this feeling of powerlessness.

In a moment of heartbreaking realization, Vanessa whispered, "Father, is that you?" Richard held her gently, offering reassurance that he knew it was a lie. As Vanessa's condition worsened, tears welled up in her eyes until she passed away. With a heavy heart, Richard closed her eyes and carried her lifeless body into the building.

The ambulance finally arrives, a welcome sight after what felt like an eternity. They arrived with Richard, Sam, Amy, Jack and many of the survivors that weren't seriously hurt. "We can take it from here," the paramedic says. Richard solemnly reported. "The dead are in the building by the waterfall."

"Thank you. We will get body bags for them. Are any of you hurt?" Richard looks around at his shell-shocked crew. Everyone shakes their heads, the acrid smell of smoke heavy in the air, as Richard surveyed the leveled buildings, the silent screams of the trapped echoing in his mind.

"One other thing." Richard looks at Jack. He goes to the paramedic. "I think that little boy there lost the last of his family. There was a woman and a little girl close to him and he mentioned being with his mother and sister."

The paramedic looks at Jack. "We'll call Child Protective Services. Thank you all." The paramedic leaves to make some calls.

Sam approaches Richard, saying, "At least it's over."

"For now. But I fear that maybe it's just begun," Richard responds with a sense of foreboding.

Chapter Fifteen

December 6, 2124

A t 9:00 a.m. EST, Melissa arrives at the Capitol building, its imposing structure looming large against the clear morning sky. Stepping out, she gazes up at the immense dome, its grandeur emphasized by the flag billowing freely between the two majestic chambers, a symbol of liberty. A surge of pride swells in her chest as she snaps to attention, the flag's colors a brilliant beacon of hope and freedom. Some offer salutes: others climb the stairs, eager to get to their offices. The surge of pride that swells in Melissa's chest causes her heart to beat faster, sending a rush of adrenaline through her veins. Her muscles tense with the physical manifestation of her emotions, causing her posture to straighten and her shoulders to square. The brilliant beacon of hope and freedom represented by the flag seems to glow even brighter in her eyes, reflecting the intensity of her emotions. As she stands at attention, and salutes, her breath quickens, her senses heighten, and a sense of determination courses through her entire being, fueling her sense of duty and commitment. Her emotional state is physically evident; she's awestruck.

Entering the grand building, the massive paintings of Washington Crossing the Delaware and the signing of the Constitution immediately strike her, their grandeur filling the space. The sight of the impressive paintings causes a rush of awe and pride to swell within her chest, her heart beating faster as she takes in the historical significance of the artwork. A tingling sensation runs down her spine; she deeply admires the leaders shown in the paintings, their determination and courage radiating from the canvas. As she stands in the grand building, surrounded by the echoes of the past, a sense of reverence and inspiration washes over her, fueling her own passion for serving her country.

Elizabeth Manchester walks over to Melissa, her heels clicking on the marble floor of the Capitol building. The air is filled with the sounds of hushed conversations and the faint whir of overhead fans. The smell of freshly polished wood and paper fills the room. Elizabeth looks at Melissa. "You seem to be in a good mood. Is there something you know about the gun safety bill that I don't?"

Melissa chuckles softly. She says, "Oh, it's not that. The Thanksgiving recess brought news. I'm becoming a great-grandmother."

Melissa is filled with joy, shown by her flushed cheeks. Endorphins make her heart race, energizing her movements. Her eyes sparkle with excitement, reflecting her inner happiness. Tension melts away, giving her a relaxed posture that spreads joy. A warm smile and positive energy radiate from her. Her laughter and open body language attract others. Melissa's joy captivates people, drawing them in. Laughter and conversation fill the room. Various scents blend in the air, creating a comforting atmosphere.

Her deeper, more relaxed breathing suggests that each inhale fills her with sweet contentment. The air itself appears to be infused with her happiness, wrapping everyone in a comforting embrace that banishes all worries and troubles. Her heartbeat slows, syncing with the rhythm of her peaceful breaths. The tension that is coiled tightly in her muscles melts away, leaving her feeling weightless and free. A soft glow emanates from her, casting a warm and calming light that soothes those around her. The room brightens as if lit by her inner joy, creating a serene atmosphere that envelops everyone in a sense of tranquility. Her happiness radiates, impacting those near her.

In Melissa's presence, it is impossible not to feel the physical effects of her joy - a lightness in the chest, a tingling in the fingertips, a smile that seems to stretch from ear to ear. Her happiness is contagious, spreading like wildfire and leaving a trail of warmth and positivity in its wake. The physical effects of Melissa's joy are palpable, almost as if her happiness has a tangible presence. Nearby, individuals experience a sense of relief. The tingling sensation in their fingertips seems to radiate a warmth that extends all the way to their hearts, filling them with a sense of contentment and peace. And the smiles that grace their faces seem to stretch wider and wider, reflecting the sheer infectiousness of Melissa's joy.

It is as if a wave of positive energy sweeps through the room, leaving everyone basking in its glow. The physical effects of Melissa's joy are truly palpable. As she beams with happiness, Melissa's joy lifts a weight from those around her, making them feel lighthearted. The tingling in their fingertips seems to signify a surge of energy and excitement coursing through their veins, urging them to join in her contagious joy. Broad smiles illuminate faces, warming everyone nearby. Melissa's presence is like a ray of sunshine on a cloudy day, brightening moods and sparking a sense of positivity in all who cross her path.

Her laughter, like tinkling bells, echoes through the House Chamber, infusing the air with a sense of jubilation. The physical effects of her joy are evident in the way her cheeks flush with color and her eyes twinkle with unbridled delight. Every movement she makes seems to be infused with an extra dose of energy, as if her happiness is propelling her forward.

"Congratulations," said Senator Richardson from California.

"I thought your granddaughter is married to a..." Senator Ted McDonnell from Alabama begins.

Melissa says. "A woman, yes, and I appreciate modern technology's beauties."

"What about modern technology?" Richardson asks.

"They explained it, but I don't understand. Something about a friend of Jessica's."

"Jessica, is that your granddaughter-in-law?" Richardson clarifies.

"Yes, she is. Look what they gave me." As Melissa proudly displays the sonogram picture, the room seems to buzz with excitement. The physical effects of excitement and anticipation are palpable in the room. Melissa's heart races with joy as she sends a rush of adrenaline through her veins. The buzz of excitement seems to vibrate through the air, causing a light tingling sensation on the skin of those present. A wave of sweet anticipation heightens everyone's senses.

Congratulations and wishes bring smiles to everyone's faces. Even reserved Republican Party members show emotions, their body language and expressions mirroring the room's joy. The moment is infectious, creating a warm and welcoming atmosphere. Melissa's happiness affects everyone, fostering unity and elation in the room.

"Well, I have to say she looks to be in good health," Elizabeth says.

"Are you kidding? He looks like he could arrive at any minute," Richardson says.

"So, are you going to keep us in suspense? What is the child?"

"That child's existence is an affront to God, and it will face the consequences it deserves. As will the parents." Kathleen Hand of Louisiana, a person in their thirties with dyed blond hair and a vocal member of the American Now party, erupts in anger, passionately denouncing the unborn child.

The American Now party members arrive, feeling angry and ready for confrontation. Adrenaline pumps through their bodies, making their hearts race and muscles tense. Their hands clench into fists and their breath quickens. They speak louder, gesture aggressively, and tremble with fury. The atmosphere shifts from joyous to tense and hostile as their anger grows.

Melissa's anger rises, making her heart race and chest tight. Adrenaline flows, causing her hands to shake. Her breath quickens, fueling her intense gaze as she faces Kathleen. Her jaw tightens, body tenses, ready for action. Her stance exudes power and protection, showing her fury. The physical effects of her anger reveal her strong emotions and determination to defend her family.

"I don't think anybody asked for your opinion. But I'm tired of you criticizing my family. From my daughter marrying a Mexican to now my unborn great-granddaughter. That ends. Mention my family again, and you'll regret it. Is that understood?"

Melissa's fierce spirit blazes, her body language a powerful display of unwavering determination. The tension in the room becomes palpable as Kathleen, observing Melissa's intensity, experiences a surge of adrenaline coursing through her veins. The presence of the America Now members offers a layer of reassurance, their support acting as a source of strength and solidarity amidst the charged atmosphere. Emotions in the room resemble a brewing storm, with waves of determination and gratitude colliding, creating a sense of urgency and empowerment.

As Kathleen vocalizes, "**You, too, will face judgment. All of you will.**" her voice quivers with a mix of excitement and nervousness. Her heart rate quickens, and a rush of adrenaline courses through her veins, with the blood pumping in her ears as she joins the other American Now members, her steps quick and resolute. The swirling emotions inside her are clear as her hands tremble slightly and her breath comes out in short, shallow gasps. Despite the physical effects of her emotions, Kathleen's resolve shines through, propelling her forward with a sense of purpose and determination.

"What is that all about?" Richardson asks.

117

"Kathleen being Kathleen," Elizabeth responds. "The biggest drama queen in the universe. Remember when she continuously heckled President Sanchez during the State of the Union last year?"

"Or what about the Muslim lasers causing the worldwide inflation," Richardson says.

"Hey, she was a member of your party before she switched to American Now."

"And we are glad to get rid of her."

Elizabeth looks at Melissa, who is still breathing heavily. "To be fair, Melissa, I don't think anyone would fault you if you pounded Kathleen to the next century."

Expressing her concern, Melissa states, "Why give her the news coverage? America Now just loves to preach hatred and violence. They literally bring out the worst in people. I won't give them the soundstage."

Elizabeth nods in agreement, responding, "Maybe, but that could be enough. We all know that some people vote against their best interests when people tell them what want to hear. I fear that America Now could one day become the dominant party America."

Melissa, looking worried, replies, "Well, I pray that day never happens. Anyway, we need to caucus."

During the Democratic caucus, everyone gathers in chairs to discuss the day's issues, or at least that is the initial plan. However, their attention quickly shifts to the sonogram, and the comments made by Kathleen Hand.

The room is filled with quiet conversations and laughter. There's a mix of coffee and ink smells in the air. People are eagerly examining the sonogram, showing curiosity and concern. Papers rustle and pens scratch as everyone is engaged. The energy is palpable, showing urgency and determination in discussing Kathleen Hand's remarks.

A light-hearted moment ensues when a freshman Senator jokingly says, "Grammy, have you picked out a tiny dress or suit for the baby's potential presidential campaign in the maternity ward?"

Laughter fills the chamber as the conversation continues playfully. Joan Stanton from Illinois jokes, "Maybe that little one will take your seat someday, Melissa," causing more laughter.

Rachel Collins, a freshman congresswoman from Washington D.C., chimes in, saying, "I shouldn't be worried for another 30 years."

Ms. Collins' raising the subject causes Melissa to become serious. "I will not seek another term for the House after this one ends." The room falls into a hush so profoundly that the mere drop of a pin would echo loudly. Everyone present stands in stunned silence.

It is Jeff Gollum, a congressperson from Oregon, who speaks up, breaking the tense stillness, "I guess your granddaughter will need someone to babysit the tyke every once in a while. Although we will miss you," he says.

Rank-and-file members express their sentiments, saying, "You are one of the House's longest-serving members." After the caucus, conversations buzz among the people as the group disperses.

Elizabeth approaches Melissa with a suggestion, "With the rising popularity of the American Now party, perhaps we should bring the Republicans to our side."

Melissa halts her. "We can't. Having three political parties ensures that America Now will not hold absolute power, which is beneficial for the country."

"But merging both parties could make America Now uneasy."

Melissa replies, "Let me propose this - as I mentioned, I plan on stepping down in two years. If our party wins, I want you to become the new Speaker of the House. Once in that position, you can work towards unifying with the remaining members of the Republican party."

Grateful for the offer and expressing her confidence, Elizabeth accepts, "Thank you for your trust in me. I will strive to unite the parties if the opportunity arises."

A couple went for a morning jog in Worchester. Rounding a corner, they stumble upon a horrifying sight in a dimly lit alley, filling them with dread. On the pavement lies the lifeless body of a woman, her feet pointing towards the street, the stench of death mixing with the damp air and assaulting their nostrils. They can't look away from the ghastly scene, noticing that the woman's pants are forcefully yanked down, revealing her pale skin, showing that someone has mercilessly taken her life. Her throat has a deep slash, and she has been disemboweled, with evidence of this heinous act lying beside her mutilated face. The police arrive, sirens wailing. Their investigation began immediately, focusing on the victim's mutilated body. Both hands were missing and her teeth were smashed.

"Dear God, what has happened here?" gasps one officer upon arrival at the scene, while another scans the area for signs of a struggle or violence.

"I find no trace of blood or a trail. I will have to say that the murder occurred elsewhere.

The first officer's pen dances across the paper, scratching out a detailed account of the blood-splattered scene, the chilling silence broken only by the scratch of his pen. "The bigger mystery is why? Perhaps the Coroner can find answers to both questions." With a grim expression, the coroner arrives, her black bag swinging, the weight of it hinting at the grim task ahead. As she approaches the gruesome sight, the stench of decay is heavy in the air and stinging her nostrils. She carefully inserts the thermometer. Its coldness was a stark contrast to the body's warmth. Only her breath broke the silence as it disappeared beneath the skin. A faint glint remained.

With a somber tone, she speaks, "Based on the chilling temperature, she met her fate around five hours ago."

"Ok, let's pack her up and get her to the morgue. Maybe they can find out who she is." The officer says.

"A DNA analysis will take time."

"Maybe we'll get lucky and someone will report her missing." The second officer says.

A ringing phone shatters the silence of the empty street. The still air, carrying dust and decay, felt heavy with anticipation.

Chapter Sixteen

After the heated House debates, Melissa is finally ready to depart, with the lingering smell of stale tea and tension heavy in the air. As she makes her way through the dimly lit corridor, the heavy scent of aged documents and lukewarm tea clings to the air. The rhythmic tap-tap-tap of footsteps echoes through the polished hallways, serving as a counterpoint to the low hum of conversation from far down the corridor. On her way to her office, she unexpectedly encounters the person she most wants to avoid, and Kathleen Hand. "Why did you postpone the vote on the election interference measure? My bill deserves a vote, same as the gun bill." The adrenaline coursing through her veins fuels her passionate speech, causing her voice to rise in volume and intensity. Her narrowed eyes and furrowed brows convey her frustration and determination, while her clenched fists emphasize her resolve. The venom in her voice adds a sharp edge to her words, making her displeasure unmistakably clear. The physical effects of her emotions are evident in her body language, mirroring the intensity of her feelings about the situation.

"Gun violence is a known issue. Those thirty preschoolers are just the latest of school shootings." Melissa's heart pounds in her chest, her blood boiling with a mix of anger and frustration as she feels the tension building in her muscles, her fists clenching tightly at her sides. The heat rising in her cheeks signals the struggle to control the urge to lash out at Kathleen, her breathing quickening with each strained inhale and exhale. Melissa felt the weight of the conversation as a physical force, the gravity of the topic and the sharp sting of each word exchanged between her and Kathleen hanging heavy in the air. The emotional turmoil she is experiencing is manifesting itself in her body, causing her to feel tense and on edge. Despite the overwhelming urge to react impulsively, Melissa knows she has to stay calm. She can feel the adrenaline coursing through her veins, fueling her fight-or-flight response. However, she also understands that violence is not the answer, no matter how strongly she feels about the issue at hand. Taking a deep breath, Melissa tries to channel her emotions into a more constructive outlet, focusing on articulating her points clearly and passionately, using her words as a weapon instead of her fists. Though the physical effects of her emotions are still present, she is determined to rise above them and engage in a meaningful dialogue.

"HEY, it's our right to carry as many guns as we can. That's in the Constitution. The right to school safety is not. Yet, we all know that these so-called 'victims' are crisis actors. We all know those kids are safe and sound with their families." Kathleen's disdain is palpable as she speaks, her features contorting into a sneer while her icy gaze narrows. The sharpness and cutting nature of her words, delivered with anger, resembles daggers. Her aggressive body language, marked by clenched fists and tense muscles, signals readiness for conflict. This negative energy creates a tense atmosphere, leaving others uncomfortable and on edge. Despite Kathleen's fervor, Melissa remains unfazed by her conspiracy theories, having heard them all before and growing weary of the repetition. Frustration washes over Melissa, evident in her rising blood pressure, stiffened shoulders, and clenched jaw. The surge of adrenaline readies her for a potential confrontation, as anger flushes her cheeks and challenges her composure.

You have no proof that anyone stole the election. Short of this so-called Cain person. I will not have the House consider these outrageous conspiracy theories. Like when you said the United States has Gazpacho police. Tell me, Ms. Intelligent, what a soup has to do with the police? Or what about the Democrats creating Wonton destruction? Also let me tell you one other thing: there is no secret, Satanic Democratic meeting hall. Not in the DNC headquarters and not at some stupid hamburger joint."

As Melissa continues to speak, her voice betrays a mix of amusement and exasperation. Her laughter carries a hint of disbelief at the absurdity of the allegations, underscored by an undercurrent of frustration at their persistence.

Melissa speaks with a mix of amusement and exasperation. She laughs in disbelief at the absurd allegations and shows frustration at their persistence. Physically, her emotions show subtly. She furrows her brow, trying to understand Kathleen's nonsensical statements. Her hands gesture animatedly as she talks. She laughs lightly but shakes her head in disbelief. Melissa finds the situation absurd and exhausting. Despite trying to stay composed, there is a visible tension in her body language, revealing the internal battle between amusement and frustration.

Kathleen's seething anger radiates off her like waves of heat, her face flushed with emotion and her hands trembling with intensity. The mention of the past speeches sends shivers down her spine, triggering a physical reaction as her muscles tense and her heart rate quickens. Her voice, usually calm and composed, now drips with venom and conviction, each word punctuated with a sharp edge that cuts through the air. The fire in her eyes betrays the deep-seated frustration and disbelief she feels, as if a storm is brewing within her, threatening to unleash its full force at any moment. The emotions she is experiencing are palpable, almost tangible, as they manifest in her body language and demeanor, painting a vivid picture of her inner turmoil.

In response to Melissa's assertion, Kathleen sharply retorts, "This is no conspiracy theory. We both know that they stole the election. Daniel couldn't possibly have lost.

Melissa counters with, "Except he did! Probably because he said on tape that he sexually abused a woman and, oh yeah, killed another, and said that he wanted to be a dictator? Yeah, there's no way he could have lost. The after losing, he declared that the Constitution should be terminated on live television."

Kathleen retorts, "Considering all that fraud... Maybe it should be."

"My life was at stake, defending your right to speak freely. When I was in the military. I did it to protect that document you said should be terminated."

"You were a military lawyer and then a judge."

"In Botswana, I oversaw the case involving the individuals behind the Kalanga massacre. I heard the bombs going off. I held a dying soldier after enemy fire destroyed my jeep. What did you do?"

"You mean you sentenced innocent people to various punishments, including Captain Stevens, to the most horrific death at the hands of the Kalanga people!"

"JAG did what it had to keep the peace."

"If Daniel was President, we wouldn't have been in that mess."

"Oh yes, he probably would have carpet bombed the entire country just to make way for a luxury resort. To hell with the people living there."

Kathleen's fuming anger radiates through her body, causing her muscles to tense and her heart rate increases.

Melissa's heart races as a wave of shock and disbelief washes over her. Her muscles tense, breathing quickens, and hands tremble at the weight of the words she has just heard. The surge of emotions creates a knot in her stomach, a physical manifestation of the turmoil raging within her. Blood rushes to her face, coloring her cheeks crimson with a mix of anger and hurt. Each word spoken feels like a dagger piercing her heart, causing a sharp pang of pain with every syllable. The intensity of her emotions is palpable, radiating off her in waves that seem to distort the surrounding air.

"What is it with you? Are you trying to get on his non-existent cabinet? **Tell me where the line is when you abandon Daniel?** Because he's done a lot of horrible things in his disgusting life.

Kathleen's fuming anger radiates through her body, causing her muscles to tense and her heart rate increases. Adrenaline floods her system, heightening her senses and sharpening her focus. Her face flushes with heat as her blood pressure rises, and her breathing becomes rapid and shallow. The intensity of her emotions is palpable as her body reacts to the perceived injustice with a surge of energy and readiness for action. The physical manifestations of her anger underscore the threat in her words, signaling a deep-seated determination to seek retribution.

"Well, it's a good thing that all the poll workers' information is secret. Otherwise, I'm sure your cult will do something about them," Melissa starts to walk away.

"We are not in a cult. America Now is a growing political movement." As Kathleen speaks, her face turns a bright shade of red, her eyes widen with intensity, and her hands clench into fists. The heat of her anger radiates off of her like waves, making those around her feel the tension in the air. Her voice rises in pitch, the words sharp and cutting, like the eruption of a volcano ready to unleash its fiery wrath. The sheer force of her emotions is palpable, leaving a lingering sense of unease in the room.

"A very dangerous one at that."

A wave of anger washes over Kathleen. Her heart pounds in her chest, and she clenches her hands into tight fists. She can feel the heat rising in her cheeks and a prickling sensation at the back of her neck. The accusation of being part of a dangerous cult stirs up a mix of frustration and defensiveness within her, causing her to stand a little taller and speak with a sharper tone in her voice.

The emotional intensity of the moment is palpable as Kathleen struggles to contain her rising emotions while trying to defend her beliefs. Melissa angrily confronted Kathleen after her declaration, "We will speak for the glory of America."

"You mean the downfall of America? You and America Now want to destroy the Constitution and various agencies. So, what if people suffer? As long as you make your friends wealthier," Melissa flings her hand in frustration.

Kathleen replies, "America Now, me included, simply desires efficient government and national purity."

"Then resign and take as many of your America Now party members as you can."

Kathleen's heart races, pounding against her chest like a drum, while her face flushes with anger, heat rising up from her neck to her cheeks. The tension in her body builds, muscles tightening like coiled springs ready to release, as she can feel the pressure building inside her, a storm of emotions swirling within, threatening to erupt like molten lava from a volcano. The breaking news alert only adds fuel to the fire, intensifying her already heightened state of agitation. With each passing moment, she feels herself on the brink, teetering on the edge of a violent emotional explosion. The blaring sound of the breaking news alert cuts through the air, mixing with the faint hum of the television.

A shiver runs down Melissa's spine as she watches the intense expression on Sean Bradley's face, his words hanging heavy in the air, creating a sense of tension and urgency in the room. Screen light washes the room, shadows playing on walls. "This is flaming hot news. We have recent evidence that proves the election of 2124 was stolen. We have obtained this recording."

"I bribed men to rig the election." The voice in the recording declares.

As the recording plays, Melissa's eyes widen in shock and disbelief, her body going cold as goosebumps prickle her skin. She feels a wave of anger and frustration welling up inside her, her fists clenching involuntarily in response to the injustice unfolding before her. The emotional rollercoaster she is on is taking a toll on her physically, causing her to feel drained and overwhelmed by the flood of emotions coursing through her.

"Confirmation at last," Kathleen looks at Melissa. "What's the matter Melissa? Not too long ago, you demanded proof. Where here it is. Now I demand that a full House investigation be convened right away." As Kathleen's anger subsides, she feels a wave of relief washing over her, calming the racing thoughts and tense muscles that had consumed her just moments ago. The release of tension in her body is palpable as her heart rate slows, her breathing deepens, and the furrowed brow smoothens. Feeling lighter and more at ease as the physical effects of her anger fade, she thinks more clearly and rationally. The contrast between the intense emotions she was experiencing before and the newfound sense of calm is stark, highlighting the powerful impact our emotions can have on our physical well-being.

"We have verified that Tracy Kincaid, who was the campaign manager of Jill Lunden, is the person on the recording. America," Sean's voice booms with clenched fists and a fiery glare.

"I don't believe it." Melissa, feeling her heart racing and a surge of adrenaline, notices a knot forming in her stomach, leading her to clench her fists in disbelief. As she covers her mouth, her breathing becomes shallow and rapid, with her chest rising and falling with each quick inhale and exhale, the tension in her body palpable, her muscles tight and ready for action. Emotions manifest physically, reflecting her disbelief.

"Now do you believe it? It's everything I have been saying since the election. We possess an audio recording. Proof positive that Jill's campaign rigged the election."

Chapter Seventeen

December 10, 2124

S teve and his children are watching a new adaptation of A Christmas Carol together, visibly relaxed as the movie plays. Their bodies lean into each other in comfort, their faces lit up with joy and wonder, eyes glued to the screen. Steve's arm is draped protectively around the kids, creating a sense of warmth and security. However, Jill's pacing sharply contrasts with the scene on the couch. Her movements are quick and erratic, hands fidgeting with the hem of her shirt. A worried expression and restless eyes reveal her inattention to the film. Her palpable tension is apparent in her demeanor, betraying a clear state of unease. Her restless energy fills the room as a stark reminder of the turmoil brewing inside her.

"Someone should give a copy of this to Daniel Thompson. If anyone needs to be visited by three spirits, it's him," Henry, Jill's son, bursts into laughter, the sound bright and joyful.

"Like he will take their advice. If he has seen any of the fifteen hundred versions of the story, he probably always prefers the old Scrooge version before the visits." Their daughter Rachel, the eldest, chuckles as she spoke.

"You're probably right,"

"Honey, what's the matter?" Steve asks, basically knowing the answer. Jill's heart pounds in her chest with worry, causing a tightness in her throat as she imagines all the scenarios that could have befallen Tracy. Her hands tremble with each failed attempt to reach her friend, the uncertainty gnawing at her gut like a pit of dread. Sleep evades her, leaving dark circles under her eyes and a heaviness in her limbs. The weight of her emotions seems to press down on her shoulders, rendering even simple tasks a monumental undertaking. Time seems to stretch endlessly as she waits for any news, her mind consumed with fear and anxiety.

"Four days have passed since my last communication with Tracy, and I am concerned about her well-being." Jill finally voices her worry, linking it to the increased violence in the nation following Daniel's accusations about the election.

"Without any proof except the word of someone named Cain."

What proof does anyone need if they are groomed to believe the person saying it? Even without proof, someone drove a car and detonated it in downtown Portland." Jill is still horrified when she hears it on the news.

She is more horrified when a person said on the news, "Too bad governor Brady wasn't there at the time." Says another, "They get what they deserve." Jill hears about a baby whose head is caved in.

"I don't understand some people. I remember when the FBI building was destroyed by terrorists, the country united. Recently, Portland, OR was bombed and some believe the people got what they deserved. What insane universe are we living in?"

Steve gets up. "That was then. This is now. **Daniel brings out the worse in people.** Years from now, they will probably review their past actions with regret."

"That doesn't help with Tracy not answering my calls. I fear that something might have happened to her."

"It's possible she finally took your advice and met someone." Jill thinks on that situation.

She knows Steve is trying to reassure her. "I'm sure she would call and tell me. I mean the many times that she told me off about leaving her love life alone.

"Perhaps she went on vacation. The election was a long haul. She may have planned a break."

"She still has her phone. I always remember her saying that her phone is her life. I wish I could track her phone as easily as the kids."

"Mom, I'm sure that Aunt Tracy is fine. Maybe she lost her phone," Rachel says.

"I remember a couple of times she runs with her phone in her pocket. It would be very easy if someone stole it," Henry says.

Jill felt conflicted between appreciation and gut instinct, creating a knot in her stomach. Mixed emotions of warmth and unease coursed through her. Despite feeling grateful for her family, a sense of foreboding weighed on her chest. This tension manifested physically, causing restlessness and muscle tension. Reflecting on proposing to Steve fifteen years ago, guided by intuition, reminded her to trust her gut feelings.

"Why don't we go to Tracy's place," Steve suggests. "If she's on vacation, her suitcase won't be in her apartment."

After considering, she conceded, "Okay, everyone might be right. Tracy could just be sick." However, even Jill herself wasn't convinced.

Their conversation was suddenly interrupted. "This is flaming hot news. We have recent evidence that proves the election of 2124 was stolen. We have obtained this recording."

A recording played, revealing a voice confessing. "Fine, I bribed men to rig the election."

"The voice was identified as Tracy Kincaid, Jill's campaign manager." Sean's voice thundered, demanding an immediate investigation, his words emphasized by clenched fists and a fiery glare. "Television off." Jill's heart pounded in her chest, blood rushing through her veins at a dizzying pace. A cold sweat broke out on her forehead, and her skin prickled with a clammy sheen. Every muscle tensed, ready to flee from the overwhelming fear that gripped her. With short, shallow breaths, the icy air filled her lungs. Reality twisted, colors blurred, and sounds faded to a distant drone. The weight of the truth crushed her as she realized the voice belonged to Tracy.

Could Aunt Tracy have stolen the election, Mom?" Rachel asked in shock, her eyes fixed on her mother.

"It's absurd. Even if we wanted to steal the election, we would lack the money and resources," Jill says, her concern for her friend deepening."Why hasn't she returned any of her phone messages?"

Her husband gasps, his voice trembling with disbelief. "I don't believe it," he says.

"You shouldn't, dear. I know Tracy. She's ambitious but not stupid," she responds.

"Then what do you want to do?" Henry asks.

A strangled cry escapes Jill's lips as she frantically returns to the phone, her voice a breathless whisper. "Tracy, please call me. We're heading for your place." The phone hangs up abruptly.

Jill grabs her heavy wool coat, finding comfort in its rough texture against her skin. "What are you waiting for?" she asks.

Jill's car pulls up to the Happy Arms Apartments, its tires crunching on the gravel driveway. She notices the dim light revealing the keypad in the garage. She punches in the code 5520, the click-clack of the numbers echoing in the quiet space.

After Jill and her family exit the car, her son asks, "Can me and sissy go for a walk?"

Jill looks at them and replies, "Fine, but be careful."

The kids leave as Jill and Steve enter the elevator, with Jill requesting, "Fifth floor." The elevator doors ping open, and they emerge, blinking in the brighter hallway light. A plush, royal blue carpet greets them, soft beneath her feet, as the air carries the intoxicating aroma of a thousand blossoms, though it does little to calm Jill's rising apprehension.

Eventually, they reach room 20, the heavy oak door looming before them. "Tracy, this is Jill," she announces as she knocks on the door, but there is no answer. Jill then inserts her card into the reader with a swipe, the magnetic strip making a faint whirring sound as the door creaks open to reveal a dimly lit room.

Steve looks at his wife, her smile a beacon in the dim light, and mentions, "I've been meaning to give this back to her after the election."

"Well, I guess it's a good thing you didn't," Jill replies. They enter the room, noticing the spotless floors and the sunlight streaming through the windows, illuminating the pristine condition. Every item is neatly arranged, creating a feeling of calm and order.

"Why don't you check the bedroom? I'll check her office," Steve says, heading for the bedroom as Jill walks to Tracy's office. The office library holds a collection of tablet books on a ledge, reflecting the light, while books line the far wall, creating a welcoming space.

Jill takes out one book and looks at the cover: Black's Law Dictionary. "I don't understand why you don't just get a computer to help you. You could probably be an eminent lawyer with the law computer," Jill recalls asking Tracy.

Tracy walks up to Jill, takes the book, and places it back, explaining, "Because, Jilly, a computer is so impersonal. Books provide all vital details, a person's emotional state, their thought processes."

Jill attempts to read a book once but struggles to grasp what Tracy is conveying. Walking up to Tracy's desk in the quiet office, the sound of her footsteps echoes softly. She notices Tracy's sleek, green palmtop, its smooth surface gleaming faintly in the dim light. The palm-sized computer, a nice small rectangle, feels cool and smooth against her skin. Adjacent to the palmtop, a small, square piece of paper with Jill's name clearly printed on it is almost hidden in the shadows. With trembling hands, she carefully unfolds the letter, the scent of old paper filling her nostrils. The message reads,

Dear Jill,

I don't know how to tell you this, but I rigged the election. You didn't come close to winning. I had to use a lot of computer connections to change your and Daniel's results. Eventually, this will come to light. I have ditched my phone and plan on leaving the country. Please do not look for me or try to contact me. Everything I've done, I've done for you.

Tracy.

With a feeling of unease, Jill looked around, sensing something amiss. Suddenly, Steve walks in and says, "Several clothes are missing, and I couldn't find a suitcase."

Jill shows Steve the letter. "I can't believe it. With her confession and this letter, Daniel has already won. He will sew discontent."

"Hi, my name is Tracy Kincaid." Jill smiles, a warmth spreading through her as she recalled the bright colors and giddy laughter of that day she met Tracy, a five-year-old's boundless happiness.

"Jill. Jill Leigh."

"Jill Leigh. Jilly."

"Jilly, I like that."

"So, Jilly the valedictorian."

"That's right, just working on my speech."

"So, I have to ask you a favor."

"Shoot Jilly. Anything."

"Be my Matron of Honor."

"So, you and Steve... It would be my honor."

A torrent of silent tears streams down Jill's face as she looks at Steve, her shoulders shaking with grief. "She didn't write this letter," Jill says, her voice filled with uncertainty.

"What do you mean?" Steve questions, his brows furrowed in confusion.

"It says Jill. She always calls me Jilly. Also look around. She leaves all these books. They are worth a fortune."

Suddenly, they hear a kitten's soft mewling. Jill's gaze sweeps the room, landing on a small gray and black kitten near a food bowl. The sight of the kitten's emaciated body tugs at Jill's heartstrings, its ribs protruding under its thin fur. The silence is broken only by the occasional whimper of hunger, the air heavy with a mix of desperation and neglect.

Jill murmurs with compassion, "Oh, you look like you haven't eaten or drank in days." She scans the pantry and finds a nearly full bag of kitten food, promptly pouring it into a bowl. Filling another bowl with water, she places it beside the food. Jill looks at the multicolored collar around the kitten's neck and then at the medallion in the center. "Ozzie," she says. A glimmer of warmth in her eyes as she watches the kitten tentatively approach the nourishment.

As Jill returned to the office, her mind raced with questions. "I didn't know that Tracy has a kitten."

Steve, intrigued, inquires, "What was that?"

"Why did Tracy leave this kitten if she never planned on coming back? I'm telling you, none of this makes any sense."

Frustrated, Jill slams Tracy's desk, the sound reverberating through the room as a hidden compartment is revealed. The musty scent of old paper fills the air as Jill's fingers brush against the smooth leather cover of a red book, a lock securing its contents. Her curiosity is piqued, and she contemplates the mysterious contents within. "What is it?" Steve asks, his eyes reflect Jill's own curiosity.

After searching in vain for a key, Jill resolves to uncover the secrets hidden within the book and find Tracy. "Yet another mystery. But I'm bound and determined to find out what's in here and find Tracy. I must retrieve something before we go home," she says, determination shining in her eyes.

The screen is shattered into a spiderweb of cracks, reflecting the sunlight in jagged lines, causing Steve to wince in sympathy for the owner. Jill leans in closer to examine the damage, detecting the faint scent of electronic components that tickle her nose. Rachel's fingers trace the fractures, feeling the rough edges of the broken glass, with the sound of the cracked screen crunching slightly under her touch filling the air. "We'll have to get home, recharge it, and see if it still works," Jill suggests.

Jill and Steve return to the elevator, with Jill hearing the purring of the kitten while Steve carries the food and dish. As the doors open, they come face to face with Henry and Rachel, who immediately notice the kitten. "Hey, nice kitten," Henry remarks.

Rachel rubs the kitten, which gets a purr. "Oh, you're a cutie."

Steve then asks, "So how was your walk?"

Rachel excitedly says, "It was great. I even found this on the side of the street." She produces a vibrant green cell phone. The screen shattered, revealing a faint light within. The screen is shattered into a spiderweb of cracks, reflecting the sunlight in jagged lines, causing Steve to wince in sympathy for the owner. Jill leans in closer to examine the damage, detecting the faint scent of electronic components that tickle her nose. Rachel's fingers trace the fractures, feeling the rough edges of the broken glass, with the sound of the cracked screen crunching slightly under her touch filling the air.

"We'll have to get home, recharge it, and see if it still works," Jill suggests. They all get into the car and head home.

Chapter Eighteen

December 11, 2124

A feeling of both fear and excitement permeates the atmosphere, as apprehension and anticipation commingle. Freshly cut grass, hushed conversations, and humming speakers filled the air. Providing a sturdy and unwavering base, the solid dais ensured stability for those who stood on it. Jill Lunden addressed the press conference to a sea of faces. As a crisp autumn wind blew through the trees, rustling the leaves, she experiences comforting warmth with her family standing close by. The press conference buzzes with chatter and the clicking of cameras, accompanied by the faint hint of autumn leaves in the air. Jill's speech was a mix of nerves and reassurance, strengthened by her family's support. The gentle and calming sounds of the wind blowing softly outside created a serene backdrop.

"I categorically deny any kind of election fraud. All agencies reported that the election was conducted fairly." With her elegant and carefully chosen words, she crafts a mysterious and shadowy atmosphere that permeated the room. Unease and desperation saturate her speech, leaving a sense of discomfort. Her anxiety grows as she tries to access Tracy's palmtop. Her heart pounds in her chest, a drumbeat of excitement echoing the thrill she felt. The green cell phone Rachel found sits on the kitchen table. The press tension is palpable, creating a heavy atmosphere. She fears the unknown and feels hopeless about Tracy's whereabouts. Her body displays physical signs of intense emotions as a response. Her heart races and sweat beads form on her forehead and palms.

Her tense and tightening muscles knot her stomach and ache her limbs as each breath becomes shallow and strained, a struggle to fill her lungs. Overwhelming emotions weigh heavily upon her, causing her significant distress and hardship. This combination of fear, hopelessness, and uncertainty creates a storm within her, leading to dizziness and lightheadedness. It feels like the world is spinning out of control, reflecting the chaos of her internal turmoil. Her heart pounds in her chest, the rapid rhythm echoing in her ears like a drumbeat of distress. The stress coursing through her veins manifests in a cold sweat that beads on her forehead and palms, a physical manifestation of her emotional turmoil. As panic grips her, her hands tremble uncontrollably, making even the simplest tasks seem monumentally challenging. The tension in her body radiates outward, causing her jaw to clench and her temples to throb with a dull ache. The weight of her emotions is a physical pressure on her chest, making it difficult to draw a full breath. Each heartbeat sounds like a heavy thud against her ribcage, a stark reminder of the intensity of her feelings. The storm of emotions raging within her manifests in a whirlwind of sensations, leaving her disoriented and unsteady on her feet. The world around her blurs and distorts as tears well up in her eyes, threatening to spill over at any moment. This overwhelming mix of fear, hopelessness, and uncertainty leaves her drained and overwhelmed, a prisoner to her own turbulent emotions.

"What about the recording?" The newsman's voice cuts through the air with a sharp and authoritative tone, filled with urgency, as he mentions the recording. The scurrying of pen over paper fills the room as he speaks about the ongoing analysis of the recording and the absence of the person involved for questioning.

Despite her best efforts to stay composed, the physical effects of her emotions were evident, making her feel exhausted and overwhelmed. Her smile trembled briefly as she left the podium, a wave of her hand barely hiding her rising panic.

Her heart races in her chest, thudding loudly in her ears as adrenaline surges through her veins. The weight of her emotions felt like a heavy burden, causing her shoulders to slump and her legs to feel weak. Each breath she took felt shallow and strained, as if she were trying to hold back a flood of tears. Her hands shook slightly, betraying the inner turmoil she was desperately trying to keep hidden. The lines of stress and worry etched themselves onto her face, creating a mask of vulnerability that she struggled to maintain. Despite her efforts to maintain her composure, the physical effects of her emotions were impossible to ignore.

"That was President-Elect Jill Lunden, denying any involvement or acknowledgement of the election being stolen. Currently, polls show that...."

"Television off." William Chavez and his wife are in the White House living room. They are sitting in plush peach seats, watching a 100-inch 8k television above an ornate fireplace. The room is cozy with a warm fire crackling and the scent of burning wood. When the television turns off, it contrasts with the grandeur of the room. Intricate details and luxurious furnishings fill the room, creating an immersive experience for William and his wife.

President William Chavez is overwhelmed by a potent mix of frustration and anger, affecting his physical health. He sweated profusely, his fists clench, and his face flushes with tension. The tension grew with each passing moment. Intense emotions caused a cascade of physical effects. His heart rate and adrenaline increases, raising his body temperature and making his heightened emotional state visible. His tightened fists, flushed complexion, and tense muscles make his movements rigid and controlled, reflecting the toll of the potent mix of emotions on his body.

"Many people believe the election has been rigged. You said that it could never happen." Amanda's shoulders slump as she exhales deeply, the weight of her words hanging in the air like a heavy fog. Her chest is tight, constricted by the weight of unspoken sadness. Each syllable she speaks seems to carry a physical burden, causing her to appear smaller and more fragile. A dull throb in her temples and heavy limbs mirrors the ache in her heart. Her resignation weighed her down, making it hard to stand.

Amanda's eyes glisten with unshed tears, her chest heaving with the weight of her sorrow. The heaviness in her heart seems to radiate through her entire body, making her limbs feel weak and her movements sluggish. Each breath she takes feels like a struggle, as if the air itself is heavy with the burden of her emotions. Her once bright eyes now appear dull and clouded, the unshed tears threatening to spill over at any moment. The tension in her body is palpable, as if she is carrying the weight of the world on her shoulders. Despite her efforts to hold back her tears, her trembling lip betrays the depth of her pain. With her gaze downcast, she appears troubled and haunted by a multitude of swirling, conflicting emotions that play across her features. The tension in her body is palpable, with her muscles taut from holding back a flood of feelings. The heaviness in her chest makes it hard to draw in a full breath without it catching in her throat. Each word she utters carries with it a tremor that betrays the depth of her emotions. Amanda's emotional weight is physically apparent; her clenched fists and rigid posture reflect the internal battle she's fighting. Her furrowed brow hints at the mental strain she's under. The unshed tears in her eyes shimmer like dewdrops, threatening to spill over and release the pent-up emotions within. Her coiled muscles, tense and ready to spring or collapse, silently express the internal storm raging within, a potent display of tension. The trembling in her voice and the catch in her breath reveal the raw vulnerability she is experiencing, laying bare the depth of her emotions for all to see.

Her hands clench and unclench, fingers fidgeting nervously as she speaks, as if seeking a release for pent-up emotions. Her voice wavers, breaking at times with the weight of unspoken sorrow. The room seems to grow dimmer around her, as if the shadows of her emotions are casting a veil over everything. Despite the physical toll of her emotions, there is a certain beauty in the vulnerability Amanda displays. In her fragility, there is strength, a raw honesty that speaks volumes about the depth of her feelings. And as she stands there, shoulders slumped and heart heavy, it is clear that she is facing her emotions head-on, bravely confronting the storm within.

"It's not possible. Every state has several checks and balances to protect their elections." The weight of worry settles heavy in William's chest, causing his heart to race and his palms to grow clammy. A knot forms in his stomach, twisting with each passing moment as he watches Amanda's expression. The tension in his muscles grows, his jaw clenching as he anxiously waits for her response. The uncertainty in the air seems to thicken, making it hard for him to breathe as he contemplates the implications of her doubts. With each passing second, he experienced a growing unease, a nervous energy that made him fidget. He's deeply troubled by the nation's turmoil.

"Yet we have a tape recording that has Jill's campaign manager saying that **she did rig the election.**" William can't shake Jill's words on television from his memory. They replay in his mind with unwavering clarity, her eloquence and conviction echoing in his ears. As he reflects on her words, a renewed sense of admiration for Jill washes over him. He acknowledges her unwavering grace under pressure and her ability to lead with resolve. Amidst the turmoil, William can't help but notice Jill's attitude. From the beginning to the very end of the election, she consistently displayed an unwavering sense of pride and confidence in herself and her abilities. At the news conference, she remains calm and defiant, yet William detects a hint of fear and uncertainty in her voice. While researching during the election, William discovers that Tracy Kincaid is not only Jill's campaign manager but also her best friend, who is now missing.

"Jill says the recording needs to be verified and I agree. Remember when Daniel publicly announces the claims of election fraud on television? When all the stations 'voluntarily' give their air space. The violent protests, including the bombing in Portland, OR. I can only imagine the violence that will happen now. The tape could be altered." Amanda's hands tremble, her knuckles white as she clutches her necklace, the cool metal a stark contrast to her clammy skin. Her heart pounds in her chest as she struggles to process the news of the bombing in Oregon, which hits her like a physical blow. The shock and devastation manifest in a cold sweat breaking out on her skin, her body trembling uncontrollably with overwhelming emotions surging through her. The weight of the tragedy settles heavily on her shoulders, leaving her with a deep sense of sorrow and helplessness. Amanda's breathing becomes shallow and rapid, her chest tight with the unfolding tragedy before her eyes, the physical effects of her emotions palpable, leaving her drained and emotionally raw.

"You're right, William. No matter what the analysts say, Daniel's people will always believe in a vast cover-up." Amanda says, envisioning the peace her husband brings about being destroyed by America Now. A sense of dread washes over her, her heart racing, palms growing sweaty, and a knot forming in the pit of her stomach. The weight of the impending turmoil is a heavy burden on her shoulders, leaving her physically drained and tense. A deep sense of despair, a heavy ache settling in her chest, overwhelms her at the thought of her husband's accomplishments being undone. The physical effects of her emotions are palpable as she grapples with a mix of fear, anger, and helplessness.

William observes the alarm in her eyes and notes his own heart rate increase in response to the intense emotion. Adrenaline courses through his body, heightening his senses and sharpening his focus. His eyes widen, mirroring the fear and apprehension reflected in hers. The tension in the air is palpable, with the weight of their shared emotions creating a charged atmosphere crackling with intensity. The physical effects of their emotions manifest subtly yet powerfully, connecting them in a moment of raw vulnerability and understanding. "So, what's next?"

As they contemplate their next steps, William says, "We do the same thing we would have done if none of these allegations and this Cain person never existed. I need to talk to my assistant and schedule a date for Jill Lunden to visit the White House to begin the process for the peaceful transfer of power." With those words, a surge of relief washes over him, easing the tension in his shoulders and bringing a sense of lightness to his chest. The weight of recent turmoil seems to lift, replaced by a renewed sense of purpose and determination.

His body language changes - he stands straighter and moves more confidently. The stress on his face fades, and he has been replaced by a slight smile as he thinks about the future. Feelings of relief and determination fill him, giving him clarity and focus. He is energized and ready to tackle any challenges, confident that he made the right choice for himself and the country.

"You're playing with fire. What if the tape is legit? You should probably hold off until we have the results." In the quiet room, William pats his wife's hand, a slight gesture of love and support, as his determination grows. His heart rate increases, and adrenaline surges through his body, fueling his resolve to act. With muscles tense and breathing faster and shallower, the intensity of his emotions is apparent due to the stress of the situation.

His palms sweating and jaw clenched, he says, "I can't let Daniel or this Cain person control the narrative. I'll order an investigation into the stolen election. Put to rest once and for all that the election was fair. I'll order an investigation into the stolen election."

"You think anything will convince people that the election was not stolen? I remember an old saying. The more you say something, the more people tend to believe it." Amanda expresses her fear. She questions if anything will convince people that the election wasn't stolen. She recalls an old saying about repetition influencing belief. William's voice carries the weight of his determination as he speaks into the phone, exuding authority and conviction. The power of his emotions drives him to make bold decisions and take control of the situation. Having hung up the phone, he felt empowered, determined to uncover the truth and fight manipulation.

With concern for his wife, William's heart rate quickens and his muscles tense. A knot forms in his stomach, reflecting the emotional turmoil within him. His body language shifts as he leans in closer, seeking to comfort and protect her. The physical effects of his concern are palpable, evident in his body's reactions to the swirling emotions. As he held her gentle hand, a soothing warmth spread up his arm, amidst the sounds of nature and fragrances of blossoms and the woodland.

William, standing alongside his wife, contemplates the strength of their shared love and companionship. Amid the chirping birds and rustling breeze, contentment washes over him. As they embrace hope in the intelligence of the American people, he knows they will face the challenges ahead with strength and unity.

"We must trust in the wisdom and rationality of the American people."

Chapter Nineteen

December 15, 2124

Agent Thomas Judson arrives at the FBI headquarters at his usual time, parks in his usual spot, and takes his usual elevator. As the elevator doors open, Judson smells the musty scent of aged wood and dust, a scent that speaks of the building's ten-year history. The new building sits atop the old one's ruins. During his FBI orientation, Judson saw the scattered bricks and twisted metal in the museum, a grim reminder of the terrorist attack. The Botswanan War begins after a terrorist attack. Nostalgia and determination washed over him as he exited the elevator. The musty scent of aged wood and dust triggers a flood of memories, reminding him of the countless hours spent within these walls, chasing down leads and solving cases. The weight of his ambition and determination to join the FBI is a physical force pushing him forward, with every heartbeat resonating with a sense of urgency fueling his drive to make a difference. He walked through the ruined building.

The lingering smoke and destruction stirred sorrow, anger, and resolve within him. The adrenaline coursing through his veins heightens his senses, sharpening his focus on the task ahead; each step towards his goal is a step towards redemption, towards rebuilding what was lost, and towards honoring the fallen officers. Pride, anticipation, and apprehension tightened his chest. The weight of his responsibility, past events, and the headquarters' tension all contributed. Judson's heart pounded; adrenaline surged as he prepared for the day. The building's history and the spirits of the old building adding to his seriousness.

"Hello Agent Michaels," Judson replies. '*Always so formal. No trace of emotion as usual,*' Michaels thought.

"Director Knighton says he needs to see you."

Despite the heaviness of the memories and the gravity of the task at hand, a sense of purpose and determination rises within Judson. The physical effects of his emotions manifest in the form of a slight tremor in his hands, a subtle tightening of his jaw, and a steely glint in his eyes. Ready to face whatever challenges lay ahead, Agent Judson carries with him the weight of the past and the hope for a better future as he makes his way to his office. Through the familiar halls, he could hear the distant echoes of ringing phones and the low murmur of hushed conversations. The flickering fluorescent lights above cast a sterile glow on the beige walls, creating a sense of urgency and secrecy in the air. The click of his polished shoes on the linoleum floor reverberates through the quiet corridors, serving as a reminder of the weight of his responsibilities. Judson is aware of the tension building in the atmosphere, a palpable reminder of the ongoing threat of terrorism that hangs over the agency like a dark cloud.

"Hello Thomas," Agent Michels greets with a warm smile that belies the ice that runs through his veins when duty calls. His eyes, usually twinkling with friendliness, can turn steely and cold in an instant. The physical effects of his emotions are subtle yet telling—a slight tensing of his jawline, a tightening of his grip on his pen, a barely perceptible narrowing of his gaze. The adrenaline rush of a high-stakes situation causes his heart rate to quicken, his palms to sweat, and his muscles to tense in readiness for action. Though his exterior remains composed, a trained eye can detect the telltale signs of his internal battle between duty and compassion.

"Hello Agent Michaels," Judson replies.

'*Always so formal. No trace of emotion as usual,*' Michaels thinks. "Director Knighton says he needs to see you."

The air in FBI headquarters crackles with tension as Trampas Knighton, forty, the head of the agency, reviews the latest case files. He is hunched over his desk, the fluorescent lights reflecting harshly off the glossy pages of the reports spread before him, a low hum filling the quiet office. Crime is rising, with a noticeable increase in violent crime, leaving residents increasingly apprehensive. The fluorescent lights flicker overhead, casting a cold, sterile glow over the room, heavy with the scent of paper and ink, mixed with a faint hint of coffee from a nearby mug. Outside, the city bustles with activity, muffled voices and distant sirens creating a constant backdrop of noise. Trampas feels the weight of responsibility pressing down on him, the urgency of the situation reflected in the furrow of his brow and the tight grip on his pen. He hears a hesitant tapping at his door, a soft knock that barely disturbs the silence. "Enter," Knighton says as Agent Judson comes in and stands ramrod straight. "Agent Judson is reporting as ordered, sir," Judson states, standing rigidly at attention, his old brown briefcase clutched tightly in his hand; the leather feels worn and familiar. Trampas just shakes his head. "This is the FBI, not the military. You don't have to stand at attention," he remarks. Director Knighton let out a breath. "At ease, and will you please sit down?" Judson finally collapses into a chair, the wood groaning under his weight. "You know, I'm quite impressed with you. You have a knack for solving cases that others had abandoned. You show great loyalty and dedication to the job. In fact, you remind me of another junior agent," Trampas says as he looks at Judson. Judson shows no pride or ambition. '*Guy's a natural poker player.*' "But that was In a different building," Director Knighton looks down, remembering the friends and mentors that he lost that day. "Because of these attributes, I have decided to give you an important assignment."

Judson, maintaining a poker face, responds, "All assignments are important, sir."

"Agreed. But this one could have national importance. I'm sure that you are aware of the accusations Daniel has made regarding the last election."

Judson casually mentions, "I'm aware that he gets most of his information from a group called Cain-inon."

Director Knighton then explains the seriousness of the situation, referencing recent events in Portland, OR, and nationwide protests, emphasizing the need to address the issue.

Judson questions, "You're going after protesters. Doesn't that violate..."

The director clarifies, "We're not going after anyone. What we are doing is a joint NSA, Secret Service, and FBI investigation into the allegations."

Judson inquiries about his orders, to which the director instructs him to collaborate with the Secret Service and the NSA, sharing and gathering information. After their conversation, Judson's departure is announced by the squeak of his shoes on the polished floor as he heads to his cubicle.

As Judson departed, a warm tingling sensation of satisfaction and amusement spread through Trampas' chest. As he smiles, his eyes crinkle with amusement, and he savors the moment. The cool touch of the window against his hand ground him, enhancing his sense of calm and contentment as he watches the scene outside. Reflecting on Judson, he thinks, '*I swear the office gossip is right. Guy is a robot.*'

Trampas experienced a surge of satisfaction and amusement, which manifested in a series of physical effects that were hard to ignore. The warm tingling sensation in his chest seemed to radiate outwards, spreading a sense of comfort and joy throughout his body. This prompted a subtle shift in his demeanor, with his smile growing wider and more genuine, reaching all the way to his eyes and creating a network of crinkles at the corners. By the window, the cool touch contrasted nicely with his inner warmth, creating a sensory experience that anchored him to the moment. The grounding force of the window appeared to intensify his peace and satisfaction, adding a layer of physical sensation to his emotional state. These physical effects were not just internal; they also played out in his outward appearance. His relaxed posture, free of tension or stiffness, mirrored his inner calm. His movements took on a gentle sway, almost as if he was dancing to an invisible melody, as he absorbed the scene outside with a newfound sense of appreciation and joy. Trampas smiled, a slow, knowing smile, rising from his chair to stroll to the window, noting the cool wood against his hand as he gazed out. Outside, the golden sunbathed everything in a warm glow, casting long shadows across the dusty street. The distant sound of laughter and chatter drifted through the open window, mingling with the gentle rustle of leaves in the breeze. The air carried a faint scent of wildflowers and fresh earth, evoking a sense of peace and tranquility. As Trampas watched the world go by from his quiet corner, a sense of contentment washed over him.

Agent Judson sat in his cubicle, smelling the stale faux coffee in the air. He turned on his computer and visited the website provided by Trampas. He quickly entered the number given to him. On the screen, two men appeared, both looking weathered with gray hair.

Agents Bryant from the NSA and Smith from the Secret Service greeted him. Agent Judson often got headaches from the bright screen and constant talking during teleconferences. This one seems even worse, overwhelming him with despair.

Listening to the agents made him tense, his heart racing and palms sweating. Stress and anxiety are a heavy burden, making it hard to breathe. A sense of dread overcame him, and his hands trembles slightly.

The flickering computer screen intensified, casting eerie shadows on his face. The stifling air in the cubicle intensified his sense of confinement. Agent Judson struggled to stay composed, but the teleconference took an emotional toll on him.

The mix of fear, frustration, and helplessness left him drained and emotionally exhausted by the end of the call.

Agent Bryant then presented the compiled NSA information, stating, "Here's everything I've gathered."

"Here's everything the Secret Service gathered. I must admit, it's not much."

Agent Judson carefully reviews each document, conscious of the information's significance. He thought about the possibility of someone else having the same documents. "I just received this assignment. This is all the FBI has. I don't think it's much."

Agent Bryant remarked as he tapped a few buttons on his computer. "I concur. It may not be a lot, but any piece could be valuable. I'll keep both of you informed," Agent Bryant assured them. Judson ended the call with a click, feeling triumphant. He grinned as he delved into the mystery eagerly.

In the heartland of America, Agents Bryant and Smith plugged in their flash drives, the hum of their palm tops creating a low thrum in the quiet motel room. A torrent of classified data from the FBI, NSA, and Secret Service flooded their screens, a chaotic stream of numbers, codes, and names. As they navigated through the flood of information, a rush of adrenaline coursed through their bodies, their hearts racing and palms growing clammy with anticipation. The intense focus required to sift through the data caused their muscles to tense and brows to furrow in concentration, a mix of excitement and anxiety brewing within them with each new piece of information uncovered. Despite the physical toll of stress and pressure, the thrill of the chase kept them on edge. Their senses heightened as they delved deeper into the web of secrets. The room crackled with energy; the air was thick with anticipation as they raced against the clock to unravel the mysteries hidden within the data. Agent Bryant, his brow glistening with sweat, remarked, "This is perfect. It's literally everything we need. All the agencies think they are working together in a joint investigation, and no one suspects a thing. While they spin in circles, we have what we need to catch all the traitors and deal with them accordingly."

Subsequently, Bryant gets on the phone. "Yes. We have everything we need, Lord Cain... Thank you." Bryant hangs up.

"What did Cain say?"

"Cain said that with the information we got, plus a confession. We are ready to up our game."

"Burn baby burn. Soon, we will eradicate this feeble nation, leaving behind only a haunting silence and a lingering sense of dread. We will bring a new America. Soon we will make things right," Agent Smith says with confirmation.

Agent Bryant's face brightened with a mischievous grin. He leaned in.

"Freedom Now." Bryant says

"Freedom Forever." Smith finishes

The room was dimly lit by a single lamp, casting dancing shadows on the walls that seemed to writhe and twist. The faint scent of old books and dust lingered in the air. A ticking clock in the corner echoed off the walls, creating a sense of urgency. The tension in the room was palpable, the silence broken only by the occasional creak of the floorboards underfoot. A cool draft brushed against their skin, sending shivers down their spines. Both men crossed their arms instinctively, sensing anticipation settle in.

The sight of the armbands catches the eye, contrasting the traditional American flag with a unique twist. In the blue sky, instead of stars, there was a prominent Christian cross. The colors pop against the fabric, evoking a sense of patriotism and religious devotion. Secure and unified, smooth armbands provide a tangible reminder of their beliefs. The smell of sweat and determination lingers in the air, adding a sense of anticipation to the atmosphere. The sound of fabric rustling as arms move in unison creates a rhythmic beat, echoing the unity of purpose among the wearers.

"For the true America." They both spoke in unison

Chapter Twenty

December 18, 2124

M elissa is in her apartment, savoring the Christmas atmosphere. The tree sparkles with the holographic lights. She enjoys the colorful decorations outside her window, the sound of rain, and the comfortable atmosphere of her warm apartment. Watching the leaves dance in the wind, their vibrant hues are a feast for her eyes. The gentle patter of rain on the window creates a soothing melody, while the earthy petrichor and the scent of her favorite autumn candle mingle in the air. The soft embrace of her blanket wraps around her, filling her with a sense of contentment and peace. Amid this tranquility, she notices her digital albums are a disorganized, chaotic mess of photos and videos spread across many platforms. Among the images, she sees holographic pictures of herself as a child, sitting on her father's lap with her mother behind them. The images flicker, looking very real, yet she cannot touch them, as they are just pixels, a reminder of lost happiness. The last picture of her father before the tragic day is etched in her memory. He was a firefighter on a mission when a building caught fire. Despite the intense fire, he saved ten people before the building collapsed, his body later found in the wreckage with smoke-filled lungs. Doctors mentioned it must have been agonizing to save those people. A monument in his honor now stands at the fire station where he worked. After this tragic event, a deep depression, marked by tear-filled nights and a profound sense of hopelessness, overcame her mother. In response, Melissa took on the responsibility of cooking and cleaning to support her mother during this challenging time.

Over time, her mother's health improved, giving hope, but then doctors diagnosed her with advanced Alzheimer's. She kept asking to see her husband, but Melissa sadly informs her of his passing each time. These conversations weigh heavily on both women, causing Melissa physical discomfort. A heavy stone settles in their guts, causing them to struggle to breathe. The news of her husband's passing brings fresh grief to her mother. The emotional turmoil takes a toll on their bodies, leaving them drained from the cycle of heartache and loss.

Melissa's mother's health declines until she couldn't recognize Melissa and eventually passes away. Melissa experiences intense grief, with a heavy sensation in her chest and difficulty breathing. The pain in her heart spreads through her body, leaving her tired and emotionally numb. Even though she focuses on work at the Judge Advocate General's office, moments of sadness and longing hit her, making her hands tremble and vision blurry with tears. Melissa understands that professional success can't replace the emptiness her mother's absence has created.

Melissa smiles as she looks at her wedding hologram photos, remembering the joy of that day. She sees herself in a beautiful white dress with Jacob in a sharp tuxedo. She then looks at photos of Erica and Roberto, and Jessica and Miranda, all looking stunning. Touching the hologram photos brings back vivid memories, making the colors vibrant and details sharp. A mix of nostalgia and happiness makes her heart flutter. The emotions make her cheeks flush and eyes sparkle with tears of joy. Melissa sighs contentedly, a bittersweet longing for those special moments to last forever washing over her. Immersed in the memories, the real-world fades away, leaving her lost in a realm of emotions and nostalgia.

Her heart beats faster, the rush of emotions causing a flush to spread across her cheeks. The memories wrap around her like a warm embrace, sending shivers down her spine. As she immerses herself in the bittersweet longing of days gone by, the weight of the world seems to lift off her shoulders. The room around her blurs as tears well up in her eyes, each drop a testament to the power of the emotions that have gripped her soul. Time seems to stand still as she relives each moment, the physical world fading into the background as the ethereal realm of memory takes center stage.

As she gazes at the pictures, a wave of nostalgia washes over her, causing a tightness in her chest and a lump to form in her throat. Jacob's warm smile and the familiar curve of his lips bring a bittersweet ache to her heart, reminding her of their shared laughter and pizza slices at the now-closed pizzeria. The place where they first meet. The melancholy of the memories tugs her, mingling with a sense of loss and longing for the past. She senses the weight of their common past in the air, as if the feelings shown in the photos have a tangible presence, she can almost touch.

"I'm sorry to see it go," Jacob says.

"It's been an important part of our lives," Melissa says, pregnant with Erica.

Flipping the page brought a shimmering hologram to life, showcasing the cherubic faces of Melissa, Jacob, and five-year-old Erica. The next hologram depicted Erica, beaming in a cap and gown; the image shimmered slightly as it progressed through high school, college, and law school graduations, each moment marked by the subtle changes in her appearance and the shifting light. She can still smell fresh diplomas and hear the sound of cheering crowds. As the page turned, Erica appeared in a bright, sterile hospital room; the rhythmic beeping of machines filled the air as she smiled, holding baby her own baby, her exhaustion evident but overshadowed by joy. "Mother, it's a girl."

"What's the little precious's name?"

"Miranda."

"Your Grandmother's name."

Erica looks around. "Where is dad? Doesn't he want to see his granddaughter?"

"Looking for a parking space."

Among the collected pictures, Melissa discovered many photos featuring herself and Emma Shelby, her dearest friend from her JAG days. Emma's dark hair was a striking contrast to Melissa's blond, and the photos seemed to radiate their infectious laughter. "I'm leaving JAG."

Melissa is stunned. "What do you plan on doing?"

"Return home. Maybe run for District Attorney in Portland, OR. Look, I served my time. It's time I do something else," Emma says.

"I wish you all the luck." Melissa, hugs Emma. Ten years after that, Melissa got a phone message.

"Hello Melissa Carthage. We regret to inform you that Emma Shelby was killed in Portland, OR." Melissa felt a weight of sorrow lifted as Jacob hugged her, bringing solace.

Her chest loosened, letting her breath freely. Warmth and support filled her as tears fell, expressing her pain and acceptance. Despite intense feelings, Jacob's presence gave her stability.

Tears fill her eyes as she recalls her last hospital visit, leaving her vulnerable and scared.

"My shaking is getting worse. Even with my meditations and medications, I can't seem to control them."

"You knew that the medication wasn't a cure. But let's get a body scan and see what we can do." The doctor says. Melissa could hear the tremor of worry in her voice, a slight catch in her breath that spoke volumes. Melissa rolls up her arm, waiting for the needle. With a gentle push of the plunger, the doctor injects Melissa with a serum, a cool liquid that promises a radiation-free x-ray, a faint scent of antiseptic lingering in the air.

Melissa rises and walks toward a massive, cobalt blue tube, its smooth surface gleaming at the room's far end.

Next to a silver table, she undresses before getting inside. The machine hums softly, filling the room with a gentle mechanical sound. Melissa senses the coolness of the tube against her skin as she lies inside, her breaths steady and controlled. The anticipation of the results weighs heavily on her mind, her heart racing with nervous energy. With a final click, the machine signals the procedure's end, and she exits, feeling both relieved and apprehensive. The room is quiet, save for the sound of her clothes rustling as she puts them back on, waiting for the doctor to deliver the news. Normally, the machine's Artificial Intelligence would give the prognosis, but Melissa always preferred a human response. A human's compassion. Even if it met getting the news later.

Melissa's eyes scanned the doctor's face, searching for any hint of bad news in her expression as she reviewed the test results. An icy dread seeped into Melissa's bones as she saw the grim expression on the doctor's face.

"I'm sorry you've reached stage three."

The doctor's words hit her hard, filling her with grief. She tries to control her emotions, feeling overwhelmed. The news weighs heavily on her, reminding her of life's fragility and the impact of emotions on our well-being.

"Stage three." A single tear traced a path down her cheek as she choked out the question she dreads. "How long do I have?"

"Two years. Five on the outside. I'm sorry, but there is nothing more we can do except to make you comfortable." Her words pierce through Melissa. Shocked by the prognosis,

Melissa recalls believing she is managing the initial twitches in her hand, the first sign of Parkman's disease.

"Thank you. Can I have some time for myself?"

"Of course. Take as much time as you need. I believe I gave you all the information you need." Melissa nods solemnly. "I'm going to write a new prescription. Once again to keep you comfortable." The doctor leaves.

Melissa's emotions show physically as she deals with her diagnosis, and limited time left. Tears express her sadness and release stress hormones, increasing her heart rate and making her breathing shallow. The doctor's prediction of five years left motivates her to make those years count. Melissa prepares for her condition's progression by reading extensively. Her trembling hands and fear of losing control show her anxiety. Jacob's ghostly, comforting touch reminds her to stay composed.

Melissa is back in her living room. Looking at the sonogram, she whispered a wish for the baby's health. As Melissa's emotions swirl within her, her body reacts in various ways. The weight of worry and concern settles heavily on her chest, causing her breath to catch as she contemplates the uncertain future. A sense of determination courses through her veins, sending a surge of adrenaline that propels her to make a vow to fight her condition with all her might.

Melissa was about to share the horrible news with her family when Miranda unexpectedly revealed her pregnancy, showing her the sonogram. Melissa tried to smile and congratulate Miranda, but her heart was heavy with a mix of joy and sorrow. These conflicting emotions caused her chest to tighten, making it hard to breathe. The weight of her own undisclosed news felt like a physical burden on her shoulders, making it difficult to stand up straight. Melissa vividly recalled shedding tears at the announcement. She was happy for her granddaughter but also saddened by her own health challenges. Miranda then mentioned needing a babysitter for the child, and Melissa struggled to respond, finally managing to say, "Count me in." Despite her efforts to conceal her true feelings, the tension in her body was evident as she grappled with overwhelming emotions.

Melissa's eyes fill with tears, revealing her deep love and longing for family moments, as she worries about missing out but tries to stay strong. The tension in her muscles and the knot in her stomach from fears and doubts weigh heavily on her. Despite her heavy heart, hope shines in her eyes as she focuses on the present moment, determined to cherish every second. Melissa's conflicting emotions create a whirlwind of sensations, with her heart pounding and throat tightening as she faces her situation, gathering the strength to persevere. "Television on," Melissa says, feeling her depression lift. With a stretch, she moves towards the window, where the view of the imposing Capitol building and the Washington Monument fills her with awe. The scene is so peaceful and breathtaking, with the soft morning light bathing the room, casting a warm glow on Melissa's face. A constant reminder of the bustling city outside, the distant sounds of traffic hum softly in the background. The air is crisp and clean, carrying the faint scent of blooming cherry blossoms. A sense of tranquility washes over Melissa as she gazes out at the majestic landmarks that stand tall against the sky, filling her with a sense of reverence and wonder.

"We have a copy of the names and addresses of the poll workers for the 2124 election," Melissa gasped, her breath hitching, eyes widening as icy dread overwhelms her, her heart pounding against her ribs. The screen displayed a scrolling list of poll workers' names and addresses, accompanied by Sean Bradley's calm, authoritative voice. "We at the Conservative News Network like to thank Cain for providing us with this information. We now go to Kathleen Hand. Welcome, Kathleen."

A wide, beaming smile stretched across Kathleen's face, the pure, unadulterated delight in her eyes making her features seem to crackle with wicked energy. "Thank you, Sean. I, too, would like to thank Cain for finding these traitors. We should have no secrets when it comes to the theft of the election. Let's have a Congressional investigation to determine how many poll workers took part in election fraud. This includes adding Jill ballots, discarding Daniel ballots, and changing Daniel ballots to Jill ballots, as evidenced by a recording. Heads will roll. They can't hide from us now," Kathleen asserts confidently, with purpose and unwavering posture. The fire in her eyes reflects her determined and righteous anger, fueling her every movement.

An icy wave of dread washed over Melissa, leaving her breathless and paralyzed with a chilling premonition. Fear begins to creep in. A knot of tension coiled in her gut. The room hums with palpable energy, a charged atmosphere cracking with emotion. As she stands near the television set, Melissa's body language betrays her inner turmoil. She shifts her weight from foot to foot, her hands fidgeting with the hem of her shirt. The glow of the screen illuminates her face, casting shadows that dance across her features, highlighting the conflicting emotions that play out in her expression.

'Dear God, how did Sean get this list? Kathleen is right. An investigation needs to be conducted. Just not the one that Kathleen hopes.'

Chapter Twenty-One

M egan Hall, a warm and smiling 38-year-old from Arizona, is cooking a hamburg-er. Then, she gently takes the french fries out of the sonic fryer, their delicious aroma filling the kitchen. She carefully arranges both items on a delicate china plate adorned with vibrant, hand-painted flowers. With a quiet grace, she walks to her table; the floorboards creaking softly beneath her feet. She sits alone at a small table, the only occupant of a quiet corner. Her gaze drifts across the table, lingering on the empty chairs, a sigh escaping her lips as the silence presses down.

"I wish Brad was here." Brad Halverson is her friend from the nine-to-five grocery store for five months. The chill that runs down her spine whenever she sees Brad isn't just a mere shiver, it is a physical manifestation of the mix of emotions swirling inside her. Her heart pounds, adrenaline surges, creating a mixture of excitement and nervousness. The unsettling effect of his smile raises goosebumps on her skin; a reaction both exciting and disturbing. As she hopes for their relationship to evolve into something more, her body responds to the anticipation with a fluttering sensation in her stomach, a physical reminder of the emotional rollercoaster she is on.

The fear in her body counters her passion for Brad. Following the release of poll work-ers' names and addresses, Daniel's supporters go after many poll workers. The thought of their capture makes her shudder.

Megan's breath hitches. Each news report of a dead poll or missing poll worker is a hammer blow against her chest, the escalating violence and talk of a stolen election painting a terrifying picture.

'How soon until they come after me?' An icy dread seeps into her bones, each breath a ragged gasp against the rising terror. She considers going to her sisters or parents, but she is afraid that they will turn against her. The thought of her family's potential scorn causes her intense emotional distress, a lump forming in her throat.

As threats against poll workers escalate, Megan barricades herself inside her home, double bolting the doors, an icy dread settling in her stomach. She slams her fork down.

"Dammit, I did nothing wrong. I did her duty following the rules that were handed down through decades. Hell, I supported Daniel. I gave money to his campaign. I would have loved to see Daniel win."

A rumbling truck approaches, its engine groaning and tires spitting gravel. Chilling cries of "DOWN WITH POLL WORKERS!" fill the air. The truck's exhaust belches out acrid fumes, stinging her nostrils. Her spine shivers as the shouts reverberate. The tension in the air is palpable, a heavy weight pressing down on her chest. The sound of footsteps echoes ominously on the pavement, adding to the sense of unease.

'Dear God, they found me.' She kisses the cross that she holds in her hands. As she races upstairs, the stairs creak under her hurried steps, the echoes bouncing off the walls. The scent of dust and old books fills her nose as she reaches the top. Megan's hands tremble uncontrollably as fear courses through her veins. The cold glass of the window sends shivers down her spine as she gazes out. The jump would probably be fatal. Even if she survives, the people down there will make sure that is a temporary situation. Adrenaline pumps through her body as she hides in the closet.

The old cross has a rough texture against her lips; the metallic flavor persists. "Dear Lord, help me in my blessed need. Please, dear lord look over me. I don't want to die," Megan prays, holding the cross.

As the sound of the front door crashing shatters the silence, Megan's body jerks in response. She can feel the blood draining from her face, leaving her pale and vulnerable. The voices that fill her home seem to echo in her ears, a cacophony of menace that further heightens her anxiety.

"Come out, come out wherever you are. You must pay for your crimes, traitorous bitch!"

Megan ponders, '*What crimes have I committed? I fulfilled my duty.*' Despite being a Daniel supporter, she has to abide by the rules with the ballots.

"Hey, the traitor has some good booze." Another says.

"Hey, her food is still hot. She has to be here."

"You five check upstairs. You guys stay outside in case. The rest of us will check downstairs. No one kills that traitorous hoe. I have plans for her." After hearing the voice, she immediately recognizes it as Brad Halverson.

Her hands trembled uncontrollably, the fine tremors betraying the turmoil within her. Blood pounded in her ears, drowning out all other sounds, intensifying the sense of impending doom. Every nerve in her body seemed on high alert, amplifying even the slightest movement or noise. The weight of the emotions pressed down on her chest, making it hard to breathe, as if a heavy weight was crushing her lungs. The world around her seemed to blur, her focus narrowing down to the immediate threat, the adrenaline heightening her senses to a razor-sharp level. Time slowed to a crawl, each second stretching out in agonizing detail as she grappled with the overwhelming surge of emotions.

'*How can he consider me a traitor?* Frequently, we engaged in conversations at the shopping center. I thought we are friends,' Megan thinks, her eyes welling up with tears, a heavy ache settling in her chest. She remembered Brad at the store.

"That dress looks stunning on you. I love the fabric." Brad says, his sandy blond hair and blue eyes attract her.

"Thanks," Megan says shyly.

Brad picks up a piece of frozen potter house steak, its icy surface cold against his fingertips. "Nice and marbled."

"Bananas are perfectly ripe," Megan says, a wide smile stretching across her face.

They look at each other. "Well, I have to go," Brad says.

"I guess I'll see you next week."

"Same place, same time." Both Megan and Brad laugh.

As she huddles in the dark closet, her heart races, her palms grow sweaty, and her breath quickens with the weight of betrayal and hurt. The surge of emotions courses through her body, causing her muscles to tense and her stomach to churn with a mix of anger, sadness, and confusion. Each word spoken by Brad echoes in her mind, stabbing at her like a knife, leaving her exposed and vulnerable.

Her hands tremble uncontrollably, the fine tremors betraying the turmoil within her. The blood pounds in her ears, drowning out all other sounds, intensifying the sense of impending doom. Every nerve in her body seems on high alert, amplifying even the slightest movement or noise. The weight of the emotions presses down on her chest, making it hard to breathe, as if a heavy weight is crushing her lungs. The world around her seems to blur, her focus narrowing down to the immediate threat, the adrenaline heightening her senses to a razor-sharp level. Time slows to a crawl, each second stretching out in agonizing detail as she grapples with the overwhelming surge of emotions.

Megan's heart pounds in her chest, the adrenaline coursing through her veins causing her hands to tremble. The heightened state of awareness makes her skin prickle with goosebumps, as if every nerve ending is on edge. A thick, heavy air makes it difficult to draw in a full breath. Her muscles tense, poised to move instantly; however, a powerful fear and unease immobilize her. Time seems to slow down as she struggles to control her racing thoughts and the powerful physical effects of her heightened emotions.

Her racing heart thuds in her chest, the sound reverberating in her ears. It seems like it is trying to break free from its confines, a constant reminder of her escalating panic. Despite her efforts to calm herself, the fear continues to grip her, leaving her helpless and overwhelmed by the physical effects of her emotions.

Sweat forms on her forehead, dampening her hair as her breathing becomes shallow and rapid. She senses her muscles tensing, a knot of anxiety forming in the pit of her stomach. Each passing second appears an eternity, amplifying her unease and amplifying the physical symptoms of her distress.

As the intruders roam through her home, their footsteps reverberate through the walls, magnifying her fear. Every creak of the floorboards sends a jolt of panic coursing through her body. Her mind races, desperately searching for a solution, but the harsh reality of her limited options weighs heavily on her.

The closet, once a place of refuge, now seems claustrophobic. The walls seem to close in on her, and the confined space seems to constrict her breathing even further. Beads of sweat trickle down her temples, her palms becoming clammy as she clutch onto the hope that the mob will soon depart.

As Megan's anxiety intensifies, her heart rate skyrockets, causing her chest to tighten and her breath to become shallow. Sweat beads on her forehead, her palms clammy with nervous tension. Her mental chaos manifests in physical symptoms, hindering clear thought and decision-making. The weight of the situation presses down on her shoulders, making her physically trapped and immobile. Each reverberation of the pounding on the door jolts her, echoing throughout her entire body. The immense power of her emotions is overwhelming, leaving her paralyzed and powerless and facing such uncertainty.

Time stretches on endlessly, amplifying the physical toll of her fear. The tension makes her muscles ache. The adrenaline that once fueled her now threatens to overwhelm her, leaving her trembling and weak.

As the fear tightens its grip on Megan, her heart races, sending a surge of adrenaline coursing through her veins. Her palms grow clammy, and a cold sweat breaks out on her brow. The tension in her muscles makes her a coiled spring, about to snap at any moment. Each breath is shallow and strained, the air heavy with the weight of uncertainty.

Despite the overwhelming sense of dread, a spark of determination ignites within her, fueling her courage in the face of danger. The conflicting emotions war within her, creating a storm of conflicting sensations that threaten to overwhelm her senses.

As she steels herself for the impending confrontation, her senses sharpen, every sound amplified, every shadow seeming to twist and dance in the dim light. The world around her slows down, her focus narrowing on the task at hand as she braces herself for the unknown outcome.

She tries to stay silent, holding her breath to stifle any betraying sounds. They storm into her room, ripping apart her bed and desk, the sounds of shattering glass and tearing paper filling the air, as they destroy her pictures and souvenirs. A man, his arms covered in intricate, colorful tattoos and his head shaved close, finds her.

His eyes, wild with malice, lock onto hers as he yanks her by the hair, a guttural "I've got you now" ripping from his throat; the roots of her scalp feel like they are tearing out.

Brad watches as someone drags Megan down her own stairs by her hair. Many times, they talk at the super center.

"Have you seen the price of milk? I swear the government needs to do something about these prices," Megan says.

"That's why we need Daniel. He says that he will lower consumer prices on day one."

"That's why we need his bold leadership, not the same old same old. We need a leader who will pick up trash," Megan says, recalling when Daniel put on a garbage man's uniform and drove around the neighborhood in a truck.

"Exactly something the Democrats and the Republicans will never do. America Now is the future of this country. They know the plight of the working man."

While working as a poll worker, she betrays Daniel. Her betrayal causes him physical pain, making his chest tight and his heart ache. Her laughter, once comforting, now reminds him of his loss. He feels anger, his muscles tense as he clenches his fists. Betrayal weighs heavily on him, making it hard to breathe as sadness washes over him. His longing turns into deep hurt and betrayal, leaving a bitter taste in his mouth.

Elliott Netty pushes Megan down the stairs. She looks up to see the fire in Brad's eyes.

"Brad please." Tears are still in Megan's eyes.

Brad smacks her across the face. He doesn't want to hear anymore from her.

"**She betrayed this country. She betrayed Daniel.**" Brad says anger coursing through his veins. "**The bitch deserves her fate**." He punches her in the stomach.

Suddenly, two men with shaved heads appear, their hands clamping down on her arms as they pull her out into the chilly night air. The chilling memory of the Wisconsin incident washes over her, bringing with it the icy grip of fear and the bitter taste of regret. "No Please. I did my job."

Despite Megan's desperate fight, the sheer strength of the men pulling her into the night is overwhelming; their rough hands and the chilling night air only add to her fear. As they descend the stairs, a wall of hostile faces meets her, along with a cacophony of shouts, stinging blows, and spittle. She does not recognize any of them but notices their armbands. It is the American flag with the Christian cross on it. They secure her legs to the truck with strong, quick knots, the rope biting into her flesh. "We'll see how she enjoys a ride." A cold dread washes over Brad as the cruel words hang in the air, each syllable a tiny, icy shard.

"No, Brad Please. I love you." Megan pleads as Brad gets in the truck and starts the engine.

Megan's fear and panic cause her muscles to tense up, intensifying the pain of the coarse rope digging into her skin. The adrenaline coursing through her body heightens her senses, making every jarring movement of the vehicle feel like a violent assault. As her heart races and her breath quickens, the engine's loud groaning seems to echo her own internal turmoil.

The group's initial cheers echo through the canyon, turning to horrified gasps as they find Megan lifeless, her still form a stark contrast to the vibrant landscape. With shredded clothing clinging to her mangled body, barely concealing gaping wounds, she is a horrifying sight, barely resembling a human.

"Oh, man. I hope the bitch has the stamina to stay and enjoy her flight," Brad says. The rough rope parts with a sickening tear as they free her bound legs; then, they carry her still form, its weight unsettling in their hands, to the Grand Canyon's edge, the wind whipping at their clothes as they fling her lifeless body into the chasm below. As the group stands at the edge of the Grand Canyon, their elation mixes with a hint of adrenaline coursing through their veins. The rush of their twisted accomplishment sends shivers down their spines, causing their hearts to race and their hands to tremble ever so slightly. The adrenaline-induced euphoria paints wide, wicked smiles on their faces, their eyes glinting with a distorted sense of satisfaction.

The group's elation is palpable, a heady mix of triumph and thrill that pulses through their bodies like a drug. The adrenaline coursing through their veins heightens their senses, sharpening their focus and amplifying their physical reactions. Their racing hearts thud against their rib cages, the rapid beat echoing in their ears alongside the sound of the wind whipping around them.

As they stand at the edge of the Grand Canyon, the rush of their twisted accomplishment sends waves of goosebumps cascading down their arms and backs. The shivers that run through them are not just from the stiff wind, but from the rush of adrenaline that electrifies their bodies.

Their hands tremble with a mixture of excitement and nervous energy, the aftermath of their dark deed still lingering in the surrounding air. The wide, wicked smiles that stretch across their faces are a physical manifestation of their distorted sense of satisfaction, their eyes glinting with a manic gleam that speaks of a thrill-seeking darkness within.

Immediately after finishing their beer... With smiles on their faces, they congratulate themselves on a successful task, patting each other on the back.

"One traitor gone, more remain," proclaims the man with the crew cut.

Elliott Netty proclaims, "For the new America, freedom now!"

Everyone cheers, proclaiming, "Freedom forever."

Chapter Twenty-Two

December 20, 2124

Jill Lunden sits comfortably on her plush sofa, sinking into the soft cushions as she organizes her itinerary for her upcoming journey across the United States with her husband. Fresh flowers in a vase on the coffee table fill the room with a sweet scent, while outside, birds chirp happily in the early morning light. Jill senses the smooth texture of the itinerary paper in her hands as she carefully arranges their travel plans, eagerly expecting the adventures they will soon embark on together. The sound of her husband's footsteps approaching brings a smile to her face.

"I still think that you should reconsider," Steve says. "I swear I will visit all fifty-two states before my inauguration and I intend to do it. Who knows, maybe this will heal the nation."

"I don't care about the nation. I care about you," Jill replies.

"That's nice, but as the President-Elect, I must think about the nation."

"What about the kids? You think they want to put their mother in danger?"

The soft cushions embrace her tired body, offering solace and comfort as the aroma of tea dances in the air, soothing her senses. The scent of well-loved travel guides adds a touch of adventure to the cozy atmosphere, filling the room with a sense of relaxation and anticipation that stands in stark contrast to the outside world of chaos and violence.

"Using the kids. That's low, especially for you," Steve remarks.

"I will do and use anything I can to save you from you."

"And I love you for that. But I have decided. After all, I have the best security in the world," Jill responds with a hitch in her breath, a tremor in her voice as she edges toward Steve, her eyes wide.

She looked at vibrant photographs of each state's diverse landscapes and iconic landmarks. The pictures burst with colors capturing the grandeur of mountains, serenity of lakes, and hustle of city streets. From the distant hum of traffic and honking horns came: A symphony of urban life. The air carried a faint scent of exhaust and the freshness of a new journey. Excitement bubbled inside her, tingled with nervous anticipation. She thought about recent events: the bombing in Oregon, the violence of Daniel's supporters, and troubling events involving Tracy.

A cold sweat slicked Steve's palms as he hesitantly played his ultimate card, his breath catching in his throat. "What about Tracy?" he asks.

Jill replays the tape of Tracy in her mind. "Fine, I bribed men to rig the election," the faint crackle of the tape and Tracy's ghostly whisper sending shivers down Jill's spine. Despite her fear, Jill's determination is evident as adrenaline surged through her body, making her heart race. She's worried about Tracy's whereabouts, experiencing anxiety and sweating, as she tried to solve the clues with a sense of tension and worry weighing on her. The uncertainty caused a tightness in her chest and a knot in her stomach, but Jill stayed strong and focused on unraveling Tracy's disappearance mystery.

"There is no way that Tracy would separate from her phone," Jill says.

Rachel found a phone on the street while Jill and Steve searched Tracy's apartment. When Jill charged the phone, she saw a picture of her and Tracy as kids. Jill's heart ached deeply upon viewing the photograph, making it hard for her to breathe. Tears filled her eyes as she looked at the picture, bringing back memories of their past. A mix of longing and sorrow overwhelmed her, reminding her of their bond. Each shared secret and moment of laughter appeared a tangible presence, stirring up emotions and leaving a bittersweet impression. Memories flooded Jill, creating a mix of nostalgia and grief, weighing heavily on her heart. The physical impact of her emotions reminded her of the strength of their friendship and the pain of loss.

As she grapples with the conflicting emotions swirling inside her, her body responds in kind. The worry manifests as a knot in her stomach, a persistent ache that refuses to dissipate, while the tension in her chest spreads like tendrils of unease, making it difficult to draw a full breath. Her heartbeat, once steady, now races in sync with the frantic rhythm of her thoughts, each thump a reminder of the uncertainty gnawing at her. Despite the warmth of nostalgia trying to soothe her, the shadow of Tracy's absence casts a chill over her, sending shivers down her spine. The juxtaposition of relief and worry creates a tumultuous storm within her, manifesting in physical sensations that mirror the complex emotions battling for dominance in her heart and mind.

As Jill wrestles with her conflicting emotions, her body reacts in various ways. The hope she holds onto sends a surge of adrenaline through her veins, heightening her senses and causing her heart to race. This physical reaction to hope imbues her with a sense of anticipation and energy, leaving her more alert and prepared for action. The bittersweet mix of relief and concern creates a tug-of-war within her chest. The relief washes over her like a warm wave, easing the tension in her muscles and causing a sense of relaxation to spread through her body. However, the underlying worry caused her stomach to tighten, leaving her edgy and restless.

In a moment of frustration and anger, she says, "No, I will not stand in the corner as terrorists destroy this nation. Damn Daniel Thompson and this Cain person." Her voice laced with venom, she hurls a crystal glass at the wall, the shattering sound echoing in the silence.

As her anger boils over, her heart rate increases, her muscles tense, and adrenaline surges through her body. The glass shatters against the wall, the sound echoing in the room as a physical manifestation of her frustration and rage. Shaking with rage, she explodes in a violent outburst. The tension was palpable.

"Ever since that monster released that list of poll workers, many people have died. I swear the first thing I will do after my inauguration is have my Attorney General investigate how that piece of trash even got that list."

"Of course, first we'll have to find out whom Cain is."

"And when I do, I will wring out that parasite's neck until he or she tells me what happened to Tracy. But my trips will happen. I will not fail." Jill looks at her itinerary from New York, her first visit,

"You go, and you'll be a sitting duck. I don't want to lose you." As Steve spoke, his heart raced with worry, sending a surge of adrenaline through his body. His hands shivered, and his muscles tensed with the weight of his fear. A knot formed in his stomach, making it hard to breathe as he pictured the worst-case scenarios playing out in his mind. The tension in his voice matched the tightness in his chest, betraying the depth of his emotions, with Steve's body language mirroring his internal turmoil, manifesting in a trembling voice that revealed the vulnerability he felt at the thought of losing someone dear to him,

"I don't want to lose me either."

As she packed, she looked at the television. On the screen were the list of places she planned to visit, courtesy of Cain, on the Conservative News Network, "Television increase sound." As the tension in the room rises, the emotions of those present manifest physically. Jill's voice, usually strong and clear, becomes barely audible as her vocal cords tighten with anxiety. The increase in sound from the television only adds to the chaotic atmosphere, causing a dissonant cacophony that mirrors the discord between the individuals in the room. The palpable tension in the air is almost tangible, as if the emotions are creating a heavy, oppressive weight that hangs over everyone present.

"We now go outside to Virginia Smart."

"Thank you, Sean. Sir, what do you think about Jill Lunden visiting your city?"

His friends surrounded the man; a sea of orange caps, each bearing the inscription **"Make America Pure"**, bobbed in the crowd. Their venomous words struck her. "We will be ready if that bitch comes."

"I hope she likes long drives and even longer falls." Another man says.

Jill hugs Steve. Her heart pounds, fear is coursing through her veins.

"I remember." Jill says in tears. "When I mentioned visiting all 52 states, everyone applauded, even calling it a bold move. Even the bombing of Portland, OR I was undeterred. I meticulously organized my schedule, coordinating every detail with law enforcement and political figures. I even arranged certain visits confidentially. How is Cain getting this information?"

The once exhilarating thought of visiting these states now brought a conflicting mixture of threats and applause. The air grew heavy with uncertainty as she pondered the challenges ahead. A gentle knock on the door interrupted her thoughts, and her Secret Service detail entered, providing a comforting sense of security.

Jill's muscles tensed, aching from the strain of her body's instinctive response to the overwhelming surge of emotions. The blood rushed to her face, causing it to flush with heat as her skin prickled with goosebumps. Her stomach churned and twisted, a knot of anxiety forming as her body reacted to the intense feelings coursing through her. The physical sensations of her emotions were palpable, each one manifesting differently as she struggled to regain control.

"You saw the television?" Jill asks.

The physical effects of the agent's emotions were evident in their slumped shoulders, which bore the weight of their remorse. Their gaze, once strong and direct, now drifted downward, reflecting the sincerity in their words. The heaviness of their emotions seemed to physically manifest in their posture, as if the burden of their feelings was too much to bear. It was a poignant display of vulnerability and regret, etched in the subtle movements of their body.

"You don't have to say anything." Jill's legs now display weakness and shakiness. They threaten to give way beneath her. The weight of disappointment and helplessness pulled at her limbs, each step to her couch a monumental effort. With a heavy thud, she collapsed onto the soft cushions, her body sinking into the comfort it provided.

"We can't guarantee your safety. Maybe when the truth is out and everyone has time to process. But right now."

'Steve is right. I would be a sitting duck.' Still, she wants to fight. "I understand. You can go." She looks at Steve. "Both of you." Steve knows what that means. She's about to explode and she doesn't want anyone to see it. He goes to Jill.

"I'm sorry dear. I know you wanted this to succeed." Steve and the agent leaves.

The fury that burns within her is a fierce inferno, consuming her from within. It surged through her veins, igniting a fire that threatened to consume everything in its path. The urge to release the pent-up rage built up like a storm, ready to unleash its destructive force.

In a moment of uncontrolled fury, Jill grabbed her pillow and unleashed all her strength, hurling it across the room. The impact against the wall reverberated through the air, a satisfying release of her anger. But even as the pillow lay motionless on the floor, her frustration remained unabated.

"God damn, mother fuckin son of Bitch. Forget my Attorney General. When I find this Cain person, I will make him or her rule the day he or she went against me." Her voice trembled with fury. Her words dripping with venom. The image of Cain, the person responsible for shattering her dreams and aspirations, fueled her desire for justice.

Her heart pounds in her chest, adrenaline courses through her veins, causing her hands to tremble. The tension in her muscles makes her feel like a coiled spring, ready to snap at any moment. A wave of heat flushes over her, making her skin feel tight and prickly. The sharp intake of breath as she holds back her scream feels like a physical strain as she fights against the intense emotions swirling inside her. The resolve in her eyes burns bright, a fiery determination fueling her every move as she harnesses anger into a powerful force for change.

As Jill's emotions surged through her, her body responded with a symphony of physical sensations. The ache in her muscles seemed to mirror the weight of her emotions, a heavy burden that she carried with every step. Her heart pounded in her chest, a relentless drumbeat of determination propelling her forward. Adrenaline surged through her veins, sharpening her senses and heightening her focus.

Each breath she took felt charged with the energy of her yearning for retribution, a palpable force that fueled her resolve. Her jaw clenched with determination; her teeth gritted against the adversity that threatened to derail her quest. Yet, beneath it all, there was a sense of calm certainty, a belief that justice would ultimately triumph.

Despite the physical toll of her emotions, Jill pressed on, each step a testament to her unwavering faith in the justice she sought. The journey ahead was long and challenging, but with every fiber of her being, she knew she was ready to face whatever obstacles lay in her path.

She goes to the window to look at the sights.

Glass shatters, shards flying in all directions.

She ducks, heart pounding in fear.

The sound of laughter fades into the distance.

Adrenaline surges through her veins.

She clenches her fists, eyes blazing with anger.

The sudden rush of fear causes her breath to quicken, her chest heaving as her heart races. Her muscles are tense, ready to fight or flee as the adrenaline courses through her body, heightening her senses. As the shards of glass scatter, her eyes widen in shock and her body instinctively ducks, seeking safety.

The laughter that fades into the distance leaves a bitter taste in her mouth, fueling the flames of anger that burns within her. Her fists clench tightly, nails digging into her palms as she struggles to contain the fiery rage that threatens to consume her. Her eyes, once bright with curiosity, now blaze with a fierce intensity, a storm of emotions swirling within her.

She finds a note tied to a rock. It reads, "You're a dead bitch. You and your family." Her heart races and adrenaline surges through her. The words weigh heavily, making it hard to breathe. Fear takes over, blurring her surroundings. Her hands tremble as she tries to understand the message. A knot forms in her stomach as dread settles in. Her resolve turns into fear and vulnerability.

Steve bursts into the door. "I heard the crash of the window. Are you ok?"

Jill still holds the note. She now believes she has aged ten years. "Hold me." Jill says and rushes to Steve.

"Forever." Steve says.

Chapter Twenty-Three

December 22, 2124

Scott Smith, the Secretary of State for Wisconsin, nervously approaches the podium bathed in bright lights on a bright autumn day. The state seal adorning the podium reflects sunlight, while the hum of the crowd mingles with the distant sound of rustling leaves, filling the air with anticipation. As Scott Smith prepares to address the gathered crowd, a mix of drama and apprehension washes over him. "I strongly deny election fraud and unprofessional actions by my office," he begins. "However, I support a recount overseen by America Now, with representatives from the Democratic and Republican parties to ensure fairness." This statement elicits angry shouts from America Now members, filling the room with intense frustration. Faces flush, fists clench, and voices raise in anger, creating a palpable tension and a charged atmosphere where emotions run high, sparking passionate disagreement.

"That was the scene from the press conference of Scott Smith, the Secretary of State, from Wisconsin. He joins the list of other states that have accepted Daniel's request for recounts. This is Sara Spencer; enjoy the rest of your day."

"And we are off," the announcer says. Sara, in a fit of frustration, flings her notes, sending them flying in all directions. Her voice cracks with fury, sending reverberations through the air as the sound of paper hitting wood echoes in the room, and she cries,

"God damn son of a bitch." The intensity of her anger manifests physically, causing her fists to clench tightly, her face to flush with heat, and her cutting words to slice through the tension in the room. The raw power of her emotions seems to ripple through the atmosphere, leaving an invisible trail of charged energy in its wake.

Mark comes over to her. "Well, it's a good thing the camera is off. Otherwise, people might think that we have an ulterior motive."

Sara's heart races as she looks up at Mark, her chest tightening with anxiety. Her hands tremble slightly as she tries to compose herself, a knot forming in her stomach. The rush of emotions is overwhelming, leaving her lightheaded and dizzy. Sara is aware of the heat rising to her cheeks, her body reacting to the flood of emotions coursing through her. Mark's concern is evident in his eyes, only intensifying the whirlwind of feelings swirling inside her. "Jackass caves just like most Secretary of States. I thought people elect courage, not people that will kiss Daniel's ass. As for ulterior motives. Everyone already believes that."

The tension in the room is palpable as the conversation turns to the current state of affairs. The weight of fear and uncertainty seems to hang in the air, causing a heaviness in everyone's chest. People exchange nervous glances, fidget with their hands, and their voices waver with emotion. Their faces show the stress of the situation, with furrowed brows and clenched jaws. Each word spoken seems to carry a physical weight, as if the gravity of the situation is pressing down on them. The emotions swirling in the room are like a storm brewing, threatening to unleash their full force at any moment.

"It's just not Daniel."

"Yeah, I forget about that Caner Cain for whom we wouldn't have problems. Has the United States lost its collective mind?" The frustration and disbelief in the statement's tone can manifest physically in various ways. Sara may clench their jaw, furrow their brow, and tighten their muscles, reflecting the tension and anger they feel. Their heart rate may increase, causing a sensation of heaviness or tightness in the chest. They may also experience a surge of adrenaline, leading to shaky hands, or a feeling of restlessness.

"And both of their followers. People fear them and, considering recent national occurrences, I can't blame them."

"Fuck, call it for what it is. Domestic Terrorism plan and simple thanks to our good friends Daniel and Cain. Cain needs to be exposed and Daniel needs prison. Neither should have any power." Sara's heart pounds in her chest as she storms off, her fists clenched in anger. The rush of adrenaline causes her muscles to tense, her jaw to clench, and her breathing to quicken. As she fumes with rage, her face flushes with heat, and her hands tremble with the intensity of her emotions. The weight of her emotions is a heavy burden on her shoulders, making her movements sharp and forceful.

Sara's anger is evident in her posture - straight back, squared shoulders, purposeful steps. Her body language reveals the intensity of her emotions, reflecting the inner turmoil she is experiencing. The tension in her body mirrors the conflict in her mind as she deals with feelings of injustice and betrayal. Sara's body shows signs of conflicting emotions through tension, heat, and trembling. Her resolute anger is clear as she walks away, signaling her determination to seek justice and hold others accountable.

"Sara." Mark runs after her. He finds her by the company RV outside the building; the metallic scent of the vehicle fills the air. He walks in to find Sara's anger clear in her voice. Mark says something.

"No, I don't want to hear it anymore. You know, Daniel calls us fake news. That we are out to get him. Hell, during the campaign he threatened to take away our press coverage and people have no problems with that. I swear he wants to be a dictator and people seem to be happy with that." As Sara speaks, her face flushes with anger, her hands clenched into fists at her sides. The tension in her body is evident as her muscles tighten and her breathing becomes rapid and shallow. Her emotions radiate heat, making the room stifling and intensely charged. The force of her words echoes through the room, carrying the weight of her frustration and disbelief. The energy of her anger is palpable, sparking a sense of unease and tension in the air.

"Well, once the audits and..."

"Then what? If he doesn't like it, he'll go to the courts."

"When the courts say he's lost,"

"Then he'll send his thugs after us. There is nothing he won't do to claim ultimate victory. I mean, look at what they did in Oregon. The poll workers. I wouldn't doubt it if Cain started posting the name and addresses of reporters." Cain's merciless tactics fill Sara with fear and anger. The intense emotions coursing through her body manifest in a rapid heartbeat and sweaty palms. The adrenaline rush from discussing such sinister actions triggers a fight-or-flight response, causing her muscles to tense up and her breath to quicken.

Sara feels anxious as she considers the idea of Cain targeting reporters by revealing their personal information. The thought of her privacy being violated makes her shiver and feel vulnerable. She hugs herself for comfort and protection. Despite trying to stay calm, Sara's voice trembles with fear and uncertainty. The seriousness of the situation affects her visibly as she tries to deal with the complexities of political manipulation.

"I see your point. But we must admit that Daniel and this Cain person are news."

"Oh, you don't have to remind me of that. Besides the recording, the terrorists' actions, posting of sensitive information, and the disappearance of...."

Mark searches his memory. "Tracy Kincaid."

"Yes, Tracy Kincaid. The person who allegedly rigged the election."

"You don't buy that despite the recording that says otherwise."

"Someone could have faked that recording!" Sara's heart pounds in her chest as anger flares up inside her. Her face feels hot, flushed with frustration and disbelief. The adrenaline coursing through her veins makes her hands tremble as she clenches them into fists. Her jaw muscles clench; her voice, a sharp, loud outburst. The intensity of her emotions is palpable, radiating off her in waves as she struggles to make sense of the situation.

"And if they find Tracy and she confirms it."

"Open your eyes. Chances are that this Tracy person is probably dead. Killed so she can't deny ever rigging the election. You know I've done some research on Ms. Kincaid. She and Jill were childhood friends. God, I sympathize with Jill."

As the conversation continues, tension rises in the room. The weighty discussion causes unease among the group. Frowns, creased brows, and jaws clench tightly as emotions run high. Adrenaline pulses through veins, causing hearts to race and palms to sweat. The mention of the terrorists' actions and the posting of sensitive information sparks fear and anger in those present, manifesting in shallow breaths and furrowed brows.

The physical effects of the emotions are palpable. The room seems to crackle with energy as the conversation delves deeper into dangerous territory. They exchange nervous glances, tensing their bodies for what might come next. The disappearance of someone only adds to the sense of foreboding that hangs in the air like a thick fog, weighing down on everyone present.

Despite the gravity of the situation, a sense of determination also simmers beneath the surface. Shoulders square, jaws set, and eyes harden with resolve as the group prepares to face whatever challenges lay ahead. Emotions swirl like a storm within each person, their physical reactions mirroring the turmoil within.

"Hey, I agree with you. The recording likely aims to manipulate public opinion against Jill regarding election results."

"Then why do you..."

"I'm just playing devil's advocate. I know you, Sara. You will investigate that recording. Consider it from all sides until you determine its validity. You will report it even at the risk of your own life."

"I hate the fact that you know me so well."

"You are an excellent reporter and we have worked with each other for two years and..."

Sara doesn't let him finish that sentence as she pounces on him. Sara's heart races. Adrenaline courses through her veins as she feels the heat of desire building within her. Her skin flushes with a rosy hue, her pulse quickening as she leans in closer to him. The intensity of her emotions manifests in the way her hands tremble slightly, yet with purpose, as she explores his body with a sense of urgency and longing. The physical sensations of passion and lust envelop her, creating a magnetic pull between them that is both exhilarating and intoxicating.

"What do you think you're doing?" Mark's voice is barely a whisper as he asks, while his fingers unbutton Sara's blouse.

Sara, breathing heavily, confessed to having a lot of pent-up rage that needed unleashing. Adrenaline surges through her body, heightening her senses and sharpening her focus. Her muscles tense and quiver with the intensity of her emotions, giving her the strength to forcefully push Mark onto the couch and tear at his clothing.

Mark gets Sara's pink lace panties off of her. While she's on top of him and continues kissing him, she removes her pink bra. As their passion intensifies, Mark and Sara's bodies respond with heightened physical effects. Their heart rates quicken, sending waves of adrenaline coursing through their veins. The skin on their bodies becomes flushed and sensitive to the slightest touch, adding to the intensity of their sensations. Their breaths become shallow and rapid, mingling in the air as they share heated kisses and gasps of pleasure.

Their bodies move in synchrony, each motion fueling the other's desire. Sara's hips sway and undulate against Mark's, creating a rhythm that intensifies with every movement. The heat between them, skin against skin, only serves to further ignite their passion. Their voices rise in a crescendo of ecstasy, blending with the sounds of their bodies moving together in a dance of desire. Moans and gasps escape their lips, contributing to the symphony of pleasure enveloping them. In this moment, mutual passion consumes them as they ascend to a peak of euphoria together.

"I see what you mean by pent-up rage, although I think I need a new outfit," he remarks, looking at the tattered remains of his pants, underwear, and shirt, the fabric hanging in ragged strips.

Sara gazes at the torn clothing scattered across the RV floor, her expression apologetic. "I'm so sorry."

"Don't be. As a matter of fact," he responds, a look of intense passion in his eyes as he reaches out to trace her chin. "I also believe I'm harboring some pent-up emotions, as well." The soft glow of the dimly lit lightbulbs creates a warm and intimate atmosphere. The faint scent of lavender lingers in the air, bringing a sense of calm to the charged moment. Sara's smile conveys a blend of playfulness and curiosity, while the rhythmic background of the music beneath them enhances their unspoken connection.

In the Massachusetts Coroner's office, the atmosphere is somber. The dimly lit room carries the faint smell of old paperwork, while the sound of papers shuffling and phones ringing creates a sense of urgency. Chief Medical Coroner Hilda Smithson feels the pressure as she races to identify the bodies before the upcoming criminal trials. The weight of responsibility hangs heavily in the air as she opens vault 220 to retrieve a body.

The Chief of Police demands immediate identification, but Hilda has five more bodies to identify and three criminal trials to attend to first. The current body will have to wait. "God, I can't wait till my assistant is back from vacation."

She gently places the lifeless body onto the cold steel gurney. The gurney creaks as she wheels it to the examination lab, where harsh fluorescent lights illuminate the gruesome scene, casting long shadows.

She turns on the recording and video. "Let's see. The victim is a female. About fifty years old. Cause of death is blunt force trauma. I notice a slash on the neck. I have also counted about twenty stab wounds. It appears someone removed the victim's entrails." Hilda, feeling the weight of sorrow as she contemplates the victim's fate, her hands trembling slightly as she replays the gruesome details in her mind. A wave of sadness washes over her, empathizing with the woman's suffering.

The image of the victim's injuries leaves a chilling imprint in Hilda's thoughts, making her stomach churn with unease. As she closes her eyes, the vivid image of the victim's entrails spills out before her mind's eye, sending a shiver down her spine. The sheer brutality of the crime fills her with a mix of anger and sorrow, her heart heavy with the injustice.

"Poor woman. What could you have possibly done to end up this way? Let's run a DNA kit to find out who you are," she says, taking out a long, gleaming needle with practiced hands, ready to begin the intricate process of DNA extraction.

Chapter Twenty-Four

S ean Bradley sits at his desk, conscious of the coolness of the worn wood beneath his hands as Daniel speaks to him on the phone. Everyone who watches the Conservative News Network hears Daniel. "I have information that supporters of the LGBTQ+ community, the Jews, the climate coalition, and the European survivors stole the election. I also have it on good authority that the FBI and various other organizations are investigating the claims. We ensure that all those who perpetrated this fraud face justice. To that end, we'll keep the pressure on to ensure the FBI doesn't cover up this fraud. We must demand full and complete accountability. It's commonly known that elites love to protect themselves. We must save America from these vermin. We will Make America Pure."

"Thank you, Daniel. We all know that we should not have allowed people from the United Kingdom and France to enter the United States."

"Not just them, but also the people of Botswana. We should have told them to stay in their radioactive country. Bringing in their diseases to this nation. But no President Sanchez just opens our country to those people,"

Laura's piercing green eyes seem to look straight into your soul, while her dark hair cascades down her shoulders like a waterfall. Her words create a sense of anticipation in the air. Sean recoils, a cold dread washing over him as he watches her slurred words and unsteady movements, fearing the consequences. "I'm also ecstatic that the FBI is investigating."

The shock ripples through the FBI agents like a sudden jolt of electricity, sending shivers down their spines and causing their hearts to race. Their muscles tense, and their breath catches in their throats as they struggle to process the gravity of the situation. Adrenaline surges through their bodies, heightening their senses and sharpening their focus as they grapple with the implications of the news. A blend of disbelief, anger, and resolve churn within each agent, evident in their jaw clenching, furrowed brows, and constricted chests. The weight of the information hangs heavy in the air, casting a shadow over the room as the agents brace themselves for the challenging investigation ahead.

"I can't believe," a female agent's voice trembles with disbelief, her hands shaking slightly as she speaks. The weight of the shocking news seems to physically affect her, causing her heart to race and her breath to quicken.

"First, I'm hearing about this," another agent's brows furrow in confusion, his body tense with the unexpected revelation. The emotional impact of the situation, their bodies and expressions, visibly affect both agents, mirroring their disbelief and astonishment.

Agent Michales looks at Judson with terror and conviction in his stance. Director Knighton, his face beaded with sweat and his eyes heavy-lidded, stands outside his office. "Television off." The television flickers, then goes black, leaving the room silent. "It is true we are investigating Cain's claims in tandem with the NSA and the Secret Service. Agent Judson has been our intermediary in this investigation." As Agent Judson stands before the group, a mix of tension and anticipation fills the room. Each person's emotions manifest physically in different ways - some shift in their seats, fidgeting with pens or tapping their feet nervously. Others furrow their brows, their muscles tensing with worry. A few individuals bite their lips or clench their fists, trying to contain their emotions.

The air in the room seems heavy with apprehension, the atmosphere charged with a sense of urgency. As the investigation progresses, the collective emotions of the group ebb and flow, causing a ripple effect of physical reactions. Some may experience a knot in their stomach, others a lump in their throat. The stress of the situation is palpable, manifesting in shallow breaths and a racing heartbeat.

"We will collect evidence and compile a comprehensive report to submit to the Department of Justice. Until then, please be cautious with your words. Thank you."

A wave of loneliness washes over Judson as the last footsteps fade, leaving him stranded in a silent, echoing room.

"So, you're the one investigating the entire stolen election debacle," Michaels remarks.

"That is correct."

"Is that why you seem to be worried lately? I mean, the last couple of days..."

"Yes, I know."

A chill runs down Michael's spine as Judson's voice, usually monotone, cracks with an unsettling tremor, hinting at something dreadful.

Agent Judson heads towards his cubicle, feeling Michaels' presence close behind him like a shadow, the fluorescent lights humming overhead.

"What's the problem, Judson?"

"What do you mean?"

"You almost bit my head off just a couple of seconds ago. That's the biggest sign of emotion that I've ever seen from you."

Judson's heart rate rises with anticipation. Adrenaline sharpens his focus and heightens his senses. His pupils dilate, making him keenly aware of his surroundings. The energy drink boosts his energy and heart rate. His legacy and responsibility, symbolized by the old briefcase in his hands, ground him and fuel his determination. The documents inside hold the key to his next move. Flipping through them, he feels a mix of excitement and nerves. The scent of leather from the briefcase and the energy drink on his breath intensify his emotions.

"Look at these. Interviews with poll workers who have confessed to the election interference," Judson presents the evidence.

"Why didn't you arrest them? Prove that Cain was right," Michaels questions.

"Because they are inconsistent. See this. A poll worker from Washington DC says that she throws away Daniel Thompson ballots and adds more Jill ballots."

"See, I knew Daniel won the election."

"Except her own employment card says she is out the day that she claims she did it. When I confronted her about the inconsistency, she confessed she lied." Judson remembered the day. He can still remember the cold sweat of the confrontation and then the tears when she finally confessed that she lied about everything. "She begged me to arrest her for giving false testimony."

"Why?"

"Because she prefers a federal prison compared to the wrath of American Now supporters. Look around you. Poll workers are mysteriously disappearing. Sometimes, people find their bodies."

"And sometimes parts of them in various states. Can't say I blame her." Michaels shares unsettling details that make Judson shiver. His fear and paranoia are evident as tension fills the room, heavy and suffocating. People show physical signs of stress like clenched jaws and trembling hands. Fear and horror fill the room with unease. Judson just shakes his head.

"I tried to get her federal protection, but my colleagues in both the NSA and the Secret Service didn't respond to my requests. Another issue is that she also disappeared." His heart pounds in his chest, the weight of worry and frustration causing his muscles to tense up. Each breath is shallow as the stress tightens his jaw and furrows his brow. The lack of control over the situation leaves a bitter taste in his mouth, his stomach churning with anxiety. As he lowers his head, a wave of exhaustion washes over him. His body physically reacts to the emotional toll of the situation.

Michaels places a comforting hand on Judson's shoulder. "She could be with her friends or family." Judson's heart races with anxiety as Michaels speaks, a lump forming in his throat. The weight of the situation presses down on him like a physical burden, causing his muscles to tense and his breathing to quicken. "I hope you're right," Michaels knows Judson doesn't fully believe it.

However, a nagging question lingers in Judson's mind. "How is this Cain person getting all this information? Jill's itinerary, the list of the poll workers, and the FBI investigation–it's as if there's a traitor among us," Judson ponders aloud. The fear of betrayal within their ranks sends shivers down his spine, a chill gripping him tightly. As they contemplate the danger posed by a potential traitor, a mix of anger and determination wells up inside Judson. His fists clench involuntarily, his jaw set with resolve. The adrenaline coursing through his veins sharpens his focus as he vows to uncover the truth and protect those he cares about.

Michaels, sensing the urgency of the situation, voices his concern, "We need to find this leak and plug it up." As Judson delves deeper into the web of deception, a sense of urgency consumes him. He painstakingly examined piles of documents, connecting the dots with feverish determination. The faces of potential suspects stare back at him from the walls of his office, mocking his relentless pursuit of truth.

Determined to address the issues at hand, Judson plans to speak with Director Knighton. Just as he finishes his report, Agent Michaels approaches him. "Listen, you know that I'm a Daniel supporter. I believe they stole the election. But you're right. What this Cain person is doing is reprehensible," Michaels admits, acknowledging the gravity of the situation.

"Not just reprehensible, but deadly. You heard all the people that Daniel said took part in the fraud. Every organization or group against Daniel Thompson," Judson emphasizes the severity of the situation.

"What about the recording of Tracy Kincaid admitting to fraud?" Michaels interjects, raising a valid point.

"And the fact that they can't find this Kincaid woman?" Judson questions, acknowledging the challenges posed by her absence.

The tension in the room rises, and a wave of anger sweeps through the friends. Heart rates quicken, muscles tense and faces flush with the intensity of their emotions. Some clench their fists, feeling the adrenaline coursing through their veins as they consider the gravity of the situation. The weight of betrayal and deceit hangs heavy in the air, causing a palpable sense of unease and distrust among them. The fear of the unknown, coupled with the simmering anger, creates a volatile mix of emotions that threatens to boil over at any moment. Each person's body language betrays their inner turmoil, reflecting the turmoil of the situation at hand.

"Well, whatever you find, I'm sure that you will investigate as only you can."

"Before I can publish his findings, I need to conduct further research. I also have to bring my theories to the Director," Agent Judson says.

"I wish you luck," Agent Michaels' voice quivers with empathy, his genuine concern palpable in the air. The weight of the pending investigation hangs heavily over them, causing a ripple of tension to spread through the room. Agent Judson's determination is evident in the way his hands clench into fists, his jaw set in unwavering resolve. As they prepare to delve deeper into the unknown, a mixture of anticipation and apprehension fills the space, creating an electric atmosphere that crackles with intensity. The emotions in the room are almost tangible, manifesting as a charged energy that seems to hum with every breath taken. "And for what it's worth. I hope you're wrong."

"So do I," Agent Judson's determination manifests physically, his clenched fists trembling slightly with the effort of containing his resolve. The muscles in his jaw stand out prominently, a visible symbol of his unwavering commitment to the task at hand.

The mixture of anticipation and apprehension creates a palpable buzz in the room, making the air feel charged and almost alive. It is as if the very atmosphere is crackling with the conflicting emotions swirling around them, creating an electric field that seems to vibrate with intensity.

As they brace themselves to delve deeper into the unknown, the charged energy in the room seems to pulse with every heartbeat, adding a sense of urgency to their actions. The collective emotions in the room are like a storm gathering strength, ready to unleash its power at any moment.

Agent Judson goes over his notes one last time. "I'm not wrong. There is a spy in this investigation. It's the only thing that makes sense."

As Agent Judson's suspicion grows stronger, a knot tightens in his stomach, serving as a physical manifestation of his anxiety and determination to uncover the truth. His heart rate quickens, pumping adrenaline through his veins, sharpening his focus and heightening his senses. The weight of his realization bears down on his shoulders, causing tension to build in his muscles as he prepares to confront the traitor lurking within their midst. Each passing moment etches the intensity of his emotions onto his face, a steely resolve masking his inner unease. As Agent Judson approaches the elevator, he feels the air around him crackle with urgency, bracing himself for the impending confrontation that could alter the investigation's course.

The weight of his suspicions bears down on his shoulders, making his steps heavier and causing beads of sweat to form on his forehead in the cool, air-conditioned building. His trembling hands betray the nervousness consuming him as the elevator doors slide open. He inhaled deeply to soothe his rapid heartbeat, stepping inside as the constriction in his chest worsened with each ascending level. The flickering lights in the elevator mirror the turmoil in his mind, casting eerie shadows on his tense features as he positions himself against the mirrored wall. Fixing his gaze on his reflection, he searches for any signs of doubt or hesitation, noticing a glimmer of fear in his usually determined eyes. Clenching his fists to steady his shaking hands proves difficult, with adrenaline coursing through his veins.

A gentle chime signals his arrival on Director Knighton's office floor, and the elevator doors slide open with a soft hiss. In a moment of reflection, Agent Judson collects his thoughts, straightens his tie, and adjusts his suit to exude professionalism despite the turmoil within him. Ready to share his suspicions with Director Knighton, he thinks to himself, *'God, I hope I am wrong.'*

As Agent Judson steps out of the elevator and makes his way towards Director Knighton's office, a knot tightens his stomach, a physical manifestation of the worry and doubt swirling within him. His heart beats a little faster, the adrenaline coursing through his veins as he prepares to reveal his suspicions. The weight of his concerns presses down on his shoulders, causing a tension to creep into his muscles.

Despite his best efforts to maintain a composed exterior, a sheen of sweat forms on his brow, betraying the nervousness he feels. His hands, usually steady and sure, now tremble ever so slightly, a telltale sign of the internal struggle he is facing. As he reaches the door to Director Knighton's office, a wave of apprehension washes over him, sending a shiver down his spine.

Agent Judson takes a deep breath, steeling himself for the conversation ahead. The mix of fear, uncertainty, and determination war within him, creating a complex tapestry of emotions that threaten to overwhelm him. But with each step closer to the truth, he finds a sense of resolve building within him, propelling him forward despite the storm of emotions raging inside.

Chapter Twenty-Five

December 23, 2124

"I would like to thank Cain for publishing all the information about the people that committed the election fraud." Sean Bradley says, standing on a podium with the Conservative News Network logo on the background. Meanwhile, Melissa, the Speaker of the House, was in her office getting ready for the day, surrounded by the smell of paper and ink, enjoying the sunlight filtering through the windows. Outside, she could hear voices and papers, reminding her of her responsibilities and the pride she took in her work. Cain, Bradley, and Daniel Thompson's lies disappoint and betray Melissa as she watches Sean on TV spreading Cain's false claims. As she dealt with conflicting emotions about a sonogram and thoughts about her future, she felt a mix of heaviness and lightness in her chest. Despite the whirlwind of feelings, Melissa found comfort in being present and accepting all the emotions that filled her heart.

Alyssa Summer, younger and energetic, approaches Melissa as the tension in the room grows suffocating. Alyssa's vibrant energy changes the atmosphere, replacing tension with curiosity. Melissa's anxiety eases as she focuses on Alyssa's question, leading to a shift in the room's energy. The contrast between Alyssa's vitality and Melissa's anxiety shapes the emotional energy in the space as the conversation unfolds.

Directly addressing Melissa, Alyssa asks with concern. "Is there a matter you wish to bring to my attention, Ms. Speaker?"

Alyssa's concern was evident in the furrow of her brow and the slight tremble in her voice. Her heart raced a little faster, pumping adrenaline through her veins as she waited for Melissa's response. A mix of worry and anticipation made her palms slightly clammy, and she could feel a knot forming in her stomach. The weight of the unspoken issue hung heavy in the air, causing a subtle tension to settle between them. Alyssa's body language betrayed her emotions, with her shoulders tensed and her eyes fixed intently on Melissa, searching for any hint of what was to come.

"Thank you, Cain? With the releasing of the poll workers and Jill's schedule, that monster has more blood on his hands than Dracula." As Melissa speaks, her voice trembles with a mixture of anger and frustration. Her words, precise and incisive as daggers, sliced through the thick tension that permeated the room, leaving a palpable silence in their wake. Her tightened facial muscles emphasized the stress lines on her face, clearly indicating her tension. A flush of heat rises to her cheeks, giving her a fiery, almost menacing appearance. The energy in the room shifts, crackling with the intensity of her emotions. It's as if the very air around her has become charged with her anger, creating an almost palpable aura of tension. The weight of her words hangs heavy in the air, leaving a lingering sense of unease in their wake.

"I am finding it difficult to form an opinion about the election, as there are so many conflicting viewpoints and a great deal of uncertainty. I didn't believe anyone stole the election until that tape recording..."

"Nothing supports the assertion that the election was stolen." As for the recording. I can't wait to the final report is done regarding that." Melissa's voice quivered with a mix of anger and frustration as she vehemently denied the false claim. Her face flushed with intensity, and their fists clenched tightly as they spoke. The emotions surged through her body, causing her heart rate to quicken and their breath to become shallow. A surge of adrenaline coursed through their veins, intensely fueling their impassioned and unwavering defense against the encroaching threat. Their body language spoke volumes, reflecting the deep emotional impact of the situation.

As the deceptive messages echoed through social media, Melissa's frustration turned into a simmering rage. The unfairness of it all, the sheer audacity of those who perpetuated these lies, fueled a fire within her. She clenched her fists, experiencing a surge of determination to uncover the truth and combat the erosion of democracy.

"I can't believe in this age of information the loud voices of deceit overshadow the truth. It's very disheartening to witness the erosion of trust in this country's democratic process to which I fought and many of my friends died to protect. I swear to be the voice of truth in the cacophony of lies."

Daniel gives an impassioned speech to a packed audience, gesturing wildly. "The establishment stole this election, and we all know it." Despite her certainty that the election is fair, demands for stricter voting laws increase in the following weeks. People wearing MAP hats echo their conviction, tirelessly repeating, "We want fair, not stolen elections and we demand that the President pass the Fair Election Act that the Senate proposes."

"Television off." Melissa pinches her nose. With a heavy sigh escaping her lips, she says. "Can you please inform me of my schedule for the day?"

Alyssa responded with "Let's see," She pulled out her palmtop, the cool smooth surface a contrast to her warm fingers and quickly located the information she needed. "The Senate passed a voting rights act the television mentioned. It is waiting on your desk."

"Oh great. I've heard enough about the Senate bill. To eliminate mail-in voting, an ethics test should be enforced at the polling stations, disqualifying individuals with names similar to felons from the voter rolls, no matter how common those names are. The House will reject it."

"The House version of the election bill will be voted on next."

"At least that makes the most sense. Think about it: a national mail voting system and voting rights for rehabilitated felons in their current state and a voter database. Instantaneous results which can't be refuted.

"The Senate will undoubtedly reject it. And even if they pass it, I doubt Chavez will sign off on either of them."

"Probably. But we have to try. The actions of Daniel and Cain are causing a significant rift and division within the nation, threatening to tear it apart."

However, the usual deadlock persists: the House resists the Senate's version, and the Senate resists the House's. As a result, the issue remains deadlocked, with no progress in sight. Her assistant, interrupting the flow of her thoughts, continued speaking.

"You have the hearings on gun violence."

Melissa knows all too well that any effort to enact gun control will face formidable resistance, likely making it futile.

"There have already been hundreds of just school shootings this year. Ten church shootings—then this."

Melissa revealed to her assistant a tablet displaying a crime scene report; a basketball game, now marred by gunfire, was the scene of the shooting. Thousands of people are dead, including players from both teams. *'What does one more shooting even matter anymore in this country?'* she thinks. As Alyssa's eyes scan the pad, her heart rate quickens and her hands tremble with shock and disbelief. The weight of the tragic news settles heavily on her chest, making it hard to breathe. A wave of nausea washes over her, causing her stomach to churn with a mix of horror and sorrow. The grim reality of so many lives lost in a senseless act of violence sends a shiver down her spine, leaving her cold and numb. Despite her attempt to maintain composure, tears well up in her eyes, blurring the words on the pad as her emotions threaten to overwhelm her. The sheer magnitude of the tragedy leaves her speechless, struggling to process the immense loss and devastation before her.

"Do you believe this will provoke a response?" Alyssa says.

"Are you kidding? Identical empty phrases will greet the nation. The tragedy is absolutely horrific and devastating. No one could have prevented the situation. Now isn't the moment to discuss gun violence and the phrase I hate the most, thoughts and prayers. **Will they can take their thoughts and prayers and all other kinds of fake sympathetic horse shit and shove them where the sun doesn't shine?**"

Alyssa is surprised by Melissa's passionate speech. Normally quiet, Alyssa keeps to herself. She sees a sonogram of Melissa's future great-grandchild and feels a rush of adrenaline. This sudden emotion makes her heart race and hands tremble. She feels lightheaded as if the ground is moving beneath her. This is the first time Alyssa has seen Melissa so emotional. Looking at the sonogram of Melissa's great grandchild, she was struck by the blurry image of a tiny hand, already perfectly formed. Alyssa feels a wave of understanding and a tingling sensation. She is amazed and tries to process her flood of emotions. The shock and wonder leave her excited and overwhelmed by the strong physical effects. Alyssa didn't know Melissa when Erica and Miranda were born or started school.

"I recess this body for one hour," Melissa banged the gavel on the polished wood desk, her voice echoing the sharp sound.

Melissa can't wait to get some lunch and good company. She will go to her favorite pizza restaurant and grab a slice of pizza. First, she will go to the restaurant where she bumped into Jacob many decades ago. She looks at the empty building, its broken windows like vacant eyes staring into the street. She looks a little to her right. The area where she bumped into Jacob. She relives that moment. She was a Judge Advocate General attorney; he, a lobbyist. Their meeting was just a pure random chance. She wasn't paying attention.

As Melissa walks down memory lane, a rush of nostalgia washes over her, causing her heart to race and her palms to sweat. The bittersweet memories of her encounter with Jacob many years ago stir up a mix of emotions within her. The sudden flood of emotions brings on a knot in her stomach, a lump in her throat, and tingling fingertips. Past burdens seem intensely real, suffocating her. Despite time's passage, lingering emotional scars evidence that chance meeting's profound impact.

Tears continue to stream down Melissa's cheeks, leaving faint trails on her weathered skin. Each droplet carries with it a story of love, loss, and the weight of responsibility. Her tear-streaked face is a testament to the depth of her emotions, a visual representation of the love and pain that has shaped her journey.

As she wipes away her tears, Melissa experiences a tightness in her chest, a physical manifestation of the torment she has been carrying for far too long.

Melissa finally arrives at the pizza restaurant, the aroma of baking dough and melted cheese hitting her instantly and grabs a steaming hot slice of pepperoni and sausage pizza and a Coksi. "Well, hello Madam Speaker." A man, roughly Melissa's age, her accent thick with the lilting sounds of Italy, says,

"Please Giovanni. You serve me pizza. You know my favorite soda and you also know my..."

"Condition." Giovanni looks down. As Melissa perceives Giovanni's gaze moving from the floor to her, a rush of warmth spreads through her body. She perceives her heart rate quickening, sending a surge of adrenaline coursing through her veins. A tingling sensation dances along her skin, causing her to shiver slightly despite the warmth of the room.

"You know more about me than my family at this point." Her voice sounded depressed, carrying a heavy weight and changing the atmosphere. The sadness in her tone was palpable, casting a somber shadow over the room. Her usual lively and bright voice now sounded muffled and distant, struggling with emotional turmoil. Those around could feel the weight of her words in the air, creating unease and vulnerability. The physical effects of her emotions were evident as her shoulders slumped, posture drooping. The heaviness of her emotions seemed to impact her physical presence, making her seem smaller and more fragile. "So please call me Melissa."

"Well, how goes the third most powerful person in the United States?"

"Please, if I had any power, Kathleen would be in the psych ward."

Melissa feels a warm, tingling sensation relieving tension and stress. Her laughter fills the room with lightness and joy. Each chuckle relaxes her muscles and brightens her eyes with a smile. The physical act of laughing also increases blood flow, releasing endorphins that boosts her mood and overall well-being. As she finishes her slice of pizza and soda, the combination of Giovanni's laughter and delicious food leaves her feeling content and at ease, a sense of comfort and connection enveloping her at the moment. "Well, I've got to go. More House business. You know you're better than a psychologist."

Melissa gets out of her seat while Giovanni says, "Am I." Melissa walks towards the door and turns around.

"Yeah. They don't serve pizza." Melissa smiles.

As Melissa stands at the foot of the Capitol steps, a combination of emotions surges through her body. The overwhelming joy of the impending arrival of her great-grandchild ignites a warm glow in her chest, causing her heart to flutter with anticipation. But intertwined with that joy is a lingering heaviness, a burden of unresolved issues that tugs at her heartstrings.

Her husband's death and her own mortality prompted her retirement from the House. She eagerly anticipates full family immersion, embracing daughter, granddaughter, and newest member.

The walk and friendship with Giovanni allow her to calm the storm within, to find solace in the rhythmic cadence of her footsteps. The cool breeze brushes against her cheeks, drying the remnants of her tears and offering a sense of tranquility.

As she returns to the majestic Capitol building, she inhales the crisp, clean air, noticing the faint scent of freshly cut grass. As usual, she salutes the flag.

Melissa thinks about the upcoming election certification, which is significant. It signifies the start of a new era with Jill becoming the President-Elect. Melissa feels hopeful for America's healing and a fresh start. She feels a sense of responsibility for contributing to this new chapter.

As Melissa ascends the Capitol steps, the warm sunlight bathes the grand building. But her astonishment grows as she reaches the top and discovers the unexpected crowd of people bustling around.

The sight strikes a chord within Melissa, a reminder of the countless lives touched by the decisions made within these walls. It reinforces the weight of her role as a representative, a steward of people's hopes and dreams. With renewed determination, she takes a deep breath and steps forward, ready to face the forthcoming events with unwavering resolve. Upon reaching the Capitol, Melissa climbs the steps, soaking in the sunlight. Much to her astonishment, she finds the Capitol alive with an unexpected crowd of people. Tourists and visitors dot the area, jotting down notes and capturing the essence of this historic place. She insists on having seen this identical crowd repeatedly this week.

Chapter Twenty-Six

December 28, 2124

The sun glints off the White House windows, casting a warm glow on the manicured lawn, where freshly cut grass and flowers fill the air with their scent. William hears the distant hum of security details and the click-clack of heels on the marble floors, as a sense of pride and responsibility washes over him. Standing at the entrance, he is ready to lead the nation.

"Think of it Amanda. Beginning in January, no more tension and life or death situations." She can feel the tension in William's embrace, his muscles tight with the weight of their impending departure. The surrounding room seems to blur as emotions swirl within them, the air heavy with the unspoken goodbye that hangs between them. The physical effects of their emotions are evident as they embrace: Amanda feels a lump in her throat, while William experiences a knot in his stomach. They both feel a warm tingle spreading through their bodies as they cling to each other, cherishing the moment in their former home.

"I'm sure the fish are already on red alert." Amanda Chavez, the First Lady of the United States, voices.

"I'm just looking forward to spending quality time with my grandchildren and creating many wonderful memories together. He finds fulfillment and warmth in sharing joy with loved ones.

"You can go on and on about that imaginary fifty-pound fish you supposedly caught."

"I caught it."

"You can only wish; it exists solely within the confines of your dreams."

As the conversation continues, a playful smirk forms on their faces, accompanied by a lightness in their eyes and a subtle chuckle escaping their lips. The mention of the non-existent ten pounder they claim to have caught seems to bring a sense of excitement and amusement to the atmosphere. Their body language shifts with animated gestures and a relaxed posture, reflecting the joy and satisfaction they feel in sharing this whimsical tale. The imagined weight of the fish seems to lift their spirits, filling the air with a sense of lightheartedness and camaraderie. The shared laughter and banter create a bond between them as they revel in the joy of a shared moment of playful storytelling.

William cast his eyes about the room, his attention flitting from one thing to another in a thorough examination of his environment. "I never thought I would say this, especially after the eight years of life it took from me. But I'll miss the place." As William and Amanda embrace, a wave of bittersweet emotions washes over them. Nostalgia and longing weigh on William's chest, a reminder of the place filled with memories, both joyful and painful. His eyes glisten with unshed tears, reflecting the internal struggle he faces in saying goodbye.

"I won't. I will finally get my husband back," she says, feeling relief as her husband's presence replaces past burdens. Leaning in to kiss him, she feels her heart flutter with joy.

"Now and forever." Their emotions manifest in subtle physical ways - a quiver in William's voice, a tremble in Amanda's hands. Intense emotions hang heavy in the air.

"I'm curious when we might expect to see Jill."

"The schedule says about ten. Just in time for lunch."

"I feel sorry for her. All this talk about the election. I heard she had to take her kids out of school because of threats."

"You remember her campaign promise of visiting all fifty-two states? She had to cancel them."

"I have no doubt about that whatsoever. I've seen the television..."

"Oh, I believe there may be a misunderstanding; allow me to clarify. Despite any reservations or concerns, her interest in going on the tour has not diminished but because of concerns for her safety, her security detail canceled the events. I hold her in the highest regard and have a tremendous amount of respect for her."

Amanda's laughter, unrestrained and joyous, fills the air with a sudden, bright burst of sound. "Not too long ago you called her that damn woman."

"I'm the President. As I gain more information and experience, I am fully within my rights to alter my perspectives and beliefs regarding Ms. Lunden. Speaking of which, computer. Television protocol. All televisions to be silenced for five hours, starting at noon."

"Your communication has been received and acknowledged."

With a steady gaze, Amanda looks directly at William, her expression unreadable. "I don't want to add more stress during her visit."

"That's why I love you, thinking about others." Amanda gives him a kiss.

"Hon, you look good." Jill feels a warm surge of happiness and love wash over her at Steve's compliment. Pleasure and embarrassment flushed her cheeks. She smiled gratefully at Steve. His affection made her glow with joy.

"I truly value your kind words and I appreciate you taking the time to say that to me. I have, however, taken the time to examine my appearance in a mirror. The person who looks back at me. I could've sworn that it was my grandmother. My children's and Tracy's welfare concern me. Oh, my goodness, I'm so worried; I have absolutely no clue where she might be right now."

The weight of worry and fear settles heavily in his chest, causing his heart to race and his breath to become shallow. He tried to appear calm, but his trembling hands told a different story. The uncertainty of the situation was making him increasingly anxious. Sadness overwhelms him, weighing down his limbs and making movement difficult. A lump formed in his throat, choking back the threatening surge of emotion. Unshed tears stung his eyes, mirroring his inner turmoil. A storm of conflicting emotions threatened to overwhelm him.

"I'm sure she's fine," Steve says. Jill can tell that he is lying as her heart races in panic and her mind fills with worst-case scenarios. The surge of fear causes her hands to tremble and her breathing to become shallow. Her stomach ties itself in knots, aching with worry for Tracy's well-being. A heavy sense of dread constricts her chest, and the unknown heightens her tension. The rush of emotions threatens to overwhelm her, her feeling physically drained and emotionally exhausted.

"Look dear, I appreciate you trying to make me feel better, but the longer she is missing, the more likely she's..."

Jill's voice trembles as she speaks, her chest constricting with a heavy weight of worry. Tears threaten to spill from her eyes, blurring her vision as her emotions take hold of her. Her heart pounds in her chest, aching with the fear of the unknown. Each passing moment of uncertainty feels like a physical burden, weighing down on her shoulders and making it hard to breathe. The stress of the situation is visible in the tension of her body, with her muscles tight and rigid with anxiety.

"Don't think like that. There's a chance she's taking some time off for a vacation, engaging in leisure activities, or simply taking a break. I want you to believe that until someone tells you otherwise. Ok."

"OK." Jill feels a wave of relief washing over her as she listens to Steve's reassuring words. The tension that has been building up in her body slowly dissipates, allowing her muscles to relax. Her racing heart slows down, and she feels a sense of peace and comfort settling within her. Holding his hands anchors her. Overall, Jill's physical state shifts from one of worry and anxiety to one of calmness and reassurance.

"Ms. Lunden, look to your right," the driver says.

To the right, the White House gleams, its white stone shimmering under the warm autumn sun, the air crisp and cool. A feeling of awe and wonder washes over Jill as she takes in the majestic sight before her.

"Breathtaking," they both whisper, the sheer scale and history of the building making them speechless.

As the car gets closer, Jill hears the cries of protesters. Some are crying 'Traitor' while others are saying 'True winner'. A person throws a tomato at the car. The sound of the impact brings Jill memories of a rock being thrown, glass breaking, and a note that says, "You're a dead bitch. You and your family." Soon after that, she calls Ms. Dissaldorph.

"While we love having Rachel and Henry and hope to have them until the inauguration, I understand the need for their safety. Tell you what, we can still teach them over their palm tops. For what it's worth, no one believes you stole the election."

"Thank you. I know that Rachel and Henry want to say goodbye to their friends..."

"We can always do a video conference. We need to arrange a time.

"That will be great."

"Please take care of yourself and be well, Jill." Ms. Dissaldorph signs off.

Jill's emotional distress manifests physically; she cries, and the tightness in her chest makes breathing difficult. Each sob shakes her body, intensifying the tension in her muscles. The weight of her emotions seems to physically burden her, as if she is carrying a heavy load on her shoulders. As her heart races with a mix of emotions, her body responds by releasing adrenaline, making her feel jittery and on edge. Her throat is so tight she can barely speak or swallow. The tears stinging her eyes add to the physical discomfort caused by her emotional distress.

The knot in her stomach, a common physical response to stress and anxiety, shows the profound impact the situation is having on her. It feels as though her body is in a state of fight or flight, reacting to the emotional pain she is enduring.

Overall, Jill's body is a canvas for her emotions, each physical reaction mirroring the intensity of her inner turmoil. The mind-body connection is undeniable as she navigates through the overwhelming mix of anger, frustration, and sadness that consumes her.

"Ms. Lunden, we are here," the driver says, which breaks her from her memory.

Jill takes a deep breath.

"Showtime."

William and Amanda wait outside for Jill's limo to arrive. William has never met Jill Lunden in person. Despite this, he deeply respects her resilience.

"You look nervous," Amanda says.

"Well, it's not every day you meet your replacement."

"Only for this job, and don't you forget it."

"Yes ma'am. Here they come."

Jill and Steve step out of the car, the gravel crunching beneath their feet. William notices the changes in Jill's appearance, showing the toll of the ongoing controversy. Her face has worried lines and a sense of weariness. Despite looking older and exhausted, Jill still displays resilience. Her posture is strong, and her eyes hold determination. She seems to have turned her emotions into a source of strength. Even in tough times, she exudes a commanding presence that captivates onlookers.

"God, she looks older than you," Amanda says.

"Have you seen the television sets? Her friend is missing. She receives threatening messages and has to take her kids out of school. The belief that the election was stolen is stressing her a lot. I remember when I won, the only stress I had was filling my cabinet. That she still goes out in public speaks volumes to me." Steve comes out. "Her husband seems fine, although."

"That's because he's not a mother." Amanda remembers the several times when she hears of a school shooting, wondering if her kids are fine.

"What does that mean?"

"It means that you are not carrying a person inside you for nine months."

"Touche." William surrenders.

Jill finally arrives at the top of the stairs. "Welcome to the White House Jill, and Steve, isn't it?" William says.

Jill looks around and then extends her hand. "Don't you mean that damn woman?" Jill says with a hint of a smile.

"Please, that is the past. Now is the time to look into the future."

Jill looks at Steve. "See, I tell you he can't take a joke." She looks back at William. "Compared to what people are saying about me now. I guess I can handle that damn woman. You must be Amanda." Jill shakes her hand.

"Will, that's what it says on my driver's license and birth certificate." Jill and Amanda laugh.

"A little Ying to his Yang."

"You know the saying about opposites? And this must be Steve Lunden, whom I have the fortune of giving the tour."

Jill looks at Amanda. "Don't forget he's taken."

Amanda looks at William and takes his arm. She says, "I've shared nearly fifty years with this. Believe me, your husband is safe."

Amanda looks at Jill and Jill can see that she can understand a joke. She says, "Well Mr. President. This is your show, so lead me on."

"Right this way."

Jill is awestruck, completely captivated by the building's timeless elegance and the sheer beauty of its design. Despite seeing numerous photos and videos of the White House in various magazines and online platforms before, experiencing it in person exceeds all her expectations.

"Quite a sight," William says.

"Yes."

"I had that feeling when Morrow showed me the tour."

"When does that feeling go away?"

"I'll let you know." They take an elevator. "This is my favorite spot. The bowling alley, but I've done my research on you and I think I know what your favorite area will be." He then takes her to the movie theater. This is necessary, given the inherent risks of a presidential theater appearance.

"You didn't do all your research. My theater comment refers to Broadway. Oh, I love the occasional movie and I'm sure my family will use this often."

"Will, I guess we can continue?" William leads Jill to the Oval Office.

Jill stands in shock. The many pictures Jill has seen of the office don't do it justice. On the carpet, they display the presidential seal in the office. The ancient lamps and couches. In the center is the Resolute Desk. A leather-seated chair sits behind a powerful desk, telephone and paperwork present.

"Want to sit in it?"

"I shouldn't."

"Please, after January 20th, all this is yours."

Jill sits in the chair, feeling the history of several Presidents and decisions coursing through her. She looks around and sees a photo that catches her eye. It is William, Amanda, and a baby in the hospital.

"Is this little Rebecca?"

"Yes," William says in sadness.

"I read your autobiography. I'm so sorry if I hit a nerve. It's just that it's a very moving chapter. Especially what happens after that?"

"I don't want to discuss it."

"I understand. When Steve is ten, a school shooting kills his baby brother. It destroys his parents. When we had a boy, he insisted on naming him Henry."

"Will, I think we're done having children." William gives a little chuckle. "However, my granddaughter's middle name is Rebecca."

"Well, last I checked, your daughter Chelsea has a boyfriend but no kids. Must be your son, Diego, or your other daughter, Maria."

"Both actually. You have read my autobiography."

"Well, I don't know about you, but I could use some lunch."

Amanda and Steve walk around the Rose Garden. "You're saying that some idiot paved over the garden for this stupid patio?"

"Yes, about a century ago."

"Too bad. Jill wants to see the garden."

"So, tell me. How is Jill? I see her on television during the campaign..."

"She attempts a brave facade. But I can tell that she's stressed over these allegations. She's also depressed over the deaths because of the allegations. Add to that the threats to the children and her friend missing..."

"Ms. Kincaid. The person who made the recording."

"I see you've done your homework. Yes, Jill is terrified about Tracy's disappearance."

"Poor woman. I remember when my best friend died. She doesn't even have that knowledge. I feel sorry for her."

Steve grabs a rock and throws it at the patio in a fit of rage. **"Well, you're in the minority.** I'm so sorry. Many people believe in this Cain person. Whoever she or he is. The worst part is that I talked her into running when the Democrats asked her about it."

"Running for President means being away from you and the kids. Especially during the primaries," Steve recalls Jill saying.

"We can make do. Besides, I know you. If you don't run, you'll wonder what could have been. Consider the future of our children and grandchildren if not for yourself."

Amanda brings him back to the present. His expression shows fury at the rumors surrounding his wife. But Amanda can also see the guilt for talking her into throwing her hat in the ring and the love he feels for Jill.

"You know, I talked William into running. He gave the same reasons to me that Jill gave to you. Maybe we should listen to them rather than them listening to us."

Steve laughs. "Thank you. I needed a good laugh. Eventually, Jill would have run, anyway. You also know that William would have. It's in their nature. It just makes me angry to see the vibrant woman who I convinced to run becoming a shell of her former self,"

Amanda pats Steve's shoulder. "You wouldn't be in love with her if it didn't."

As Amanda speaks, Steve feels a surge of warmth spreading through his chest, a mix of affection and protectiveness for the woman he loves. The anger he feels towards seeing her change is like a fierce fire burning within him, causing his muscles to tense and his heart to race. He can almost feel the weight of his emotions physically, as if they are tangible forces pushing and pulling at him. Amanda's comforting touch on his shoulder provides a momentary sense of relief, a grounding reminder of her presence and support in the midst of his turbulent feelings. The intensity of his emotions is palpable, leaving him with a sense of both vulnerability and strength as he grapples with his love and anger intertwining within him.

"Thank you. Jill has been determined to find Tracy and I fear for her and our children's safety. Kind of hard talking to her about everything." Steve and Amanda walk towards the house.

She then looks at her watch. "Well, it's time for lunch."

Chapter Twenty-Seven

T he scent of freshly cut flowers and polished wood creates the welcoming atmosphere of the dining hall. Inside the grand room, the soft clinking of silverware against plates echoes, while intricate designs and sparkling crystal glasses adorn the table, exuding elegance and refinement. Past events linger in the air, adding a touch of nostalgia to the ambiance, as the flickering candlelight casts a warm glow and creates dancing shadows on the walls. Plush velvet chairs invite guests to sink into their softness, while delicate floral arrangements add a pop of color to the elegant setting. Tantalizing aromas from the kitchen fill the air, hinting at the culinary delights to come, making the overall atmosphere a feast for all the senses.

Jill suddenly realizes she has never been in this dining room before. Memories return, causing her heart to beat rapidly and sending waves of adrenaline through her veins. A knot forms in her stomach, weighing her down like lead, as her palms grow clammy and a cold sweat breaks out on her forehead. The tension in her muscles makes her keenly aware of the immense burden she carries, and every breath is shallow and strained, as if her lungs couldn't fully expand. The emotional turmoil takes a toll on her body, manifesting in physical reactions that mirror the intensity of her feelings.

Inside, Amanda and Steve are already present. Steve appears more relaxed than during the tour, with his shoulders no longer tense and his jaw unclenched, exuding a sense of calmness and releasing stress. Amanda's unchanged expression may hide a storm of emotions swirling beneath the surface, possibly a mix of anxiety, apprehension, or uncertainty.

As Jill approaches her husband, she senses the palpable shift in his energy, recognizing the weight of his newfound relaxation and finding comfort in his improved state.

"Nice tour and talk."

"You can say that although someone in the past paved over the Rose Garden."

"I could have sworn I told you that ages ago. When I first visited the place."

"You might have. I just hoped that someone would have restored it."

"I'll do that during my first ten days in office," Jill says. Jill's laughter catches in her throat, causing her chest to tighten with fear. This makes her heart race and her breathing quicken. A cold sweat breaks out on her forehead, and a wave of nausea washes over her. Her hands tremble as weakness and unsteadiness overcome her body because of the surge of adrenaline in reaction to her growing fear. The physical effects of her emotions are palpable, manifesting in a cascade of physiological reactions that leave her feeling overcome and vulnerable.

"What about you? Did you have a friendly talk with the President?"

"You know, I must have been in the White House several times, but I never remember it being so glorious. I guess that's the difference between being a professional in the building and being a sort of tourist. It feels, new," Jill says.

"It's amazing how perspectives change based on our roles and experiences, isn't it?" Steve says.

"Wait till you're the President," William says, overhearing everything.

"January 20th can't come soon enough," Jill responds.

Everyone takes their seats.

The lunch menu delights William, with the sizzle of the steak filling the air, accompanied by the mouth-watering aroma of cooking meat. This makes his stomach growl in anticipation as he savors the familiar scent. The sight of the perfectly cooked steak and eggs makes his mouth water, and he can almost sense the juicy flavors just by looking at them. Curious, he asks, "Do you always have steak and eggs for lunch?" Steve responds with a delighted chuckle, savoring the flavor, and a bright smile spread across his face.

"No, my daughter and my head medical pain in the ass have me on a diet. But she's not here right now." Amanda's gaze pierces through William, her eyes burning with a mix of frustration and disbelief. The tension in the room is palpable, causing a tightness in William's chest as he tries to decipher the emotions swirling in Amanda's eyes. His heart rate quickens, the adrenaline coursing through his veins, as he braces himself for her next words. Her intense gaze acts as a physical force, pressing down on him as he struggles to maintain his composure.

As Jill takes a bite, she suddenly leaps in her seat when the chef appears beside her, his metallic red body gleaming in the sunlight. He reaches out with outstretched hands, his robotic voice a monotone hum asking Jill a question. Her adrenaline surged as her heart pounded. Her hands tremble as she struggles to swallow the bite of food, her breath quickening in response to the unexpected presence of the chef. Goosebumps prickling her skin, a wave of fear washes over her, causing her muscles to tense up. The sudden jolt of surprise also makes her lightheaded, as if her body is trying to process the shock of the moment. To compose herself, Jill experiences a mix of emotions swirling inside her, from anxiety to curiosity, all resulting in various physical reactions.

Jill recovers herself. "Oh, you're cute." Jill's heart flutters as she blurts out the words, feeling a rush of warmth spreading through her body. Her cheeks flush a rosy hue, and a radiant smile illuminates her face, her eyes sparkling with adoration. The physical effects of her overwhelming emotion are clear in the way her body seems to tingle with excitement, her pulse quickening as she gazes at the object of her affection. A surge of happiness envelops her, filling her with a sense of lightness and joy.

William says, "Meet my other health professional, the Chef. My daughter programmed him to make foods that would lower my cholesterol."

Steve looks at the steak and eggs. "How do you explain this, then?" Steve asks.

"I've worked around the chef." Amanda gives William another look.

"And when Chelsea finds out..."

As Amanda's words sink in, a knot forms in William's stomach. "She'll watch me like a hawk. We'll cross that bridge when it comes." He can almost taste the bitterness of the impending confrontation with Chelsea, the weight of his actions settling on his shoulders. His appetite diminishes as the thought of no longer indulging in his favorite dishes looms over him, a pang of regret tugging at his heart. Heavy air hangs, charged with unspoken consequences of his choices. William knows a storm is approaching, and he senses the storm clouds gathering above him, casting a shadow over his usual carefree demeanor.

"I'm sorry if I startled you," the chef says to Jill.

"No, I need to apologize for my reaction," she says, her voice still carrying a hint of tension.

"If you must. Since you will take over the duties of Mr. Chavez in January. May I ask about your preferred choice of dishes, are Mrs. Lunden?"

Despite her lingering unease, Jill maintains a polite demeanor. She understands that her initial reaction might have seemed exaggerated, and she doesn't want to cause discomfort for the chef. Deep inside, however, she can't rid herself of the sensation of constantly being cautious, forever prepared for the unforeseen. "The kids will eat anything that comes their way. Steve is allergic to Strawberry seeds." Steve looks a little embarrassed. "But my favorite dishes are mostly seafood. I haven't really thought about it. I will have to program a list after the inauguration."

"As you wish," the robotic chef leaves.

William looks at Jill. "You have to forgive the chef."

"I have nothing against that cute robot. I just never think about a White House menu," she says.

"I know he likes to spring things," Amanda says.

"Are you okay, hon?" Steve asks.

"I'm fine." Slamming her hands on the table with a combination of fear and anger heightens Jill's senses. She becomes more aware of the sounds and movements around her, her breathing, turning shallow and rapid, her muscles tense and ready to react at any moment. Her body language exudes alertness, with her shoulders slightly raised and her back straight.

Jill notices everyone looking at her. She takes a bite of her steak. "This is very good."

After lunch, Jill and William stand silently behind two chairs, the only sound being the gentle ticking of a nearby clock.

William points Jill to the right chair, and he takes the left one. They share a glance and continue their conversation as the press takes pictures.

"So, what are you planning on doing after you leave the White House?" a press agent says.

"As I told our lovely first lady, I plan on spending as much time with my family," William replies.

"Jill, what do you plan on doing during your first few months?" the same agent asks.

"That's easy. I locate Cain and discover his information source," Jill responds. William can see a look of defeatism in her voice as she speaks.

'She doesn't think that she will find Cain and I can't blame her. My best people haven't found that asshole yet.'

"What about the recording and the convenient disappearance of Tracy Kincaid?"

Jill's composure impresses William as she reacts to her friend's name, her intense focus and vigilance reminding him of a military general always on guard for potential threats.

"I don't know what has happened to Tracy. Perhaps she's vacationing," Jill replies. She feels her pulse race and a cold sweat appear on her brow. The uncertainty of Tracy's whereabouts weighs heavily on her, manifesting in a furrowed brow and clenched fists. The subtle tremor betrays the lack of conviction in her voice and in her hands, a physical manifestation of her growing apprehension. With each passing moment of silence from Tracy, Jill's body tenses, ready to spring into action at any sign of trouble.

"Thank you. That's all we have for today," William says as he gets out of his chair. The reporters leave.

William looks at Jill. "I'm sorry for that."

Jill is saying softly, "You don't think I haven't heard the rumors. That I killed Tracy. That I paid her to leave the United States. I just want her back. She's like a sister to me." As Jill speaks, her voice quivers with the weight of her emotions, her words laced with a mix of desperation and sadness. The muscles in her face tense, her brows furrowing as she struggles to contain the storm of feelings raging within her. Her racing heart mirrors the chaos within her mind. The tears welling up in her eyes spill over, tracing a path down her cheeks as her body betrays her, unable to hold back the flood of emotions any longer. A lump forms in her throat, making it difficult to speak as the raw intensity of her emotions threatens to overwhelm her. Each breath she takes feels like a struggle, as if the weight of her emotions is pressing down on her chest, making it hard to find solace amid her turmoil.

"I understand." The memory floods William with a bittersweet mix of emotions as a wave of grief washes over him. It manifests as a heavy ache in his chest and a lump in his throat, causing his eyes to well up with tears and blur his vision as he recalls the delicate touch of Rebecca's tiny hand. The weight of sorrow seems to press down on his shoulders, making it difficult to breathe. Amidst the sorrow, a sense of tenderness and warmth spreads through him, gently reminding him of the love for his daughter. Mixed with this sorrow is a flicker of hope, a fleeting thought that one day he will see his beloved daughter again, at least knowing the fate of his daughter. In contrast, Jill doesn't even have that for her best friend.

"I want to thank you for keeping the televisions off. I know Jill has felt pain in her chest every time someone has died because of Cain," Steve says.

"You and Jill take care. We'll see you at the inauguration," Amanda says and gives Steve and Jill a kiss on the cheek.

William looks at Jill. "You know, during the campaign I thought little about you, as you can recall. You were going up against my Vice-President. But I must admit. With everything you have gone through. I doubt I could go out into public, let alone do press conferences."

"It is difficult. Everyone is thinking the worst of me. I just hope that Tracy comes back and announces the recording as fraud. I also hope that following the inauguration, our country can find its way back to normalcy."

With a laugh, William responds, "Whatever that may be." The physical effects of her anxiety dissipate, replaced by a pleasant and soothing sensation. The laughter eases her troubled mind, providing a temporary escape from the chaos.

"Amanda goes to Jill. I hope your friend also shows up. I've had friends in my life. Some are still alive and some are dead. But I never had one like the way you describe your friendship with Ms. Kincaid. It must be killing you, the unknown."

"Every day."

"Take care." Amanda gives Jill a hug. Then Jill and Steve head back to the limo.

William and Amanda go back into the White House.

"She's a sturdy woman," William says.

"Maybe," Amanda says, expressing her hope that Jill's friend will indeed come back. She can't fathom the anguish Jill must be enduring. Amanda's inquiry, the one everyone avoided, finally surfaces: "What do you think the chances are of her still being alive?" William, grasping his wife's hands, reveals his pessimism about the situation.

Hilda Smithson anxiously awaits the DNA results for the unfortunate woman, whose death triggers memories of her studies on Jack the Ripper. She ponders the identity of the victim as she reviews her notes, questioning who could have committed such a heinous crime. In pursuit of a clue, she investigates other cases and finds a like pattern - a woman named Laura Kelly experienced a similar demise. Ms. Kelly, she learns, was once Daniel's former campaign manager. Despite the instant availability of results through eye mail, Hilda still prefers the traditional paper copies. When asked about her preference for avoiding eye phones, she explains, "Those things give me painful headaches, not to mention I like things I can hold in my hands."

"Your just old fashion." her assistant says frequently. She wishes he were here and not on vacation.

The only mail carrier, a male about twenty-five years old, delivers the mail. She expresses her gratitude as she grabs the envelope, and he departs. She then looks through the papers. After a moment, she spots what she is searching for. "Well, that can't be a coincidence," she remarks.

Chapter Twenty-Eight

T he sight of the planes gleaming in the evening light is mesmerizing, with anticipation mounting as the intensifying hum of engines fuels excitement that fills the air. The crisp autumn air, scented with jet fuel, invigorates the senses. A gentle breeze suggests adventure, and the temperature seems ideal for a new beginning. Upon arrival on the plane, someone is waiting for them. Jill immediately goes on alert, looking for any sign of trouble.

"Mr. and Mrs. Jones." the person says, which calms Jill a little. Jones is the name that the Chavez's give Jill and Steve rather than their real names.

"Are you sure that's really necessary?" Jill asks while planning with William Chavez to visit the White House.

"Given the current climate of uncertainty and concern, I am strongly convinced this is an essential step."

Without a moment's hesitation and with no reservations of any kind, Steve readily offers his complete agreement.

"That's us," Steve states matter-of-factly, showing him and Jill with a subtle nod of his head.

"The plane is ready and we can lift off when you are ready."

Jill and Steve step onto the plush carpet of the private plane, the scent of leather and expensive polish filling their nostrils.

"Ladies and Gentlemen, please buckle up as we are preparing to taxi." With a surge of power, the plane rapidly speeds up down the runway, and then suddenly, they are airborne, the ground falling away beneath them.

Steve says, "It's kind of President Chavez to find a personal airplane for us."

Jill's heart rate quickens, her chest tightens, and a rush of adrenaline courses through her veins. A whirlwind of emotions clouds her mind, making it difficult for her to focus on anything but the overwhelming feelings. Lost in the intensity of her emotions, she sees the world blur, and her inner turmoil consumes her.

"What's the matter, dear? I thought William and Amanda were excellent hosts."

"They were. It's just..."

"You're worried about the kids."

"Well, of course I am. I removed them from school because America Now supporters threatened them. The rock broke that window, the incident in Portland, and all those poll workers that were killed or missing..."

"None of which is your fault. You intend to blame someone, put it on Cain, Daniel, or both."

"It's not just that. What if Tracy did rig the election? Suppose that recording is authentic. What if Tracy's departure was caused by her actions? I thought I knew her. Yes, she is pretty loose in following the rules, but I thought she was honest. Remember, during the election, how she always blew up? What if she left because she stressed about rigging everything?"

"Hon, you said yourself that Tracy or anyone else has enough money or resources to rig an election. Even if by some chance Tracy rigged one state, she couldn't rig all of them. You win because you're a good person and the best choice for the United States. Can you imagine if Daniel wins the election? He would destroy the United States in two months. That's why the people elect you. Because intelligent people see through Daniel's bullshit."

Jill looks outside. She sees only land below. Nice green land. "You know, from my vantage point, everything appears calm. You can't tell that the country is tearing itself apart. If I can, I would love to have my entire term in the air."

"You are a person who is relatable to others. To understand their needs and act in their best interest."

Jill snuggles close to Steve. She can hear his heartbeat. Their gaze rises to the television, where they see "breaking news."

"Television increases sound factor 40," Jill says.

"We can now confirm that the recording is that of Tracy Kincaid." A wave of despair washes over Jill, leaving her breathless and numb with despair. "However, we have confirmed that the sentence syntax is off. We conclude that the recording in question was a spliced conversation."

The expert, a man with short, white hair, meticulously traces the lines of the diagram, explaining each detail. It's all things outside Jill and Steve's understanding, technology too complex for their minds to grasp.

"So, you're saying that the recording is not valid?" Jill recognizes the anchor as Mark Esper.

"It's a fake. Brought together by changing the sentence structure of the words. I have brought this up to the five most distinguished sentence structure professionals in the world and they agree with my findings," the white-haired man says.

"Well, thank you."

"Television off." Jill's voice, thin as a spider's thread, barely registers above the silence of her sorrow.

"Well, there you go," Steve says, intertwining his hands with Jill.

"The recording is a fake. Tracy didn't rig the election," Jill's voice rings with a bright, infectious cheer, her eyes sparkling.

"I can't believe the nightmare is over."

"It's not over. Do you believe America Now will simply accept that statement?"

The realization sets in that the nightmare might not be truly over. A chill runs down her spine, sending shivers through her body. Fearful anticipation of what is next makes Jill's heart race, breath quicken, and hands tremble. The emotional rollercoaster she's on seems to have no end in sight, leaving her depleted and overwhelmed.

"They really have no choice," Steve says. Silently, he admits Jill is right. Supporters of Daniel Thompson will accept nothing short of surrender. "On January 6th, they will confirm you as the next President of the United States."

"Tracy is still missing." Jill moves her head to see Steve 's face. Jill experiences her heart fluttering in her chest, a gentle rhythm that mirrors the love that surges within her. The warmth of their touch spreads through her veins, calming the chaos that surrounds them. Despite the uncertainty of their circumstances, a sense of solace washes over her, knowing that Steve is by her side.

"Remember until we hear otherwise? She is on vacation," Steve says, watching Jill, experiencing admiration and affection, hindering his speech. A warmth diffuses through his body, and he senses a tingling in his fingertips, as if their connection is electrifying.

"You don't believe that any more than I do,"

Jill looks at Steve and his expression confirms what she says. He is just trying to protect her.

"Thank you for saying those things. I love you, Steve. I just want nothing to happen to you and the kids," Jill says as Steve just looks at her. He still sees sorrow and fear in her eyes.

"Nothing is going to happen to me or our family. Despite everything that is going on. I can't picture my life without you," Steve says. They continue to hold hands.

"Ladies and gentlemen, please fasten your seatbelts for our final descent," the pilot calmly announces. The plane begins its descent, the engine's hum fading as the air pressure changes.

Vice President Bill Nelson and Amanda walk into the Oval Office; the hushed reverence of the room is remarkable, a silence broken only by the gentle ticking of a clock, William sitting silently behind the Resolute Desk.

"Did you hear the news?" Bill says.

"I hear a lot of things. So, you have to be more precise."

"The tape recording is a fake. They spliced the recording from some conversation."

"Give me a couple of minutes and then have my press secretary come in." Bill leaves the room. William looks at Amanda.

"While it's the first good news in some time, I doubt it will change anything."

"You think that Daniel's supporters people won't believe it?"

"Tell something long enough. Soon people will believe it. Daniel has been saying that the recording is genuine. Someone stole the election. Many people believe it and we've all seen where that leads to. But enough about Daniel, Cain and America Now. I wonder where Jill and Steve are right now?"

As Amanda checks the time, the city's vibrant, chaotic hum nearly obliterates the faint tick of her watch.

"They should land anytime now. Chef says dinner should be ready in five minutes."

William's warm hand envelops Amanda's, his reassuring pat, a spark of happiness in her otherwise bleak week.

"I'll be there soon. I just have one thing to do."

"Don't be too late, you know chef hates to reheat." Amanda's kiss is a burst of sunshine, a warm explosion that leaves William breathless and smiling.

With Amanda gone, William pulls out the first draft of the letter but quickly discards it. He then extends his hand towards the shelf, grabs a fresh sheet of paper, and begins writing.

President Lunden, by the time you read this letter, I will have already left the White House. I understand things appear bleak at the moment. Based on what I have seen today, you are the ray of light that will keep America running. I am certain that you have what it takes to rise to the challenge. I do not envy you. Be true to yourself and recognize that not everyone will approve of you. We expect that. You may fall but also be two inches taller when you pick yourself up. You have my respect.

Sincerely, William Chavez.

William folds the letter, seals it in a cream envelope, and then puts it in his heavy mahogany Resolute desk.

The drive home appears endless; The familiar streets blur in her vision as her mind replays the worst-case scenarios of what could have happened to Tracy. Fear and disgust war within her, twisting her gut into a nauseous knot that threatens to send the little food she has consumed rushing back up.

"I can't wait to see the kids and give them the gifts from President Chavez. I want to hold them in my arms and know they are safe. Can't we just go get them?" Jill says.

"Let them have the time to spend with their friends. Might be their last."

"You're probably right. Cain may know travels plans, poll workers and Secretary of State addresses. But that monster wouldn't know the addresses of our kids' friends. I hope." The uncertainty causes Jill's hands to tremble as she attempts to put her finger to the door. The weight of anxiety presses down on her chest, making it hard to breathe. Her heart races, pounding against her ribcage as if trying to break free. The threats in her voicemails echo in her mind, heightening her fear and causing a cold sweat to break out on her forehead. Upon arriving at their house, the once comforting surroundings now appear suffocating. Jill's steps falter as she moves from room to room, searching for any sign of danger. The lack of communication from Tracy only fuels her imagination, creating nightmarish scenarios that seem all too real.

"We can contact the children. Will that ease your anxiety?"

Jill's nod is a weak, trembling affirmation, her gaze distant and hopeless.

"Phone call Rachel and Henry. Three-way communication." Steve says.

"Hi mom and dad." Both kids say.

"How was the trip to the White House?" Rachel asks.

"Did you get us anything?" Henry jumps in.

"Everything went fine." Jill's voice, now lighter, dances with unrestrained glee, like a bird taking flight.

"Are you ok?"

"I'm fine. Just listening to some music." Rachel says.

"Watching a science fiction show," Henry says.

"We'll pick you up at ten, isn't it?" Steve says.

Henry says, "Actually, can you make it noon? Ms. Sanderson wants to take me to see some old fashion movie at the retro theater. Something about computer programs being people."

As Henry speaks, his excitement is palpable, his eyes lighting up and a wide grin spreading across his face. The anticipation of spending time with Ms. Sanderson and watching a movie that piques his interest causes a rush of adrenaline, making his heartbeat faster and his hands slightly tremble with excitement. The thought of delving into the world of computer programs and their human-like qualities fills him with curiosity and intrigue, adding a touch of nervous energy to his already buzzing emotions.

"Sounds good and strange. Will do. Love you."

Jill repeats. "Love you."

"Love you." Both kids say and sign off.

"See, the kids are fine. They're having a wonderful time."

Jill's voice, barely a whisper, trembles with unspoken terror as she says, "Phone, messages. Specifically, those of Tracy Kincaid."

"No messages found," the computer says.

Jill's eyes dart to Steve, her breath catching in her throat as an icy dread washes over her. "Phone, delete any messages mentioning the threats to my life," Jill says.

"1550 messages deleted."

Jill lies on the couch, feeling exhausted from fear, anxiety, and uncertainty, as constant heightened emotions drain her energy. Despair overshadows her vibrant spirit, trapping her in fear and hopelessness, making her wonder how to find peace in the chaos of her life. Threatening voicemails and Tracy's absence haunt her, leaving her desperate for answers and hope.

In this moment, she looks at Steve, noticing he's speaking. "I'm sorry. What did you say?" she says as she walks towards the bedroom.

Steve notes, awed by the grandeur of the White House meeting, "It is impressive." Reflecting on President Chavez's mannerisms, he says, "During the election, he called you a little…"

Jill interjects, "Yeah, I'd rather forget that" as she unpacks her belongings, hearing the soft rustle of fabric and the clink of glass. The presents of President Chavez fills the quiet room.

"I know President Chavez has shown no acts of kindness during the campaign. Something I remind him of. But as he says, that is now in the past."

"Now that the recording is a confirmed fraud and I know the kids are safe. My one concern is to find Tracy." Jill throws her bag on the floor and cries. With a regretful sigh,

Jill says, "Look, I apologize for that outburst and any others over this long week. Tracy is still missing, and I haven't been getting much sleep." As she kicks off her shoes, Steve approaches her from behind, his arms wrapping around her midsection, offering comfort and security.

As he rubs her shoulders, his soothing voice fills the room. "Your shoulders are tense."

"Yours would be too if you had 1550 death threats. But then again, I only say those related to me." Steve understands the implications. He comes closer to her, his warm breath brushing against the curve of her ear. "Can I help ease your tension?" Jill looks at Steve.

As their lips meet, Jill senses a surge of electricity running through her body, the warmth of Steve's touch sending shivers down her spine and intensifying the fiery embrace between them. In a flurry of motion, she unleashes her pent-up energy, ripping the buttons from Steve's shirt with a satisfying rip. He gently removes her shirt, the silky fabric falling away to reveal her leopard-print bra. Feeling the light touch of her lips on his chest as she leans in, her body warm against his, he swiftly pulls off her bra. His mouth immediately covers her left breast, suckling and massaging her right breast, causing her nipples to become erect, her voice filled with excited cries. Just as she reaches for his belt, the phone's shrill ring pierces the air, and she curses under her breath, torn between desire and duty.

With a growl of frustration, she is saying, **"Phone answer."** As she sees herself topless. "No video." As her frustration intensifies, her heart rate quickens, causing her chest to rise and fall rapidly with each breath. The heat of desire flushes her cheeks and sends shivers down her spine, heightening her awareness of her own vulnerability. The raw intensity of her emotions is palpable in the way her body tenses, muscles coiled like a spring ready to release. Steve's longing gaze only adds fuel to the fire, his dark eyes reflecting the depth of his own desire, creating a charged atmosphere thick with unspoken longing and tension. The physical effects of their emotions manifest in subtle gestures and expressions, creating a silent dance of desire and restraint between them.

"Hello, this is Hilda Smithson, the Chief Medical Examiner for the State of Massachusetts. Am I speaking to Jill Lunden?" the voice on the other end asks. Jill's hand shakes as she snatches the receiver. The sudden silence amplifies the frantic beat of her heart.

"Yes, this is Jill Lunden." As she listens, her face blanches, the color draining from her cheeks. Her trembling hands reach up to wipe away the tears that continue to cascade down her flushed face. She drops the phone, her hands trembling. Steve's gaze sharpens, sensing danger in the air. Jill grabs the phone again. "I'm on my way." She chokes out.

"What is it?" Anxiety washes over him as he speaks. His heart races, palms sweat, and muscles tense. His body is on high alert for the response he expects, as Steve feels a knot forming in his stomach, a physical manifestation of the unease that grips him. Though he knows the answer, its potential consequences frighten him. This fear, a raging inner storm, sends shivers down his spine, each flash of uncertainty sparking adrenaline. A combination of anguish and disbelief overwhelms Jill, her pulse racing, and her breathing becoming shallow and irregular, while the room seems to spin around her, making her surroundings blur. Every part of her aches with distress, causing her body to slump under the weight, as the air in the room feels heavy with sorrow, making it suffocating. Gathering her strength, Jill steadies herself, knowing she needs to stay strong.

"They found Tracy. Someone murdered her." Jill's body trembles with a mix of fear and grief, her heart pounding in her ears as she struggles to process the news. The tears stream down her cheeks, feeling hot against her skin, contrasting with the chill that runs down her spine at the thought of facing the reality of Tracy's death. The weight in her chest seems to press down on her, making it hard to breathe as she tries to steady herself.

As she hurries to dress, her hands shake uncontrollably, fumbling with the buttons and zippers as her mind races with a jumble of thoughts and emotions. The cold sweat that coats her skin makes her clammy and weak, adding to the sense of disorientation and panic that threatens to overwhelm her. Each breath is shallow and strained, the air tasting sharp and metallic in her mouth.

"They're asking me to go to the coroner's office." A cold sweat slicks Jill's skin as she frantically tugs her clothes back on, her breath catching in her throat. "I will call when I know more."

"The hell you will." Steve looks for a fresh shirt. "I'm going with you."

"I can handle this on my own."

Steve takes Jill's shoulders. "I know you can. I'll be there to provide moral support."

Jill quickly kisses Steve, then they leave. Despite the turmoil raging inside her, Jill tries to focus on the task at hand, pushing aside her overwhelming emotions to prepare herself for the arduous journey ahead. The uncertainty of what lies ahead looms large, casting a shadow over her every movement as she braces herself for the painful truth awaiting her at the coroner's office.

Chapter Twenty-Nine

The rain beats against the windshield, creating a hypnotic rhythm, while the air is heavy with the scent of wet asphalt and freshly fallen rain. A knot of tension forms in Jill's stomach as the car races towards their destination, with the sound of the wipers swishing back and forth adding to the sense of urgency. Her fingers tap nervously on the armrest, her eyes fixed on the road ahead as the car's engine hums steadily, drowning out the sound of the rain outside. "It can't be her," Jill says, while Steve holds her. "That's it. It must be some mistake. Who would want to kill Tracy? She didn't have any enemies." She pushes the button. **"Can't this car go any faster?"**

Jill's heart races with anxiety and fear, her chest tight with the weight of disbelief and shock, as adrenaline courses through her veins. Her hands tremble as she grips her seat belt, urging the car to move faster. The blood drains from her face, leaving her pale and clammy, as the realization sinks in that someone, she cares about could be gone. Steve senses Jill's body tense against his, her breathing shallow and rapid, as she struggles to process the overwhelming emotions crashing over her. The world blurs around her, the outside noise fading into a distant hum as her focus narrows on the road ahead. She is desperate to get to the truth, to find some semblance of closure amid the chaos of the moment.

"We are going as fast as the law allows. Ms. Lunden."

"Thank you." Jill slams the pad.

"Jill, you might be right. Maybe the Medical Officer made a mistake. We will get there and it won't be Tracy and then we can go back home."

"You don't believe that for a second, do you?" She looks at Steve's eyes and face and knows the truth. "Hell, I'll go on public television and admit that I stole the election just to have Tracy back alive and well."

"Don't say that. Tracy wouldn't want you to say it. She will want you to fight Daniel and this Cain person with everything you have."

Jill wipes away more tears. "You're right. Tracy would be the first person to smack me across the face to bring more sense into me. Just dear lord. Don't let it be Tracy when we get there."

Jill's chest tightens with anxiety, her heart pounding in sync with the rapid breaths she takes, as the weight of her emotions manifests as a physical burden. It is hard for her to stand upright as she wipes away the tears that blur her vision. The tension in the air is palpable, causing Jill's muscles to tense up in anticipation of the impending confrontation.

Steve and Jill arrive at the Massachusetts Office of the Chief Medical Officer's office, which bustles with activity. The sound of ringing phones and shuffling papers fills the air, mixing with the faint aroma of green tea. Feeling a sense of urgency, they approach the reception desk, their hearts pounding with anticipation. Behind the desk, a young woman with vibrant pink hair furiously taps at her company palmtop. Her name tag says Katheryn and her frustration is evident in the sharp thuds. "Sorry, things are always on the fritz and they keep saying we will get upgraded. I'll be old and gray before that happens," the woman Katheryn says. "How can I help you?"

"We are here to see Ms. Hilda Smithson."

Steve says while Jill is near hysterics. "And you are?" Katheryn says.

"Jill Lunden. I got a call." Each word is a painful gasp, Jill's voice cracking with unshed tears and silent grief.

"You mean the President-Elect. Look, I don't think you stole the election," she whispers. "I think that what Daniel is doing is sick." Aloud she says,

"Take a seat and I'll contact Ms. Smithson."

"Thank you," Steve says, his arm wrapped around his wife, as they walk toward the comfortable, inviting couch. **"I don't give a fuck about Daniel or Cain.** I just want to see Tracy," Jill says.

Steve gently pats her shoulder, offering a silent reassurance.

The soft glow of the lights casts gentle shadows on the tear-streaked faces, while down the hall, faint murmurs of voices mix with quiet sobs. The air is heavy with the scent of perfume and the lingering presence of salty tears, as Jill's trembling hands clutch a tissue and Steve's eyes dart nervously toward the approaching woman. "Hello, I'm Ms. Smithson," she says. "You must be Jill and..."

"Steve."

"Sorry, we have to meet under these circumstances."

"Will that's ok? You must be mistaken anyway," Jill says.

"I wish I were. We identified Ms. Kincaid through DNA. As you know, we extract a little blood when a person is born. We ran the body through the DNA identifier and it came up to Ms. Kincaid."

"Well, the results are wrong," Jill looks at Hilda. "I'm sorry."

"Think nothing of it. You're not the first person to yell at me. I doubt you will be the last. However, I ran the test three times. If there was an issue, it would have popped up."

"I still think you're wrong. I want to see for myself," Jill says, her face contorted with a mix of anger and desperation, tears streaming down her cheeks as she sobs. Her chest heaves with each breath, her body trembling with the intensity of her emotions. Her voice cracks as she screams, the sound raw and filled with pain.

"Are you sure? You don't even know how we found..." Hilda, is trying to remain calm, but her own emotions is clear in the tightness of her jaw and the furrowed brow. She is aware of her heart racing, adrenaline coursing through her veins as she tries to reason with Jill.

"I want to see!"

"Very well. Follow me."

As the echoing footsteps of Ms. Smithson, Jill, and Steve fade into the oppressive silence of the long hall, their destination weighs heavily on their hearts. Hilda's badge beeps as she places it against the panel, noting the cool smooth surface against her skin, before she speaks into it. In the elevator, Steve breaks the silence with a question, asking, "Can I ask why you called us?"

"Your wife's name is in our records of death or emergency calls."

"Of course it is. Tracy used to be my contact information until I married you." Jill's red and puffy eyes are evidence of the emotional storm she is weathering. The weight of her sorrow seems to be physically draining her, leaving her with a heaviness in her chest and a lingering ache in her bones. Her tear-streaked face shows heartbreak and loss, leaving her with hollowness and emptiness inside. The absence of tears now only serves as a reminder of the pain she has endured, a silent testimony to the depth of her emotions.

The elevator doors slide open, revealing a dimly lit room where ghostly shadows dance on the walls, a musty odor hanging in the air. The air is heavy with the scent of disinfectant, along with a subtle metallic undertone. Jill, Steve, and the Chief Medical Officer's steps reverberate across the sterile expanse, contributing to the disquieting ambiance.

As Jill scans the room, she can't help but admire the careful attention to detail in the arrangement of each item. Finally, Hilda approaches a cold, imposing metal wall with its shelves tightly shut, hinting at the corpses within. She explains, "We keep the bodies in stasis until someone claims them or a week has passed."

"What happens after that?" Steve asks.

"We turn them into mulch. Nutrients for the plants."

"Thank god I married you," Steve says.

With a decisive press of her badge against the panel, the Medical Officer hears the satisfying click as the handle disengages, revealing what lies beyond. Immediately, a table silently slides out, the white blanket concealing the body beneath slightly rumpled. Hilda unveils Tracy's face, revealing a grotesque and contorted expression, her eyes wide and vacant, sending chills down Jill and Steve's spines. A wave of revulsion and nausea, accompanied by a cold sweat, washes over Jill, making her feel instantly ill. Observing several jars filled with murky formaldehyde, in which various organs seem to float, Jill notices the pungent smell of the chemical stinging her nostrils. The sight sends shivers down her spine, making her skin crawl, and a deep sense of unease washes over her, like she has stumbled upon a secret world hidden in plain sight. A macabre fascination emanates from each jar, the contents, barely visible through the dusty glass, hint at the unknown, their stillness unnerving. Jill's mind races with questions, her curiosity battling with a growing sense of dread. "What are these?" Jill gulps, scrutinizing the jars brimming with an assortment of liquids and materials.

"Ms. Kincaid's entrails. Investigators found them on the street next to her body," the Medical Officer says. Jill can't believe what she is hearing. The Medical Officer continues, "It seems that her murder took place in a different location. Through forensic analysis, we may uncover the story of her death, including the exact location. To preserve the evidence, it is necessary to secure her entrails in these jars."

Jill's blood is boiling, a fiery rage erupting within her, threatening to consume her with its incandescent heat. The intensity of her emotions leads to a heart-wrenching, screaming sob escaping from her lips. **"Are you telling me they brutally mutilated her and then gutted her like a pig?"**

As the rage threatens to overwhelm her, Jill's chest constricts, making it difficult to draw in a breath. The torrent of emotions wells up inside her, manifesting in a gut-wrenching sob that racks her body with each anguished cry. Tears stream down her face, hot and stinging, as the emotional turmoil manifests physically in her trembling limbs and quivering voice. The sheer intensity of her emotions leaves Jill feeling drained and raw, her body trembling with the aftermath of the emotional outburst. These physical effects of her anger and grief are clear in the way her body reacts, a visceral response to the overwhelming emotions that threaten to consume her. Turning back to face the Medical Officer, a mix of determination and vulnerability is clear in Jill's expression. She takes a deep breath, trying to steady her trembling voice, and speaks with sincerity. "I am truly sorry for my reaction. It's unjust to point it at you. I apologize."

Hilda nods, her eyes filled with compassion. "I understand when I took this job that many people will have their emotions take control. It's a challenging job, and it takes a toll on everyone involved. I appreciate your apology. I thought I saw all forms of horror in this job. Then I saw the body."

"Which is where?" Steve asks.

The medical officer gives the location five inches from where Rachel found Tracy's cell phone.

Jill looks at Hilda. "Can I have some time with my friend?" Jill looks at Steve. "Alone."

"Of course. I have to get the paperwork for you to fill out."

"Paperwork?"

"To take custody of the body."

"Of course." Then Hilda and Steve leave Jill to be with Tracy.

A shudder runs through Jill as she takes a deep breath, steeling herself against the awful sight of her friend's lifeless form. "Tracy, I apologize for ever doubting you. It's clear now that they must have murdered you to silence you about the fake tape. You'll always be my good friend and sister. **I promise you; I won't let them get away with this.**" She leans down, her lips brushing Tracy's forehead in a silent farewell, then carefully and slowly spreads the blanket over her lifeless face. The weight of the fabric feels heavy in the room's stillness.

Hilda and Steve return to the room. Steve goes up to Jill. "Are you ok?"

Jill looks at Hilda. "Once she's ready, I will give you the details of the funeral home they can manage." Jill gives a gulp. "The body."

"Very well, if you can sign these. We will prep and release the body." Hilda hands the forms to Jill. Jill signs the forms and hands them back to Hilda. "Oh, I almost forgot. Here are her possessions."

A single tear traces a path down Jill's cheek as she listlessly picks up the heavy envelope. Hilda then says, "For what it's worth. I wished things turned out differently."

Jill says, "I hope you don't take this personally. But I wish I never saw you."

"I get that a lot," Hilda says, head low.

"What are you doing?" Steve's confusion and concern manifest in furrowed brows and a furrowed expression, his body language subtly reflecting his emotions.

"What I should have done in the beginning!"

The rain, now a torrential downpour, beats down on Jill and Steve as they make their way back to the car, the air thick with the smell of wet earth. Jill is tight-lipped as Steve holds the door for her and gives her a kiss on the hand. Afterward, he enters the car and apologizes, saying, "I'm sorry. I wish for a better result," Steve says and gives Jill a squeeze of her hand.

"They killed her." Jill says between sobs. **"They faked a tape, then cut her open and gutted her. Then they threw her down the street as if she's nothing. SHE WAS MY FRIEND, and it got her killed."**

Jill's body trembles with grief as new tears stream down her face, her chest heaving with each sob. The weight of her sorrow seems to physically crush her, her shoulders slumping forward as if unable to bear the burden of her emotions. Steve can feel the tension in her hand as she squeezes his, her fingers trembling with a mixture of anger and despair.

"We don't know that. Now that they find Tracy's…" Steve says.

"What. They will look for the people responsible. **We know who is responsible! And I'm tired of not just having my name thrown in the mud, but Tracy's. I'm tired of jumping at shadows and I won't cower in fear any longer."** As Jill speaks, her voice quivers with a mix of anger and frustration. Her hands tremble slightly, betraying the intensity of her emotions. Her face flushes with a combination of defiance and determination, her eyes sparking with resolve. Pent-up emotion coiled every muscle in her body, creating palpable tension.

Jill hits a panel. "Ryan, call a press conference." As Jill's anger flares up, her heart rate increases, adrenaline surges through her body, and her muscles tense. Her hand stings from the impact of hitting the panel, and her breathing becomes rapid and shallow.

"What are you doing?" Steve's confusion and concern manifest in furrowed brows and a furrowed expression, his body language subtly reflecting his emotions.

"What I should have done in the beginning!"

Chapter Thirty

J ill and Steve arrived home to find the lights already on, casting a warm glow against the rain-lashed windows. Outside, the relentless rain drummed against the glass, punctuated by distant thunder. A damp chill clung to Steve's coat as he entered, while Jill, shaking off her umbrella, felt a wave of relief wash over her. This relief was short-lived, however, as she declares, **"I'm going to find Cain, and when I do, I will make that cancer pay for every life that monster took. If that person thinks it knows what pain is like, it has seen nothing yet!"**

Steve responded dryly, "What are you going to do, fling Cain to the sun?"

Jill's eyes darted to Steve, her breath catching in her throat as a cold dread washed over her. A fierce determination, mirroring a grief too deep for words, burned in her eyes—a sorrow he couldn't comprehend. **"Don't give me any ideas,"** she snaps, her burning rage fueled by the replay of Tracy's torment, a thirst for vengeance searing through her.

"How are you going to find Cain? I doubt that he or she is in any listing.

Undeterred, Jill vows, **"Come hell or high water, I will find Cain and make that monster pay for everything."** Steve retreated slowly, knowing this resolute side of his wife all too well. Shedding her heavy, red coat—its damp fabric clinging uncomfortably—Jill noticed an envelope from Hilda fall to the floor. Her hands trembled slightly as she picked it up, her knuckles bone-white against the pale paper. A shallow gasp escaped her lips as a wave of nausea rolled over her, clenching her stomach.

"All that Tracy was is now here..." Jill says, tears welling in her eyes. The grief was a physical weight, pressing down on her shoulders, making it hard to breathe and stand upright.

"That's not true. Tracy is still alive inside you." Tears of love flow from Steve's word. Her fingers, deft and sure, worked quickly to open the envelope, the anticipation growing with each passing moment. The paper crinkles and the contents spill out on the table: Bubble gum, a friendship bracelet Jill gave her when they were ten years old, and a key fall onto the table. The bracelet felt heavy and cold against Jill's skin, a stark contrast to the warmth of the memories it evoked.

"Friends forever." Tracy said.

"Always and forever." Jill agreed.

Tucked away in Jill's jewelry case, among other treasured trinkets, was her friendship bracelet; its vibrant colors are still bright.

Then she looks back at the tiny, golden key, its intricate details catching the light.

"What is this?" Jill picks up the key; its smooth surface feels cool beneath her fingers.

"Safe deposit box?" Steve wonders.

"Could be. But I think they are all finger and eye scanned now." Jill says, still looking at the key. "It's not for her car. That operates by her fingerprint."

"Could it be her apartment?"

Jill ponders the matter, turning it over in her mind. Most houses and apartments use the fingerprint system, but those over one hundred years old still prefer the key system as a bit of nostalgia. Some use the finger system while still having key locks. Tracy likes the key doors, finding them aesthetically pleasing and well-made, not to mention keys didn't break down.

Jill searches her worn leather purse, its contents smell of old receipts and lotions. She finds her copy of the apartment key Tracy gave her and compares it to the one on the table. "It's smaller and the dents are different." Jill confirms.

"Then what is it for?" Steve asks.

Jill rises from the couch and goes to the back shelf. She touches the cool wood as she takes down the red book, a reminder of her and Steve's find in Tracy's apartment. She carries it to the glass table, carefully inserting the gleaming golden key into the keyhole. The key fits perfectly, and with a gentle turn, the lock clicks open, bringing a smile to Jill's face. "Voila."

"Well, that's one mystery solved." Steve says.

Jill carefully examines each page, turning them over one by one.

'I write this now as my diary which my father gave me. My name is Tracy Kincaid, and I was born on March 5, 2075.'

"Oh shit. This is her diary." Jill says.

"Should you be reading it? Those things are private."

"You're right. But I need to confirm one thing."

Jill walks to another glass table; its surface gleams under a protective cover. The cover comes off with a soft click, and she nestles the book inside the glass case before putting the cover back in place. "Computer, scan the document."

"Scanning," the computer says. "Scan complete."

"Look up any references to rig or stole." '

'April 7, 2084. I jury-rigged the dryer to heat the clothes faster. I don't know how much longer the dryer will last; it's already on its last legs.'

Jill remembers Tracy's lighthearted mention of the incident—a happy memory that warms her heart. However, the dryer surprised Tracy by lasting a full five months. There were five different mentions of Tracy jury-rigging several other electronics. "She sounds like quite the engineer," Steve says.

"Jack of all trades," Jill says. Although Jill always believed Tracy could have been a talented engineer or mechanic, Tracy choose not to follow in her father's footsteps.

June 10, 2193: My innocence has been stolen from me. All I know is that I had one drink. Later, I felt woozy and nauseous and then I blacked out. The next thing I know, I was awake and naked on a hotel bed. I go to the bathroom and find some bruises on my body. I take a shower and start having these foggy memories of a man taking me upstairs. He lays me on the bed and rips my clothes off. As the shower continues, I can see the same man on top of me as he...'

"Computer off!" Jill screams.

In a flash, Jill's eyes dart to Steve, a quick, almost imperceptible movement that betrays a sudden shift in her attention. Jill's hands cover her face, hot tears streaming through her fingers, silently falling. An icy dread washes over Jill as the horrifying implications of Tracy's words sink in, leaving her breathless and paralyzed with shock. "The Steele party."

"The what?" Steve asks.

"George and Samantha Steele invite every member of my school's student government and a plus one to a party. At the time I wasn't seeing anyone, so I invited Tracy." Jill remembers Tracy at the party. Her short dress, made of a sheer, delicate fabric, leaves little to the imagination, with her silky purple bra peeking through. Jill wore a crisp blue blouse and a swirling red skirt.

"After an hour, I was woozy; a wave of dizziness washed over me as the world seemed to spin." Jill goes back to that day.

Tracy asks, "You want me to drive home?"

"No, I'll just take a cab. Have fun."

"Well, take care."

Jill looks at Steve. She sees concern and horror on his face.

"What's the matter?"

"I believe someone intended you to be the rape victim. Everything you mentioned. Tracy mentioned it in her diary."

The reality gasps Jill, an icy fist clenching her chest. Her heart hammers against her ribs, a frantic drumbeat mirroring the terror blooming in her stomach. She is pale and clammy; Steve's words, heavy and suffocating, hang in the air—each syllable a physical blow. Muscles tense, primed for fight or flight, yet her body feels frozen, trapped in fear's icy grip. A tremor, a surge of adrenaline, courses through her, leaving her weak and shaky. "Soon after that, something changed in Tracy. She became more of an introvert. She stopped going to parties and talking about having relationships. How could I have not known?" Jill says, hugging Steve.

"She probably felt embarrassed and wanted to put it in the back of her mind."

"When that recording of Daniel's sexual assault came out, Dear god Tracy was there and heard it."

"It must have brought a flush of memories back. No wonder she screamed during the election party."

"Especially when I mentioned meeting a nice man and having kids. I just wish she told me." Jill's hands tremble as she closes the reader, the cool plastic a stark contrast to the heat rising in her cheeks. A wave of nausea rolls over her, leaving her stomach churning. The memory of Tracy's shrill scream and wild eyes haunts her, causing a physical tightness in her chest from the anxiety that remains.

"We talked about everything. Her fears of the doctor. My insecurity during the Senate hearings. We talked about everything, or I thought we did. I thought knew her."

"You did. You knew the kind-hearted person who always gave Rachel and Henry gifts. The person who stayed at your bedside when you were sick. The person who was by your side when the Senate grilled you about President Cracker. The person who held your hand while your parents passed away was on my way to you. There was just another part of her she didn't want anyone to know."

Jill, overcome with affection, leans in and gives Steve a tender kiss. "You're right. There could be several reasons she doesn't confide in me."

The phone rings. "Phone answer. Yes."

"Ms. Luden, I have arranged a press conference for 2pm at Hyde Park."

"Very good. Thank you. Phone hang up."

"Well, I guess we better get to bed. It looks like you are going to have a full day tomorrow."

Jill walks around, the place strangely familiar. A wave of nausea washes over her as someone offers a drink. She frantically searches for Tracy but finds her nowhere in sight; her desperate yells are unanswered. Then, a powerful grip yanks her into a dimly lit room, the rough wood of the door scraping painfully against her arm. Thrown onto a bed, she recognizes Daniel Thompson, and a shadowy figure looming behind him, aggressively tearing at her clothes. Chilling laughter drowns her screams as icy fingers trace her skin, their echoes a cruel symphony celebrating her terror. In a mirror, she sees the grotesque sight of Tracy's mutilated corpse; a single finger presses against her lips in a silent, desperate plea. Jill stares at Tracy's lifeless eyes, her mouth opening only to release blood. As Daniel leaves and the shadowy figure moves, panic constricts her throat. The sight of the shadow and its serrated knife sends a fresh wave of fear through her as it lunges, razor-sharp steel flashes. Jill screams,

"NO!" She awakes with a start, drenched in sweat.

"What's the matter?" Steve asks.

The terror of the dream leaves Jill trembling, her heart hammering against her ribs, a frantic drumbeat echoing in her ears. Cold sweat slicks her skin despite the warmth of her bed, and her breath hitches in ragged gasps, each inhale burning. Tense and shivering from the lingering cold of the icy laughter, goosebumps rise on her arms. Her eyes dart around the room, searching for any trace of the horrifying vision; the vividness of Tracy's mutilated body threatens to overwhelm her with nausea. The residual adrenaline makes her hands shake uncontrollably as she tries to speak to Steve. "Hold me tight and never let me go,"

"You got it,"

December 29, 2124

At 2:00 p.m. EST, Jill walked toward the podium, the afternoon sun glinting off the polished microphones. Their metallic sheen contrasted with the murmuring crowd, whose scent of freshly cut grass mingled with the sharp tang of nervous sweat, unsettling Jill. The weight of expectation—heavy, palpable, a tangible presence alongside the eager whispers and keyboard clicks, the ethereal glow of flickering holo-video screens amplified —, promising a global broadcast. The previous night's dream lingered in her mind: Daniel attacking her, Cain approaching with a knife, and Tracy, eyes lifeless, mouth bloody, a finger pressed to her lips, signaling silence.

Further fueling her unease, Jill reread a passage in Tracy's diary: *When I told my parents about what happened, they told me to keep quiet. That we can't have the publicity.'* A surge of righteous fury—the injustice of the situation clenching her fists and boiling her blood—gave way to understanding. She now understood why Tracy had avoided her parents until their death in the car accident, and she realized Steve had been right.

Tracy's subsequent entry pierced Jill's heart. *'I feel so embarrassed and mortified. Jill was right in that I should never have worn that dress. I messed up by having that drink and everything is my fault.'* Looking up, Jill whispers, "You could've told me, Trace. I wouldn't have judged you," wiping away more tears.

"We are ready whenever you are," her press agent, Ryan, announced. Jill smoothed her hair one last time, checking her reflection before approaching the podium. With a gentle tap of her finger, she tested the microphone; all systems are a go.

"Thank you for coming today. I will keep my statement brief. A tremor runs through her as she inhales sharply, her chest constricting to still the frantic fluttering of her heart. **"Last night, I saw the body of my good friend and campaign manager, Tracy Kincaid. She was murdered and her body dumped in the street.** For the sake of America, let's end this violence and destruction. This violence claimed not only my friend but also several poll workers and protesters. Furthermore, numerous secretaries of state have received death threats, as have judges who dismissed Daniel's election fraud cases. You tried to smear my name with a fraudulent tape, and, even worse, I allowed it to happen. **That ends today."** She pounds her fist on the podium. With each word at the press conference, Jill's voice grew stronger, her conviction unwavering. Her initial pallor gave way to a deep crimson flush as her anger intensified. The muscles in her jaw tightened, a visible tremor running along her jawline. Her chest heaved with each forceful exhalation, her heart hammering frantically against her ribs. Veins bulged slightly in her neck as she strained to project her voice, the exertion visible even from the back of the room. Initially clenched into fists, her hands gradually relaxed slightly as her passion gave way to controlled fury, though a subtle tremor remained. "None of these deaths should have happened," she declared. **"Cain, whoever you are, I will find you and make you pay. Daniel, Tracy's blood, and the blood of everyone killed in your crusade, are on your hands and the hands of your supporters. I hope you are happy."**

Chapter Thirty-One

T he television, perched above the roaring fire, casts a flickering light that competes with the flames, the sounds of the show mix with the crackling fire. Andrew Utter and Daniel Thompson watch Jill Lunden's press conference regarding the death of Tracy Kincaid. An icy dread seeps into Constance Utter as the chilling parallels between Laura and Tracy's deaths strike her, leaving her breathless and trembling.

"Murdered. Mutilated and gutted, just like Laura Kelly."

Constance's heart hammers against her ribs, a frantic drumbeat mirroring the accusations swirling in her mind. Her clammy, stiff hands clench into bone-white fists; a tremor spreads from her chest, making her teeth chatter despite the room's warmth. Her breath comes in shallow, rapid gasps, a stark contrast to her usual rhythm, as the blood drains from her face, accentuating her sharp jawline. A nauseous knot tightens in her stomach, threatening to bring up the bile, while Daniel's presence feels suffocating, the air thickening and pressing on her chest. Dizziness washes over her, blurring her vision as suspicion threatens to overwhelm her. Daniel Thompson glares furiously, his voice grows low, growl, fists clenched, knuckles white against reddening skin. Unspoken threats crackle between them; a palpable tension hangs heavy in the air. Constance's breath hitches again; a cold fear grips her, contrasting with his simmering rage. Only the frantic drumming of her heart and the furious pulse in her temples break the silence.

Never mention that turncoat's name again. She gets what she deserves. Just like everyone that crosses me.

Daniel's face flushes a deep crimson as he speaks, the veins in his neck and temples standing out like angry cords. A slight tremor runs through his hands, clenched into fists at his sides. His breathing is shallow and rapid, his chest constricting with the intensity of his remembered rage. The satisfaction he feels, however, manifests differently. A slow, predatory smile spreads across his lips, pulling the corners of his mouth back to reveal his teeth. His eyes, dull, gleam with a cold, hard light, the pupils constricted to pinpricks. A faint sheen of perspiration appears on his forehead, contrasting with the stark dryness of his mouth. The pleasure he takes in Jill's pain is apparent; a subtle flexing of his jaw muscles, a slight tightening of his shoulders, betrays the visceral thrill he derives from her suffering.

Beneath the surface of Constance's composure, a storm rages. Her heart beats faster, a subtle tightening in her chest mirroring the knot of unease in her stomach. This is a familiar response to Daniel's volatile moods; her jaw clenches, and her meticulously manicured fingertips itch with a barely perceptible tremor. The coolness of her skin belies the rapid fire of thoughts racing through her mind, a stark contrast to the heat that flushes her cheeks whenever she considers the implications of Daniel's actions and their potential consequences.

"You can tell that she's been crying, the poor soul," Andrew says. He looks at Jill on the television. Her eyes are red and swollen, the skin around them raw and slightly puffy. A faint, reddish flush remains on her cheeks, a stark contrast to the overall pallor of her face. Her nose is congested, and she keeps dabbing at it with a tissue, leaving damp smudges. Her shoulders slump, and her breathing seems shallow and uneven, as if the sobs are still catching in her chest. There's a slight tremor in her hands, and her whole body seems to hold itself, as if bracing against further emotional pain.

"Well, of course she's been crying. She lost her best friend..."

Daniel looks up. "Or worse, enemy. The only person who can confirm that the tape is, in fact, real." Daniel's face is tight, jaw clenched, a vein throbbing visibly in his temple. The force of his throw sends a splatter of ketchup across the pale kitchen wall, mirroring the chaotic turmoil in his gut. His breath comes in short, shallow gasps, his chest constricted with a mixture of anger and anxiety. His hands tremble as he wipes at a stray tear that escapes, unnoticed, down his cheek, leaving a glistening streak against the grime already present there. He bunches his shoulder muscles, tensing them. His heart hammers a frantic rhythm against his ribs, a frantic drumbeat accompanying the silent scream trapped in his throat.

"**Don't you have any compassion?** Andrew, imagine what would happen if you lost me." Constance says.

"He'd be a lot better off. **As for compassion, those bitches took what is rightfully mine.** Why should I have any compassion if one of them is dead?"

"I can't deal with him." Constance looks at Andrew and throws her arms in the air, a gesture of frustrated helplessness. Her chest heaves, her breath coming in ragged gasps as her shoulders rise and fall rapidly. A faint tremor runs through her body, a physical manifestation of the barely contained rage bubbling beneath the surface. Her face flushes crimson, the blood rushing to her cheeks, and her hands clench into fists, the knuckles whitening under the strain.

"**Then leave.**" Daniel screams.

"Don't worry, I'm going." Constance's face is flushed, the blood rushing to her cheeks and neck, a visible testament to her rising anger and frustration. Her breath comes in short, shallow gasps, her chest tightening with each uncontrolled exhale. The muscles in her arms and shoulders are tense, bunched tight with the residual energy of her frustrated gesture. Daniel's scream makes her flinch, a visible tremor running through her body as his shout momentarily jolts her nervous system. Even as she speaks her response, a slight tremble remains in her voice, a physical manifestation of her inner turmoil. The tension visibly eases from her shoulders only slightly as she leaves, although her hands still clench and unclench, revealing the underlying stress. Andrew's intervention causes a further subtle shift; her muscles stiffen again; her heart rate likely increases as a surge of adrenaline courses through her system.

"I will talk to him. As for the other thing, I cannot imagine losing you." As Andrew's words sink in, his wife feels a surge of fear and uncertainty wash over her. Her heart races, pounding against her chest as a rush of adrenaline courses through her veins. The weight of his words hangs heavy in the air, causing a knot to form in her stomach.

"You go down the road he's going down. You just might."

She feels her hands trembling slightly as she clutches onto Andrew, seeking comfort and reassurance in his embrace. A sense of vulnerability washes over her, making her feel exposed and raw.

Despite the warmth of Andrew's touch, a chill runs down her spine at the thought of losing him to Daniel. The mere idea sends shivers down her back, causing her to hold on to him even tighter, as if trying to anchor herself to the present moment.

The emotional turmoil manifests physically, with tears welling up in her eyes, threatening to spill over at any moment. The intensity of the moment makes her breathless, as if someone knocked the air out of her lungs.

As they stand there, locked in a tight embrace, the physical effects of their emotions serve as a poignant reminder of the deep connection they share and the fragility of life.

"Just remember, I told you this would happen if you let him play with his ego rather than give the facts."

"I know." His voice cracks slightly on the last word, a tremor betraying the raw fear constricting his chest. His grip on his wife tightens, his knuckles whiten as he tries to convey the depth of his anxiety. A frantic rhythm pounds against his ribs, his rising panic mirrored in the drumbeat of his worried heart. He senses the familiar clenching in his stomach, a knot of dread that threatens to overwhelm him. His wife's presence is a lifeline, but even her warmth doesn't entirely quell the icy fingers of fear that creep up his spine. His breath catches in his throat, shallow and rapid, a testament to the turmoil within.

Constance seeks Daniel's wife in another room; the quiet hush of the hallway contrasts with the sounds she left behind.

Daniel remains on the couch, the cushions sinking under his weight as he speaks. "I don't know what you see in her. If you ask me, you're better off without her."

Andrew walks back to Daniel. "You may hate it, but she is right. If you want to win the people over, you need to show some remorse. Otherwise, it's just a replay of Laura."

"Why would I give this any of my time? Like Laura Kelly, it will go away with time."

The flames crackle, spitting embers that dance in the screen's periphery's blue light. A low hum from the television mingles with the rhythmic crackle. The scent of wood smoke hangs heavily in the air, contrasting sharply with the sterile, almost clinical tone of Lunden's voice. A knot of tension forms in Andrew's stomach.

"...is on you and your supporters' hands. I hope you are happy. The fact is that you lost, and I will assume the presidency on January 20th. As for you, I couldn't be less concerned. Return to the dark, musty hole from which you emerged. Try to regain your television personality or become a news correspondent. I don't care. Just leave America alone, Thank you." Jill finishes her speech, head held high, as she departs from the podium.

Andrew looks at Daniel. "You were saying. You know Jill is not going to 'let this go.' Tracy was her friend from birth. At least that is what I heard."

Daniel's face, a mask of fury, contorts with uncontrollable wrath; veins throb like angry serpents beneath his crimson skin, his breath coming in ragged gasps. Lava seems to burn in his eyes, each vein a river of fury. His jaw sets like granite, knuckles white as he squeezes his fists until they ache. His heart hammers against his ribs, a frantic drumbeat threatening to shatter the cage of bone, while the muscles in his shoulders and neck tighten, rigid and tense, as if bracing for a physical blow. Despite the chill in the air, a sheen of sweat slicks his skin, betraying the internal inferno. A barely perceptible tremor in his hands betrays the rigid control he desperately attempts to maintain, as the blood roars in his ears, drowning out all other sounds except the furious pounding of his pulse.

"I don't give a fuck if they were from the same womb. The audacity of that fucking bitch to speak to me in such a manner is unbelievable. Schedule an interview for me. **Immediately.**"

Daniel walks toward his favorite seat at the Conservative News Network; the bright lights warm his face. Despite the intensity of his emotions and the sweat trickling down his heavy, overweight body, he composes himself in front of the camera, his demeanor shifting from rage to a calculated and confident one. His breath comes in ragged gasps, his heart hammers a frantic rhythm against his ribs, but his voice, though sharp with barely controlled anger, remains steady.

"Jill Lunden has spread false rumors about me. I want to clarify that I did not cause her friend's death, nor did anyone who follows me. I'm deeply sorry for the tragic loss of the only person who could confirm that the tape is real. That the Lunden campaign or even the whole Democratic party bribed the 'inspectors' itself? I wouldn't put it past them to stop trying to make America Pure. Everyone knows they and what's left of the Republican Party are Americans in Name Only. They would like nothing better than to help their rich donors at America's expense. But we won't let them. We must make sure that each Secretary of State recalculates their votes to make sure that illegals didn't sway the election. To make sure your vote is counted, we must flood each of the Secretary of State's offices. We will prevail in court. We will make America Pure."

"Wait a minute. Are you saying that Jill Lunden killed her own best friend?"

"As I mentioned, it just seems strange that the person who could confirm the tape's authenticity just winds up dead. I know that the tape is real and that Jill will silence anyone that stands in her way to power. Even her so-called best friend. After all, she sold out Charles Sport to get herself out of trouble. Kill her friend and then say that either I or the true loyal Americans that want to see a pure America did it. Jill, no one is fooled," he says.

"Well, we know the FBI still scours mountains of evidence of voter fraud." Sean says. He doesn't know if there are mountains of paperwork, but he knows what gets ratings, and making Daniel happy is the key. That is why the Conservative News Network is the number one news network, despite admitting under oath that they lie on more than one occasion.

Daniel's jaw clenches, a physical manifestation of his suppressed rage, causing a barely perceptible tremor in his cheek muscles—noticeable only to a keen observer. The coldness in his eyes, a product of intense focus and emotional withdrawal, constricts his pupils, sharpening their predatory look. A subtle tightening of his throat, reflecting the effort to maintain such rigid control, mirrors the lack of resonance in his voice. His still hands, deceptively calm, mask considerable muscular tension, clear in the slight whitening of his knuckles. Even his shallow breathing, a conscious effort to regulate his autonomic nervous system, results in a slight pallor around his lips and a noticeably increased pulse, detectable beneath his skin. Beneath this carefully controlled exterior, however, a physiological storm brews, revealing a body on high alert.

"**They are not doing enough**. They need to arrest everyone that was involved in the election's fraud, including governors, and if they don't act, then the people need to, for the good of this country. So, to those people, I say. Stand back and stand by."

The glaring lack of evidence supporting his accusations is immediately obvious. He utters the words, leaving the rest to his followers; his pronouncements hang heavy in the air, creating a palpable sense of unease. His accusations, coupled with his lack of remorse, paint a chilling portrait of ambition—a man willing to exploit any situation for personal gain. Even as the camera continues to roll, capturing his impassioned speech, the physical manifestations of his emotion subside, replaced by a carefully cultivated calmness. Yet, the lingering traces of anger and resentment etched on his face serve as a stark reminder of the darkness underlying his composed demeanor. '*I will have my revenge.*' Daniel thinks.

Chapter Thirty-Two

December 30, 2124

Arizona Secretary of State Sydney Cain, her face etched with the weight of years beyond her thirty, stepped into the glare of flashing cameras. With evident apprehension, she carefully and slowly approached the podium, her nervousness betraying her. Her voice trembled slightly as she announced, "Five recounts confirm Jill Lunden's victory in Arizona. Our comprehensive investigation revealed no evidence of illegal voting activity. Therefore, upholding the voters' will, we officially declare Jill Lunden the winner. There will be no additional comments provided at this time, nor will there be any further statements released. Signs reading "Vote for the Right Person Or Else," "We know where you live," "Stop the election rigging," and the ominous "Vengeance is mine, saith the Lord," underscored their dissent. Marci Waller commented, "That was Sydney Cain confirming the end of the Arizona recount, but, as you can see, some people disagree. Back to you, Sarah."

"We've also confirmed that many other states have completed their recount audits, with several showing results consistent with the initial election numbers. In others, recounts revealed that Jill Stein won more votes than initially reported. There is breaking news to report: vandals have attacked multiple campaign headquarters, resulting in significant damage. We now go live to Samuel McCoy in Little Rock, Arkansas."

"From my position behind the Democratic headquarters, I see the damage—broken windows, and a crudely painted 'A.I.N.O.' sign. We can only determine that means American in Name Only, as Daniel Thompson said during his interview with Sean Bradley. We also see the same thing in the Republican Party headquarters."

"Anything from American Now headquarters?"

"Nothing so far," came the reply.

Sarah found it convenient. "I'm told you have an eyewitness," she said.

"Yes, I do," Samuel replied. "This is Susan Winters. Susan, please describe the events you observed." A woman in her late fifties, her silver hair neatly pulled back, stepped forward with quiet, elegant grace.

"I was driving by the building and I noticed these people in black suits with a strange armband marching towards the building. Suddenly, they threw a brick and started pounding on the door. Fortunately, nobody answered. I then saw a fingerless person, apparently using spray paint. I left and called the police, hoping no one saw me."

"Thank you."

In a hurry to leave, Susan ran away as fast as she could.

"We also have some footage of an event that happened at Clyde's Steak and Grill. A place popular with Democrats and Republicans, transcending political divides. I must warn you that the video is pretty graphic."

As people watch the news, they see Clyde's, a one-story red brick building radiating a warm, inviting glow from its windows. Inside, people gather by a crackling fireplace, their voices and the clinking of glasses mingling as they discuss upcoming events. However, as the crowd disperses, a group in orange hats lingers, their taunts echoing. Someone even attacked a prominent House member. Screams pierce the air as the orange-hatted mob surges forward in a brutal melee. The House member fights back desperately. Then, a bottle shatters, its explosion accompanied by a shower of sparkling fragments and a sharp crack. A woman screams, her high-pitched cry piercing the sudden quiet. Someone shouts, "Police!" The mob retreats, leaving behind a scene of carnage.

"I am happy to report that Representative Smokey James only has minor scrapes and rests in his home. Despite the serious nature of the situation, local law enforcement authorities have not yet made any arrests, nor have they offered any public statements regarding an ongoing investigation into the matter. A person comes to Sarah with some paper. "This just in. By an 8-1 decision, the Supreme Court has declared that all recounts are to cease. The courts have ruled Daniel lacks standing to bring cases before them." Sarah looks at the screen, eyes defiant. "Daniel, the states are against you, and the courts are against you. With the election results so clear, don't you think it's time you gracefully concede and showed respect for the democratic process? At this time, you seem pathetic using fake evidence and some mysterious person who has yet to bring any proof of the 'stolen election'. This is Sarah Spencer saying have a great day." Sarah takes off her eye prompter.

She gets up from her silver anchor chair and bumps into Mark. "Hey, where are you heading? I was hoping we could get some lunch." Mark asks.

"Raincheck? I have to do some research."

"Research?"

"I want to find Cain." Mark looks worried.

"Are you sure?"

"I have a bad feeling about that person."

"I just want nothing to happen to you." Mark takes her hands. "You're special to me."

Sarah looks at Mark, her eyes lingering on his smile, though worry flickers in his own. Yet, a lightness fills her, each delicate heartbeat a song of pure, unadulterated happiness. She hasn't known he feels that way about her; her heart soars, a wave of unexpected joy washing over her as a new possibility bloom. "Mark, I didn't know you felt that way."

"I don't think I knew until you mentioned going after Cain. Then I visualized you lying in a dark street the same way Laura Kelly and Tracy Kincaid were. I'm unsure how I'd react if this should happen to you.

Now Sarah gets that vision, and the thought horrifies her. Her heart hammers against her ribs, a frantic drumbeat that echoes in her ears. A cold sweat slicks her palms, making the newspaper she holds damp and slippery. Her breath catches in her throat, a tight, constricting band around her chest. Her stomach clenches, a nauseous twist of dread.

"I'm a journalist and Cain is a story. Professional curiosity, a burning need to under-stand, to uncover the truth. Could I be in danger? Hell, I'm in danger every time I get behind the camera." Her fingers, despite the tremor in her hands, begin to tap a frantic rhythm against the leg, a counterpoint to the erratic pounding of her heart. "But if you're worried about my safety. You are welcome to help. Say my place during dinner." She sees excitement in Mark's eyes. She walks up to him and whispers. "The computer might process many leads throughout the night. However, will we pass the time?"

Mark's excitement is palpable, his heart pounds, adrenaline surges as his hands tremble slightly. The sparkle in his eyes intensifies, mirroring the anticipation building within him. His breath hitches, shallow and rapid, as he processes the whispered words, a mix of nervousness and exhilaration flooding him at the prospect of a night of research. The air crackles with tension, charged by their shared anticipation and curiosity. As he drew near, eager to catch every word, Mark's body language betrays his racing mind, already brimming with possibilities for their shared night.

Several people are marching over various cities carrying signs that say, 'Jill cheated.' 'Daniel is the President.' 'Death to poll workers and Secretary of States.' 'Thank You Cain.'

Thomas Hunter was at his anchor chair for the American News Network, giving his report. "Massive violent protests to support Daniel Thompson currently grip the United States. However, with the Supreme Court saying that the recounts should end and Tracy's taped confession proven to be a fraud, it seems that Daniel has run out of miracles. My question is this. Amid the violent clashes and unrest, a concerning lack of police presence and subsequent action is clear. That's all for the news. This is Thomas Hunter signing off."

"Great work. I'm sure Gregory is looking down on you and smiling," Christian Silverstone says.

"Thanks. But the Conservative News Network is still slamming us."

"All glitz, no actual news,"

"Maybe, but it's an outlet for Daniel, and that's where most people are getting their news. Perhaps it's time we added some glitz to our own programs."

"I'm not sure I understand; could you elaborate? Because I refuse to report false news and give fake videos."

"Nothing like that. Just a few ideas."

Intrigued by Thomas's ideas, a warmth spread through Christian's limbs, igniting a spark in his chest. His pulse quickened, a subtle tremor running through his fingers as he leaned forward, captivated by the vivid pictures Thomas's words painted in his mind. His pupils dilated slightly, his focus intensifying, and a blush rose on his cheeks, mirroring the burgeoning excitement within.

"This matter requires corporate review and approval before I can act on it. But I like it."

"We are in a difficult situation and it has become apparent that immediate action is required."

"Today, glorious protests occur as people continue to complain about the stolen election. Meanwhile, paid demonstrators by both the Democrat and Republican parties continue to incite violence, especially at Clyde's Bar and Grill. Even a Democratic Representative from California's fourth district, Smokey James, pretended to take one for the team." Sean shows a video of the fight at Clyde's, especially the punch to Representative Smoky James. "As you can see, the fist didn't even make contact." Sean Bradley had to admit, albeit begrudgingly, the skill and artistry of the individual who had so cleverly manipulated and altered the video footage. It appeared Smokey was only pretending, as his actions appeared to be more of a playful charade than an actual threat. "Facing imminent certification and a Supreme Court failing to act. Let me clarify this. Daniel, you have a responsibility to continue this fight and to uphold the values our founding fathers fought for. The USA stands with you."

"Television off." Daniel says in the place he likes to call the war room. All around, loyal staff are calling Senators, House members, even Governors trying to fight for Daniel.

Everyone is busy today, even Andrew is currently engaged in a phone call. "Seriously, all we need is a 1500 more votes and Daniel will win...No. How do you know the election's results are legitimate? You already sent out of the delegation." Andrew hangs up the phone. "Governor Richard Brady was not willing to pay ball," Andrew says. '*I knew he wouldn't.*'

"Hey, you're doing better than me. The Senator from Louisiana just laughed at me."

"The Governor of Washington just ignored me."

Daniel walks around and stops by Andrew. Andrew sees Daniel's defeated look.

"What's the point? Sean Bradley is the only person on the news for me. Everyone has abandoned me. Maybe I should accept that I lost. I can't keep saying the same thing."

Constance felt a surge of joy as Daniel finally made sense, but her elation quickly faded as she watched Andrew violently slap him across the right cheek. Her heart raced, a knot tightening in her stomach as the heavy tension filled the room, the sound of the slap lingering in her ears.

"I am sorry, but I did not give up my Senate position to have this pity party. Courageously, stand for righteousness. Assert with absolute certainty that the establishment stole the election. You will not surrender. Consider our nation, even if it's not for you. Would you like to see a cheater leading this country to ruin?"

Shock and anger surged through Daniel as he stood there, his cheek bearing a vivid handprint. This was the first time he'd seen Andrew so animated, and the pain radiating from his injured cheek was a harsh reminder of their disagreement. Fighting back the urge to retaliate physically, he placed a trembling hand over his reddened cheek, trying to soothe the sting.

"I won't throw you across the hall at the moment, **because you're right.** We can't let any cheater, nor a woman run this country. That bitch would ruin this great nation of ours. We'll become a global joke. We must fight for our rights as men."

Constance's disappointment deepened as she heard Daniel's response, his words dripping with resentment and disdain for women. Further disheartening was Andrew's echo of Daniel's sentiments, reinforcing the belief that women were incapable of leading the country.

"You know what you should do? Hold a rally on January 6th. Show that you are not going to take this lying down."

"I'm way ahead of you." Daniel looks at a map and makes a circle. "The rally will be held at Monument Park."

Constance finally spoke, breaking the silence that had settled over the room. Her voice shook with a tremor that betrayed her inner turmoil and nervousness. "Daniel, this isn't about gender or leadership. It's about justice, equality, and fairness. We must uphold the principles founding our nation. The destructive nature of violence leads to division, fostering an environment of animosity and mistrust that hinders unity and understanding. The necessity of discovering common ground and achieving a shared understanding is paramount to success."

Daniel glares at her. **"Get that fuckin bitch out of here!"** he screamed. Andrew escorted her out.

"Are you going to let him talk to me like that?"

"I will talk to him."

"Don't bother." Constance's heart raced with a mix of anger and disbelief as she stormed away from Andrew. Her face flushed with a combination of frustration and sadness; her fists clenched tightly at her sides. The weight of Daniel's hurtful words hung heavy in the air, leaving a bitter taste in her mouth.

As she walked away, the weight of Andrew's betrayal pressed down on her with each heavy step. Her mind whirled, struggling to make sense of the situation, but her emotions threatened to overwhelm her reason. Tears welled up, blurring her vision as she fought back the rising tide of grief. The impact of his betrayal left her feeling exposed and defenseless. Taking a deep breath, she fought back the surge of anger that threatened to overwhelm her. Even in the face of significant opposition, she will resolutely and steadfastly defend the beliefs she holds dear. A sudden surge of resolve and determination ignited within her, filling her with a newfound sense of purpose and ambition. Constance vowed to fight for herself and other women, to prove them wrong and rise above their prejudice. She envisioned a future of gender equality and respect, and as she left Andrew and Daniel behind, a sense of hope emerged. Despite the pain, her strength and resilience would carry her forward, empowering her to challenge the archaic beliefs holding society back. Constance, recognizing her voice's power, resolved then to build a world where women were neither dismissed, belittled, nor underestimated.

He came back to Daniel. The timetable revealed the certification schedule. Once they finished their impromptu planning session, Daniel sent a message. It stated there would be a *"Stop the Steal" rally on Jan 6, 2125, at Memorial Park at 9am EST. "Will be crazy."* Andrew and Daniel looked at the message and hit deliver.

The meeting ended. Andrew went outside. Constance was comforting a grieving woman. "Constance, are you ready to go home?"

Constance directed her attention toward him, her eyes meeting his. The extent of her anger is completely undeniable, leaving no room for doubt or question. "Wouldn't you want to stay here with Daniel? After all, you're like two peas in a pod. Look at that poor woman. Do you remember her? She's the individual who unfortunately lost her son during the torrential rainstorm. Do you believe Daniel harbors any feelings of sympathy, empathy, or compassion for others involved? To feel sympathy, one must possess a heart full of compassion and understanding for others. Daniel's manipulative actions have victimized countless people, a fact that is somehow overlooked in your decision to support him as our nation's leader. Also, the way you agreed with him about woman. Hell, you started that conversation."

"I only told him the things that I knew would please him and make him happy. I also didn't mention women, but cheaters."

He was prepared to concede, acknowledging that victory was no longer within his grasp. Why did you slap him? Is the Vice-Presidency that important to you? You know Jill didn't cheat. Her victory was completely legitimate; she won the election through skill and fair play. You were encouraging and goading him on. And then this rally. The people will be both angry and armed, presenting a dangerous situation.

Andrew just gazed at her. "We were talking about taking security measures. Not to mention it is just Daniel's last gasp and blow off steam. What's the worst that can happen?"

Chapter Thirty-Three

December 31, 2124

Agent Judson sits at his computer, the quiet hum of the office shatters with a sharp, insistent beep and Agent Michaels' voice. "Director Knighton suggests proceeding cautiously." The air hangs thick with the smell of stale tea and ozone from the ageing computer equipment. Judson experiences a prickle of unease; the fluorescent lights hum a discordant counterpoint to the rhythmic tap-tap-tap of his own fingers, suddenly stilled.

The weight of the pending investigation presses down like a cold, heavy blanket. His shoulders slump; the muscles tense and bunch under the imagined burden. His breath hitches, shallow and rapid, a constriction in his chest mirroring the tightening knot in his stomach. Clammy sweat slicks his palms; his heart hammers a frantic rhythm against his ribs; each beat a painful echo of the impending doom. His jaw clenches: muscles strain; a subtle tremor runs through his body. "Says we need to gather more proof before we bring anything to the public. Makes sense after that incident in Wyoming," Judson says.

"You mean the Disciples of the Way. It was a tragedy."

"It was a massacre, and the agency fired ten agents because of it."

"I'm aware!" Michaels shouts, emphasizing his knowledge of the matter. "My mentor was one of them. He ended his own life not long after the incident, succumbing to overwhelming despair and hopelessness.

"I sincerely apologized for my lack of knowledge regarding this matter. I only read the historical section. How the Disciples, under the leadership of Thomas Scott; killed two Republican governors and their families. Later, he appeared on television and claimed that his followers did it because the messiah instructed them to, stating that America was a godless country."

"You only knew a small part of the story. There was so much more. Things you didn't know or would ever know. Their actions, what they did to those governors, their wives and the children. I was there. Having recently graduated from Quantico; I was eager to start my career. I saw them. They displayed the bodies in a horrifying and disturbing manner, arranged in an unsettling and grotesque way. The stench of blood and decay filled the air, mingling with the metallic tang of fear. Similarly, Nevada's governor and her family experienced the same fate. "Their faces showed horror, etched with deep, unsettling fear."

Even now, a lingering, subtle sense of death, barely perceptible, still clings to Michael's senses. Eventually, they traced the Disciples of the Way to the farm in Wyoming. The guards, in a terrifying demonstration, ignited themselves before the FBI could even arrive at the initial gate; Upon entering the compound, what they found was far worse than anything they could have imagined—a scene of utter destruction, with shattered remnants and eerie silence. A horrific scene unfolded: corpses, eyes vacant, limbs rigid in rigor mortis, faces contorted in silent screams, lay amidst a litter of overturned soda cans; their metallic scent was a stark contrast to the nauseating odor of death. Subsequent lab tests revealed strychnine, a clear, odorless, and extremely toxic alkaloid, in the soda. "The victims of Thomas Scott and his Disciples of the Way beliefs still haunt my nightmares—not just the governors, but also the blindly devoted followers. I will always remember the charred remains of the guards and the faces of the poisoned soda drinkers. The sickly-sweet scent of the poisoned soda triggers a phantom constriction in his chest, mirroring the victims' last agony. "My sleep is restless, punctuated by sudden starts and gasps, my body betraying the terror my mind struggles to comprehend."

"I am curious what happened to Mr. Scott's so-called Messiah."

Michael's breath came in ragged gasps, a desperate, choked sound. "Never existed. That was simply Scott's rationale, a flimsy justification, for the taking of human lives."

Making his way across the room, Agent Judson arrived at Michael's side. "I can't imagine what you experienced, but at least Thomas Scott can't harm anyone else and perhaps my concerns are unfounded...."

"You don't sound convinced."

Agent Judson's breath hitched, a cold sweat clinging to his skin as he braced himself. "I must concede that your assessment is accurate, and I agree with your perspective. I received information about a shadowy paramilitary group months ago. The likes the United States had ever known. Picture, if you will, the Disciples of the Way, but amplified, enhanced, and supercharged to an almost unimaginable power and intensity.

A tremor runs through Michael's body, a ripple of cold fear that starts in his gut and spreads outwards. His breath catches in his throat, making his chest constrict. Despite the comfortable ambient temperature, goosebumps rose on his skin, a peculiar reaction that hinted at something more than just a chill. A frantic rhythm, a drumbeat of anxiety, pounded against his ribs. His muscles tensed to prepare for fight or flight, yet neither option seemed viable against this nameless, worse threat. His hands clench into fists, the knuckles whitening under the strain.

"I started making inquiries, uncovering statements targeting Jews, women, and the LGBTQ+ community. In fact, I took the time to write a few of them myself. The sheer number of showers I've taken since is uncountable." Agent Judson's hands tremble slightly; the phantom sensation of soap underscored his compulsive cleansing ritual. His chest tightened, constricting his breath, each inhale a struggle against the weight of guilt. His face paled, his skin clammy despite the cool air, and nausea threatened to overwhelm a physical manifestation of his moral turmoil. The hateful words were like a brand seared into his soul, the shame radiating outward. "But my efforts yielded results; someone gave me an address and part of a name—Something Forever—though I never heard from him again." Michaels, mirroring Judson's distress with a clenched jaw and trembling hands, reached out unconsciously, as if to offer comfort. His shadowed eyes reflected the unspoken weight of the situation and the profound implications of Judson's statement.

"Look I'm sorry. But something forever can be anything."

"I remember there were four words, and the last was forever."

"Doesn't sound like any paramilitary group I ever heard of. I wonder if it might be an expression or a common saying of some kind."

"Could be anything or nothing! A prank perpetrated by several individuals." Michael recoiled, a surge of anger building at the uncontrolled rage displayed before him.

"You don't believe that?"

"To answer your question, no, I do not, and I offer my sincerest apologies for my inappropriate behavior." Judson's brow furrowed slightly, a subtle tightening of the muscles around his eyes betraying his worry. A faint tremor ran through his normally rigid posture, a barely perceptible shift in his weight. Conversely, Michael felt a tightening chest, shallow breaths, and anxious prickling skin. His heart pounded a little faster, a rapid drum against his ribs, mirroring the sudden surge of adrenaline.

"I wouldn't be worried. If this group is the same as the Disciples of the Way…"

"Its destructive capacity surpasses that of the Disciples; The only question is how much more destructive." Judson shudders, a tremor running through his frame. The muscles in his jaw clench, and a faint flush creep up his neck, spreading a warmth that contrasts with the chill that seems to have settled in his bones. His breath hitches, a shallow, rapid intake of air, evidence of the anxiety constricting his chest. "I believe Cain leads this group." His heart hammers a frantic rhythm against his ribs, a trapped bird struggling for release. A cold sweat slicked his palms, making the already-damp newspaper he held slip in his grip. His muscles tensed, shoulders drawn up towards his ears, as if bracing for a blow. The fear radiates outward, a chill that seeps into his very bones, leaving him trembling slightly.

Agent Michaels reacts with utter shock and surprise at that revelation. "Cain, why do you say that?" Michael's eyes widened slightly, his pupils dilating as a surge of adrenaline spiked his heart rate. His face paled, a fine sheen of sweat breaking out on his forehead despite the cool air conditioning. His hands clenched into fists, the knuckles whitening under the strain. A barely perceptible tremor ran through his body, betraying the turmoil of his emotions.

"Let's just say from what I heard their philosophy follows that monster's."

"Alot of people's beliefs follow Cain's. I believed the election was fraudulent." He kept that to himself. Despite Daniel's protests and legal challenges, the election was fair, and he lost.

It's more than just that. I would like you to look at some messages that I recently came across.

"That looks pretty old," Michaels says as Judson looks at the briefcase, a smile on his face. The aged leather creaked a low protest under Judson's touch, its surface worn smoothly by time and travel. A faint scent of old paper and pipe tobacco hung in the air. The cool metal of the clasps felt reassuringly solid against his fingertips; a sense of quiet history emanated from the worn object. The only sound was the gentle ticking of a hidden clock, a rhythmic pulse against the silence.

"Family heirloom. Both my father and grandfather and several generations of Judson's were attorneys. My father was hoping I would follow the family tradition. I wanted to be a law enforcement officer. He lived long enough to see me graduate from the FBI academy. He concluded by expressing pride, regardless of my path, presenting me with this briefcase."

"That's touching. My father is still alive, but we are not close," Michaels says with pain in his voice. His throat tightened, and a slight tremor was noticeable in his words. His shoulders slumped, a visible weight settles upon him, and the muscles around his eyes tightened, betraying the effort it took to maintain composure. A faint flush crept up his neck, a betraying sign of the suppressed emotion threatening to overwhelm him.

"Why?"

"He disagrees with the federal government and with everything it stands for. To him, I'm just part of the problem with the United States. He also supported the Disciples of the Way."

"That's sad. You should try to make amends. Before it is too late. Time goes by quick." Michaels has a new appreciation for Judson. He saw him, not a computer in human clothing, but a complex person whose traits included efficiency.

Suddenly, Judson's government-issued palmtop beeped, a sharp, insistent sound cutting through the silence. The men were surprised.

"What is that?" Michaels blurts.

"Remember when I said I was looking into that group? Well, I've been monitoring emails." Judson puts his hand on the palm top and instantly the email appears on a screen in front of Judson and Michaels.

"Demonstration at federal and state capitol buildings, bring party supplies."

"That sounds ominous," Michaels says.

"What do you think they mean by bring party supplies?" Judson gulps, fear taking over his voice.

"My guess. It isn't ballons and party hats. It could just be signs and noise makers. After all, it just says demonstration. You know, a peaceful protest."

"I studied this group long enough to know that peaceful is not in their vocabulary. Look at these papers." Judson hands Michaels some documents.

"Papers. Who uses papers anymore? Why didn't you use the information web storage system?"

"I do. I also like to have a hands-on copy. Now the papers you are holding. In the system, they just disappeared."

"Convenient."

"I thought so. Anyway, this person is a suspected member of United We Stand. This person belongs to Divided We Fall. Both are mortal enemies with only one thing in common. They support Cain and his wild theories. They have plane reservations to Washington, DC, on January 4th."

"Yeah, they also support Daniel's MAP ideas. Michael says, "I remember people suspected Carl Gailson, the leader of United We Stand, of mass murder at a Georgia gay bar."

"Suspected and even though there was enough evidence to convict, including several eyewitnesses, the District Attorney refused to indict him. Talk about turning a blind eye." Judson says.

"But it doesn't have him going to Washington..."

"Enough about this Gailson person. Look at this." Judson hands Michaels more sheets of paper. Michaels looks at Judson. "You can see this has schematics to not just the Capitol building but every state Capitol building as well." Michaels can see Judson's point of view.

As Judson delved deeper into the list, a knot of anxiety formed in his stomach, causing a wave of nausea to wash over him. His hands trembled involuntarily, a visible manifestation of the fear and concern that gripped him. Every name he encountered seemed to send a chill down his spine, leaving him with an unsettling sense of foreboding.

"Why don't you respond? Maybe whoever is emailing can give a little more information that you can use."

Judson returns to his computer. "Rest assured. I won't miss it. Those politicos will finally get what's coming to them," he hits send. The response was immediate and frightening,

"Don't you know it?" The reply came back.

Judson and Michaels both looked at the screen. "Will, that's even more chilling?" Michaels says.

"That's what I've been saying. I have a dreadful suspicion something will occur in January."

"That's in a few days. What do you think it could be?" Michaels says.

"I don't know. But it more than likely has to do with the Capitol. Why would they have the schematics?"

"They have plans for all the state ones. What do you think they are going to do? That's insane. There would be enough warning." Michaels says.

Judson's heart rate quickened, pounding in his chest like a drumbeat as he realized the potential danger that awaited those who innocently planned their trips to the nation's capital. A cold sweat broke out on his forehead, dampening his brow as the weight of the situation settled heavily upon him.

Judson's mind was a maelstrom of racing thoughts, colliding in a chaotic whirlwind. He imagined the violence that could erupt if these individuals carried out their nefarious plans, his breathing growing shallow and erratic, the air suffocating. The troubling discovery increasingly tormented him; its weight pressed down with each passing moment, intensifying a sense of responsibility to prevent harm to innocent lives. His muscles tensed, his body rigid, as if expecting an imminent threat.

"I don't know what anybody's planning on doing. All I know is that I need to show this to Director Knighton."

"Well, he's in a meeting with the President to give an update on the election fraud."

"Damn, that means I'll have to contact him tomorrow."

Judson's heart hammered against his ribs, a frantic drumbeat that echoed the rising panic in his chest. A cold sweat slicked his palms, leaving the phone in his hand clammy and slippery. His breath hitched in ragged gasps, his lungs burning with a mixture of fear and adrenaline. His muscles tensed, coiled tight as springs, ready to react—to report, to fight, to do whatever it took. The blood rushed to his head, making it feel heavy and throbbing, while his extremities grew numb with a chilling sense of dread. His stomach churned, a knot of anxiety tightening with each passing second.

Chapter Thirty-Four

In a dark and gloomy room, illuminated only by the flickering glow of a CRT monitor and intermittent lightning flashes outside, Agent Bryant hunches over his keyboard, the rhythmic tap-tap-tap of his fingers punctuating the low rumble of thunder. The air hangs heavy with the metallic scent of ozone and the musty odor of old paper and dust; a chill permeates the room despite the oppressive heat radiating from the computer–a stark contrast to the electric crackle of the storm raging outside. This contrast mirrors the tightening in Bryant's chest, a mixture of anxiety and the cold pressure of the impending deadline. '*Demonstration at federal and state capitol buildings, bring party supplies.*' He hits enter.

Several responses appear on his screen, but one catches his eye. The one from Bugs Capone. "Rest assured. I won't miss it. Those politicos will finally get what's coming to them," the email states.

"He's getting dangerously close. He may expose the entire organization soon." Agent Bryant's heart hammers against his ribs, a frantic drumbeat against the silence of the observation room. A sheen of sweat slicks his palms, making the grip on his coffee mug precarious. His jaw clenches, muscles tightening in his neck and shoulders as tension coils in his spine. The blood rushes to his head, a throbbing pulse in his temples mirroring the frantic pace of his thoughts. He forces a calm exterior, his face betraying none of the turmoil raging beneath the surface, but the subtle tremor in his hands gives him away. His breath hitches, shallow and rapid, a stark contrast to the controlled rhythm he usually maintains. The icy grip of fear threatens to paralyze him, yet adrenaline courses through his veins, sharpening his senses and fueling a desperate need for action.

"Don't you know it?" He types and then turns off his palmtop. The cool plastic feels smooth against his palm as he switches it off. He enters his bedroom, which has a faint scent of lavender and dust, to put on the red jump suit. He carefully positioned his armband, a modified American flag displaying a Christian cross instead of stars, on his right arm. In the mirror, he gazes at his reflection, a blend of determination and nervous energy staring back. His jaw is tight, a subtle clenching betraying the resolve burning within. A faint tremor runs through his hands, barely perceptible but a giveaway of the anxiety bubbling beneath the surface. His breath hitches slightly in his chest, a shallow inhale and exhale betraying the rapid beating of his heart. The skin around his eyes feels taut, a slight sheen of sweat highlighting the sharp angles of his face. "For the new America." He says. He sees his black car, the engine's low hum vibrates through the car as he pulls away, the gray building shrinking in his rearview mirror. The crisp morning air smells of exhaust fumes and damp earth. A sense of purpose, tinged with apprehension, fills him as he drives.

Agent Bryant arrived at the meeting hall. Except for the occasional jagged lightning illuminating rain-lashed windows, the only light came from the digital clock on the wall, which showed 23:58. Then came a bone-jarring clap of thunder, vibrating through the floor and followed by a torrential downpour. The air was heavy with ozone and the damp fragrance of the old building. Despite his thick overcoat, a chill ran down Bryant's spine; the silence between thunderclaps felt heavy with anticipation. He approaches the door, rapping six times, pausing for six seconds, and rapping six times again. A wave of nervous anticipation washed over him; his palms grew slick with sweat, his heart hammered frantically against his ribs, and a faint tremor ran through his hands. Suddenly, a screen appeared, it's cool, smooth surface a stark contrast to the prickly heat now prickling his skin. His breath hitched, his muscles tensed, and his wide, focused eyes drank in the image: "Freedom Now," a voice said. Agent Bryant gave the response code, "Freedom Forever."

The screen dissolved, revealing a boy in a blue jumpsuit who snapped to attention, saluting Bryant with a precise, military-like movement.

"Would you like me to take your coat, Major?" Agent Bryant's eyes scan the boy's uniform, settling on the small, almost insignificant insignia of a private.

"Very well." With a sigh of relief, Agent Bryant removes his damp coat and gives it to the waiting private.

"The meeting is just down the hall and the guest speaker should be here in ten minutes." Agent Bryant ignores him and goes down the hall.

Down the hall, he sees the person he wants to talk to. "Lt. Colonel."

Agent Smith turns his head. "What is it?"

"Agent Judson, from the FBI…"

"Yes, I remember him. What about him? Is he still trying to find out what the NSA and the Secret Service know about the stolen elections?" Smith's laughter, a mix of relief and nervous energy, reverberates through the room. His heart races, pumping adrenaline through his veins as he struggles to maintain his composure; the tension is palpable, tightening his stomach into a knot. Sweat beads on his forehead, a physical manifestation of his anxiety. The mere mention of Agent Judson and the investigation sends shivers down his spine, a cocktail of fear and uncertainty coursing through him. His shoulders tense, his hands fidget—his body language betraying the calm facade he tries to project. The weight of the situation leaves him exhilarated yet on edge, a turbulent mix of emotions reflected in his physical reactions.

"I think he's on to us. Or more likely this group."

A cold dread washes over Smith as the words hang in the air. "Are you sure?"

"Yes sir. I sent the email that you ordered. The one about the demonstration and bringing party supplies."

"I know about the message. What does that have to do with Judson?" As the tension in the room escalates, the air seems to thicken with an almost tangible weight. Smith's voice quivers slightly, betraying a hint of nervousness, while beads of sweat form on his brow, reflecting the dim light of the office. His hands fidget nervously, tapping on the desk in a rhythmic pattern, a physical manifestation of his anxiety. The weight of the unspoken words hangs heavily in the room, creating an atmosphere charged with anticipation and uncertainty.

"Look at this." With a slight tremor, Bryant gives Smith the crumpled paper.

"Bugs Capone. He can't be serious." Smith reads more. "I see your point. He's asking a lot of questions. Didn't he hear what curiosity did to the cat? I tell you we should have taken care of Jerry Allan, but he escapes our claws. As for what you have told me, I will have to talk to my next in command. I see what he has to say."

"But if Judson keeps asking about us and starts piecing things together..."

Smith checks his watch, the secondhand sweeps past the minute mark with a quiet click. "That can wait. Our meeting is about to start."

Smith and Bryant enter the dark convention hall and hear the murmur of hushed conversations and the distant click of heels on the polished floor. All around, they see lonely officers in faded blue jumpsuits, their faces etched with weariness, and high-ranking officers in crisp yellow jumpsuits, their bearing stiff and formal. Despite the bright red jumpsuits clearly visible on the meeting's screen, the Generals remain undercover and absent. They conceal their faces, and their modulated voices lack warmth. Colonel Smith only knows of the one General he communicates with over secure channels; the General's voice, crisp and authoritative, is the only one he ever hears. The Generals are anonymous figures, their true identities hidden from the public eye.

Everywhere around Bryant, the Confederate flag is prominent, carried proudly, its movements a blur of color and fabric. Nearby, others bear the crisp white Christian flag, catching the morning breeze, while some display the American flag upside down—a sign of distress—its red stripes limp in the humid air. Even the Nazi flag of World War II is present. This diversity of banners, however, belies a common thread: the red, white, and blue of the American flag, along with the simple elegance of the Christian cross displayed on their armbands, clearly identifies them as members of Freedom Forever, a group dedicated to bringing about a new vision of the United States—one that will erase the sins of the past and restore America to its former glory. The loud clang of a gong reverberates through the air, instantly silencing the murmuring crowd. A hush falls as all attention turns towards the imposing podium.

Three figures emerge from the shadows, their robes the color of midnight, the air thick with the scent of incense. Two people, one on each side of a figure holding a large book aloft, carry blazing torches, illuminating the scene with a warm, flickering light. With a determined stride, the person in the lead marches past the ancient altar, the scent of incense heavy in the air, and turns, the torch casting long shadows. The man with the missing fingers positions himself at the altar's rear, holds the book up. Bryant can see that it's a leather book with precious jewels around it.

The man lowers the book and then proceeds to the center of the altar, setting the book down and then bowing. The person in the rear holds his position, the silence amplifies the tension in the air. Everyone recognizes the three figures as the prophets of Cain; their dark presence casts a shadow over the hall. Whispers circulate about a fourth member, allegedly killed in a brutal terrorist attack, the details shrouded in secrecy. The sight of the prophets brings shivers and respect to the group.

A low hum from the voice modulator accompanies the book's opening; the sound is almost mechanical. "For a long time, we have waited for God's chosen Messiah. A person who will bring us from the oppression of the enemy. The LGBTQ+ community, immigrants and the leftist court system that even today tries to find and imprison God's true messenger to Earth." That receives several boos from the crowd. Missing fingers held up his hand. "But the true messiah has always stayed one step ahead. Fighting tirelessly against the corrupt government of the United States, including the last election. A person who brings out the truth." The speaker slams his hand on the altar. "My followers welcome the true messenger of God, Cain."

A figure emerges from the shadows, clad in dark, flowing clothes that seem to absorb the dim light. The phantom's body remains completely hidden, only the glint of something metallic at its hip. The air hangs heavy with the smell of incense and the burning torches. Silence, broken only by the gong which amplifies the rustle of the garment. Ice-cold dread seeps into the onlookers as the figure looms, their breath catching in their throats. The phantom's masked face pulses with a dark, angry energy, the shadows themselves seeming to bristle with rage. As the crowd collectively inhales the stench of fear, a heavy silence descends, broken only by the frantic beating of hearts. A bone-chilling stillness descends; the only sound is a whisper of dread crawling through the air.

The phantom's imposing figure looms above the crowd, its dark cloak swirling around it like a storm as its booming, modulated voice commands their attention. "My true patriots, my name is Cain. As you see, there is a rally on January 6th." The crowd cheers. "For too long, we have been quiet. We see this nation fall to disease, war, depressions, anarchy, and corruption. We wait no more. On January 6th, we will reveal ourselves to the disease that is the United States government. We will make sure that our so-called leaders hear our voice. January 6th starts the new age for the United States," Cain passionately speaks, hands waving emphatically, and its voice rises and falls with emotion.

The crowd cheers. Cain continues to look around, impressed by the size of the crowd. Cain even looks at the screens. The phantom then raises its arms.

"But no matter what the government does, someone created a more heinous crime." Cain's head nods, and the two flanking prophets advances, their torches casting flickering shadows on the man's missing fingers. Seconds later, they return, dragging a man between them—his clothes torn and bloodied, his hands secured, his bruised head bowed low in complete surrender. Smith and Bryant identified him as Jerry Allan. They positioned him on the altar, the cold stone pressing against his skin, and bound his arms and legs. They went back to the man with the missing fingers for their torches, then resumed their positions.

"This filth that we entrusted in our care tried to betray us." A cold sweat slicked Jerry's palms, intensifying the chill of the unforgiving stone. His heart hammered frantically against his ribs; each beat a painful counterpoint to the tightening ropes. Panic constricted his chest, making breathing difficult, and a tremor, amplified by gnawing fear, ran through his body. His muscles, tense and aching from the bonds, strained against the rough rope, each strand a searing line of pain that eclipsed the initial cold. His vision swam, blurring the torches and the faces of his captors. A faint whimper, lost in the rising tide of his terror, escaped his lips.

"This vermin went to an FBI agent and told him about us. But with his blood." With measured steps, Cain approaches the man with the missing fingers, who prostrates himself and offers the apparition a bone-handled knife. The torchlight flickers, making the knife's glint seem almost alive as shadows writhe and dance around them. Cain then returns to the altar and says a silent prayer. The phantom raised the knife high, then brought it down with brutal force into Jerry's chest. The blade tears through flesh with a sharp sound, followed by a sickening thud and a gush of warm blood, its coppery stench filling the air. Jerry lets out a low moan before falling silent, the only sounds now the crackling and spitting of the torches in the darkness. A chilling dread hangs heavily in the air. **"This is the heart of a traitor."**

Cain hoists Jerry's heart; its rhythmic thump-thump echoes in the silence, a macabre metronome marking the end of a life. In a horrifying instant, the altar explodes in a raging inferno, its flames licking at Jerry's body with terrifying speed. The heat is suffocating, the screams unimaginable. Cain casts the heart into the flames; it lands with a soft thump, instantly consumed by the orange and yellow inferno. The crowd responds, fists pounding their chests as they chant, "Hail Cain!" repeatedly. Meanwhile, in a dark corner of the room, the American flag hangs motionless.

Afterword

All hell will break lose as Cain's plan is implemented in

Nazi America Insurrection

Please check out our website at or join our mailing list and receive the latest novel updates and exclusive access to the short stories that take place before the novel.

CHECK OUT THE PODCAST Please join our unscripted conversations on the Dark World Conversations with RJ Kelsay podcast; where we discuss various topics sometimes of current and historical events and sometimes just fun discussions of fictional worlds from the movies and literature that we enjoy. Remember, those who don't learn from history are doomed to repeat it. Join the conversation! The podcast can be found on YouTube, Spotify, Amazon Music,

Audible and more!

Please join our newsletter by sending a request to rjkelsay@gmail.com where you will get up to date information on upcoming stories as well as mini stories. Coming soon.

About the author

RJ Kelsay grew up in the Pacific Northwest as part of a multigenerational military family. He received a bachelor's degree in political science and combines his knowledge in the field with his passion for writing. RJ resides in the Pacific Northwest with his wife and two children.

www.ingramcontent.com/pod-product-compliance
Lightning Source LLC
Chambersburg PA
CBHW020416110726

47899CB00006B/2014